PRAISE FOR
THE CONNECTIONS SERIES

Connected

"I was pulled in from the first word and felt every emotion...An incredibly emotional, romantic, sexy, and addictive read."

—Samantha Young, *New York Times* bestselling author of *Before Jamaica Lane*

"Emotional, unpredictable, and downright hot."

—K. A. Tucker, author of *Ten Tiny Breaths*

"This book had all my favorite things. Sweet, all-consuming romance, smart and real characters, and just enough of every emotion to keep me unable to put the book down. This was one of those holy-smokes kind of books!"   —Shelly Crane, *New York Times* bestselling author of *Significance*

"It's been two weeks since I finished *Connected* and Dahlia and River are still in my head."   —The 2 Bookaholics!! (5 stars)

"I am now in awe of Kim Karr."   —Shh Mom's Reading

"I can't say enough about this book! I LOVED IT! You will be sighing, swooning, and smiling often but you will also be crying, yelling and you will have your jaw drop to the floor once or twice."   —The Book Enthusiast

"I can't wait for more of [Karr's] books!"   —Aestas Book Blog

"Grabbed my attention and held on to it from beginning to end. . . . The romance, the heat, the angst, the storytelling, and the characters are all captivating and very well-balanced."   —Bookish Temptations

"A sexy, emotional, and wonderfully romantic debut. . . . Kim Karr has a fantastic 'voice,' which will only continue to grow and refine."

—Swept Away by Romance

CONNECTED

The Connections Series

KIM KARR

New American Library

NEW AMERICAN LIBRARY
Published by the Penguin Group
Penguin Group (USA) LLC, 375 Hudson Street,
New York, New York 10014

USA | Canada | UK | Ireland | Australia | New Zealand | India | South Africa | China
penguin.com
A Penguin Random House Company

Published by New American Library, a division of Penguin Group (USA) LLC. Previously
published in an InterMix edition.

First New American Library Printing, February 2014

 REGISTERED TRADEMARK—MARCA REGISTRADA

LIBRARY OF CONGRESS CATALOGING-IN-PUBLICATION DATA:
Karr, Kim.
Connected/Kim Karr.
p. cm.—(The Connections series ; 1)
  ISBN 978-0-451-46827-7 (pbk.)
I. Title.
PS3611.A78464C66 2014
813'.6—dc23   2013037145

Printed in the United States of America
10   9   8   7   6   5   4   3   2   1

Set in Bulmer MT
Designed by Spring Hoteling

AUTHOR'S NOTE

Music means a great deal to me, so I spent many hours searching for songs that reflect the content of this book. I hope that listening to these songs before you read each chapter will enhance your experience. Please visit my Web site www.authorkimkarr.com for song links to Spotify.

Connected Playlist

Chapter 21

♪ Lifehouse (featuring Natasha Bedingfield)—*"Between the Raindrops"*

Chapter 22

♪ Within Temptation—*"Memories,"* The Smashing Pumpkins—*"Perfect"*

Chapter 23

♪ Yellowcard—*"Miles Apart"*

Chapter 24

♪ Ivan & Alyosha—*"I Was Born to Love Her"*

Chapter 25

♪ Rihanna—*"Diamonds"*

Chapter 26

♪ Avenged Sevenfold—*"Victim,"* Citizens—*"Amazing Grace"*

Chapter 27

♪ Sara Paxton—*"Connected"*

Epilogue

♪ The Script—*"Breakeven,"* Go Radio—*"Go to Hell"*

CONNECTED

I have visited this place many times, but today it's different. I'm alone. There are no comforting arms around me. My body trembles. Not from the cold, but from the realization that fate hasn't worked in my favor. A single tear slowly drips down my face as I look into the night and scream, "Why couldn't we just stay together?!"

As the wind moans in the distance, thunder crashes and lightning strikes. I stand here hoping the impending storm will carry me away and erase the shadow that looms over me. A slow, soothing rain falls from the blackened sky, but it provides no relief for my ravaged soul. A mist slowly rises into the night, and the cold air sends shivers down my spine.

I huddle to the ground, feeling lost and alone. As my tears merge with the rain, they fall into the darkness. No one is here to see me. No one knows where to find me. Only the vultures notice me as they fly swiftly overhead, seeking shelter against the cold rain. I'm not looking for refuge in this place I now despise, but I have nowhere else to go. I have no hope. I have no future.

PROLOGUE
Crazy

August 1999

This was the best place on earth. Music roared through the speakers, electricity filled the air, and crowds of people rushed to find their seats. My father and I stopped quickly to purchase our concert T-shirts. Clutching our tickets tightly, we made our way through the crowd.

The excitement around us was almost indescribable. We sat down, mesmerized by our surroundings. It was impossible to take everything in. Being so close to the stage was intoxicating. I was frozen with shock, and my eyes flickered through the rays of the spotlights as they made their way up the stairs.

Bono encouraged thousands of fans to wave their hands and nod their heads. Eventually, I began to absorb my surroundings as U2 began to play "Beautiful Day." Slipping into an almost hypnotic state, I closed my eyes and swayed to the pulse of the beat as the vibrations of the music penetrated my body. I remained in this state throughout most of the concert, just as I had many times before.

Going to the Greek Theatre, or the Greek, was an experience like no other. It was the largest outdoor amphitheater in the area. Celebrities, unknown bands, known singers, groupies, and concertgoers gathered here from miles around, but they had all come for the same reason: to listen to the best music ever.

My father was the general manager of the Greek. He loved music, mostly rock, from the eighties and nineties. He'd been going to concerts since he was thirteen and always bought a T-shirt. To say that he had a few concert T-shirts was putting it mildly. He started working at the Greek at a young age and never left because he loved his job. He always knew the inside scoop about bands and lived for sharing his stories with me. I was even lucky enough to have one of the Wear Purple ticket stubs from Prince's sold-out Purple Rain concert in my possession.

But there is one concert that will forever hold a place in my heart. It was the Nirvana benefit concert for Bosnian rape victims. They opened with "Rape Me," and the emotion in that song made me fall even more in love with music than I already had. After I left the concert that night, the Greek was not only my father's favorite place to be, but mine, too.

My mom was not into music; she preferred clothes to concerts. She taught me to sew, and together we made a quilt with the concert T-shirts I outgrew. Between my father and me, we collected over two hundred pieces of music history.

Trying to figure out what I wanted to be when I grew up was always hard. I was torn between my father's love for music, my mother's love for fashion, and my love for photography. I thought maybe I'd have a music career or go to the New York School of Fashion and Design like my mother had. But whichever career path I chose needed to provide me with the freedom to take pictures.

CHAPTER 1

Out of My Head

October 2006

Walking through the Greek-lettered doors of Kappa Sigma, I felt like I'd just stepped onto a movie set. It was Halloween, everyone was wearing costumes, holding red Solo cups, and dancing . . . well, not everyone.

I looked twice to be certain, but sure as shit, there was a large, dark blue ice luge in the center of the living room. The guy at the bottom of the channel was my boyfriend, Ben, and the person in line behind him was my best friend, Aerie. I didn't go to a lot of fraternity parties, and looking at the two of them now, I knew why.

Frowning at the two drunken idiots on the receiving end of the ice luge, I headed toward the kitchen to grab a beer. As I crossed back into the living room, I saw Ben sucking on a lime and squinting his eyes with his nose scrunched as he moved his head from side to side. While shaking my head, I passed by a couple playing beer pong and laughed. Clearly she'd had a few too many drinks.

Noticing me, Ben shot a wicked smirk in my direction and crooked his index finger, gesturing me toward him. He strode a few steps closer, his gaze holding mine as the crowd cleared the way.

Standing face-to-face, I could see that his forget-me-not blue eyes were slightly hooded, allowing me only a glimpse of his dilated pupils. But his sly grin was still present, meaning he was in a somewhat coherent state of mind.

Raising an eyebrow, I pointed to the dark blue ice sculpture. "Hey, how many times did you hit that?"

Feigning confusion, he raised his hands palms up. "Not sure," he said as he cocked his head to one side while shrugging his shoulders.

Ben took the cup out of my hand and set it on the table beside us. He snaked his arms around my waist and pulled me to him. "Hey, Dahl. What took so long?" he asked as he placed his strong hands on my behind.

Wrapping my arms around his neck, I rested my forehead on his chin and let out a slow sigh. "Photo shoot took longer than expected. Drake had a meltdown when the models' outfits weren't the shade of purple he'd asked for."

Ben groaned and dipped his head to kiss me. "Drake's a fuckin' pansy-ass. He'd better hope you find a new internship for next semester because he's really starting to piss me off."

Flinching a little at his words, I leaned back to place my hands on his hard chest before looking into his slightly glazed eyes. "Ben, promise me you'll stay away from him."

"Will do. Promise, Dahl." He chuckled, the smell of alcohol strong on his breath.

I sighed and ran my hands up to his hair, combing my fingers through it.

Looking at me with concern, he whispered, "You okay?"

"Of course. The wrong color purple isn't really the end of the world."

He studied me and hesitated before responding. "Dahl, you know that's not what I mean."

I stiffened. I knew what he meant, but I didn't want to talk about the anniversary of my parents' death.

"Ben, I'm cool. Let's have a good time," I muttered. I broke our embrace, grabbed my beer, and looked around the room for Aerie.

Ben nodded, his sly grin returning while he watched me chug the entire contents of the Solo cup before chewing on the ice cubes. Beckoning me to the center of the room, he pointed to the luge. "This way, gorgeous."

Having refilled our drinks, we stood at the liquor-filled ice dispenser. The party was in full swing, and I watched Ben hit the luge yet again. When I excused myself to use the restroom, I glanced around at the crowd and pushed through the chaos. There were wall-to-wall people in every room. I stumbled into a tall guy with red hair, and I knew he was beyond drunk when he tried to kiss me. I shoved him and giggled when he tripped over his own feet and fell on his ass. I continued making my way to the stairs. They were filled with students drinking, making out, or doing way more than I ever needed to see.

The room smelled like alcohol mixed with sweat, and I suddenly felt like I couldn't get out of there soon enough. Weaving around the crowd on the stairs I was thankful to finally make it to the bathroom.

After splashing my face with water, I headed to Ben's room for a much-needed mental break. This particular day was the hardest one of the year for me, but being around friends always seemed to help me through it. As I headed toward his bed, I noticed the tickets he had given me this morning. I knew he meant well by buying us Greek tickets to see one of my favorite bands, Maroon 5. He thought he would brighten an otherwise dark day, but I couldn't go back there.

Sighing, I threw myself on the bed. Yes, he meant well and he really wanted to be the one to take me there, but he knew I would never go back. I've told him this. The U2 performance was the last concert I went to with my family before my mother, my aunt, and my father died in a small plane crash coming home from Mexico.

I'm not sure how long I stayed in his room thinking about my parents until I finally decided to rejoin the party. I first stopped in the kitchen to grab a third beer, and then headed back into the living room. All the lights had been turned off and orange candles glowed everywhere as the sound of haunting music filled the room.

I felt a strong arm wrap around my waist and Ben nibble on my ear. "Where you been, Dahl?"

"Just grabbing a beer," I answered, holding my Solo cup up in the air and twisting around in his arms.

Loud screams pulled my attention back to the ice luge where Aerie was jumping up and down, grabbing her throat, and squealing in pain. Motioning my head toward her, I set my cup down on the banister. "What's she drinking?"

Clutching his arms tighter around my hips, he pulled me closer. As he slipped his long fingers inside the waistband of my black leggings, he fingered the lace of my panties and whispered in my ear, "Don't know." Then he placed one of his legs between mine and asked, "Want some?"

I shook my head no but was nearly panting as I responded. "I promised Aerie I'd go with her to the bar and listen to some new band. One of us should stay somewhat lucid—at least until we get there."

He trailed his hands across the top of my panties; the fingertips of his one hand grazed from my backside across to my hip bone. Before I knew what was happening, his fingers started drifting down into the front of my pants.

"I didn't mean the luge," he said coyly before plunging his tongue into my ear and grinding his hips into mine.

I pulled back from him and removed his hands from inside my leggings. I needed to stop this very public display of affection before I couldn't. I brushed his blond hair away from his seductive blue eyes and asked, "You coming?"

Grinning fiendishly, he answered, "I hope to be soon, gorgeous!"

I laughed and shook my head. "Ben Covington, you're impossible."

I reached around his neck and tugged his head down to mine, connecting my mouth to his.

Ben pulled his soft lips from mine and groaned in my ear. "My room now. I need to fuck you."

I leaned back and stared at his incredibly irresistible grin. Summoning all of my willpower, I tried to decide what to do.

Before I could respond, Aerie tugged my ponytail. She swayed slightly and slurred, "There you are, girlfriend! You ready?"

Separating myself from him, I shrugged my shoulders and mouthed, "Sorry. Rain check?"

He exhaled and muttered under his breath to Aerie, "Nice fucking timing."

Aerie, being Aerie, thumped him in the forehead. "Watch the language, asshole," she quipped as she reached for my arm.

Leaning back toward Ben, I gave him a swift kiss. With Aerie forcefully tugging me toward the door, I managed to say, "Meet you back here later." Walking backward and giggling, I blew Ben a kiss and waved goodbye.

Rocking back on his heels, he stood with both hands in his pockets while biting his lip and shaking his head at me.

⬤

The cool night helped to settle the heat Ben had ignited. Sounds of Halloween echoed from every direction as we walked down fraternity row. We only took a taxi part of the way; then we walked the rest. Once we got out of the taxi, I glanced at Aerie, or more specifically, at her devil costume. She must have been plastered when she got ready because it wasn't something I could have ever imagined her wearing: a very short red sequin dress, a devil tail, high heels, and all the accessories to match. It could barely pass as an acceptable red-light-district ensemble—let alone a Halloween costume.

As we walked toward the bar, I grabbed a stumbling Aerie by the arm before she landed on her ass. "Have a nice trip?" I laughed, knowing full well she didn't like to be made fun of but not really caring.

Aerie shrugged, pulling her beautiful wavy blond hair back and fastening it with the clip she had been fishing out of her purse when she missed her step. "Be nice," she quipped, stopping me so she could readjust her shoe. "At least you can't call me a nonconformist!"

I never told Aerie that Halloween was the anniversary of my parents' death. Ben was the only one who knew I never wanted to camouflage my feelings with a costume.

I sighed and wrapped my arm around her shoulder and put on my very best Vincent Price voice from "Thriller." "Ahhhahhahaaahaaa, you know I never conform. It's against my religion."

We continued walking—Aerie in red high-heel vixen pumps, me in black Converse sneakers—and she tripped again, leaving her shoe behind her. "Aerie, really, I think your outfit could have done without those shoes. They're too big, you dumbass." I turned around and picked up her shoe. "What size are these?" I asked, squinting to see inside.

"Don't worry about it; it's not like you'd ever wear them anyway, Miss I-Always-Have-to-Wear-Comfortable-Shoes. It was the only pair of red shoes left, and one size too big is hardly an issue when they match your outfit perfectly," she announced, yanking the shoe out of my hand. "You know it's all about the look. I'd sacrifice comfort for style any day. Ahem . . ." She cleared her throat while looking down at my shoes.

Shaking my head at her, I couldn't help but roll my eyes. "Whatever."

I walked a little slower so she could keep her shoes on. Aerie said in a much sweeter voice, "Thanks for taking me out. Now, come on. Let's get moving and have some fun. It's girls' night out after all, and I have a broken heart to mend."

I gave her a little smile as I squeezed her arm. "Sweetheart, I think you started the mending process hours ago!"

Aerie shuffled down the sidewalk to hold her shoes in place, and I knew this was going to be an interesting night. Aerie, my best friend since freshman year, broke up with her boyfriends like I changed the flavor of my coffee creamer—often.

Aerie was type A, even though you would never have known it from her drunken state. She strove for perfection—not just with herself—but with her boyfriends. Which explains why she broke up with her last boyfriend yesterday. Tonight she was looking forward to new options, and I was looking forward to hearing a new band.

CHAPTER 2
Next Lifetime

We walked through the open door to the University of Southern California Campus Bar and Aerie pulled her tail up. "At least they aren't playing that Halloween crap in here," she yelled a little too loudly. As my ears adjusted, I heard a velvety soft voice singing an unfamiliar yet captivating song.

Aerie stopped to put her devil horns on, and I glanced around the large room recognizing a lot of students, while trying to get a look at the band. I shouted directly into her ear, "They sound really good. Have you heard them before?"

She was on her toes trying to see over the crowd. I laughed at how short she was until her pointy devil horn hit me in the eye. "No, but I love their sound," she responded, still trying to see the stage and almost falling over.

I had been coming here for the last three years and couldn't ever remember it being so crowded. I could barely see the long wooden bar to my right, and with the mass of bodies bumping and grinding on the dance floor, I couldn't even catch a glimpse of the stage.

"Do you know their name?" I asked Aerie.

"I think they're called the Wilde Ones." She hiccupped and laughed. She winked at me as she started to dance her way toward some friends on the dance floor and yelled over her shoulder, "By the way, I love them! Great name and an even greater sound."

"I'll get drinks and meet you out there in a bit," I said to no one since she was already gone. When the bartender acknowledged me, I ordered two beers, one with ice and one without, and tacked on two shots to help Aerie drown her misery.

The live music stopped and typical Halloween songs were blasted through the speakers. I turned my back to the bar and scanned the crowd for Aerie. You would think she would be easy to spot in her red sequin devil costume. She said she was out for vengeance and if her outfit was any indication, she would be vindicated.

I didn't see her anywhere but I did spot an attractive guy. He was still too far away for me to zero in on any specific feature, but something—no, everything—about him drew my attention.

I watched how he moved; his confidence captivated me. He seemed relaxed, like he knew exactly where he was going. And as he headed in my direction, I became mesmerized. Biting my bottom lip, I was unable to focus on anything but him. My head was still a little foggy from the three beers I'd consumed earlier and I was clearly not thinking straight when I made eye contact with him, and then slowly studied his body from head to toe.

As the distance between us narrowed, I could see that he was alarmingly attractive: long, lean, and muscular but not bulky. He wore a black beanie hat with his light brown hair sticking out. When I looked into his eyes, they undid me. Although I couldn't see their color, I could feel their intensity. I almost feared that if I looked into them for too long I might never walk away. His eyes aside, the words *handsome* and *gorgeous* weren't strong enough adjectives to describe this man.

My mind wandered to where it shouldn't. Knowing better than to compare this guy to my boyfriend, I did it anyway. I felt incredibly guilty, but I couldn't help myself. Ben was all surfer. He was attractive, hot, and sexy with an ego to match. This guy was equally as attractive, hot, and sexy, but there was something else—something more. I couldn't quite put my finger on it.

Easing his way through the crowd, he removed his beanie and ran his hands through his hair. When our eyes connected it felt like minutes, but only seconds passed. Suddenly I felt an electric pull forcing me to keep looking at him. Everything I felt indicated he was dangerous. I knew I should look away, walk away, but I didn't. I couldn't. He was just too alluring.

He was finally close enough that I could tell his gleaming eyes were green. I was instantly drawn to his smile. It wasn't a full smile, more like a half grin emphasizing his dimples. His skin was smooth with no facial hair and that made me weak in the knees. His full lips were begging for a kiss. I'd never looked at a guy like this before, not even Ben. So why was I eyeing him this way, and why was I unable to avert my gaze?

Aside from his overall sex appeal, his clothing made him even more irresistible. He wore faded jeans, a black Foreigner concert T-shirt, and black work boots. I had to laugh a little when I saw the concert T-shirt because I was wearing one, too—my dad's U2 T-shirt, knotted on the side, hanging off my shoulder.

Having made his way through the crowd much better than I had, he was now standing in front of me. His face was breathtaking; he had a strong chin; a small, straight nose; perfectly shaped eyebrows; and long eyelashes. He was a vision of utter perfection and I couldn't help but smile.

The bar was crowded and there was no room on either side of me.

Putting both hands in his pockets, he smiled back at me. Then, running his tongue over his bottom lip, he asked in a low, sexy voice, "Were you staring at me?"

I pouted my lips and rolled my eyes. I took a deep breath as I straightened my shoulders and placed my hands on my hips. "No, I was just looking for my friend while I waited on my drinks. You just happened to be in my line of vision."

He chuckled a little then said, "That look was hot."

I huffed out a breath and tried not to laugh. *Did he really just say that?*

When the bartender brought my order and set it in front of me, my phone started ringing in my pocket, but I ignored it as I continued to stare at him. "Why would you think I was looking at you, anyway?"

As the person beside me settled her tab and walked away, he moved to fill the empty space and tossed his beanie next to my drink. His proximity caused my pulse to race and my heart to pound faster. Leaning sideways, he rested his hip against the bar. With his eyes still locked on mine he answered, "Because I was staring at you, hoping you were staring back."

I looked directly into those powerful green eyes, so full of intensity, and I instantly lost my train of thought. With the electric pull only growing stronger between us, I feared I wasn't going to be able to get out of this encounter unscathed.

He dragged his teeth across his bottom lip and his eyes scanned my body. The expression on his face told me he wanted to do more than just talk. I wanted to do more as well.

A moment of comfortable silence passed before he cocked his head to the side in the most adorable way and grinned. "With all this talk about who was staring at whom I think we forgot the basics. I'm River," he said as he extended his hand with the most devilish grin on his face.

Feeling bewitched by him, I put my hand out to shake his but quickly pulled it away. Unfortunately, I also bumped into the person standing next to me and accidentally spilled his beer.

He gave me a dirty look and swore under his breath. River's grin quickly turned into a frown, and he gently moved me away. In a clipped tone he apologized, "Sorry, man. Just an accident, but let me buy you another."

The now drinkless man with a wet shirt looked at him and nodded. River pulled out his wallet and handed him a ten. "Buy two." The man took the money and walked away, muttering something under his breath. River immediately returned his attention to me, and I bit the corner of my lower lip and smiled at him.

There we were, standing face-to-face, with only a few drinks separating us. Sliding one of the beers toward him, I took a sip of my own even though the ice had melted. "Thank you, that guy sure as shit wasn't happy with me. In fact, he kind of acted like an asshole."

Taking a sip of his drink, he started to laugh, almost spitting it out. Skimming his finger over my bare shoulder, his eyes locked on mine. "You're more than welcome."

Quivering from his touch and intense gaze, I took a step back, fearful of where this might lead.

Moving forward, he traced my last step. He was not going to let the distance widen between us. He stared intently into my eyes. "Now, where were we? Do we need to start over?" He waited for my response as he watched me swallow my drink.

I pulled my lower lip to the side with my teeth and smiled playfully. "We were introducing ourselves."

"Okay, so let's try again. I'm River and you are . . . ?"

"I'm not sure you need to know that information right now. I'm kind of thinking you might be a stalker."

His eyes widened as he laughed. "You're not serious—are you, beautiful girl?"

Unable to control my own laughter, I simply said, "Maybe I am," but my laughter subsided when I registered the sweet name he'd called me.

Leaning toward me, he was close enough that I could inhale his fresh scent. It was a soapy, just-out-of-the-shower smell.

"What? If you're not going to tell me your name then I get to call you whatever I want."

Averting my eyes from his gaze, I looked down.

After taking another sip of his beer, he set the mug down. He hooked my chin with his finger and tilted my head up toward him. His touch seared my skin and left it tingling. He stared at me with his intense green eyes and chuckled. "Can we talk about you thinking I'm a Jack the Ripper type? I just want you to know, I'm definitely not. In fact, I think it's safe to say you were staring at me first, but in no way do I think you're a stalker."

My mouth dropped open. I was unsure of what to say. I knew he was right. I had stared first.

"So we can get past this; let's just say I was staring first. Not that it really matters."

We were looking into each other's eyes as the bartender passed me my bill. When I turned to pay for my drinks, our connection was broken. Handing my money to the bartender, I thanked him and told him to keep the change. This distraction gave me some time to think about how to handle this potentially dangerous situation.

I watched River as he ordered two more beers, and realized I had to work out my conflicted feelings. I pushed my guilt aside and handed him one of the shots.

"Cheers."

"It's a beautiful day," he replied before shooting back the shot.

I tried not to show how turned on I was that he had just quoted lyrics from one of my favorite songs.

Setting his shot glass down, he put his hand in his pocket. "So, does this mean you forgive me?"

His voice was strong, but soft, and made him even more tempting. I found myself thinking that he was not only adorable, but unlike anyone I had ever encountered before. I knew I shouldn't be doing this. I had a boyfriend who I loved waiting for me.

I raised an eyebrow and asked, "Forgive you? Forgive you for what?" I was having a hard time concentrating on the conversation and honestly had no idea what the apology was for.

He shifted on his feet. "You know what? Never mind," he muttered in my ear. His warm breath brushed my neck and I wanted to feel it everywhere.

Looking me up and down, he changed the subject. "What, no costume?"

Continuing our dangerous flirtation, I glanced down, motioning with my hands from head to toe. "How do you know this isn't my costume?"

While tugging on my T-shirt and pulling me a little closer, he seductively whispered, "If that's your costume you're definitely taking first place in the contest because it's the sexiest one I've ever seen."

We were silent for a minute; not even our heavy breathing could be heard. The noise from the bar and the crowd around us had quieted, but his words, his touch, they inflamed me, excited me, and sent fire through my veins.

"Where'd you get this, anyway?" he asked, tugging at the knot on my shirt, pulling me closer.

It felt like the room was spinning and I wasn't sure if it was him, the alcohol, or the fact that he had just asked me a question I didn't want to answer. "My dad managed the Greek and was a collector of concert T-shirts," I said, trying to push back the emotions welling up inside me.

He seemed to understand my hesitation before nodding, clearing his throat, and he once again changed the subject. "So, have you ever seen Foreigner play?" he asked, now pointing to his own shirt and grinning.

As I looked at the bold white letters across his chest, I pushed aside my sadness and refocused on our conversation. We were just two people who had a lot in common—or at least that was what I wanted to think. When our drinks were gone, he ordered another round. As I finished the shot, I accidentally slammed the glass on the bar, and the bartender glowered at me. "Sorry," I mouthed.

River reached out and grabbed a strand of hair that had come loose from my ponytail. He very slowly tucked it behind my ear, sending shivers down my spine. Circling his index finger around my ear, I lightly tugged on my lobe. He sparked a fire in me that never before existed.

Gulping the drink I didn't need to be drinking, I hoped to extinguish the flame. I hoped no one had seen him touch me that way. Ben would be fucking furious. He was ridiculously jealous. We had many arguments about other men, all unjustified. At least until now.

As the strobe lights started to flicker and I leaned my hip against the bar for support, he put his hand on my waist and turned me so my back was against the bar. I wondered if he noticed me almost lose my balance from the flashing lights and drunkenness. Moving to stand directly in front of me, he put his hands on either side of me and pressed his palms into the bar. He was enveloping me, but I didn't feel trapped. I didn't know what I felt, but I knew my heart was pounding out of my chest; my stomach was doing flips, and I became lightheaded as goose bumps emerged on my skin.

I thought he was going to kiss me as he stared intently into my eyes. I closed my eyes preparing for it but I felt him abruptly pull away. Immediately, I heard a high-pitched voice squeal, "River, don't forget we're leaving right after the show," and before I could catch a glimpse of the girl, she bounced away.

Smirking at me he said, "My little sister has the worst timing."

I was going to respond when I heard a drumroll echo through the bar. Glancing around, I tried to figure out what it was for. Amused, he rolled his eyes before looking at the stage and then back to me. "That would be for me," he laughed, leaning in so we were face-to-face. "They want me back onstage. I've gotta go unless you'd rather I stay and we finish what we started? Because that certainly would be way more fun."

I really hadn't heard anything he said, but everything seemed to finally make sense. He was the voice I heard when I came into the bar. He was so charming, so captivating, and so aware of me. I was pretty sure I was drunk because I was feeling things I should not have been feeling. As I stared into his powerful green eyes, I knew I should've been trying to escape them.

Before I could say anything in response, he moved his head slightly back, lifted my hand, and slowly kissed it. Then he leaned into me and whispered in my ear, "Guess not. Not yet, anyway." My hand was on fire, my ear scorched.

That same drumroll rumbled through the sound system again and he quickly turned his head back to look at me. "I gotta jet."

He was still holding my hand, as he looked straight into my eyes. "You'll wait for me until after the show."

It wasn't a question. It was a statement. And then motioning between us, he added, "Because this isn't finished."

At that moment I realized that what had started as harmless flirting had turned into a situation that had gotten way too dangerous.

He placed his hands back on the bar and waited for a response. Since he hadn't asked a question that I wanted to answer, I just smiled and said, "If you're in the band, you'd better go. You shouldn't leave your fans waiting."

He gave me one last heart-stopping grin and then leaned in and kissed me. My body reacted strangely; a rush of something I couldn't identify surged through me. At first he only lightly touched my lips with his then for a few short seconds he pressed a little harder before pulling away. I didn't kiss him back, but felt light-headed.

"I hope you've become a fan," he said, winking at me before grabbing his hat. Then he turned and walked away.

I brought my fingers up to my lips and watched as his silhouette disappeared through the crowd. I became vaguely aware that "Superstition" was playing, but my mind was focused on him.

I shook my head, trying to rid myself of the thoughts that shouldn't be there. I knew I had to leave, or I would end up doing something I would regret. I loved Ben, and Ben would fucking kill River just for looking at me the way he did. And then there was the kiss; yes, Ben would certainly kill him.

Knowing these things, I wondered why I hadn't walked away in the first place. For a moment there, I felt as though I believed in love at first sight, which I didn't. And how could love at first sight even exist when you were already in love with someone else? I didn't want to keep thinking about what happened because I was confused as hell, and I knew the meaning of it all wasn't what I wanted it to be.

I smiled about our encounter. He definitely was not a stalker. He was adorably charming and utterly charismatic, a guy who had a simple ease about him that I really liked, and a guy I didn't ever need to see again. This I knew for certain.

With thoughts of River swirling through my head, I made my way through the crowd to the dance floor where I found Aerie with some kind of pink drink in her hand. "We have to leave. Now!" I shouted at her while pulling her off the dance floor.

"What? Why? Are you sick?" she asked, struggling for words.

Then she turned and pointed to the stage. "Because if you're not, I want to see that hot guy sing first."

I turned to see where she was pointing and sure enough it was him, River. I then realized I'd never even told him my name.

Pulling Aerie through the crowd under protest, I heard the audience chanting, "River Wilde, River Wilde." I glanced up to the stage just in time to see him grab the microphone. Before the live music started we exited through the door, and Aerie started yelling obscenities at me. As we walked away I found myself thinking I had just had the most magical encounter and might never be the same because of it.

CHAPTER 3
It's Not My Time

March 2010

I looked in the mirror, trying to decide whether or not the pearl necklace would take the edge away from my deep V-necked black cocktail dress. The bathroom counter was covered in different necklaces, our laundry was in a heap on the hamper, and dirty towels were thrown all over the floor. I smiled when I glanced up and saw Ben's reflection in the mirror. He was leaning with his shoulder on the bathroom doorframe, a wicked grin on his face, and a wild glimmer in his piercing blue eyes.

"Pearls or no pearls?" I asked as I watched him come toward me. I had known him since I was five years old, but for some reason the way he looked at me then left me breathless.

Ben wrapped his tan arms around my waist and started to kiss my neck. I could feel the soft, warm skin of his freshly shaven face. "Dahl, I'd prefer nothing at all, to be perfectly honest," he muttered while he began to unzip my dress.

"Hey, we're going to be late," I said. "L.A. is at least an hour drive." I tried, unsuccessfully, to wiggle out of the one arm he still had around my waist as he continued to unzip my dress with the other.

Watching Ben in the mirror, I saw him bite his lip as he let out a little groan. "Well, it's my party, and I can be late if I want to," he whispered in my ear then resumed kissing my neck. He looked incredibly hot in his black tuxedo, slicked-back hair and clean-shaven face. I felt a slight stirring through my body, which prevented me from wriggling out of his arm. Instead, I turned around to look at him.

I was so proud of how successful Ben had become in this short time. He had landed a job at the *Los Angeles Times* right out of college and proved his ability in only a few short years. Even though the commute from Laguna was tedious, he didn't mind doing it, especially since he wasn't required to go into the office every day. Now my fiancé was going to be receiving California's Journalist of the Year award at a prestigious dinner in L.A. for his brilliant work in underground crime investigation. I knew I wasn't the only one full of excitement, even if I was the only one who showed it.

Ben's lack of enthusiasm wasn't like him. In fact, he hadn't been acting like himself all week and I had been trying to figure out what was going on. I wasn't sure if I should be concerned or touched by his behavior. He had been sweeter than he usually was; he sent me flowers, he bought me candy, he spent every night at home with me. He had even shown up at my office every day to take me to lunch.

Ben was never the type of boyfriend to dote; he wasn't a flowers-and-chocolates kind of guy, and I wasn't the kind of girl who needed that. I liked my independence and so did he. He had always taken care of me and loved me in his own way, but never in all our years together had he done those types of things.

Once before, he came close to acting like a doting boyfriend, but technically he wasn't my boyfriend at the time.

The event leading up to our breakup will forever be ingrained in my mind. I remember clearly the day I popped into Ben's room at his frat house. It was the end of the first semester of our senior year at USC. I stopped by to tell him I'd finally gotten the internship I really wanted at *Sound Music*. I was so happy that I wasn't going to have to intern for Drake anymore, and I knew Ben would be thrilled. He wasn't in his room when I got there, so I sat down at his desk to send his sister, Serena, a quick e-mail to share my news with her. I knew she'd be excited for me.

I pressed the space bar on his computer and his e-mail account was already open, so I figured I'd just type my quick note from there. Instead of hitting COMPOSE I accidentally clicked on the TRASH folder and noticed the date October 31 straightaway. As my eyes scanned the screen, the words *Reply to: S'belle, later tonight, green eyes, touch, copper, and your apartment* were all that registered before he came over and quickly left-clicked, hitting the DELETE button. He startled me. I hadn't heard him walk into the room. I hadn't had a chance to read the whole thing, but I knew he must have been hiding something. *Was he really making plans with another girl? Plans that were not in the least bit platonic?*

He admitted to e-mailing this girl but assured me nothing sexual had actually happened. In the end, he confessed that their relationship was inappropriate. He swore he had ended it, and I'm sure he had; but I couldn't trust him, so we broke up.

Over the next three months, he tried so hard to convince me to forgive him. He left notes on my car, flowers at my door, messages with profuse apologies, text messages confessing his love. He showed up anywhere he knew I would be, and even bought me a silver-plated coffee cup that said "To brighten up your mornings" along the side.

It was a long, hard three-month separation. I never realized just how much I would actually miss him, but I did—a lot. So I decided to trust him and move past his dishonesty. I really did love him, and I knew he loved me. Perhaps I also felt a little guilty about my own encounter with a certain singer.

So, yes, the doting alarmed me, not that I didn't appreciate his kind gestures, but it made me think something was wrong. Was there something not right in our relationship? It had had its share of ups and downs. Maybe this behavior was just one of the ups, or maybe it had something to do with wanting to get married since we had never talked about setting a wedding date.

The one thing I was sure about was our love and commitment to each other. We had grown up together. We had been boyfriend and girlfriend since we were sixteen, and we had been engaged for two years. We may have disagreed on many things and argued more than I preferred, but we always fell back on our commitment; especially since the root of most of our disagreements stemmed from something I could not fix. Our arguments were usually the result of Ben's jealousy. Ben would be jealous if another man so much as looked at me, which was ironic because Ben was always very flirtatious. He was also self-centered. This trait was more a function of who he was—a man with drive, determined to get ahead—although sometimes I wondered at what cost.

Shaking my head, I had no idea what was going on with Ben. However, I made an effort to push aside the disconcerting thoughts and just embrace the moment.

"Today is your big day," I said while looking into his eyes. I gave him a large, happy smile, full of pride. I diverted my eyes from his and said, "And your party or not, it would be rude for the main speaker to be late." I kissed him on the lips to help soften my words. "Now zip my dress back up, and tell me what you think."

Ben flashed me a dangerous smile but didn't move. "You can be very bitch . . . y. Oh, I mean boss . . . y. I think you look fucking gorgeous," he snickered, finally turning me back around to zip up my dress.

I looked at him in the mirror and saw him still grinning at me. "No, the pearls, silly! Should I wear them or not?" I asked while holding them up to my neck again.

Ben's smile faded a little as he took the pearls from my hands. "No pearls. They remind me of your grandma. Not that I didn't love your Grammy, but I love you in a totally different way. I don't want Grammy images popping up in my head while I'm fucking you." He turned me back around and kissed me right on the chest where the pearl necklace would have sat. Then he ran his hand up under my dress. I shivered, and he smiled.

I laughed and said, "Stop it, Ben Covington! You can't do that after talking about Grammy—it just seems wrong." I moved aside and started to leave the bathroom to put on my shoes. I tripped over a towel on my way out and said, "Maybe you could try cleaning up after yourself a little," but he knew I was kidding since I was much messier.

"I love you, you know," Ben said while he followed me out of the bathroom.

As I sat on the bed, still unmade from our afternoon romp, I slipped on one of my shoes before pulling my leg up onto the bed. "I know, and I love you, too." Once again, I wondered: Why the onslaught of affection?

Ben stood over me to help fasten the ankle strap on my left shoe. I noticed his facial expression change again, turning a bit more serious. "No, Dahlia, I really, really love you. Never forget it, no matter what."

"Dahlia? You never call me that," I said as I wriggled my foot and ran it up his stomach, trying to lighten the mood.

Ben smirked, set my foot down, and walked over to his dresser. I was at a loss for words as he reached into one of the drawers and pulled out a Cartier box. Walking back to the bed, he handed me the box and said, "I bought this for you because it says what I never seem to be able to say."

Surprised by the lavish box, I looked at it for a few seconds before opening it. Inside was a stunning white gold–and–diamond bracelet. It had four hearts engraved around the edge. I knew it well because I had written a paper about that piece of jewelry for one of my style classes in college. The bracelet was created by Cartier in the 1970s and designed to be locked firmly onto a loved one's wrist by the giver with the aid of a golden screwdriver that the giver keeps. Looking up at him, my eyes started to fill with tears, and without words I put my hand out for him to fasten the bracelet around my wrist.

Staring at the beautiful piece, I was overcome by emotion, but tried not to cry. "I love it," I said while swallowing hard. He leaned down and kissed me softly on the lips. I gazed at him and noticed his eyes were slightly weepy, and his forehead was creased.

I kept watching him as he turned around and walked toward what used to be my mother's hope chest. It was old, and the creamy white paint was almost completely peeled off. Ben's strides were slow and deliberate. This display of emotion was unusual. I had never seen him that overcome, not even when he asked me to marry him. It just wasn't his nature.

Turning the key that I always left in the keyhole, he opened the lid to the chest and said, "I don't see why you'd ever have to take off the bracelet, but just in case I'll put this"—he held the screwdriver up in the air—"in here so you know where to find it, okay?" He winked at me while pointing to the chest. I knew he never liked how unorganized I was, but he knew I could always find anything of importance in that chest.

I watched as Ben carefully looked for a place to put the screwdriver. He decided on a small square located in the red-velvet-covered tray that was hinged to the lid. From the bed I could see all the items that were meaningful to me. I smiled when I saw my dolls, yearbooks, diplomas, and various pictures. I finished putting on my other shoe, stood up, and walked behind him. I wrapped my arms around his waist and squeezed. He grabbed my arms and squeezed back for a few seconds before placing his hands on the lid. As he closed it, I saw Malibu Ken lying on top of all the other items, and my mind wandered back to the first time we had sex.

We were out surfing at our favorite spot, miles away from other people and cars. The swells were small so the surf was unburdened. It started to rain, but we continued to ride the most perfect waves. When the rain fell harder we swam to shore, boards attached to our legs, and it was almost pouring when we made a run for the car. Ben carried both of our boards while I carried all the other gear. A crack of thunder took him by surprise and made him fall with the two boards toppling down. I stopped to help him, throwing all the gear I was carrying to the ground. He just looked at me and laughed. "Fuck it." He put both boards together in the sand to make a teepee.

We were sitting under it, watching the rain hit the waves like sheets of glass shattering on the ground, when Ben leaned in and kissed me. We had kissed so many times before, but never like that. I pulled away at first, not sure where we were headed. I'd gone on the Pill a couple months before in anticipation of having sex for the first time. And as the tide creeped up I knew the time was upon us—I knew the time was right.

Ben brought my lips back to his and thrust his tongue to meet mine. I closed my eyes, craving his touch. I could smell the salt from the ocean on his warm skin and taste it on his tongue. He pulled me as close as he could and when we stopped kissing, I opened my eyes.

We were both breathing heavily, almost panting as the drumming of the rain continued. He gazed at me with his lips slightly parted. I pressed my fingers against his lips and he kissed them. Then I ran my fingers down his bare chest and across his well-defined stomach. I heard a slight intake of breath and with hooded eyes he kissed my lips again, this time a little harder. As his tongue entwined with mine, he slipped his hand inside my bikini top, rubbing circles around my nipple with his thumb.

The wind picked up, blowing my hair across our faces. Moaning into his mouth and straddling his lap, I felt his erection as I ground my hips into his. I ran my hands through his wet hair and down his bare back, hard enough that I could feel the grit of the sand rubbing against his skin.

Kissing his way down my throat, Ben whispered, "I love you, Dahl," before moving his hand behind my neck and tugging the string that held my bikini top in place.

My head fell back as he lightly kissed each of my now fully exposed nipples. I arched my back as his kisses turned into sucks and licks, sending a jolt of pleasure through my core and a shiver down my spine. I could feel his smile against my skin as I whimpered, "I love you, too."

Flashes of lightning lit the sky off in the distance, but the real spark was right here on the beach. As I reached down, pressing my hands against the outside of Ben's board shorts, he moved his hands to the inside of my knees and spread my legs open wider.

After outlining his erection with my fingers, I hooked my hands in the elastic of his shorts, wanting to lose the wet barrier between us. As my hands descended, Ben pulled away. "I want you—now."

"I want you, too," I responded as I leaned back from him so I could see his face, leaving my hands where they were.

As the ominous storm assaulted the beach, we continued to explore each other's bodies. When we were both panting uncontrollably, he stood up and reached for my hand, pulling me up, out of our shelter and into the pouring rain.

"Come on, let's go. I'll come back and get our shit later," he managed to say while pulling me close enough so that I could feel the raindrops from his body mix with mine. We stood there touching and kissing as he pulled me into his hardness, running his fingers inside the back of my bikini bottom.

Pulling away, I looked around the deserted beach. "Let's stay here."

Ben didn't need any more convincing as he pulled me back under our surfboard teepee and we had sex for the first time.

I remembered looking at him that day so long ago, with his blond hair and perpetual tan. When we stood there in the rain, about to take our relationship to the next step, I thought he looked more and more like my Malibu Ken doll. Ever since then I called him Malibu Ken or Ken for short. I remember he reacted by saying, "Shit, Dahl, people are going to think I play with Barbies." Then, with a wicked grin he continued. "But that's okay as long as you're my Barbie." He knew I was.

That night, before he closed the chest, I pulled out my Malibu Ken and set him on my dresser. When he saw it, he asked with an amused look, "Barbie belonged to Ken, right?" I nodded. "It's cool then."

I thought about how he tolerated my nickname for him over the years, even though he never really liked it. He just knew my Barbie dolls were a lifeline to my lost childhood—they photographed well, they let me style them, and they reminded me of happier times.

Ben suddenly shut the lid and the memory dissipated. Blinking my eyes, I returned to the present as he turned and hugged me tightly. I don't remember the last time we hugged like that, and again I felt a bit alarmed until he looked me in the eyes and said in the softest whisper, "Please, Dahl, I want to fuck you, make love to you, before we go."

With all the emotion and love I felt for him, I really didn't care how late we were, so I whispered back, "How can I turn you down when you asked so nicely?" Then in a half-joking, half-serious voice I added, "But make it quick!" I grabbed the back of his head and pulled him down for a kiss.

Ben kissed me differently than he had ever kissed me before, and then he made love to me differently than he had ever made love to me before. He was full of passion, like usual, but I also felt a need in him I'd never sensed before. He loved sex, and we had it often. He was usually quick and to the point, but now he took his time, his eyes never left me, and he never said a word. The look in his eyes and the way he touched me told me everything I needed to know.

Afterward, we held each other for a little while before he got up and went into the bathroom to get dressed again. I heard noises in the bathroom that sounded like sobbing. Ben had never cried—ever—but knowing we were going to be late, I vowed we would talk about his strange behavior when we came home that night.

●

The ominous glow of the headlights shone through the rain. I sat in his BMW and glanced over at him. Ben hated listening to Top 40 music, but he turned the radio station to 102.7 for me anyway, which made me smile. We were listening to Gavin DeGraw's "In Love with a Girl." I was singing along to the lyrics and was surprised when I saw Ben singing the words as well. Sensing me watching him, he turned, quickly looked at me, and stopped singing. "If I ever wrote a song, this is the one I'd have written about you," he said. Then he turned the radio up louder, and the lump that I had in my throat earlier returned.

We had been together so long that sometimes I lost sight of what I loved about him. At this moment I knew it was just everything; the way he carried his six-foot frame, his short dirty blond hair, his dimples, and the way he commanded attention from everyone with his confidence. Sometimes it seemed to border on arrogance, but it only made people notice him more.

Growing up he was all surfer, and as an adult he still was. I smiled, thinking that as a kid he had such a bad mouth, was hotheaded, and most teachers said he had a poor attitude, but I never thought so. That was just his way. As I looked over at him driving on the freeway I realized it still was his way, and God, I loved him.

He looked at me as he pulled off onto the streets of L.A. "What?" he asked while turning the radio down as the song ended.

Grinning at him, I reached over the console and placed my hand on his thigh before I ran it up his leg. "We're going to be late to your first award party, and it's all your fault."

With a shit-eating grin on his face he said, "So fucking worth it," as he changed the radio station.

We stopped at a traffic light, and I took my hand off his leg to turn the radio station back. I heard tires squealing, and when I looked up, I saw a big black SUV with heavily tinted windows jackknifed in front of us. Its passenger door opened, and a man in a ski mask jumped out holding a gun.

I screamed at Ben, "Oh my God, he has a gun!"

Panic set in instantly, and I struggled to breathe as he approached Ben's side.

"Get the fuck out of the car!"

I was frozen in place with fear. *What's going on?* In my panicked state, I hit the LOCK button on the door, but it was already locked. My sweaty palms were shaking, and I grabbed for Ben. He looked at me, and I knew he was trying to contain his emotions. "Just keep calm, Dahl."

My eyes were locked on the gunman as his eyes shifted to me. Terror shot through me as he tapped his gun against the window a couple of times and then pointed it at my head.

Frantically, I started beating the dash and was screaming, "Drive, Ben, drive!"

He pounded the steering wheel with his fists. "We're fucking blocked in."

He grabbed my hand tightly, while his other moved to open the car door. "Call nine-one-one!"

I was petrified. "What are you doing?"

"Whatever happens, don't get out of this car." His voice was deep and quavering. "Do you hear me?"

I heard the click of the door and screamed, "Ben, don't!"

He stepped onto the pavement and I yelled, "You don't have to be the hero! Come back!"

Not taking my eyes off Ben, with trembling hands I managed to dial 911 before the phone slipped through my fingers.

I heard a shot. Ben fell to the ground. "No! No! Noooo!"

My vision started to blur as I swallowed back the bile that rose in my throat. My screams faded into squealing police sirens. The sirens grew louder as I grew numb, and "It's Not My Time" by 3 Doors Down played on the radio while my world came crashing down.

CHAPTER 4
The Diary of Dahl

Black is everywhere. It's the ground where he fell, it's the bag his beautiful body was taken away in, it's the color of the dress I wore to his funeral, it's how I feel, and it's the color of the journal I have kept since I was ten. The journal he talked me into keeping because he had been keeping one of his own. Even then, he loved putting words on paper. I never got a thrill out of it, and now it just plummets me further into the darkness.

●

3 days after . . .
March 6
The funeral. His sister, Serena, took care of everything. His best friend, Caleb, was in town. I didn't even know he was back from his tour in Afghanistan. He helped Serena. His mother, Grace; his sister; his nephew, Trent; and I sat together. That's really all I remember.

3 months later . . .

June 9

Each day is a test of will. Will I get out of bed, will I take a shower, will I leave the house, will I eat dinner, will I sleep on the couch, the floor, or in the spare room? Because there is no fucking way I'm going back into that bedroom. When I go in there—I see him everywhere—and when I sleep in there I can't stop dreaming about him. The thing is, they are not dreams; they are nightmares because when I dream, I dream he's here with me, and when I wake up—I'm alone.

I had my first dream about a week after he was killed. I woke up in the middle of the night, and he was lying next to me. I laid my head on his chest to hear him breathe. I ran my hand up his stomach to feel his hard muscles. God, he felt so good and I missed him so much, and here he was. So I laid my head on his chest, happy to have him back, and fell back asleep. Of course, when I woke up in the morning, he was gone.

I had my second dream after Grace insisted on taking me to the doctor because she knew I wasn't sleeping well. The doctor prescribed Ambien, and that night I decided to sleep in *our* room. Grace stayed with me, as she often did, and I fell asleep easily. I woke up in darkness. He was leaning over me, kissing me, running his hand up my thigh and under my shorts. He moved my panties to the side and plunged his finger inside me before removing my panties. Then he removed his boxers and slid inside me easily, moving slow at first, then faster, his thrusts increasing until he found his release. That is when I woke up and realized he wasn't here, I was alone again and my dream was just a sweet memory of what we had done so many times before he was killed.

The nightmares of his death come no matter where I sleep. They are of that night, the road we took, the stoplight, the gun, the loud echoing sound of the bullet that fired out of its chamber, him calling me by my full name, and him falling to the ground—blood everywhere. In my nightmares we take different roads and stop at different lights, but the outcome is always the same. He calls me by my full name and then he dies. Dahlia. Death. Those two words have echoed in my head almost every night.

The police called Grace last week to let her know they had arrested the man who killed him. They found the gun he used. His fingerprints were all over it, which led the police directly to him. He later confessed to the shooting. Serena came by to let me know because Grace couldn't talk about it. She was just too upset. Caleb stopped by later to check on me and ended up sleeping on the couch. He's worried about me so he crashes here a lot lately.

●

6 months later . . .
September 15
I haven't been coping well with his death, with life without him. I know this. I still can't say his name. He was my friend, my love—my everything. When my parents died, I was only fourteen years old and even though I moved in with my uncle, I would have felt really alone if it hadn't been for Ben's tender affection.

My uncle was a shell of a man who had lost his wife and only brother in the plane crash that took them all from us. The crash that not only ended my life as I knew it, but also any dreams of performing; performing at the Greek where my father wanted so much to see me onstage. I never thought I would recover from losing my parents, but even at fourteen, Ben was not only my best friend, but also my sole source of comfort. We spent every day together in the year following my parents' death and we formed an unbreakable bond.

When tragedy struck again, there he was: my rock, the mountain I depended on to give me strength. I don't really remember my parents' funeral. I think I blocked out most of that devastating time. But I do remember him sitting next to me when my uncle died, staying with me, taking care of me just as he had done when I lost my parents. But he couldn't do that when he died.

I remember my uncle's funeral well. I was kneeling in the pew of the empty church, crying as Ben came to sit beside me, pulling me onto the bench. Smoothing out the wrinkles in my black skirt, he said, "I've looked everywhere for you, Dahl. What are you doing here so early?"

Looking around, I noticed there was no one else in the church and thought how appropriate that was. I looked into his blue eyes and cried, "I'm all alone now."

I shifted my gaze quickly to look somewhere else, anywhere but at him. I didn't want him to see me crying. I was stronger than that. I was a girl who knew death well. As I looked back to the front of the church I caught sight of Jesus on the cross. The colors from the stained glass windows reflected on the statue, and Jesus suddenly looked amazingly beautiful and tranquil. I wished I could feel that much at peace.

Cupping my chin, he turned me to face him as he looked at me with his crystal blue eyes. "You will never be alone; you will always have me. You know that, right, Dahl?"

But I don't have him. He's gone, just like the rest of my family, and I'm alone.

9 months later . . .
December 18

Recently, I've started leaving the house, but I feel like I have no hope, nothing to look forward to. I haven't gone back to work. I don't really have to work, for the money anyway. Not that money matters to me in the least. Between what my parents left me and what he left me, along with the mortgage insurance that paid off the house, financially, I'm secure. Emotionally . . . that's a different story. I can't seem to care about anything.

Grace and Aerie stop by almost every day. Serena comes as often as she can. Caleb brings dinner at least once a week and stays to watch TV until I fall asleep. These are the only people I have left in the world now. I've had many friends, but these are the only people I've stayed close with. They try to get me to go out with them: lunch, movies, errands even, but I can't seem to go anywhere without breaking down.

My last breakdown was mid-October. Serena brought me to the farmers' market to get apples because she wanted to make an apple pie. I didn't want to go but she insisted. When we got to the market I saw that the outside was decorated with pumpkins and bales of hay. Off to the side of the entrance was a huge display of ghosts and goblins. I didn't open the car door. I couldn't. I told Serena to go in without me. She was used to my mood swings and didn't argue anymore, so she went on ahead.

As I stared at the Halloween display with tears streaming down my face, I remembered our first Halloween party together as freshmen in college. His fraternity house was having a party and at the last minute he told me we had to dress up. I was so pissed because he knew I didn't dress up for Halloween, and even if I did, we didn't have costumes to wear.

I was so mad at him, I was seeing red. My mouth started spewing nasty words before I could stop myself. "Why do you always have to do things last minute? Can't you get your shit together just once and think ahead?"

Not answering, not arguing back, not even looking at me, he strode over to the bed and grabbed the two sheets off it. He still hadn't said a word even as my yelling continued.

As I watched him, my fury only grew. "What the fuck are you doing now?"

Taking the sheets into his bathroom, he came out holding a pair of nail scissors.

He walked over to me with the sheets in his hands; he started cutting holes in one. When he was done he grinned at me. "Here, you be a ghost," he announced, while tossing the cut-up sheet over my head, "and I'll be a goblin," he said while cutting the other sheet into strips and wrapping his body with it.

"I'm not wearing that. I'm not wearing any costume. I hate Halloween," I hissed at him as I pulled it off my head. He knew I hated Halloween and I knew he knew why. Of course he knew why. "Fine then, be your own fucking gorgeous self," he said, grinning as he pulled me to him and kissed me hard. "Now let's go to the fucking party and have some fun." And just like that, we went to the party.

He didn't take my shit; he just took care of the situation, of me, always. So as I sat in Serena's car missing him and remembering that day, I thought, *God, he definitely had his flaws, but he always knew how to win me over.*

I wish I could have done the same for him, but it never worked out that way. When he was mad at me, his anger would linger no matter what I tried to do or say. It could last one hour or one day. I had learned to just stay away and let him come to me when he was ready. He didn't express his love in words very often, but his gestures more than made up for it. At the end of the day he always made sure I knew how much he loved me. That's just one of the many things I miss every day.

●

12 months later . . .
March 4, 2011
Grace insisted I stay with her for a week and she took me to see my therapist every day. She received an update on his killer. The police told her the shooter would be standing trial within the next twelve months. I didn't mind staying with her because loneliness and heartbreak were eating away at me.

Yesterday was the anniversary of his death, and after visiting the cemetery Grace sat me down and told me it was time to take my ring off. She handed me a long white gold chain she had bought and told me to wear the ring around my neck until I felt I could take it off and put it away forever. She reminded me that the ring, and Ben, would be a fond memory that I would have forever, but it was time to start living my life. She cried more that day than I'd seen her cry in the past year and I realized just how deep her grief ran, too.

After arriving home, I sat outside on the stone patio I love so much. It was quiet and peaceful—my own private oasis with a pebble stone path that leads to a pool. I noticed the purple flowers from the salvia had bloomed. Most of the wildflowers were starting to bloom. I started to cry thinking spring was here already. Another season alone.

Walking down the pathway, I saw that butterflies were everywhere. I sat in one of the Adirondack chairs on the back of the patio and looked at the dazzling ring on my hand. He picked out the 2.5-carat Tiffany bezel princess-cut ring himself and told me it reminded him of me. The platinum-set diamond is elegant, modern, and simply radiant.

As I twisted it around my finger, I thought back on the day he proposed. I'd just graduated from grad school, and he was already working full-time at the paper. We had both been really busy, so I insisted he take off work the Monday after my graduation, and he surprisingly agreed, saying we needed to spend some time together. Having just moved into our house in Laguna Beach, we decided to get some things done on Sunday and make Monday our fun day.

We woke up early that morning. I stepped into the backyard to watch the sunrise and I recall the way my skin pricked from the chill in the air. I remember the light breeze that swept through my hair. As he walked in front of me I could see the waistband of his board shorts slightly peeking out from his jeans. I threw on my favorite J.Crew black-and-white-striped sweater over my bikini.

We packed up the BMW M5 Touring with all our gear and headed to Rockpile Beach. I didn't really care for the surfing there, but he loved it. "The coast has a sick reef break right now. Depending on the conditions, we could catch a right at the north corner, and if it comes together it will be cranking. Come on, Dahl, it only happens maybe three times a year and right now is one of them." He was so excited I couldn't possibly say no.

When we arrived at the beach, I looked out at the waves and gasped. The paddling channel was to the south of the beach where the rip allowed easy access to some very big, thick, and grinding waves. He took his aviator sunglasses off and watched them. They looked rough, about eight feet high. A lot of water was rushing into the small cove. We didn't even get out of the car. He knew there was no way I was going to be able to surf those waves without getting crushed.

"Go ahead, go. I'll watch you," I said, staring at the waves crashing against the rocks.

"Nah, I don't have a death wish today, another time, Dahl. Let's head down south," he said with his hand cupped over his blue eyes, squinting out into the vast Pacific. He put his sunglasses back on and pulled onto US 1. It was a beautiful day. We had the windows open, and I could feel the heat of the sun soaking into my skin. The Cure was blaring through the speakers. "You hungry? I'm starving. Taco Bell first?" he asked with a huge smile on his face. For some reason he only liked that particular Taco Bell.

Rolling my eyes at his choice, I smiled and nodded my head. "Sure, why not, but I get to pick the dinner spot."

"Sa-weet," he said, laughing.

After lunch he surprised me. "What do you say we grab some towels and head down to the beach where it's a little quieter? We might even catch some Zs?"

"You don't want to surf?" I asked as I looked out onto the blue of the Pacific, the waves ripping radiantly out to the horizon, and many surfers already on their boards.

"Nah, not feeling it," he said, grabbing my hand and leading me to the car to grab the towels. We then walked down to the never-ending beach of glistening sand.

We headed out a couple of miles until we were far away from the crowd. He threw a towel on the sand and picked me up, making like he was going to throw me on it. I screamed in protest as he gently laid me on the towel, bracing himself on top of me to kiss me. It was so quiet I could hear the birds squawking as they dove into the water to catch their prey.

"I've missed this," he whispered while dipping his head

down to kiss my neck, tickling me with his unshaven face, "and I've missed you not being around." He continued running his hands down the length of my body.

"I've missed you, too, you know. At least I'm finally done with school forever!" I began running my fingers through his blond hair. "Now I'll be out in the real world; no homework, no internships, no thesis. Just plain everyday work and I'm so looking forward to it," I said as I pulled him back down to my lips and ran my hands down his back.

He braced himself on his forearms, and stared at me for a long time.

"What?"

"You," he replied. "You're just so fucking gorgeous."

I shook my head and smiled at him like I always did when he said that to me.

"Really, you are. I could look at you, be with you, for the rest of my life," he said while standing up to reach into the inside pocket of his board shorts. He pulled out something silver and shiny but I couldn't quite see what it was with the sun so bright and my sunglasses off. Maybe it was a coin or his watch, I couldn't tell.

Then he sat back on both knees and pulled me up off my back and onto my knees. "Dahl London, I have loved you my whole life and don't ever want to know what it is like to live without you. Marry me!"

The wind blowing though my backyard brought me back to the present. I stopped twisting my ring as I stood up and reached into my pocket to retrieve the necklace Grace had given me. With tears in my eyes, I walked over to the flowers and sat on the grass to smell them. After I inhaled their beautiful scent, I picked one, a silent tear rolling down my face and I decided—yes—it was time.

15 months later . . .

May 18

I woke up in the spare room, the room that has become my room. But when I woke up today I felt different. I felt a little better than I did yesterday and much better than I did last month or the month before that. I looked out the window and the sun was shining. I decided I needed to get up, and as I did, I looked at the bare walls and my clothes thrown all over the floor. Maybe today would be the day that I go in our room—no, that room. I hated this room I was in, but couldn't help feeling that its drab, lifeless personality properly reflected how I felt.

After we moved in, I never got around to decorating it. The walls and carpet are still a gloomy shade of off-white, the windows are bare, and there is very little furniture. The room has no personality; it looks exactly the same way I've been feeling.

I pulled myself out of bed and walked down the hall to the bathroom, thinking about how much I hated it as well. Maybe I should go back to that room today. My room, I mentally corrected myself. My therapist wants me to call things in the house *my* instead of *our*, but I can't do that yet.

I walked to the closed bedroom door at the end of the hallway, and when my hand touched the doorknob, I considered whether or not I should open it. I remembered the dreams I had when I slept in there and how real they seemed and I knew his presence was in there—everywhere.

I mentally pushed myself to open the door and look in. It was unchanged; I hadn't let anyone go in there, not even Grace. The bed wasn't made. My dress was thrown over a chair in the corner. My many strands of white pearls and a single strand of black pearls were strung over the mirror attached to my dresser. They were my aunt's most cherished pearls, handed down from her mother, left to me when she died. I saw my running shoes under the chair as I walked across the room, touching various items on my way to the bathroom. I actually laughed as I looked at the necklaces, remembering his *pearls remind me of Grammy* comment.

I started to feel like maybe time had stood still, but I knew that wasn't true—it only did in here. I looked around at all of our things and knew it was time. It would be strange not having his things here to remind me of him, but I would always remember him, he was a part of me, he *is* a part of me, a part of my heart, a part of my soul, a part of my everything. Always.

As I stood at the dresser, I looked at his things. I grinned as I spotted his bottle of cologne, the cologne his sister bought him so long ago, the cologne he hardly ever used. He used to say, "Cologne is just a masculine name for male perfume; either way it's made for chicks."

I laughed a little at his need to redefine words as I caught a glimpse of myself in the mirror: gaunt cheekbones, light splattering of freckles, unkempt hair, and tired hazel eyes. I remembered that he would always tell me, *You're so fucking gorgeous.* I wonder what he'd say if he saw me now. Probably something like, "Dahl, get your shit together already." Even at that I laughed because his use of obscenities wasn't really vulgar, it was just a part of his everyday vocabulary, and over the years had become a part of mine.

I looked in the mirror and I saw my engagement ring hanging around my neck and the bracelet encircling my wrist. I was aching inside at the thought that this ring wouldn't hang around my neck forever, but I knew I would always wear my LOVE bracelet. I will wear this bracelet, not just because he gave it to me the day he died, but because he gave it to me and said, *This says what I never seem to be able to say*. I never doubted his love, but that gesture more than proved it. Thinking about it almost brought me to my knees. So as I looked at the bracelet, I promised myself that it would be a constant reminder that I would always say what needs to be said—no regrets.

The mirror seemed to only reflect a messy room. It is not our room, it is not that room, and it is not my room. It was just a messy room. Grace wanted to clean it up a million times, but I wouldn't let her. I wasn't ready for the memories of that beautiful day, our last day together, to be erased, but now I knew the memories could never be erased because they were ingrained in my mind forever.

Moving away from the dresser and looking around the room again, I asked myself, "What have I become?" But I already knew the answer. I'd become empty, almost completely void of emotion and I didn't want to be like that anymore. I needed to let time back into this room. I knew I had to put that day away. I needed to become me again. With that thought, I reached down and grabbed my running shoes. I headed toward the door and smiled, but not before snatching my iPod. I would start my day with a run and listen to some music. I would run and clear my head. Then maybe when I came back I'd start what I knew I should have already started.

CHAPTER 5
Every Storm Runs Out of Rain

Present Day

Fall is in the air. There is a cool breeze all around me blowing orange, yellow, and red leaves in circles. As I exit the park to head back to my house, I pass a bunch of kids raking leaves into piles and watch as they jump in, carefree, with no worries about what lies beneath. I wonder what I would feel if I were to jump into those leaves.

I have been running almost every day. Running makes me feel human again; it sets my mind free and allows me to forget everything. I ran five miles this morning and felt like I could have pushed myself another five, but I promised Aerie I would meet up with her. We've been meeting for lunch at least twice a week and for dinner almost every Friday night.

Walking through the front door I notice the boxes, some labeled, some still empty, piled in the corners and know I should finish packing up his things. Maybe later. I've started sleeping in my room again. On the nights that I wake up thinking he is still here, I end up sleeping on the couch, but it is happening less and less these days and so are the nightmares of his death.

After taking a shower, I go out to the garage where his car is parked next to mine, our surfboards are in the corner, and our surfing gear is piled on the shelves. He's everywhere, but nowhere at all.

On the drive to the restaurant I pass things that remind me of him, as I do every time I leave the neighborhood. He's at the corner bus stop where he would drop off Mr. Langston, our elderly neighbor, every Wednesday morning. He's at the drugstore, where he would go whenever he ran out of something, always in a hurry.

As memories flood my mind and thoughts of what used to be cloud my vision, I finally realize what I have to do to move on. Today, as I drive down my street—what used to be our street—I finally realize it is time for my own personal storm to end. No umbrella can stop me from getting wet while living in that house, what used to be our house. It's like the thunder has finally stopped crackling in my head, and as the clouds begin to move away, tiny rays of sunshine start to filter in. I know I have to move out of the home we once shared.

Walking into the restaurant, I smile as I spot Aerie in her jet-black suit and bright pink blouse, all buttoned up and put together. I glance down at my jeans, Converse sneakers, a Bon Jovi 1987 concert tour T-shirt, and my leather jacket and I'm already anticipating the concerned look she's going to give me.

I sit at the white linen–clothed round table in the middle of the restaurant; she's on her cell phone, no doubt giving orders to someone. Aerie hits the END CALL button and places her phone on the table as she stands to greet me. As expected, she looks me up and down before hugging me like I'm made of glass and might break if she squeezes too tight.

"Still not eating," are the first words out of her mouth before lifting a piece of my hair as she wrinkles her nose. "Dahlia girl, I'm taking you to see my hairdresser tomorrow, and I don't want any lip from you. Your hair isn't even blond anymore."

"So nice to see you, too. How are you? Glad you could meet me for lunch."

I continue. "Seriously, maybe you could start out with something like that before laying into me." I try to keep a straight face but I can't hold back the giggle that escapes, sounding more like a snort.

I know she's worried about me, but we have gone through this little exchange every time I meet her and really, enough is enough. Last week she took me to get my nails done after having grabbed my hands and wincing at the dirt still stuck under my nails from gardening. In my defense, she called me at the last minute when I was weeding the flowerbed and I only had time for a quick shower. It's not like I'm walking around dirty and unshowered, for Christ sakes.

I decide to move on and tell her my decision.

"I had a revelation on the way over here."

"Really? And what would that be?"

Attempting to restrain my voice as much as I can manage, while fighting back the tears, I say, "I'm going to sell the house."

Concern is written on her face as she responds, "Are you sure? I mean, are you sure you're ready? The last time Grace talked to you about the idea, you shut her down flat."

I shift a little in my chair and take a sip of water. "Yeah, I'm sure. Everything about the house reminds me of Ben, and it's not just the house, it's the whole damn neighborhood. I need to do this. I know I do." As I tell Aerie how I feel, as I finally start to open up to her for the first time in a long time, I realize that I just said his name. I actually used his name. I said Ben. I said the name I must have said over a million times until almost two years ago, and I know I'm starting to heal. My body tenses from the realization, and my eyes fill with tears. I try to relax and will them not to spill over.

Aerie reaches across the table and gently wipes at my cheek where a few of the persistent tears flow against my will. She takes a deep breath, and I see her eyes start to fill, too. "I think it's a good idea. I think you need to remove yourself from the things that prevent you from moving forward."

I take my napkin and wipe my mouth for no reason. "I know I need to, I just don't know if I can really do it."

The waiter approaches and takes our order. Once he leaves, Aerie looks directly at me with concern still etched on her face. "Yes, you can. You are stronger than you think, and you have me. You have Grace and Serena, too. We will all help."

Putting her napkin on her lap, she gives me a slight smile. "I think moving is the best decision you've made in a while."

Her voice cracks a little as she adds, "And this is none of my business, but you know that has never stopped me before, so I'm just going to throw this out there for you."

She pauses for a minute, looking anywhere except at me, and then continues. "I was thinking, why don't you give his car to Trent?"

Her words come out fast and I can see the tears begin to well up in her eyes again. After all this time, Aerie still hasn't been able to say his name to me, probably out of fear that I will break down.

I'm sure I'm going to surprise the shit out of her with my quick response.

"You know what? That's a great idea. In fact, I'll call Serena and see if it's okay. I have actually been thinking about that for a while, since Trent turns sixteen next week."

I take a piece of bread and rip off the crust. I dunk it in the olive oil, hoping that the distraction will stop the stinging in my eyes.

"I think Ben would have wanted his nephew to have his car. He loved that car and he loved Trent. I know Trent misses Ben, too, surfing with him, and driving to the beach with him. Trent always told Ben his car had so much power and he loved to ride anywhere with him."

Shaking my head and laughing a little, I think about how happy this will make Trent. I'm also trying not to cry at the thought of Ben's car not being parked next to mine, as I chew the piece of bread that I feel I might choke on.

Aerie laughs a little, but tears are rolling down her cheeks. She picks up her napkin and dabs the tears off her cheeks. "God, he did love that damn car."

Her laughter fades as she reaches her hand across the table and sets it next to my plate, silently asking for mine.

"Dahlia, you know how much he loved you."

She pauses a minute like she's trying to decide if she should say something or not as she starts to pat my hand.

"And because of how much he loved you, you know he would want you to move on and live your life. I think he would be happy with your decision."

Removing her hand from mine, she clears her throat. Smiling, and just barely laughing now, she adds, "I also know if he were here, he would have kicked your ass for not making that decision sooner."

Aerie pauses again, raising her water glass and waiting for me to do the same. Then she clinks her glass to mine. "To bright days ahead, Dahlia girl. I know they're coming."

And before either of us can cry, our food arrives.

We spend the rest of lunch chatting about nothing important, and I enjoy the food and the company. As we finish, Aerie's tone suddenly becomes more serious. "I need a favor," she says, tilting her head to the side and smiling at me. "Tom quit yesterday, and I need you back at work. I'm really short-staffed in the photo department at the magazine. Dahlia girl, please, I need you."

I sigh, knowing I'm not ready to commit to anything full-time, and without thinking, I quickly answer, "I'd be happy to help you out until you get someone else."

"No, I mean come back to work full-time. Take Tom's job. I need you."

Crossing my arms and leaning back in my chair, I gaze at her slightly wavy bright blond hair, her perky little nose, and petite, toned body. But underneath that beauty I know lurks a beast. I have a feeling I'm about to see that side as I bring this conversation to an end.

"Aerie, come on, don't ask me to make such a big decision. Don't say you need a favor and then not like my answer, it's not fucking fair."

She knows I can never resist a request when someone asks with such need. I'm just a sucker like that—always have been. "I only just decided to sell the house. Let me get through that first and then we can talk about work, okay?" I look her straight in the eyes and add, "But I will help you on my terms. So, is working only on an as-needed basis okay for now?"

Surprisingly, Aerie's irritation seems to settle quickly. Sighing, she takes a sip of her water and looks at me. As she pushes her plate aside, she smirks and says, "That's called freelancing, and in my defense, I didn't know you were going to come here and tell me you decided to sell your house. So I'm sorry. Okay?" She sticks her tongue out at me for good measure.

I smile as I roll my eyes at her. "Whatever. Do you want my help or not?" She laughs and so do I.

Aerie started working at *Sound Music* right out of college while I went to grad school. She worked her way up the ladder quickly and now manages the main features department. Once I graduated I went to work for her as a photo stylist. My love is photography but my passion is music, so with my degree in place I was able to meld my love and passion together into what became a dream job. And maybe now is the time to return to work.

❧

A week later, and it's Thursday night. My routine consists of putting on my pajamas, brushing my teeth, and lying down on the couch to watch *Vampire Diaries*. Every Thursday Ben and I used to watch it together. He told me he hated the show, but he always watched it with me anyway. I used to think he secretly had a crush on Elena. We would pop popcorn, get my quilt and pillows out of the closet, and lie feet to feet on our giant sofa. I've continued the tradition, only without the popcorn since Ben was always the one who ate the whole bowl anyway.

Just as I settle on the sofa, with the quilt my mom and I made together, and turn on the TV, my cell phone rings. Aerie's name flashes across the screen and I roll my eyes. "What do you want?" I answer.

"I know, I know. *Vampire Diaries!* But listen, and do not say anything, and do not say no. I have you on the eleven o'clock flight tomorrow morning to McCarran International to conduct the initial photo-style interview with River Wilde."

"What? Are you crazy? No! No fucking way!" I tell her, shaking my head for emphasis even though I know she can't see me.

Aerie ignores my outburst and tells me she's already arranged for me to meet the lead singer of the Wilde Ones at *Sound Music*'s corporate headquarters in Las Vegas tomorrow afternoon. She stresses, "The lead singer, you know, River Wilde," in case I'm suddenly suffering from amnesia. Aerie tells me River is in Las Vegas for some kind of promotional event and had a last-minute change in his schedule. She has no one else to do it and he only has a small window of time for the magazine to meet with him on Friday. Then she says, "And, Dahlia girl, this is a huge opportunity for me and the magazine, so please."

Turning down the volume on the TV and looking around at everything I have to pack, I tell her, "I can't go on such short notice— you know that. I just put the house on the market."

"No, I know no such thing. Having your house up for sale isn't the issue. Being gone one night won't make a difference. I'm not dumb. I know you. I know what's going on in that pretty head of yours, and this has nothing to do with your crush, I promise."

She stops a minute, then continues. "You're afraid to see him, your secret rock star crush, but come on, Dahlia. He probably won't even remember you." She says it so matter-of-factly I actually feel a little hurt.

I think to myself that actually River Wilde was my crush before he was a rock star, and no matter what she says, she's obviously setting me up so I can't say no. Aerie knows I secretly swooned over him after we met at the USC Campus Bar many years ago. She knows he's the singer whose songs were always on repeat, not only on my iPod, but also in my head. And she knows he was the one singer I never talked to Ben about, and now she wants me to meet him, again.

"You are going to owe me so big—you know that, right? I'll do it because I'm sure he won't remember me anyway and even so it's not like anything embarrassing happened, you know?" I finally manage to croak out.

"Thank you so much. I really do love you, Dahlia girl," Aerie croons, and then spends the next hour telling me the highlights of River's career to prepare me for the interview.

After we hang up, my mind wanders back to how I felt that night I met River. That was still the only time someone's touch sent goose bumps up my arms. I clearly remember the feelings I felt then, feelings I have long since buried. I hope to God they don't resurface tomorrow. But how could they? Those were a young college girl's feelings. A girl who was in love with someone else anyway.

Every now and then I have thoughts about our intense connection that night and wonder if it might have been more in my mind than it actually was. More like it was okay to want to believe in something you knew couldn't possibly be.

Besides, even if the connection was real, River is somewhat famous now and I'm sure he has a lot of women after him. What does any of that matter anyway? I'm still a broken girl struggling through my grief, trying to reenter the real world without the man who is still a part of me.

I haven't paid much attention to River's career since Ben's death. Curiosity takes over and I do an Internet search for his name. I read a few articles about him, backing up what Aerie already told me, and download his latest songs. I slip into my bed around eleven, not even realizing I never watched *Vampire Diaries*.

CHAPTER 6
Begin Again

Peeking through Nevada's desert haze is the most dynamic city on earth. As my plane circled the airport waiting to land, my stomach was in knots with a mixture of nervous excitement and downright fear. I'm nervous because this is my first day back at work in almost two years. But I'm excited because I finally feel like I'm doing something productive after so long. And I'm fearful because of who I will be interviewing. Well, not really fearful so much as uncertain and apprehensive—or, dare I say, eager to meet with him.

We've been circling for almost forty-five minutes. I'm listening to the music I recently downloaded. Looking out the window and past the clouds, I can see the famous Las Vegas strip and I'm trying to comprehend how I allowed myself to be talked into this job. How is it that in just a few short minutes I'm going to be seeing River again?

Earlier this morning Aerie texted me a list of hygiene tips I might want to consider before hitting my first "freelance" job. These things included shaving my legs and blow-drying my hair, both of which she knows I've done very infrequently since Ben's death. She also rudely advised me to put some thought into my wardrobe selection.

Last night I carefully picked out what I was going to wear today. I'd decided on a white blouse, a black pencil skirt, and standard high-heeled black pumps. I woke up dreading the day ahead of me, but after listening to the Wilde Ones' album this morning, their music had energized me.

I'd happily showered and used my favorite grapefruit-scented shampoo. I not only took extra time to lather it in and repeat the process, but I decided to ditch my chosen business attire in favor of something more fun. My showers are usually the five-minute quick in-and-out variety, but today it lasted much longer. I felt different, maybe even excited. I'd actually danced around my bedroom before getting dressed and I can't remember the last time I did that.

Feeling concerned about my appearance for the first time in a long time, I decided casual was better than trendy, and then decided sophisticated was better than casual, and in the end went with a mix of all three. I had selected black skinny jeans and my most loved white swing top with THE KINKS scripted diagonally across it and LOLA underneath in black faded letters. I also threw on my gray moto leather jacket with the hoodie snapped off, and a pair of black open-toed wedge booties. I hadn't been shopping in so long, I don't even know if the shoes were still in style, but they're comfortable. After adding some eyeliner, mascara, and lip gloss, I was ready to go.

Now as the plane finally lands, I take a deep breath, and walk down the Jetway. I laugh as I read the sign at the end of the walkway that says, WHAT HAPPENS IN VEGAS, STAYS IN VEGAS. As I make my way through the airport, I smile again at the noise of the slot machine handles being pulled and bells ringing for lucky winners. After collecting my luggage in baggage claim, I set foot on Sin City's pavement and wait for a taxi to take me to my destination.

It's early November and the weather is crisp and mild. As I sit in the backseat of the taxicab, I can feel the bright sunshine through the window permeate my skin. I want to embrace the warmth and take a few deep breaths, trying to curb my sudden onset of jitters. I feel so many emotions running through me as I consider the two possible extreme outcomes of meeting River today. How will I feel if he doesn't remember me? How will I feel if he does? The answer to both questions: I have no idea.

Knowing I'm in a hurry, the driver tells me he will take the fastest route he can. As he's explaining that it is the longer distance around the strip, but much shorter timewise, I zone out. God, what if he doesn't even remember me when I've never been able to forget him? Or what if he does and we still have that strong connection? Is he still adorably charming and utterly charismatic? Why am I even thinking this way? I'm here to do a job and that's all I should be thinking about. River is just a person I have to interview to prepare for a photo shoot. I've done this job a thousand times. "Just do your job, that's all you have to do," I say to myself over and over again.

I watch the crowds of people walking down the sidewalk, men and women, couples and families, winners and losers, and I think about how they're all here to forget about their everyday lives. This is the perfect day for me to do the same. Today I'm Dahlia London, the photographer. I can be that girl. I was that girl. I am that girl. I will not be Dahlia London, poor girl whose fiancé was killed in front of her.

The sunlight streaming through the cab window is reflecting off the diamonds of my bracelet. As I look out onto the street I see a man dressed in a suit, walking while checking his phone, and I can't help but think of Ben. Ben was always multitasking, and he was able to accomplish more in a single day than I ever could in a week. I smile at the memory of the man who was so driven and so successful at such a young age. Taking deep, cleansing breaths, I look at my bracelet again and remember the reason I will never take it off. The promise I made to myself: to have no regrets. Those thoughts are what I will take with me as I interview the one man I had an almost dalliance with once, a long time ago.

The taxi is approaching the office building on East Harmon Avenue, just a few blocks east of the Hard Rock Hotel where I will be staying. Since I'm running short on time, I decide against dropping my bags off at the hotel first.

I hop out of the cab and as I do, I hear my phone ring. I answer it while grabbing my suitcase and messenger bag and make my way into the building. With my shoulder holding the phone to my ear, I open the large double doors. The lobby is quiet; it's Friday afternoon, so I suspect many employees are gone for the weekend. Aerie is on the phone frantically screaming that I'm late and telling me to get up to the seventh floor immediately because River is already there. After reassuring Aerie that I've arrived and am on my way up, I exit the elevator and hit the END CALL button.

Practically running to get to the conference room, I trail my suitcase behind me. I turn the corner and start down the hallway where I can see through the conference room's glass wall. There he sits, River Wilde, looking down at his phone. My heart is pounding at the mere sight of him, and the feelings I felt five years ago come flooding back.

I slow down my pace, take a few deep breaths, and pause to straighten my jacket. The shift of my body weight causes my messenger bag to fall off the top of my suitcase and it hits the marble floor with a loud noise. Looking around the empty hall, I pick up my bag and continue walking, but as I lift my eyes and River Wilde comes into view, he's no longer looking at his phone. He's looking at me. He's still just as captivating as he was so long ago, but this time the word *dangerous* no longer applies.

My legs are shaking and my stomach is doing flip-flops as I make my way to the conference room. I'm not a nervous person by nature, but the fact that I asked myself, *Could love at first sight be real?* when I met him that night makes me nervous as hell. The silence in the office adds to my anxiety; the only sound is my shoes clicking across the tile floor.

As I approach the door, I can see him running his hand through his hair. He's walking around the conference table toward the door, and we reach it at the same time. With a nervous grip, I grab the door handle, dropping my eyes from his as my bracelet hits against the glass, causing a sharp pain to radiate through my wrist.

I wince as I stumble into him. When our bodies meet, my nervousness evaporates. I'm so close to him. I can smell his soapy, just-showered scent that I remember so well. I can feel his hard body, and as I look up, I see the smooth skin on his face, and my knees buckle beneath me.

Goose bumps run up my arms and down my legs. Our collision has awakened something in me. Something I haven't felt in a very long time. Desire.

I'm sure I'm staring as I continue to gaze into his eyes, searching for that look he gave me long ago, but before I can find it, our connection is broken.

He takes a step back and I notice his gleaming green eyes looking me up and down. Remembering I'm supposed to be Dahlia London, the interviewer, I try to calm my nerves. I drop my eyes to escape his intense gaze and begin to speak a mash of garbled words that make very little sense, even to me. "Excuse me," "I'm so sorry," "Thank you," and "Oh shit."

Shifting my eyes into the room, embarrassed by my lack of professionalism, I somehow manage to look at him again. I take in his faded jeans, black Doc Martens and gray T-shirt with FENDER written across it in black. He's still so overwhelmingly attractive. He looks exactly how I remember him; no, he looks better.

Still grinning, he chuckles and crosses his arms. "No apology necessary. That's the kind of collision I wouldn't mind having every day."

Giving him a polite nod, I continue to stand there, and I'm wondering if he really doesn't remember me.

"Let me get your bags for you," he says as he moves to take them out of my hand. Crossing into the room, he sets my black messenger bag on the table in front of us before picking up my suitcase and sets it in the corner of the room next to his guitar case. I can't help but notice that his walk is still full of confidence.

Turning around, he strides back to the conference table, showing no sign of recognition, and I begin to feel a little deflated. He stops at the table where I first saw him and we stand across from each other, with the table between us.

Glancing at my suitcase and pointing to the glass wall he asks, "Are you sleeping here? Because there isn't much privacy."

I let out a soft laugh and he laughs, too.

Trying to decide if I should mention that we've met before, I decide against it. I'm not sure he remembers me; actually, I'm pretty sure he doesn't, so why embarrass myself more?

Since I'm here to do a job, I remove my jacket, stand up straight, and extend my hand. "Hello, I am Dahlia London from *Sound Music*. I'm so sorry I'm late."

River extends his hand to meet mine, and I think I see a little glimmer in his eyes but I'm not sure. "Dahlia, hmmm . . . a flower. Well, it's nice to finally meet you," he remarks as his lopsided grin returns.

"Aerie has been texting me your location for the past hour," he says, glancing at his phone.

"You already know who I am, so we can skip that part of the introductions. Agreed?" he asks, smirking, as he sits down and motions for me to do the same.

"Sounds great," I say, and take a seat. Reflecting back to that night so long ago, which now seems like yesterday, I try to see through his words. Is he playing with me? Well, this time around, I'm not playing a game. This is a business meeting, so I need to get down to business. I unzip my bag, take out my tablet, pen, and paper, and avoid looking into his eyes at all costs.

The room only includes a conference table, chairs, and a credenza. There is no whiteboard, no easel, nothing to take notes on. Pulling a larger tablet and colored pencils from my bag, I place them in the center of the table. River looks inquisitively at the items. "For our final layout," I say with a grin.

Leaning back in his chair and placing his hands behind his neck, River says, "Whatever you say. As long as I'm not the one drawing, anything goes."

"I won't grade you on your inability to draw a simple diagram," I retort, flashing him a half grin.

I start the interview by asking River for a brief history of his band. I continue with questions about the band members, their likes and dislikes for clothing and locations, and their favorite memories from their first tour. This takes about thirty minutes and our conversation remains professional.

Moving past the band's history, I ask him questions about the new album. Before answering, River gets up from his chair and strides across the room to the credenza to pour us each a glass of ice water. The room is quiet as I watch him walk, relaxed and confident. It is the sexiest thing I have ever seen—aside from him. And as I'm staring at his backside, I notice his ass seems a bit flat because his jeans hang a little and it's also the sexiest thing I have ever seen.

River circles the table and sits next to me. This move surprises me and makes me lose my train of thought. He turns his chair to face me, points to my shirt, and says, " 'Lola' ranks in my top ten all-time-favorite songs. It's actually on my phone." He takes his phone out of his pocket, touches the screen a few times and shows me, in case I doubted him.

"That's cool, we obviously have similar taste in music," I say while trying to catch a glimpse at what else is in his music library.

"Where did you get that T-shirt anyway? It looks like the actual shirt sold when *One for the Road* was released in 1980," River asks as he stands up and pulls me up with him.

I shiver as he tugs on the hem of my shirt and says, "Turn around, let me see something." He twirls his finger in case I didn't understand his words.

I give him a questioning look before I comply. Without even thinking I jump into his game headfirst. His scent, his closeness, the way my body reacts to his touch have paralyzed me and I welcome the chance to turn around so I can escape his eyes on my face. God, he's just so mesmerizing, and I need to pull myself together.

His phone rings, but he ignores it. With my back to him he pulls the collar back on my shirt and reads the tag. "Holy shit, this is an original! Do you have any idea how long I've been searching for one of these?" Then he makes me laugh when he apologizes. "Sorry. My mother taught me better than to swear in front of women."

"Don't worry about it. I say *shit* just about every other sentence." And it dawns on me that River is flirtatious and charming and he must connect with many women. Accepting this, I relax and sit back in my chair as I start telling him about my father and his obsession with music and concert T-shirts. I make sure not to repeat what I'd told him that night so long ago. I'm not sure why. Talking to him now, I realize that our conversation that night so long ago was just one of many intimate conversations he has probably had in his lifetime. It's his nature; it is who River Wilde is.

I continue to talk freely with him because, honestly, I haven't felt this comfortable in a man's company in a long time. I try to keep in mind that it doesn't matter if he doesn't remember me; I'm having fun.

And besides, I was the one who ran away from him that night. Seriously, how memorable could one conversation and one kiss with one girl in a crowded bar be anyway?

Glancing at the clock on the wall I notice it's almost five o'clock and I have only just started the interview I needed to prepare for the Wilde Ones' upcoming photo shoot. River must have seen the concern on my face because he casually asks, "I don't have any pressing plans for tonight. We could finish the interview over dinner?"

I have spent the last hour discussing everything music with this attractive man. I told him about all the concerts I have been to, he told me about all the bands he has seen, and we listed our top songs, top artists, top singles, and top albums. Throughout our conversation, he continued to stare at me with those twinkling green eyes, grinning occasionally, even when what we were talking about wasn't funny. He played air guitar when I mentioned a song with a great strings solo and mocked playing drums when we talked about an artist who was known for his drumming ability. He seemed very playful and I was enjoying myself immensely—actually, I was having a blast. I'd even grabbed a pen and pretended to sing my favorite Britney song, which really made him laugh. So dinner . . . why not?

Just as I start to answer him, my cell phone rings in my purse. Picking the purse up off the table, I accidentally dump all of its contents.

"Shit!" I yell, holding up my index finger. "Sorry. Give me a sec. That could be my boss." I roll my chair back and kneel on the floor under the table to gather my things. I find my phone first, right in between River's feet.

As I reach for it I hear River clear his throat. "I can get that for you," he says before peering his head under the table. "But on second thought I think I like this better," he says, pointing at my head between his legs.

I move back a little to look at him and end up staring right at his crotch. I move quickly, trying to remove myself from this very awkward position but as I do, I smack my head on the table.

Standing back up, I hold my phone up and laugh a little before patting my head and saying, "Sorry about that, but I got it."

He chuckles again. "Do you want me to get the rest of your stuff or do you want to do it? I'm good either way."

Biting my lip, I say, "If you don't mind, I'll let you get it."

Staring intensely at me, he runs his tongue over his bottom lip. "You sure, 'cause I was enjoying myself." Then, not waiting for an answer, he scoots out of the chair, and starts to gather everything.

His mannerisms, his tone, his facial expressions, and his body language . . . it's all so charming—disarming. He's the same as I remember. And right now, as he's putting my things back in my bag, all I can think about is how much I want him.

Once everything is back in my bag, he asks, "And dinner?"

I bite back a smile. "Sounds great, but we really need to get going. The offices close at five on Fridays."

"That's no problem." Then pointing to the large tablet in the center of the table he says, "I was really looking forward to Pictionary. Later maybe?"

I put the rest of my things away and say, "Let's go."

He gestures for me to lead the way and looks me over from head to toe. "Do you want to drop your stuff off at your hotel before dinner?" he asks while grabbing his guitar and my suitcase from the corner.

"Yeah, I'll just grab a cab and head to my hotel. I can meet you for dinner later."

He runs a hand through his hair and looks at me. No, he's actually glaring at me. "Is that a nicer way of brushing me off?" he asks.

I cringe, remembering that night, but since he doesn't even remember I don't know why he suddenly seems aggravated.

"What? No."

"It's settled then. I have my car here. We'll just swing by your hotel first."

His annoyance seems to have dissipated and he no longer waits for me to take the lead. Instead, he grabs my hand, leading me to the elevator and out of the building.

CHAPTER 7
Where We Belong

Ben is the only guy I've ever held hands with before and we usually only held hands when we were in public. I don't really know if it was a gesture of affection or a way for Ben to let others know he was my boyfriend. Either way, when we held hands, we were palm in palm. Our hold was loose enough that if we needed to let go to allow someone to pass it could easily be dropped.

Why does River's hold feel so different? It's tight, our fingers are laced, and he's rubbing circles along the top of my hand with his thumb. It feels intimate.

Absorbed in my thoughts as we walk through the parking garage, I barely notice it's just as empty as the building. With his guitar slung over his shoulder, he runs his other hand through his hair, taking the lead as he heads toward what I assume is his car. It's a vintage black Porsche. He turns as we walk and I see him crack a genuine smile. He has the cutest dimples. It's the first full-blown smile I've seen from him, and it's absolutely adorable.

Arriving at his car, he gently lets go of my hand to reach into his front pocket for his keys. He unlocks my door and opens it for me to get in. He clutches my hand to assist me into the very low seat and once I'm seated, he lifts my hand and kisses it. Instantly, I feel a sense of déjà vu, as if I'm back in the bar that night I met him so long ago.

I sit quietly while he closes my door and walks around to put my things in the trunk. He opens his door and tosses his guitar in the small area behind us before he gets in. Grinning crookedly, he raises an eyebrow and gestures toward the car. "So do you like it?"

I bite my lip and raise my eyebrows. "Isn't this James Dean's car?"

He shakes his head and laughs. "Well, this one isn't his actual ride, obviously, but it's modeled after his 1955 Little Bastard."

I giggle at the nickname, and I remember my dad's love for James Dean. We were both avid James Dean fans, so much so that we must have watched *Rebel Without a Cause* over a hundred times. I think I knew all the lines by heart. I probably still do.

He looks over at me curiously and says, "Can I ask what you're thinking about?"

Sighing at the memory, I lock the thoughts of my dad away. "Dream as if you will live forever, live as if you will die today."

He places both hands on the steering wheel and glances over at me. The intensity of his powerful green eyes captures my full attention. "I love that movie, and that's definitely one of my favorite lines."

I put my seat belt on before twisting sideways to face him. "James Dean was my dad's favorite actor, and he always loved his car. So how fitting that I get to ride in a Spyder in my lifetime."

"Hmmm . . . ," he responds as he puts on his seat belt.

Giving him a thumbs-up, I say, "Hey, I really do like your car. It's actually pretty cool."

His huge grin returns and his dimples resurface. Then, just as I remember him doing all those years ago to avoid awkwardness, he changes the subject.

"Where to?" he asks as he pulls out of the garage.

I tell him where I'm staying, and after what feels like only a few minutes, we pull up to the Hard Rock Hotel. He puts the car in park and glances over at me. "Stay there. I'll get your door."

Walking around to my side of the car, he points and nods to the valet, indicating that he'll open my door. After pulling it back, he braces his hands on each side of the doorframe and leans in. He surrounds me with his intoxicating scent and overwhelming sexiness before he reaches for my hand.

I shake my head and roll my eyes at his over-the-top chivalrous gesture but thoroughly enjoy it. Stepping out of the very low car, I clutch his hand and laugh a little. "Thank you, kind sir."

He guides me forward to close my door. Then, half-grinning, he looks away, almost shyly. "You're welcome."

He's so adorable.

Standing very close, he gingerly pushes me back against the car, again bracing his hands on each side of me. He's close, but still not close enough. His eyes shift back to mine; piercing me, sending shivers down my spine. As he leans in toward me, he whispers in my ear, "Sir. Yeah, I think I like the sound of that."

I roll my eyes at his comment.

He stares at me with his mesmerizing green eyes, then chuckles and asks me, "What, a guy can't be a gentleman?"

I smile, actually impressed, and laugh. "I never said that."

He hands his car keys and some cash to the valet. "Just the bags in the trunk go to this beautiful girl's room. We won't be long."

Hand in hand again, he leads me to the front desk. He stays close to me and I feel his hand occasionally, maybe accidentally, brush against my outer thigh. Giving my name to the cute female clerk, he checks me in. She flashes him a flirty smile and asks if a credit card should be left on file for incidentals. He immediately hands over his card. When I protest he just shrugs and winks at me. "Doesn't matter, I don't think you will be charging anything."

I've always been an independent person; with Ben, I would often get really upset if I thought he was infringing on it. Strange how for some reason, I'm not the least bit upset that this adorably charming man took control of getting me checked into my room. Actually, it's turning me on.

Before handing me the room key, he looks at it while sliding his tongue over his lower lip and dragging his teeth across it. "I'll wait in the bar, unless you need some help getting to your room."

I stare at him and try to control my heavy breathing. I choose to focus on his flirty comment and not his overwhelming sex appeal, and just shake my head at him. Flirting back, I bite my bottom lip and look over his long, lean body in a very obvious manner. Then, cocking my head, I say, "I'm good, thanks."

He responds with a slight groan, and his eyes flicker at me. I quickly turn, laughing to myself as I walk to the elevators without glancing back. As soon as I reach my room, I call the concierge and arrange to have my bags delivered. While waiting, I lie on the bed and try to figure out what is going on with my emotions. I feel a connection to River. We have the same ease we did the first night I met him. He's adorably charming, beyond charismatic, and more than attractive. All of the same qualities that made me want to stay with him that night at the bar and have me wanting to spend more time with him now. It's like he's reenacting parts of that night even though he doesn't seem to remember it.

I look around my hotel room at the pictures of guitars on the walls, and thoughts of wanting someone to touch me, kiss me, be intimate with me flood my mind. Glancing out the window, I begin to question what I'm doing with River. Am I betraying Ben? How much time is enough time? Am I ready to be with someone else? I have only ever had sex with Ben; what if I suck at it with somebody else? Is this dinner actually a date, or is this just a business dinner? Am I prepared for a one-night stand with the man who twice captured my attention faster than anyone I have ever known? With everything racing through my mind, I'm only certain of my answer to the last question. I am.

A knock on the door brings me out of my thoughts and jolts me off the bed. Oh yeah, my luggage. I ask the bellman to wait a sec while I get some money out of my purse. Answering quickly, he tells me it has already been taken care of by a man wearing a Fender T-shirt and black leather jacket. All I can do is smile.

As I close the door, the hotel room phone rings and I slide across the bed to answer it. River's seductive voice comes through. "Just wanted you to know I made dinner reservations at N9 Steakhouse, in case you want to change, or not. They couldn't fit us in until eight, is that okay?"

"Sounds great, actually. I'll change and come down."

I can hear him chuckling on the other end of the phone. "Do you need help?"

Giggling, I roll over and stand up so I can hang up the phone. "I'm good. Thanks, though. I'll be down in a few minutes."

I hide my face in my hands. I can't help but laugh out loud. In no way would I ever classify our conversations as professional. He's flirting with me and I'm flirting back. It's fun and exciting and I feel like I'm finally living again.

Thanking God that I packed extra clothes, I'm happy that I had trouble deciding what to wear this morning. I packed a few different outfits in case I wanted to change before the meeting, along with clothes for a quick morning run.

I take out a dress from my suitcase. It has a crisscrossed silk top with an asymmetrical black leather miniskirt bottom and a drawstring waist. It's edgy and short, perfect for dinner with an almost-famous, adorably charming rock star. I pair it with my black ankle strap pumps and silver clutch.

Since I never change my jewelry, my wardrobe for tonight is set. I have worn the same jewelry every day for as many years as I can remember: a pair of two-carat diamond studs, given to me by my parents for my thirteenth birthday; my grandmother's vintage watch with a black satin band and diamond surround; my aunt's white pearl and black pearl bracelets; my most recently added Cartier bangle; and the engagement ring from Ben that I still wear on a chain around my neck.

Looking in the mirror as I quickly strip down to jump in the shower, I wince at what I see. Knowing actual clothing choice is irrelevant to men but looking sexy certainly isn't, I shake my head at myself. That's definitely not sexy looking back at me. My tall, thin frame is now soft. I've lost most of my muscle tone along with the definition I spent years working on at the gym and in Pilates classes. What is left is merely skin and bones. My legs have very little shape and any semblance of the small chest I once had is now gone. Even the bra I just removed is too big. Suddenly I have doubts that the hot, attractive, and charming man waiting for me downstairs will even want what I'm willing to give.

But I've decided to just let fate take its course, so I take a shower, brush my teeth, fix my face, spritz on some body spray, and put on my too-big black bra and panties, before slipping on my dress and shoes. I look in the mirror again and flip my hair over to brush it so that my now ashen blond hair falls in a cascading mess down my back, and then I give myself a self-assuring smile.

As I look away from the bathroom mirror, I turn back and decide I probably shouldn't wear my engagement ring when I go out with another man. It just doesn't feel right. Just for tonight, I should remove my necklace. As I do, visions of Ben slipping it on my finger come to mind, and I try to suppress them, but that was a happy time for me, and I actually smile at the memory.

After I remove the necklace and kiss my engagement ring, sadness fills my heart. I swallow hard to hold it back. I almost feel like I should be begging his forgiveness for my thoughts, my wants, and my needs. As I continue to look at the ring, a constant reminder of Ben, I know I will never forget him, but I have to put him away just for now. So I kiss my ring one more time and turn to lock it in the safe, saying a soft *I will always love you.*

While gathering my things, I hear a faint knock on the door. I open it without even looking to see who it is. He's standing there, leaning against the doorframe with his head down and a beautiful grin on his face. I can't help myself as I quickly look over his long, lean body. He's tall, slightly muscular like a swimmer, and has crazy light brown hair with copper strands. He's insanely attractive. When my eyes meet his, he simply undoes me, completely mesmerizes me.

For the first time today, I feel the same electric pull that I felt between us that night. I also finally realize what the *something else* was that I couldn't figure out back then; what was driving me to him. It is awareness. Not only am I completely aware of him, but he's also completely aware of me.

Still standing in the doorway, I catch him studying my body, and then he leans in toward me. Unable to control myself, my body sways closer to his, and a small noise escapes my throat. I hear him inhale in response. We are so close, I think he's going to kiss me, but instead he rests his forehead on mine and I can feel his breath on my jaw. Our foreheads remain connected for a few short seconds before he glides his nose over my cheek. Exhaling a heavy breath as his mouth lightly grazes my ear, he whispers, "You look beautiful—perfect, really."

His intimacy catches me off guard. My stomach is filled with butterflies. I didn't expect his contact nor did I expect his kind words. I have to bite my bottom lip and swallow hard to resist the urge to pull him over to my bed and just be done with it. Instead I decide to take a step back and wrap my arms around myself to stop my uncontrollable quivering.

With his gleaming green eyes gazing at me so intensely, I manage to find my voice and say in an octave or two higher than usual, "Thank you, kind sir. Did I take too long?"

Before he can respond, his phone rings, but he ignores it. The distraction is fine with me because it keeps him from noticing my reaction to his touch. He continues to look at me with that mesmerizing gaze. I almost feel like he's deciding if he wants to eat me for dinner, which would suit me just fine.

Stepping back, he braces his arms on both sides of the doorframe and shakes his head. "No, I just wanted to make sure your bags were delivered."

I smile warmly at this thoughtfulness and inhale his intoxicating scent. "Yes, they were. Thank you very much."

Stepping under his arms and into the hallway, I turn to glance at him as the door closes. "I'm ready."

I grin when I hear that *Hmmm* sound from him again. Already I've figured out that he makes that sound when I do something unexpected or when he finds something I said or did funny.

He takes my hand and leads me to the elevator. Exiting the building, we walk to his car waiting for us out front.

Driving out of the parking lot, he pulls his car over to the side of the road and cocks his head toward me. "Did I tell you how amazing you look?" His voice is soft with a rough whispering, raspy tone.

Losing myself in his green eyes, I answer honestly, "Yes, actually, you did, but I don't mind hearing it from you again."

With his eyes locked on mine, he nods his head. "Just wanted to make sure you knew." Grinning, he turns back to face the road and pulls out of the hotel parking lot. "Mind if I change before we head out?"

He pauses a second to look at me, and when he sees me shake my head, he continues. "You can grab a drink while I take a quick shower."

Then, thumbing to the backseat where his guitar is, he says, "I have to drop my guitar off anyway, I had a photo shoot before our meeting and they wanted pictures of me with her."

I giggle, despite myself. *Her? He calls his guitar "her"?*

"What?" he asks in mock offense.

Still giggling, I ask, "Does your girl have a name?"

Laughing back, he answers, "Stella, her name is Stella, and don't make fun. She's the only girl I have ever really counted on."

Having stopped my giggling and replaced it with appreciation, I say, "I'm not making fun, I actually get it. I feel the same way about my camera." And for good measure, I laugh a little and say, "Maybe I should name him."

The humor having entered back into our conversation, he chuckles along. "'Him'?"

"Him, her, I don't know. I've never given it that much thought, but having a girl sleep in my room with me every night isn't my thing." I know this will elicit a reaction.

He's full-out chuckling now. "Hmmm . . . you should see the picture I have in my head right now, no pun intended."

Pouting my lips, I raise my eyes upward. "I'd rather not."

"That look was hot," he says after letting out a soft groan.

We stop at a red light and my gigglefest is over. As I glance over at him and he's looking at me, I wonder if he can see into the future because the look he's giving me tells me he sees what I see.

His phone rings again from his pocket, and he ignores it again. He slowly reaches over, grabs a strand of my hair, and very slowly tucks it behind my ear, sending shivers down my spine. Circling his index finger around my ear, he lightly tugs on my lobe, sparking a heat within my body that I have only felt once before. My body starts to quiver. I look up to meet his hooded eyes and decide to just come out and ask him if he remembers me, but before the words can come out, horns start honking. The light has turned green and I close my mouth.

As we enter the Palms Place Hotel and Spa driveway, he continues to tell me about his new album, but I'm having a really hard time concentrating on anything other than how attracted I am to him.

He stops the car and peers over at me. "Dahlia, did you hear me?"

Blinking at him, I shake my head. "Sorry. Should I be taking notes?" I have no idea what he just said, and the funny thing is I really am interested in his new album, and not only for work.

"Yeah, this is really important stuff." Then, grinning mischievously, he says, "I asked if you have ever stayed here before?"

My door opens and the valet is standing in front of me. River meets me on the sidewalk and continues his teasing. "So did you get that down?"

I pout my lips and roll my eyes. "No, I have never stayed here." I smirk and then add, "Smart-ass." With a little more boldness than I intend, I say, "And don't say it."

Cocking his head to one side he asks, "Say what?"

"That my look was hot."

"First of all, what makes you think I was going to say that? And secondly, it was."

A greeting from the doorman helps distract him. I'm grateful because I knew what he was going to say. He said the very same thing to me today—and the night we met.

With our hands together, we walk through the lobby of the hotel. But as we wait for the elevator, I realize he's still holding my hand, and we're no longer walking. We are standing still, holding hands as he looks at me with his intense green eyes and rubs circles on the top of my hand with his thumb.

He's explaining that he likes staying here because it's close to everything, but peaceful and quiet. I can see what he means. This place immediately puts me at ease.

Dropping my hand as we approach the elevator, he reaches for his wallet and takes out his room key so he can put it in the key slot and push the button for Penthouse A. I'm relieved that he doesn't have a single room like mine, because what am I supposed to do while he showers, sit on his bed and drink?

As we ascend, he leans against the elevator door with his foot on the wall, his hands in his pockets, facing me. He smiles slightly, and I can see traces of his dimples. Then out of nowhere he breaks out in song, singing an ode to the T-shirt I wore earlier today. He seems lost in the song as he sings "Lola." He's so attractive, and watching him sing makes my breath quicken and my insides tighten.

When he reaches the line about cherry cola, he grins crookedly. His voice is amazing, and I just close my eyes and listen, trying to control my breathing. He stops singing before he gets to the next line about sipping champagne.

I'm hyperaware of his closeness without even opening my eyes. He comes to stand directly in front of me, and his breath is noticeably quicker. He places a kiss on my hand before leaning into my ear and whispering, "Do you like cherry cola?" Then the elevator doors open, and the moment is lost.

CHAPTER 8
Something More

I can't stop thinking about everything that has already happened today as we exit the elevator. River grabs my hand and leads me down a magnificently decorated hallway. The floor is checkered in varying tones of white tiles, the walls are a spa blue with creamy-white-colored frames equally spaced apart, each housing different photographs of the desert, secured by glass panels.

Walking down the hallway, I begin to wonder about the *something more* as my mind drifts back to the question I asked myself so long ago. Does love at first sight really exist? If I had asked myself that question five years ago, I'd have said absolutely not. The love that Ben and I had for each other evolved over our many years together. I can't even remember when our love went from the love between two friends to falling in love.

Then one drunken girls' night out, I met the man who is now leading me to his hotel room and I wondered to myself: *Could I suddenly believe in love at first sight? How could love at first sight even exist when you were already in love with someone else?*

But now, after River's serenade in the elevator, I'm asking myself that very same question. Only this time, the man I was in love with is gone. Ben is just a beautiful memory.

Ridding my mind of any thoughts about love, I choose to focus on lust instead. My body begins to tremble slightly and I feel an ache that seems to radiate from everywhere. I want this man to touch me. I need him to touch me. Honestly, I want more—a lot more. I'm fairly certain he wants that, too. All I have to do is finish my interview first so we can move on to what I've wanted to do since I first saw him.

River pauses at the door while he takes the key that's in his hand and slides it into the key slot. He drops his hand and puts it on the small of my back as he guides me into the suite. Walking in, I mentally take back my thoughts that he's almost famous. This suite is definitely for famous people. It has floor-to-ceiling windows along the entire back wall. The living room is decorated similar to the hallway, with soft color tones and a fireplace. The dining room has a light beech-wood table for twelve, and the kitchen is equipped with white marble countertops, a built-in coffeemaker, and even a gas stove. The hardwood-and-marble flooring is like nothing I've seen in a hotel suite before. There is even a small swimming pool with a hot tub on the balcony overlooking the strip. The suite is bigger than my house.

Setting his guitar down in the corner, he leaves his hand on my back while guiding me toward the window. He stands still for a moment, and I wonder what he is thinking. Before I can speak he slides his tongue over his bottom lip in an insanely hot manner. We're so close that I can feel his warm breath on the nape of my neck. I admire his gorgeous face and smooth skin. I can almost touch his defined abdominal muscles through his T-shirt. He is so unbelievably good-looking. I feel my heart quicken and if he gets any closer, I might just free-fall out the window, but I continue to look at him. His facial features are so alluring: He has a strong jaw, a sculpted nose, an extremely toned body, and his personality is captivating.

"There isn't another view in Las Vegas like the one from this window at night," he says while unlocking the sliding glass doors and opening them. "I hope you plan to stick around to see the city light up." Not waiting for an answer, he brushes by me to walk toward the kitchen, but not before dragging his fingers across the span of my back. His soft touch sends tingles all the way up to my neck.

On his way into the kitchen, he texts something on his phone, but I don't ask what.

Watching River walk that walk to the kitchen, I can only smile. "Is that an invitation? Because I didn't think I needed one," I tease.

"You don't," he says as he turns back to catch me staring at his backside. He winks at me, and then grins so wide his dimples are almost pulsing.

❦

River plugs his phone into an iPod dock on the counter and U2's "Beautiful Day" surrounds us as he glances at me, a small grin curving from his lips, and he hums along to the song. *What is he doing?*

Opening the refrigerator, River pulls out two bottles of beer and lifts one up. "Is this okay? I'm not really a good bartender, but I can try to whip up something if you want."

I nod, still smiling. "It's perfect. Can I get a glass of ice, please?"

"Hmmm . . . ," I hear River say, grinning at me and shaking his head.

He starts opening and closing a few cupboards until he finds the glasses. He pulls down two and places them on the counter. After filling one with ice from the dispenser on the refrigerator door, he walks toward the large L-shaped sofa and motions for me to come over and have a seat.

As I walk toward him, I can't help but notice how hot he looks. He's like a magnet, and I'm being pulled toward him against my will.

Raising an eyebrow, he says, "What are you smiling about?"

"Nothing. Everything. I don't know," I say, shrugging my shoulders and trying to resist his pull.

"Hmmm . . . ," I hear again as he walks closer to me. He motions with one hand for me to sit. I do as he suggests, and he hands me my drink. "That's not very definitive."

"It wasn't meant to be."

Now I'm distracted by his messy but perfect hair. I want to ask him if he has any idea how attractive he is. *What's wrong with me?* I'm giddy like a teenager, for Christ sakes!

Taking a large sip of my drink to cool down my overheated body, I immediately feel it; a brain freeze. I squint my eyes trying to stop it, to will it away.

"Much colder with ice . . . ," I hear him start to say, but the end of his sentence trails off.

I look up as he sets his glass on the table. He must have noticed my brain-freeze face because he says, "Close your eyes."

I look at him quizzically while squinting.

"Brain freeze, right?"

I nod my head and close my eyes.

Placing his fingers on each side of my temples, River firmly presses into my skin and massages in circles.

I feel his nose in the crook of my neck, but this time on his way up to my ear he allows his lips to skim the most sensitive flesh of my neck. When he reaches my ear, he whispers, "Better?"

Nodding my head slowly, I open my eyes, aware of how close we are. My breathing starts to speed up. Does he realize what that move does to me? I really want to grab him, but I restrain myself, remembering dinner and the interview. Yes . . . dinner and interview.

Pulling back to a safe distance, River once again changes topics. He asks me about where I grew up, what I was like in high school, where I went to college, and what my life is like now.

My mind drifts back to Ben time and time again. I'm finding it difficult to not mention him, as he occupies my every memory. I'm talking to River, but Ben is in my head. I start to wonder what the hell I'm doing.

A knock at his door distracts me from my thoughts of Ben, for now.

"That must be the food," River says. A waiter wheels in a table full of plates covered with silver domes. After River hands him a tip, I shoot him a questioning look.

"Yeessss?" he says as he removes the domes to reveal an array of nibble-size bites.

"When did you order food?" I ask, squinting my eyes and pouting my lips.

"Texted down to the kitchen," he says, making a slight groaning noise, and with his eyelids half- closing he adds, "That look is hot." *I knew he'd say that.*

All I can do is shake my head because what I really want to do is lie him down on the couch. *What's his game?* He's driving me to the edge and there is no way he isn't there, too. He was almost panting after his last move.

Pushing aside my desire for him, we talk for almost another hour while we continue to drink and eat.

When we have both finished our second beer, mine with ice, his without, River stands up. "Feel free to make yourself at home while I take a quick shower."

I'm watching River leave the room, admiring that walk that I can't get enough of and the way his hair sticks out in the back, when he turns around and winks at me. Having caught me staring, he mumbles something I can't really hear, but sounds strangely like: *You could join me if you want.*

Disappearing into what I can only assume is the bedroom, I consider joining him. I really want to, but I'm here for work. Damn, I really need to get my shit together and get that interview done.

I make my way over to the balcony and I step outside. Horns are blowing, lights are flashing, and people are everywhere. As I look down at all the chaos, I think about how I want so badly to just feel alive again. But everything still reminds me of Ben. Even here, with this incredibly hot, yet adorably charming man, my mind wanders back to when we took a trip to Las Vegas after I finished graduate school.

A group of our friends planned a couples' weekend, but it was more like a guys' weekend and a girls' weekend combined. As soon as we arrived, the guys hit the casino and I never saw Ben again until he came stumbling into our room around four in the morning, drunk and not ready for sleep. The next day, we spent the morning together in our room and he met the guys in the afternoon. Then I didn't see him again until he stumbled into our room just in time to catch a cab back to the airport. That was the way we were, and honestly, I had a great time with my girlfriends that weekend. We played blackjack, did some shopping, ate fabulous food, and went clubbing at night.

Suddenly, a pair of strong arms surrounds me as River places his hands on the railing, suspending my memories of Ben. I want to lean into him, to feel his hard body against mine. Instead, I inhale his now-familiar scent and close my eyes. Every nerve in my body is electrified. Two years of neglect has my body screaming for this man to touch me.

"Should we catch the sunset before we head out?" River says, standing so close, yet way too far away.

"I would love that. The sky is so clear, the sunset is going to be gorgeous." I don't turn around, barely moving a muscle, because the pull of my body to his is so strong right now, I can hardly restrain myself.

"Yeah, it is."

I can tell by the way his warm breath is hitting my ear that he's not looking at the sun, and that thrills me. Being surrounded by River and watching the sunset feels so right that I try to rid my mind of any thoughts of Ben so that I can focus on River. But focusing on anything right now is hard to do. He's so close to me that it's driving me crazy.

After we watch the sunset, River moves back, leaving one hand on the rail next to me. "Ready?"

"Yes," I say, glancing up to his gorgeous face.

When I turn completely around, I see him for the first time since he emerged from the bedroom. He's wearing frayed black jeans with a gray button-down shirt that reveals a hint of his defined muscles, a belt, and black work boots. I notice that he is about the same build as Ben, maybe just slightly taller.

River grins as he notices me staring. "Do you see something you like?"

Before I can respond, I stumble slightly and River's mouth is at my neck, only because that's where I landed.

River doesn't hesitate to use the opportunity to glide closer to my ear and whisper, "Hey, gorgeous, you okay?" I feel his breath, his lips slightly grazing my neck. But unlike the last time, he doesn't pull back immediately and the electric pull intensifies.

Responding in a very raspy tone, I start, "Absolutely, I'm . . ."

River doesn't let me finish my sentence; he gently pushes me back against the rail. His arms are extended on either side of me, he's caging me in, but once again, I don't feel trapped. He never moves his lips away from my neck as he repositions us. My breathing is hitched and my heartbeat has doubled as I tilt my head back to allow him full access to my neck. He's softly running a trail of kisses from my neck up to my mouth, slowly, lightly licking, softly sucking, until his lips finally meet mine.

Parting my lips, I think I hear a groan from the back of his throat, and I know I hear a small moan of my own as his mouth presses against mine. I'm frozen, unable to move, not even able to lace my arms around him because I'm wrapped up in a different emotion. It's happiness growing inside me, overshadowing the sorrow. I feel my darkest days slipping away, right here, right now, with him—and I'm paralyzed.

My body starts to tremble, and I put my hands on his chest for support. He's gently kissing me, sucking my bottom lip before he suddenly presses his mouth harder to my lips, his tongue colliding against mine. As soon as I start sliding my hands down his chest, he groans again, louder this time but then draws back. And just like that, our first *real* kiss is over.

But it wasn't just a kiss. It was so much more. When our tongues met, it felt like our souls connected with each other. This soul mate feeling confuses me, but looking at him makes me smile. He grins back at me as he takes my hand, leading me through the living room and out the door without a word.

Standing in the elevator, our hands still connected, each lost in our own thoughts, we don't look at each other, and we still don't speak. Memories of Ben flood my mind, but these memories are fleeting. I can't remember my body reacting to Ben's touch like it just did to River's. He's so seductive and alluring, he makes me want more than the kiss we just shared. Then I remember how skinny and frail I must appear. I shake off my self-doubt because I'm not a needy, insecure girl. Maybe it's time to cut my losses and run; finish this interview and take the next plane home.

As the doors open, River asks me if I'm hungry and I am brought back to the present. I nod my head in response. We exit the elevator and walk through the lobby toward the doors; I'm thinking, *Just finish your job and leave.*

I stop abruptly when I remember that I don't have any of the materials I need. I left my messenger bag in my hotel room when River knocked unexpectedly on my door. "Shit, I forgot my bag and I need it for the interview."

River laughs, leans in quietly and seductively whispers, "Could we do the interview thing tomorrow? Because you're looking far too sexy for me to concentrate on anything other than you."

My emotions are a tangled mess as he signals for a cab. "Are you playing some kind of game with me?"

"What do you mean?" he asks, running his hands through his hair. He sounds genuinely confused as he opens the cab door.

Trying to keep my voice down I say, "What do I mean?" Then I point to the top floor of the building as we scoot into the cab. "What was that up on the balcony?"

River tells the cabdriver, "N9 Steakhouse, please.

"That was a kiss and I think . . . No, I know you know what that is." His tone is suddenly much harsher.

My eyes open wide and my mouth drops open. I'm at a loss for words.

I don't have to speak because River does first. "We've met before, you know."

I look at him, perplexed, and a little hurt that he didn't mention it before. I nod my head, indicating that, of course, I remember. Then in a low, raspy voice I answer, "You remember meeting me and haven't said anything until now. Why?"

In an equally low voice but with the harshness seemingly gone, he says, "Why haven't you, Dahlia?" He's looking at me with his powerful green eyes and I know there's no seeing the future in them right now.

With honesty pouring out of me and thankful that he actually does remember me, I answer, "I just didn't think you remembered me, that's the only reason." And I wonder why he seems to think there is more to it than that.

"Right," he says almost with a laugh, his harsh tone returning. He clenches his fists as he leans his head back on the cab seat.

I stare out the window to avoid his gaze. We are sitting still in traffic. I'm trying not to cry and I'm feeling conflicted. I don't know what to think. After all the flirting, the attraction, and now the bitterness, I know I have to remove myself from this confusing situation.

With sudden clarity, I turn my entire body to face him. Doing this with a dress on isn't easy. I brace my hand on the seat in front of me so the slick leather bottom of my skirt doesn't slide across the bench and I cross my legs. The cab starts moving again; horns are blowing and bright-colored lights are flashing everywhere.

"River, I don't want to play games. I don't know what is going on here, but let's just go back to my hotel, let me get my stuff, finish the interview, and then we can say our goodbyes." I let him know this in as flat a tone as I can manage, knowing this is not what I want but what needs to happen.

Ignoring my request, he turns toward me. With his elbow up on the ledge of the window and his knee slightly bouncing he says, "Dahlia, I'm not playing any games here. I'm just trying to figure things out. So let's start with the night we met, okay?"

I nod but think this isn't going to go well at all.

Sitting up and in a monotone he asks rather harshly, "Why did you leave the bar that night with another guy?"

"What are you talking about?"

Staring at me he says, "Dahlia, come on, just tell me the truth."

"I didn't leave with any guy. I left with my girlfriend Aerie. So what are you talking about?"

Running his fingers through his hair, he hisses between his teeth, "After my gig you were gone. I thought we had some intense connection. Then I had to go back onstage and you said you'd wait for me, but you didn't. You just left. Later that night I had to stop by my brother's frat house to look for my sister who left without us and I saw you there. You were standing with some guy near the stairs and he was sucking on your neck."

He says the last part with disgust and I start to feel a little queasy. Never did I think my worlds would collide like this. With my eyes pleading forgiveness I say, "River, that wasn't just some guy. That was my boyfriend, and I was afraid of what might happen between you and me, that's why I left when I did."

"That's fucking fantastic news to hear now. That wasn't something you thought you should share then?"

My eyes start tearing up as I say, "It's not like that, you don't understand."

He curls his lips into a sneer as the cab starts inching its way to nowhere. While gritting his teeth and looking at the floor he says, "Really, because I think I understand pretty well. You were out for fun and looking to have a good time."

Raising his gaze to meet mine he continues with, "Do you have a boyfriend now?"

I flush, swallowing back my tears. I'm a little pissed myself now at his bitter reaction, so in a slightly clipped tone I answer, "No, Ben was my boyfriend but he died almost two years ago, and, actually, he was my fiancé."

His eyes flash to mine and I see compassion and maybe a little bit of pain in them. He studies my face like he's trying to bring back the last five years but doesn't know how. "Is he the same guy? The boyfriend from the party and your fiancé?"

"Yes, Ben was my boyfriend since we were, like, five. Well, not really but it seemed like it. We actually knew each other since we were five."

"Hmmm . . . ," is all River says at first. Then after a few beats he looks at me. His eyes are a little softer, and he seems more sympathetic. And just like that, the charming man who captivates me is back. "That explains a lot. Why . . . ?" He doesn't get to finish his question as the cabdriver announces our arrival at the restaurant.

I put my hand on his knee. I'm a little shaken by our exchange but for some reason drawn even more to him. I don't know if we can recover from this and honestly I'm afraid to go too much further in case we can't. "River, let's just end this here."

Taking my hand from his knee, he lifts it to his mouth and lightly kisses it in the same way he has done before. My goose bumps return and I have to swallow a few times to get the huge lump out of my throat. Still holding onto my fingers, our hands now resting on his leg, he lifts my chin with his other hand and rubs his thumb over my lips. "Dahlia, please stay and have dinner with me? You owe me that much for standing me up that night. Then let's see what happens." He says this very softly, almost like a whisper as he continues to run his thumb back and forth over my bottom lip. The cabdriver gets out of the cab and opens my door. I'm sure it's to move us along.

As resolutely as I can, I say, "Okay, fine, dinner and then the interview." But I know that's not all I meant. It's time to remove our masks to see if there is really something more between us, but in order to do this I have to get my emotions under control. This is easier said than done around River Wilde, especially because, as I get out of the cab, I can still feel the searing heat left behind on my lips from his touch.

CHAPTER 9
Hold My Heart

There were some things I expected when I landed in Las Vegas this morning: casinos, alcohol, slot machines, crap tables, neon lights, and even River Wilde. What I didn't expect was the bitter conversation that had just taken place in the cab.

He leads me to the elevator inside the large glass building. While we stand in silence, I take the opportunity to collect my thoughts as we rise the forty floors to the restaurant. First, he remembers me. Second, he is, was—I'm not sure which—upset with me for leaving that night. Finally, he went to the Kappa Sigma party to look for his sister and saw me with Ben.

The facts are easier to sort than the feelings that accompany them. It's my feelings I can't seem to get a handle on. They're intensifying with every word he says to me. And although I don't really know him, this doesn't dampen the unspoken truth that I feel more connected to him right now than to any other living man.

These feelings drive me to stay here, to not walk away. But the biggest reason keeping me here is that I actually get him. He's mad right now, but what I see are his struggles between his emotions and his charm. I can see through his anger to his wounded pride from being stood up. He's hurt. The fact that I get him intrigues me, it captivates me, and makes me want him more.

These thoughts swirl in my head as I exit the elevator into the restaurant. We walk hand in hand and I'm wondering how this can be real. Doubts start to cloud my mind. Is he on the up-and-up or is he trying to get back at me for leaving that night? Is this all a game? Or can we put the past behind us? Can I tell him about Ben? Why is he asking me to stay, while pushing me away at the same time? My doubts mix with my certainties, but what I'm most concerned about is that every time he looks at me it feels like he's seeing through to my soul.

I'm desperately trying to shut out thoughts of Ben, but for some reason the conversation keeps leading back to him in my mind.

As the hostess leads us to a secluded U-shaped booth, I notice the beautiful view of Las Vegas. Our booth faces the interior of the restaurant, and a wall of glass stands to our right. Sliding into the booth, I turn to look out at the view and long for peace of mind.

I stay very close to the edge of the booth, not allowing River access from my end. He smirks at me when I don't move in but doesn't say anything. He just nods as he gets in from the other side and sits down.

The restaurant is dimly lit, but there is an ominous glow coming from the candle in the center of the table and I swear from River, too. As we sit in silence, I know he's staring at me. I can feel it, but I don't look at him. Instead, I shift my eyes down to study my menu.

When the waiter approaches, he asks what I would like to drink, and I order my trademark cocktail. "A filthy Grey Goose martini with extra olives, please."

River orders a bottle of beer and starts chuckling.

Looking at him for the first time since we sat down, I ask, "What's so funny?"

He's staring at me, and my gaze shifts to meet his eyes as he says, "Filthy. That sounds really hot."

I smile coyly at him, but I don't break our eye contact. I decide to join in the banter and ignore the sexual undertone. "I only drink three types of drinks." Then, holding one finger up in the air, I say, "Beer with ice." Holding a second finger up in the air, "Martinis." And finally, holding a third finger up, "And champagne, but only with a strawberry."

Then I decide to go for it and mention something from our first meeting. "And oh yeah, an occasional shot, but then you already knew that."

Running his hands through his hair, he raises an eyebrow. "Yes, I do. I remember that very well, actually."

And there it is again. A mélange of shuffled signals where words and body language aren't always in sync, but our emotions and body language seem to be oddly connected. Finally deciding to just cut to the point, I say what's running through my mind.

"River, what kind of game are you playing? Is this your way of luring me in, because if it is, I'm not interested. I'm not a groupie." I feel relieved as soon as the words are out there.

He inches closer to me, but is still a good distance away. Putting his fingers on the table, he starts tapping it. He looks at me intently and says, "Dahlia, I'm not playing any game. I'm just interested in you, and I know you're not a groupie."

His fingers stop tapping the table, and he reaches over to where my hand is clutching the hem of my skirt. He takes it and rests both of our hands on my leg, his over mine. I notice he hasn't laced our fingers together, though. He clears his throat. "I'm just trying to figure that night out. Believe me, the facts are pretty clear, but it's the whys I'm struggling with."

River looks at me for a beat, dragging his tongue over his lower lip before continuing, "The night we met, you didn't say anything about having a boyfriend or not being able to stick around." With his eyes still piercing through me, he pauses as if waiting for a response even though he hasn't asked a question.

The restaurant seems very quiet as I return his gaze and just nod my head in agreement. All the while I know what he said is the truth and that he hasn't asked for the explanation.

Before River can continue, the waiter returns with our drinks and asks us if we're ready to order. River asks him to give us a few minutes. Once the waiter leaves he raises his glass and out of politeness I do the same. "To beautiful days," he says, and clinks his glass to mine. I can't help but smile about him remembering the concert T-shirt I wore that night, but this also infuriates me.

"That's what I mean!"

"What?" he says, looking confused.

"That! You're so back and forth with me, with your actions, with your emotions. You act like you don't remember me, then spring on me that you do. You flirt with me and then you stop on a dime. You kiss me and then you pull away as soon as I touch you. You're mad then you're not." I don't stop to take a breath or let him speak before finally raising the hand he's holding and letting it go. "You're holding my hand, then . . . ," I trail off, not sure of how to finish that thought. Tearing my gaze from his, I try to rein in my emotions, to wipe the flustered girl up off the floor.

Pulling myself together, I look over at him again and decide to continue. As I'm about to speak, I can't help but notice that he seems to be contemplating everything I just said. I can read it on his face. So I stop and give him a chance to respond.

He doesn't speak at first as he quickly slides in next to me and suddenly his lips are on mine. He's kissing me very softly. He tugs at my bottom lip before he leans away and moves back into the center of the booth. He rests into the bench and puts both hands behind his head. When his eyes shift back to mine he says, "Here's the thing, Dahlia: You confuse the shit out of me. Boyfriend or not, I really thought we had some epic connection and then you bagged out without even giving us a chance." When he finishes he shakes his head and gazes out the window into the night. His eyes are darker now, almost sad.

The waiter returns and we order our food. I'm not the least bit hungry anymore. My stomach is in knots, and I feel uncertain about why we are still discussing this. I just want this conversation to be over. And if we leave together I have no misconceptions that this attraction is going to lead to anything but a one-night stand. But I'll put aside my confusion and just be with him. I'm craving intimacy: a touch, his touch; a kiss, his kiss; and so much more. But this bittersweet conversation is blocking the way to satisfying my needs.

Oddly enough, the desire I feel for him is only becoming stronger from our emotional conversation. What I see in him is so real. I feel like I know more of him, of his soul, than I knew of Ben's in a lifetime. That draw is irrefutable, but also confusing. *Why do I feel like this?*

If tonight happens, I know I will have to deal with tomorrow's emotions because I'm certain this flame won't be doused. But to get to tonight, we have to get past this bitterness. We have to speak the unspoken words about Ben. I'm not sure I can.

Soft music is playing overhead, and the candle flame has burned out, but River's ominous glow is still strong, and he's still sitting in the middle of the booth. As I glance over at him, I see sadness in his face, and my desire to be closer to him is overwhelming.

Knowing that I'm the cause of his sadness makes me want to close the distance between us. Physically and emotionally. So I move just a little closer to him. As I do, he shifts his gaze to mine and the corner of his mouth lifts slightly into a charming half smile.

When I'm close enough, I grab his hand, lacing my fingers with his, and say, "I'm sorry. I don't expect you to understand why I didn't say anything or stop what was happening between us then because I didn't—I still don't—understand it myself. All I know is, I was a young college girl who flirted with an insanely attractive guy at a bar and had to leave because she felt like the cosmic universe had crashed down on her. And she couldn't accept that; she had a boyfriend."

When I finish my speech, I take a deep breath and exhale, clutching his hand a little harder to help contain all my emotions.

River pauses for a moment to watch me and then flashes his charismatic smile. "Hmmm . . . you flirted?" Then rather seductively he continues. "I think I was the one flirting with you, and I couldn't stop because you were perfect. You still are."

Bringing my hand to his mouth, he softly kisses it. "Beautiful girl, of course I remember you. How could I not? You're unforgettable."

Our food arrives and I try to contain the tears welling in my eyes. Before he lets go of my hand he squeezes it and with the utmost of charming looks, he winks at me. With that one little look I can feel the tension between us washing away.

Then he does the most adorable thing I have ever seen a man do. He holds his right hand to his heart and draws an X over it as he says, "Dahlia, I was never mad. I could never be mad at you, I promise."

I decide for now to believe him so we can leave that conversation behind—and like River does so well, I change the subject. As we eat, I ask him about his childhood, his family, and his career. We talk again with the ease of familiarity. He casually touches me whenever the opportunity presents itself and before I know it we've finished our meals and our second round of drinks.

The waiter returns to ask if we want dessert. I pass, but River orders chocolate mousse. Once the dessert arrives he offers his spoon to me and I sample it in the most seductive way I can. Taking the spoon from my lips, he leans into me, licks some chocolate off my upper lip with the tip of his tongue, and then leans back.

I'm not sure if it's the alcohol, or just him, but the sexual tension between us is so strong, and every fiber of my body is screaming for him to touch me. I can't take it any longer. I bring my hand to River's neck and pull him to my mouth, pressing hard, not caring that we're in public. I allow his tongue to meet mine just once before I pull back.

Sitting back and grinning, I can see he is looking at me in that intoxicating way again. He leans into me once more and whispers in my ear, "Are you ready to get out of here? Because I am."

I want to scream, "I was born ready," but I restrain myself and simply move to stand up. Swallowing hard and nodding quickly, I say, "Excuse me while I use the ladies' room."

When I return to the table, he is standing against the wall, foot propped up, and head down, grinning. He's so sexy with his long, lean, toned body and killer smile. He looks up at me and grabs for my hand. He then surprises me by gently backing me up to the wall. He kisses my forehead before moving his mouth down to my nose and kissing it, too. He moves to my mouth and tenderly but aggressively bites down on my lower lip and then looks straight at me. I close my eyes as he sucks my lip into his mouth, sending overwhelming sensations throughout my body. Pressing his lips firmly to mine, he starts to kiss me in the most erotic way. First, he starts lightly, then opens our mouths together and exhales. I inhale his sweet breath. He runs the tip of his tongue over my lower lip before slipping it into my mouth and firmly pressing his lips to mine. I'm left breathless as the kiss ends and he takes my hand.

Before we leave the restaurant, River takes me out to the terrace to watch the craziness below. We are both leaning over the stone wall, gazing below, when he steps back and turns me to face him. He has one hand on the small of my back and the other behind my neck. "You are so beautiful," he says, then leans in to kiss me again in a way that I have never been kissed. There is emotion, compassion, and lust all wrapped together in his kiss. The kiss is slow and full of promise. Our mouths move in sync with our tongues, but unlike before, he doesn't press harder or move faster. He goes slower and, in turn the kisses intensify my burning desire for him. As our lips part, he doesn't stop. He whispers something I can't hear. I think I might be purring. I know I am breathless. I'm almost panting as he peppers my neck with kisses, nipping and gently biting his way up to my ear, whispering, "I want you so much."

I pull him to me, crushing my lips to his. He responds instantly. He licks my top lip then sucks on it; he does the same to my bottom lip before locking his mouth on mine. He moves his hands down my backside and presses me closer to him so I can feel his strong body against mine. He slides his tongue over the roof of my mouth, and I know I'm moaning as I step back.

"Where did you learn to kiss like that?" I manage to say breathlessly.

He shakes his head, and his dimpled grin returns as he breathlessly responds, "I wasn't just kissing you. I was whispering in your mouth," he says, laughing. "Do you want lessons? Because I might be able to swing something for you."

We're laughing together now, both out of breath and panting. He laces our hands together. "I want to tell you something before we go," he says, pulling me back into his body. "Do you know my band's song 'Once in a Lifetime'?"

I nod my head because I know that song very well. It's one of the ones I used to listen to repeatedly on my iPod.

"I wrote that song about you. About meeting you that night."

While trying to swallow the emotion forming in my throat, I manage to verbalize only a fraction of my appreciation for being his muse. My words are short and clipped, and I don't care about whether this is a one-night stand or not. "You wrote a song about me? Really?" It's all I can say before throwing my arms around his neck and crushing my lips to his. I kiss him hard before whispering, in my most seductive voice, "Take me back to your hotel. Now!"

River sighs as he stares at me for a few seconds. "You're just so beautiful." He grabs my hand even tighter, if that's possible, and we ride the elevator back down the forty floors, this time experiencing a different kind of silence—one filled with mesmerizing gazes and exhilarating touches. He quickly leads me down the strip, having opted against a cab because at this time of night, we can walk to the hotel faster than a cab could get us there. As we walk, I notice he has lost that swagger that I admire. Instead, he's walking fast, with purpose, and I'm finding it hard to keep up.

When we reach the hotel lobby, he sits me in a chair and tells me to stay put as he walks over to the front desk and has a short conversation with the clerk. The lobby is quiet and just a few people are passing through. I don't even know what time it is. I watch him as I sit back in the chair and think, *God, he is so hot.*

I see him hand the clerk a bunch of cash and wonder what the money is for; does he pay his bills in cash instead of with a credit card? As he walks back over to me, he's smiling and I melt again. He reaches for my hand, pulling me out of the comfortable chair, and leads me through the lobby.

The closer we get to the elevator the more nervous I become. My breathing accelerates as memories of Ben flutter in my head, and my stomach starts to flip-flop with thoughts of River.

My mind is shouting at me to proceed with caution. *What am I doing with this man?* I have slept with one person my whole life. Am I betraying Ben by deciding to have a one-night stand? I know this cannot possibly be more. River is a player.

Am I ready to be with someone who isn't Ben? While my mind echoes, *Don't take that path*, my body is screaming, *Yes, take the road less traveled*. My body is telling me I want this man, his touch, his kiss, everything he has to give and more. And the longer we walk into the unknown, the more my mind starts to agree with what my body wants.

But as he pushes the elevator button, my internal light turns red. I can't do this. I can't sleep with him. Sensing my nervousness or even my apprehension, he caresses my cheek, gliding his thumb over it and asks, "What's wrong?"

When the elevator doors open, I clear my throat and yank on the hand guiding me down the wrong path. Looking down at the shiny marble floor, I drop his hand and manage, "I am so sorry, River. I'm not sure I can do this—that I can be with you."

He gently repositions me so my back is against the wall, and he's standing in front of me. Placing his thumb on my chin, he guides me to look into his powerful green eyes. While intently staring at me he says, "You know the song I wrote about meeting you? Have you ever really listened to the lyrics?"

I shake my head. I know the song well, but right now I can't recall any specific lyrics. My mind shuffles between thoughts of *Ben, River, River, Ben*.

He is quiet as he removes his hand from my face, then places both his hands against the wall on either side of me. I know what I just said to him, but his proximity makes my heart race.

He continues to talk, and I continue to listen. He has my full attention when he very softly starts to sing:

You were my once in a lifetime.
This I knew from the moment your eyes met mine.
You were my once in a lifetime.
This I knew the first time I whispered into your ear and my heart
*   stopped.*
You were my once in a lifetime.

This I knew when your face touched my spirit.
You were my once in a lifetime.
This I knew when I kissed your lips and felt it in my soul.
So where did you go, where did you go?

As he sings, tears start streaming down my face.

Moving a little closer, he places his leg in between mine. With a strained voice he whispers, "Those lyrics tell the story, Dahlia—our story. I wrote that song five years ago and even now when I sing it, your face is the face I see. You're unforgettable, Dahlia. You're perfect, really."

My body quivers as he leans in and lightly kisses my forehead, sliding his lips down my temple to my ear. "I just wanted you to know because I felt connected to you that night in a way I've never felt connected to anyone. Then today, when I saw you again, that connection I felt years ago instantly returned."

Feeling light-headed, I close my eyes. I'm unable to speak. His words are so moving, so raw, so emotional.

He kisses each of my eyelids and with his mouth hovering over mine, he talks around my lips. "Ever since I met you, no one else has been worth thinking about."

I open my eyes, and he presses his forehead to mine as he continues. "I feel like fate has brought us together again. I also believe that one night, so long ago, just wasn't the right time for us. But tonight is."

I close my eyes again and stand motionless, still unable to speak. When I open my eyes, I drink him in, all of him, everything about him, especially his beautiful words.

I find him gazing back at me as he says, "Dahlia, you don't have to apologize for anything."

With a small grin, he motions his finger back and forth between us. "And even though I'm sure you can do this, it's okay if you don't want to right now. We can just hang out, talk, or watch a movie. Whatever you want. Just stay with me, don't interfere with fate now that we've reconnected."

And with that, I nod my head, turn to press the elevator call button, and realize I never spoke a word. I didn't need to. Because somehow, he knew exactly how I felt.

CHAPTER 10
Fade into You

Keeping things professional has not gone as seamlessly as I had hoped.

Dahlia the photographer and Dahlia the girl whose fiancé was killed in front of her have mixed together, and I'm standing next to the person responsible for blending the two.

We are on the balcony staring into the night. Looking up into the heavens, I notice the sky is the deepest shade of blue, and the stars are brighter than I've seen them in a long time. He is next to me, leaning over the railing and gazing up at the stars. I smile to myself as I realize that I'm no longer struggling to feel alive.

River nudges me with his shoulder, and with just our arms touching, I can feel an electric current traveling through my body. My heart beats a little faster. I look over at him and smile. His head is cocked to the side, preventing me from seeing all of his gorgeous face. He flashes me a smirk that is so sexy I want to lean over and kiss him. He has to be the most attractive man I have ever seen.

Sure enough, true to his word, the view from where we stand is the most spectacular view of Las Vegas. The wondrous mountains, the clear night sky, and the flashing neon lights from the strip below surround us as we discuss his band and his growing fame. I've discovered that River is down to earth and not in the least bit pretentious. So I'm curious about how he deals with his fans. "How do you feel about being famous? Being asked for autographs? Do fans follow you?"

He looks confused for a second, then laughs, "I'm not exactly famous."

I softly clear my throat and then insist, "Yes, you are! Your picture is all over the Internet. Your band has a huge fan base, and I wouldn't be here with you now, prepping for a photo shoot to announce the launch of your second album if you weren't."

Grinning at me, he asks, "How do you know my picture is all over the Internet?"

"I had to do some research before coming. I'm a professional, you know," I answer, laughing.

"Did you find any good ones?"

Feeling like I might be blushing, I avoid his question. "So have you had to sign anyone's bra yet?"

Shaking his head, he snickers a little. "I don't sign and tell." On a sigh he adds, "When the band is together, sure, we get asked for autographs. And sometimes when I'm walking around L.A. someone will recognize me. But really, I mean it when I say it hardly ever happens. When we toured, we had fans following us around. To tell you the truth, I'm not really sure how I feel about it. Part of me just wants to stay unknown. The whole touring thing was hard. It was constantly infringing on my personal life. That's why I've put off doing a second album for so long. There's just so much . . . You know what? Never mind. And don't get me wrong; it's not that I'm ungrateful." He laughs. "If it weren't for the fans, I wouldn't be here—with you—trying to set up promotional shots."

I'm impressed by his honesty. "Sure, I can see how all of that can wear on a person. It always sounds so glamorous, but I'm sure it can get old."

He seems to get lost in his thoughts, so I try to lighten the mood. "Well, no one seems to recognize you here."

He looks out at our surroundings before answering me. "I think people who come here aren't looking for anything but themselves. Everything around them is just irrelevant."

I repeat the adage I saw as I exited the airport this morning: "What happens in Vegas, stays in Vegas."

He shakes his head and smirks. "You've been watching too many commercials."

Giggling, I playfully nudge him. "Yeah, yeah, I have.

"So when you're home in L.A., fans really don't recognize you on the street?"

Turning around, he leans his elbows on the railing and thinks for a minute before answering. "Sometimes they do. It happens randomly, though. I can be going for a run and someone will come up to me, tap me on the shoulder, and shove a pen in my face. But most of the time, unless I'm with the band, people are cool and just leave me alone."

He seems a little saddened by my question and somewhat distracted by his answer. I want to ask him why, when there is a knock on the door.

"Hold that thought," he says as he turns to head back inside.

I can't help but watch him as he goes through the living room to answer the door. His walk, that sexy swagger, gets me every time. Once again, he turns around and catches me staring; and just like before, he winks and grins. I shake my head and laugh to myself. It's been so long since I've smiled and laughed like this—I didn't realize how much I've missed this feeling.

He opens the door, and one of the hotel waitstaff wheels in a dining cart with two bottles of champagne and a huge bowl of strawberries. I want to gush a little that he remembers I like champagne with strawberries.

I'm surprised to see the waiter pull my suitcase and messenger bag out from under the cart as River tips him. Really? How? When? That must have been what he was doing at the front desk. This kind gesture melts away any remaining apprehension I have about being with him. My mouth drops open and I take a step inside. "How did you get my things?"

Cocking his head, he breaks into a breathtaking grin as he uncorks the champagne bottle. "I knew you wanted to complete the interview, so I asked the front desk to do me a favor and have your hotel send your things over." He pauses, looking a little concerned. "I hope that's okay?"

I bite my lip and nod my head as I walk over to him. "Of course."

He pours the champagne into the first glass and looks at me with an unyielding gaze. Getting as close as I can while he's filling one of the glasses, I stroke his face with my thumb before softly kissing his cheek. "That was really sweet of you."

His breath quickens, but as passion fills his eyes the champagne overflows and spills out the top of the glass. We both take a step back and laugh.

"I told you, bartending isn't my thing," he says as he sets the glass down and begins to fill the other. Once both glasses are full he drops a strawberry in each, and they sink to the bottom. He wedges another strawberry on the rim of each glass, picks one up, and hands it to me. His grin widens and he shrugs as he says, "I'm not sure which way you like it, in or out?"

Giggling, I take the glass and place my hand over his for a few seconds. "Usually I only put the berry on the rim, but I kind of like it your way."

I look at the glass I'm holding and smile. "The way you did it is perfect, and now I have a new way to order champagne; not one, but two strawberries."

I get the feeling he wants to say something else, but instead he lifts his glass and clinks it to mine. "To chance meetings."

I smile at him. "Yeah, to chance meetings and scheduled interviews."

Taking a sip of his drink, he licks a drop from his bottom lip in that sexy way he has.

Out on the balcony we sit in separate chaise lounges. I rest my head back and drink my champagne, enjoying the air and his company. I think we both must be trying to regain our composure. After a few quiet minutes, he twists his body sideways and faces me. "Do you want to wrap up the interview?"

As I turn my head to answer, I see just a hint of skin at his waist where his shirt has come untucked. I can't help but grin at how sexy he is. His body makes me light-headed. *There is no way I could do the interview now.* It takes me a second to compose myself. I then remove the strawberry wedged on the side of my glass, and while looking directly at him, I say, "Absolutely not! I can't focus on work right now with the fabulous view. It's breathtaking out here. I'd much rather just sit and enjoy it, if that's okay with you?" I smile at him and slowly lick my strawberry before taking a bite.

Watching me intently as I chew, he turns to sit up. I notice his breath catch and he clears his throat. He places his feet perpendicular to mine and rests his elbows on his knees. In a low and husky voice he says, "Sounds good to me."

His head is down, but the way his eyes pierce me makes me anxious. He puts his palms together, laces his fingers and inhales a deep breath. "Can I ask you something?"

"Sure." I dig my feet into the mesh underneath me in an attempt to stop my jittery nerves.

Bringing his head up, he runs his hands through his hair. "Have you dated anyone since he died?"

"No," I whisper, and say nothing else as my body suddenly goes cold.

Clearing his throat, he blinks thoughtfully and resumes his gaze. "Have you ever slept with anyone else?" he asks, then moves to lean back in his seat. Putting his arms behind his head, he stretches his legs before adding, "Besides him, I mean?"

"No," I whisper again, this time turning to look up at the clear sky. "Sounds pathetic, doesn't it?"

With concern in his voice, he says, "Hey, Dahlia, look at me."

As I turn my head, his expression is one of compassion and maybe a little unease. Swallowing, he holds his gaze steady. "That's not pathetic at all. It's a beautiful thing, being with the same person, caring about someone enough to want to get through all the shi . . . crap that life throws your way with them."

He's talking to me about Ben, and it's a little overwhelming at first. Strangely, I find comfort in being able to openly discuss my true reason for not waiting for him after his gig the night we met. I also find his concern and honesty extremely touching. Oddly enough, the mention of Ben's name right now does not send me spiraling back into thinking about him. My mind is focused on River, and my body starts to quiver at that thought.

"Yeah, he was there for me through all the shit life threw my way."

I pause, taking a moment to collect myself and think that just for tonight I'm pushing Ben aside and letting River in.

"Ben might be the only man I have ever slept with, but he's not the only man I've ever wanted to have sex with."

He starts to say something, but I don't let him. Instead I put my finger to my lips. I stand up to take that one big step keeping us apart. Once I do, I straddle myself on his lap. Watching him, I can't tell if the look on his face is shock or surprise, but when he sighs, his arms instantly loop around my waist and I don't really care anymore what his facial expression means. Enjoying our closeness, I lean in and whisper into his ear, "That's why I left the bar five years ago, because I wanted what I shouldn't. I didn't care about anything else. I wasn't thinking about consequences, so I had to leave."

When I lean back a little to look at him, he gasps. His breath is shallow and quick as I wrap my arms around his neck and look into his eyes. That's when I know it's time to jump in. Running my hands through his messy hair, I press a soft kiss to the corner of his mouth. "I've never wanted anyone like I wanted you then, like I want you now."

Grabbing my face, he tries to pull me to his lips, but I resist. I need a minute longer to finish saying what needs to be said. "I think you were right about timing and fate." I stop for a second to lightly kiss his soft lips before I finish. "And I know you were right that I can do this, but, River, what you don't know is that I *want* to do this more than anything."

I feel him shudder beneath me as a groan echoes from the back of his throat. I'm finished with words, so I move to kiss his neck, inhaling his fresh scent and enjoying the smoothness of his stubble-free skin. Then I take my tongue along his throat, making my way to the top of his chest. His head drops back, but as soon as I nip his skin, he sits up a little straighter and grabs my hips, pulling me into him. My leather skirt rides up to just below my ass and I know he's noticed when the palms of his hands glide down my backside and I hear another groan, louder this time.

As I trail kisses back up his neck, I can feel his lips in my hair and I can hear him pull air through his nose as if capturing the citrus scent of my hair. My lips head toward his mouth and when I reach his jawline, I again feel the amazing smoothness of his skin. I stop to gaze at his perfect face and when he looks back at me with desire in his eyes, I know he wants me as much as I want him.

When I press a little harder into him, I smile because I can feel his arousal. This only ignites me further and pushes the limits of my own desire, the desire that has been in hibernation for so long. Before I make my way back up to his mouth, he dips his head and slams his lips over mine. With both of us panting heavily, he stands up, taking me with him. He wraps his arms around my thighs, urging my legs around his waist. I grab the hair behind his head and hold on.

Walking through the living room door, he pauses and drags his tongue up my neck before whispering close to my ear, "Are you sure?"

"I've never been more sure about anything," I say right back, without a shred of hesitation. And it's true. I want him. I need him. This is never truer than right now as he's touching me, running his hands over my ribs, over the almost nonexistent curves of my chest, and up and down my body, searing my skin. Just as I know that I haven't been touched in almost two years, I also know I've never been touched like this before. As he continues to touch me, the searing turns into burning, and I know only he can cool it.

Instead of going to the bedroom he takes a step toward one of the unopened glass doors. With my legs still around his waist, I'm surprised when I feel the slight chill of the glass against my back, and I gasp. My dress has ridden up to near waist-level and my panties are completely exposed. Loving the feel of his hard body now pressed against mine, I deepen our kiss. My lips feverishly slide along his. My tongue moves in and out of his mouth with the same urgency as his.

We stay like that for I don't know how long. He presses his body to mine, sliding his hands up and down my body. Both of us kissing, tasting each other, tangling our tongues together. My hands are still in his hair, tugging harder as our kisses become more frantic. I'm moaning when he pulls back and sets me down.

As he pushes aside a lock of my hair, tucking it behind my ear, he seductively whispers, "Dahlia, I want you. I want to kiss you, touch you, make you come over and over again. I've never wanted anyone as much as I want you."

Goose bumps cover my body and I'm so thankful for the hard glass that is supporting me. I'm shaking so badly right now, I'm not sure I could support myself. He starts to trail kisses down my neck, and over my breasts. Then he slides his tongue over my nipple, still covered by my dress. Pushing the fabric to the side, he holds it in place and his teeth nip the lacey material of my bra. He starts sucking my nipple, tasting me, circling his tongue around and around, occasionally blowing out a cool breath of air. He does this over and over again until I begin to moan and a jolt of pleasure flickers through my body.

I can feel his smile as he kisses his way back up to my lips. He nips and sucks my sensitive skin along the way. With the hand that was holding my top to the side, he skims my navel and his fingertips brush over the top edge of my panties.

He slides his leg in between mine, pushing my thighs apart. His hand continues to move and his thumb lightly touches the sensitive skin of my inner thigh. My core is aching for his hand to move back up.

Sucking in a breath, I sweep my fingers up and down his back. I slip my hands in the waistband of his jeans and skim them along the elastic of his boxers. Letting out a light moan, I slide them all the way around to the fly of his pants. Taking in a quick breath, he swallows as I unbutton his jeans.

He presses light kisses across my jawline and whispers, "You are so beautiful."

With heat and desire pooling in me, I can't take any more foreplay. I reach around to his lower back and untuck his shirt. I slide my hands up his chest to the top button and begin slowly unfastening each one.

He's practically panting as I undo the last button. His head falls back ever so slightly before it dips back down to mine. He sucks on my lower lip before kissing me, then flicks his tongue against mine.

His hand moves back up my thigh. Pushing my panties aside, he starts drawing circles across my flesh. My breath is coming in shorter gasps as he plunges one finger inside me, slowly moving it in and out. My head falls back, hitting the glass when his thumb strokes me, but the throbbing sensation spreading throughout my body masks the pain.

He whispers in my ear as his lips explore my neck, "Come for me," and that is my undoing.

My fingers claw into the front pockets of his jeans as my muscles clench into a tight ball, and my body explodes into a thousand pieces. I hear him talking, but his words are masked by my cries of pleasure.

He pushes my body back against the glass with force. He rests his forehead on mine and places both of his palms against the glass on either side of me. His breath is just as erratic as mine.

My body is screaming for more. I want him inside me. I need for him to relieve the desire that has been missing for almost two years. With panting breaths, I bite my lip as I move to unzip his fly. As I finish, he lifts me up again and carries me into the bedroom.

Once inside, he kicks the door shut, sets me on my feet, and turns me around. He moves my hair aside and kisses my neck, seductively whispering, "God, I need you now," while unzipping the back of my dress. Pulling my dress down, he kisses my right shoulder. "Your skin is so soft." Pulling down the other side, he whispers, "You smell so good."

He turns me back around to untie the belt at my waist, then kisses each of my eyelids. "I love your eyes, their color, how you look at me." He moves to sit on the bed and pulls me between his legs. Motioning for me to lift one foot, and then the other, he unbuckles my ankle straps and removes my shoes. "There's just something about you that I haven't been able to forget." While still sitting on the bed, he tugs my dress all the way down and it falls to the floor. He kisses my stomach softly. "I haven't been able to stop thinking about you for five years."

As the moonlight streams through the windows, I struggle to find my breath as all the air leaves my lungs from his words, his charm, his everything. He leaves me breathless. Standing up, he stares at me in just my bra and panties and then he quickly removes my bra and slides my panties off my hips. He continues to stare for a few more seconds before running his eyes down my body.

I stand there completely naked, vulnerable, and unable to move. I'm shaking as he steps closer and touches me. His hands wander from my hips around to my backside and he pulls me to him. "Do you want me?"

"So much."

Pressing my body into his, it almost feels like we're about to perform an erotic dance. I rip his shirt from his body, and it falls to the ground. Sliding my hands up his hard, smooth chest, I push him down on the bed and fall on top of him, kissing his throat as he groans in my ear. Running my hands further down the deeply etched V in his abs, I slide one hand into his boxers. I finally grasp him, moving my hand up and down his length as he moans louder, panting my name.

Gently rolling me on my side, he sits up and quickly removes his shoes and socks. I prop myself up on my elbows as I watch him standing there, taking off his jeans. He reaches down to the floor to pick them up and pulls a condom out of his wallet, tossing it on the bed, before removing his boxers.

He's standing in front of me, gloriously naked, and I can't help but smile. He really is the sexiest man alive. His body is just amazing. He has chiseled arms, hard abs, and taut muscles. He grins back at me as he bends down and kisses my lips, my jaw, my ear. He lightly sucks on my lobe and then returns to my lips.

I pull him on top of me as his hands go from my hips, to my breasts, to my hair, and then clutch my face as he groans loudly. "I want to touch you everywhere, all of you, Dahlia. I want you."

Trying to handle words, I hoarsely say, "I want you, too."

Shaking his head, he lets out a low, husky laugh as he responds, "You're just too sexy."

Drawing away for a mere second, he lets go of my face and rolls us over. I cannot wait any longer; I reach across the bed, pick up the condom wrapper, and tear it open. His eyes glaze over as he watches me, his breathing heavy. I move to the side as I attempt to put the condom on him. I can feel his body trembling under my touch, and my body quakes in response.

I've never put a condom on a man before, and my hands are shaking so badly I can't possibly do it. Leaning into him, I laugh against his mouth. "I've never done this, you're going to have to help me."

And with that, he laughs and says, "Dahlia, you are . . . amazing. Yeah, I can do it." He reaches for another packet and tosses it on the bed as he throws the unused condom to the floor. Then, gazing at me with his powerful green eyes, he says, "But there's something I have to do first, something I've been wanting to do for a long time."

Then, gently, he rolls me over onto my back, easing my head onto the soft pillows. He moves his leg over my body. Hovering over me, he looks down with a wicked grin and says, "Dahlia, I need to taste you."

CHAPTER 11
Closer

Photography is all about finding the moment, but it's nice to know when to put the camera down. Sometimes I'll ask myself, *Do I want to photograph this, or should I just experience it?* Right in this moment I know I want to experience every second of it.

With his last words, our momentary lapse into laughter quickly fades and an entirely different emotion emerges—pure desire. He's standing in front of me while I'm sitting on the edge of the bed, speechless. Emotions are sailing through me as we embark on this course, seeking the beautiful horizon. I want him. No, I need him—badly. But, as quickly as a sail goes up on a windy day, a surge of nervousness wraps itself around my desire like an anchor, dragging me down. He wants to taste me? Thank God Aerie took me to the salon! I haven't slept with a man in almost two years.

Is it like riding a bike? Do I remember how to do this? God, what am I doing naked in front of this delicious man? Should I stop now before embarrassing myself?

He must sense my apprehension because as he leans into me, he whispers, "Don't worry. We'll take it slow." His words do extraordinary things to me. They give me the courage to continue the course we have charted, to dive into this sea of desire so welcoming, so warm, so inviting.

Moving between my legs, he rests on his forearms as he begins to softly kiss my lips. Snaking my arms around his neck, I pull him closer to me, arching my back and pressing myself up into him. I want him inside me, now, but he seems content taking it slow. I'm aching for him, not only because I've been abstinent for so long, but also because I have wanted him for far longer.

As my hands slide along his taut muscles, feeling the smooth skin of his back, they make their way around his hips. Before they meet their destination, he stops kissing me. Raising his head, breathing heavily, he lifts himself back up onto his arms and looks at me pointedly. "Not yet," he whispers, shaking his head and kissing my nose before gliding his lips down my throat.

As I try once again to slip my hands around his hips to feel his hardness, he slides his body further down mine. I can feel his grin as his mouth connects with my hard, wanton nipple, circling it, sucking it before moving to the other. The feeling overwhelms me, and I'm shocked that I feel like I can come again so quickly. Knotting my fingers in his hair, I begin tugging on it as if it's a life raft pulling me ashore.

My hold is lost as he descends further down my body, my breath increasing at an alarming rate. I can feel his tongue on my stomach, jetting in and out of my navel, as small moans escape me. River mutters, "You taste so good."

As his mouth lingers on my slick flesh, my core starts to pulse in anticipation, and a much louder "Yes" escapes my lips.

Hearing his hitched, ragged breathing as he slowly sucks, lightly strokes, tastes, and licks my most sensitive skin, I start to moan his name. As his tongue plunges inside my core, going as deep as it possibly can, moving in and out in a constant rhythm, his eyes flick up at me. He notices I'm watching him. "Fuc . . . Dahlia, you're just so hot," he moans with a devilish grin.

When he starts circling his tongue around me, I lose all ability to function. He then presses his tongue harder while slipping one finger inside me. "God, you taste so sweet."

And when he slides a second finger in, I can no longer even remember my own name.

I start to grind myself against his mouth, his fingers. "Oh God, River," I cry out as I come harder than I've ever come in my life, momentarily leaving this planet behind.

As I float back down to earth, he's slowly, seductively making his way up my body, still licking and tasting every inch of my skin. His mouth meets mine and I can taste myself. It is the most erotic feeling. He lightly licks my bottom lip from the outside around to the inside. I open my mouth further, and his tongue brushes against mine. He gently bites down then flutters his tongue.

As we continue to kiss, I trail my fingers down the deep line of his abdomen. His stomach clenches beneath my fingers as I pass over his sensitive flesh. I hear him let out a sharp breath as I wrap my hand around his girth, making my way down to the base.

Shifting my body, I'm now hovering over him. Breathing hard, panting, almost gasping, I can feel each and every pulse radiating from his hardness. I can barely hear the music in the background, but I think I hear "Sex Therapy" playing from his phone. How appropriate. As my hand finds its own rhythm, I begin sucking on his lower lip, moving to his upper lip, before running my tongue over the roof of his mouth, making him groan even louder.

Stopping only to look into his powerful green eyes, which are darker, filled with deep desire, I pull back to a sitting position. I can hear his breathing, fast and unsteady, nearly uncontrollable, much like my own right now.

"River," I say while reaching for the condom packet, tearing it open and handing it to him. "Do you know how much I want you?" I feel like a spider caught in his web of seduction, or maybe it's my web.

"God, Dahlia, I want you so much," he whispers to me as one corner of his mouth lifts, and he grabs the condom. Watching as he rolls the condom on, smiling and more than ready, I move to align my sex with his. His face is a picture of clear passion.

He smiles, grips my head, and pulls my mouth to his. As he deepens the kiss, I open my mouth further to welcome the softness of his eager tongue. His fingertips press into my hips, searing me, as I lower myself onto him.

Watching him closely as he fills me completely, I think that this is the most satisfying thing I have ever felt. I begin to move faster. He clutches my hips trying to slow my pace, but I don't let him.

Sucking in a deep breath, he bites his bottom lip before closing his eyes and cringing in ecstasy. "You don't know how long I've waited for this," he manages through gritted teeth.

Opening his eyes, he rolls us over, still connected. I'm now under his beautifully hard body. While moving inside me with slow, even thrusts, he's kissing down my neck, touching my arms, cupping my breasts, thumbing my nipples. I like that he doesn't know what part of me he wants to touch.

Fire burns through my veins as a blaze of arousal flames through my body. Moans of passion flood the room as my fingertips claw his muscular back, urging him to move faster.

My head falls back as I suck in a breath. The lyrics from Robin Thicke's "Sex Therapy" echo from the other room and River sings me his own version of the song.

Moving slowly, precisely, intently, he momentarily stops kissing my neck. "Dahlia, you feel so good."

Gazing at me as his hips continue to slowly roll, he kisses one cheek then the other, my nose, then my eyelids in turn. He reaches under me, and pushes me upward, allowing himself to plunge deeper inside. It's much more intense.

"Oh God, don't stop," I cry as I wrap my legs around his waist, our bodies fitting together like they were made for each other. Moaning himself, he starts to pick up the pace as he grabs my hand and pulls it to his heart.

The moonlight is luminescent through the windows as I moan louder now, feeling the buildup approaching from within me again. And when I look into his face I know he's there, too.

I feel him start to explode. Groaning low and intensely, he stills for a beat as I scream out in pleasure from the mind-blowing orgasm that rushes through my body. Cupping his chin with my free hand, I pull him to me as every fiber of my being tingles from my head to my toes. As the intensity of our kiss calms, our lips rest together. Panting against each other, he gently trails his fingers up my cheek and brushes my hair back from my face before resting his forehead to mine. "You take my breath away."

As our breathing becomes more controlled, he gently rolls off me and lies by my side. Removing the condom, he ties it in a knot, and tosses it to the floor alongside the unused one. Then he pulls me into his arms. Caressing my cheek, he turns to look at me with his gleaming green eyes. "That was amazing—definitely worth the wait."

I nod my head because words momentarily escape me. *Oh my God, why didn't we do that before?* But I remember why. Ben. I think about how glad I am that I didn't succumb to my desire for River that night at the bar because I unequivocally know I would never have recovered from it, from him, and even now I'm not so sure I ever will.

Needing to rid my mind of my inability to see this for what it probably is, a one-night stand, I stare back into his eyes and say, "If your definition of amazing is incredibly hot sex with an equally incredible partner, I definitely agree."

He looks at me with a smirk on his face that says more than words possibly could.

With my arm draped over his chest, I stroke his smooth skin as he rubs circles on my back. I glance up at him, wanting to clear the room of the waves of passion that are still knocking at my door and say, "Was that Robin Thicke I heard playing from your phone?"

Rolling onto his side, his eyes meet mine as he circles his finger around my earlobe, tugging on it before leaning in to kiss just the corner of my lips. Then as he raises an eyebrow, the biggest grin crosses his face. "I'm willing to explore your naughty side. Are you willing to let me unleash mine?" He follows up with an adorable wink.

As I laugh at his halfhearted attempt to once again revise the words of a song, he grabs my hips and a new hunger surfaces between us. He rolls on top of me, and I think that this time we won't be taking it slow.

CHAPTER 12
Say

After staying awake most of the night, we lie quietly together, entangled in a mess of sheets. My head is on his chest with one of my legs wrapped around his, and I'm trailing my fingers down his body as he nuzzles his nose in my hair, caressing my lower back.

Never having had a one-night stand, I didn't know what to expect, but I didn't expect this. Plenty of my friends have experienced casual sex. They've always described it as a quick fuck, sometimes followed by a sleepover. Either way, both people want to be out the door as soon as possible in the morning.

And yet, I don't want our time to end. Last night was amazing. River and I were together in a way I've never experienced before, not just the sex and the multiple orgasms, but also his constant tender touches, the heat I felt surging throughout my body, his softly spoken words. I find myself hoping that he asks for my phone number and that we will see each other again.

Wondering if all new sexual encounters are this satisfying, I try to keep in mind that Ben and I were together for so long that our lovemaking became routine. I also remind myself that I haven't experienced a man's touch in a long while, so of course my sexual reawakening thrills me.

I know I shouldn't be comparing Ben to River, but I do it anyway. I thought my sex life with Ben was fulfilling, but after what I experienced last night, it seems like it may have been a little empty. I think about how wrong it is of me to compare this man—who's very much alive and breathing—to Ben, who is no longer here on earth.

Am I always going to make comparisons to Ben? I already know the answer is yes. But usually anytime I compare something to Ben, Ben always wins out. If I make stir-fry, I think, *Ben made it better.* If I read an article in the paper, I think, *Ben would have written it better.* I have to stop this line of thinking. I have to remember Ben was my life, but River is in it now, too. I also have to remember that River and I were supposed to be one night of amazing sex.

But I'm failing miserably at trying to convince myself that I should be happy with a one-night stand because running through my head are all of River's endearing qualities: his sexiness, his charm, his concern for me, his playfulness, and his awareness—our awareness of each other, he of me, and me of him. Seems odd to feel this connected to someone who I may never see again.

Trying to escape these thoughts, I force myself to run through the list of things I need to do this morning: finish the interview, say goodbye to River, get to the airport, and board the plane that will take me far away from this bliss.

But I think about the way he makes me feel—as if he really cares—and it is clouding my judgment. And then I remember my Google search. River appeared just as attentive in picture after picture with different women on his arm, and that brings me back to my senses.

Sitting up, I attempt to slip out of bed but River pulls me down and crushes me to the mattress as he leans over me. "Where you going?" he asks, his voice raspy from lack of sleep.

With an equally raspy morning voice, I smile up at him. "To the bathroom and then to watch the sunrise from this beautiful spot."

As he nods his head in response, I wonder how it's possible that someone can look even sexier in the morning. Then he kisses me softly on the nose and releases me. "Coffee or tea?"

Furrowing my brows, I wave my finger from head to toe, pointing to my very disheveled self. "Do I look like a girl who drinks tea in the morning?" And for added effect, I say, "And please, God, don't tell me you drink tea!"

Leaning back against the headboard, he puts his hands behind his head, his naked body illuminated by the faint glow of the bathroom light. Shaking his head and chuckling, he says, "I'm not sure you need to know that information. Right now, I'm still trying to figure out if you're a stalker."

I slip on his button-down shirt and laugh. He just spoke the same words that mimic my own response from so long ago. I turn to see him laughing just as hard as I am. Oh yeah, add *makes me laugh* to my list of endearing River qualities.

Entering the bathroom with none of my toiletries in hand, I sit for a while and just think. Having decided to at least wash my face before going to get my bag, I look in the mirror and run my fingers through my hair. Then I see his toothbrush. *Why not?*

Coming out of the bathroom, I grab my phone and give Aerie a quick call.

"Why haven't you called me back? I must have called you ten times," Aerie says immediately, and I know a quick call is out the window. I was hoping she'd still be asleep and I could just leave her a message.

In a low voice I answer, "I'm sorry. I'm calling you back now."

"Dahlia, where are you? Why are you talking so softly?"

"I'm in Las Vegas. You know that."

"No. Where are you right now?"

Knowing it's easier to just tell her, I whisper, "In his suite."

"River's?! You are? And?"

"Umm . . . well, it's kind of a long story, and I will tell you later, but . . ." I am trying to choose my words carefully. Then I just blurt it out. "We went out to dinner and then I spent the night with him."

In a cautious tone, she asks, "Are you telling me you had sex with River Wilde?"

"Yes, Aerie, that is what I'm telling you."

"You're shitting me," she says, her voice full of skepticism.

"No, I'm not. What? Is it that hard for you to believe he'd be interested in me?"

"Of course not. Men are always interested in you, Dahlia. It's you I'm surprised about. You're not exactly Miss One-night Stand. Were you drunk?"

"No, and can we talk about this later, please? Like I said, it's a long story."

"Well, at least tell me how it was? Was it good?"

"Aerie, I'm hanging up now."

"No, Dahlia, wait. Are you okay?"

"I had sex, not surgery. Of course I'm okay."

"That's not what I meant and you know it. We both know you had a crush on him. I just want to make sure you're in the right frame of mind. Having sex with someone is one thing, but having sex with someone you already know gets around is another."

"And how do you know he gets around? Anyway, it was one night. We'll say goodbye, and I'm sure I'll never see him again." I decide not to tell her I haven't even finished the interview yet.

"Okay, Dahlia girl, I get it. And I don't know he gets around, I've just heard he doesn't keep a girlfriend for long."

"Aerie, I'm fine, and I'm hanging up now. I'll call you later. Goodbye."

"Bye, Dahlia, and don't forget to call me this time."

I hang up the phone and think about Aerie's comment a moment before glancing over to the open sliding glass door where the sun is starting to rise. Pink and purple waves of color paint the horizon over the mountains and I really want to watch them, so I decide to get my toiletry bag later.

My pulse quickens as I see him sitting in a chair, wearing only his jeans, one knee crossed over his other leg. Walking toward him, I notice a pot of coffee and croissants sitting on the table beside him. He grins at me and pours two cups of coffee. "Cream and sugar?"

Standing at the door, watching him, and smiling larger than life, I say, "Cream only, kind sir," and then with my hand on my hip I continue. "And I'm so glad you're a coffee-drinking kind of man. Now that I know, I can stop stalking you."

He winks at me while pouring cream into one of the cups and he says, "Oddly enough, a sexy woman with stalking tendencies doesn't bother me."

Crossing my arms and leaning a hip against the doorframe, I can't help but laugh. "I just bet."

"And here I thought you'd be a cream-and-sugar kind of girl with all your sweetness."

I move my hands to my hips. "What, I'm not sweet enough already?" Then, throwing caution to the wind, feeling so comfortable with him, experiencing not an ounce of unease, I stroll over to him as he motions me to sit on his lap.

The early dawn turns into a hazy morning. A beautiful yellow glow streams from the east. I sit on his lap with my knees bent and feet resting on his knee. We drink our coffee as he feeds me pieces of a croissant since one of my hands is glued to my morning coffee and the other is wrapped around his neck.

We continue to kiss and talk even after the sun has fully risen. Dazzling beams of sunlight reflect in his tousled hair. I look at him in awe. He catches my gaze and kisses me a little longer and a little deeper.

His touches also become more intimate. I try to calm the overwhelming feeling of desire creeping throughout my body. As his fingers drift up my leg, I suddenly become fully aware that I'm pantyless. I grab his hand and say, "Come on, we have to do the interview," then pull him through the door heading toward the living room.

Stopping in the bedroom, he grins and nods toward the bed. "You can interview me while we lie in bed."

Looking at his gorgeous smiling face, his smooth chest, well-defined abdominal muscles, and gleaming green eyes now ablaze, I know I should say no, resist the temptation, but I can't, so I shake my finger at him in warning. "Okay, but you'd better behave. I need to finish this interview."

I walk into the living room to get my small portable notebook, and I hear him mutter behind me, "I promise nothing."

I can't help but smile as I reach for my things. Before going back to the bedroom, I walk over to the kitchen counter, press PLAY on the docking station, and hit the room-change button to direct the music to the bedroom. Immediately, I hear the band Fuel singing "I Should Have Told You." I love this song.

In the bedroom, River is lying on his side, leaning on a pillow. His head rests on his hand, the other arm slung loosely over his hip. His legs are slightly bent with one propped up, and he's watching me intently. *He is so hot.* He starts to anxiously bite his thumbnail and I can't handle this complete vision of perfection any longer, so I avert my eyes. I know I won't be able to concentrate if I'm too close to him; I decide to sit at the foot of the bed.

Taking my portable notebook out of my bag, I turn it on and pull up the list of questions we started on yesterday. He takes the thumb he was just biting and starts rubbing circles up my legs. His still-moist touch sends shivers up my spine. I can't even think about my interview.

"Behave," I admonish as I glance at him from behind my computer screen. With my hand over his wandering one, and in a more playful tone, I say, "*Sound Music* paid me to come to Las Vegas and do an interview, not to have a one-night stand and return empty-handed." The last few words are in a much more teasing tone to help lessen the blow.

Removing his hand from my hold, he quickly sits up and grabs the notebook from my lap, placing it on the floor. Wrapping his fingers around my wrists he pulls me right up to him, face-to-face, eye-to-eye. He slides his nose across my cheek to my ear, and in a low, quiet, almost harsh tone, he says, "Dahlia, this was in no way a one-night stand for me. Was it for you? Because if so, I totally misread this, you—us." As he says this, he continues resting his cheek and his lips against the side of my head.

His words momentarily take my breath away as unexpected emotions surge through my mind, my body, and within my soul. I'm not sure what to say or what to do, but I feel strangely at peace. So tugging my arms from his grip, I grab his face and look into his eyes, knowing I can make this better, that I can take the sting out of my words. Words that were thought, and spoken, to protect myself from what I thought was only a night of casual sex.

With my heart beating faster than the music, I respond with only fragmented thoughts. "I'm sorry. I just thought . . . No, not a one-night stand on my part. I wasn't sure . . ." Then sitting up straighter, gently sweeping the hair from his eyes, I point between us. "I just thought you did this kind of thing all the time."

A frown appears on his face. He shakes his head no as Coldplay's song "Yellow" starts to play throughout the room.

He lightly brushes his lips across each corner of my mouth. "No, I don't do this all the time." He glides his lips to my neck. "In fact, I don't think I've ever spent the night in a hotel room with a girl and shared breakfast with her the next morning. And I'm glad we feel the same way," he finally whispers before pausing his kisses and directing his gaze at me. Then, with a huge grin, "So now is it okay if I misbehave?"

It's my turn to rest my head on his, both hands gripping his strong jaw, and in an effort to right my wrong, I tell him, "You know every time you move your nose to my ear like that, it drives me crazy."

Pulling back, softly gripping my arms with his hands, he nods and a slight grin appears, more like a smirk. "Yeah, I know that."

CHAPTER 13
Living for the First Time

The throbbing beat that travels through my body every time he kisses me grows stronger as his kisses turn into more, and his lips meet my most sensitive spots. Every time he touches me, he makes my breath quicken, my heart beat faster, and my temperature rise. Never have I felt like this before.

We didn't finish the interview. My plane departure time came and went. We fell asleep sometime in the late morning. After more amazing can't-get-enough sex, River asked me to stay the weekend with him, and without any doubts, I agreed. How could I not? I feel alive again—living, breathing, and experiencing life like I never had before—because of him. He took me to places I've never been, and I wanted to experience more.

When he made it clear that our first night together wasn't just a one-night stand, the sorrow, grief, and sheer loneliness I was carrying with me for almost two years seemed to disperse. It's as if I'm heading into spring, and winter is finally fading behind me. I notice the leaves turning green; no longer are they brown and lifeless on the barren ground. I can hear the chirping of the birds, they are no longer flying south, and as the harsh hot gales of the Santa Ana winds morph into gentle warm breezes, I feel alive again.

As I wake, I glance to look at the clock; it's almost noon. Lifting my head from its very comfortable position, I look up and see River. He's awake and grinning at me. His hair is a mess, but still so sexy, and my stomach flip-flops. He nods his head toward the nightstand. "Your phone is vibrating over there," he says in a wicked tone as his gleaming eyes divert back to mine and then down to the bed.

Smiling, I lay my head back down and snuggle into his chest. I wonder how he can turn an ordinary sentence into something so sensual, erotic. I mumble, "Yeah, it's probably Serena. I really should call her back and check on her son. He was sick before I left."

He sits up and pulls the sheet from our naked bodies as he leans over and softly kisses my stomach, gliding his hand all the way up my chest with his fingertips as he stands. Reaching for my phone and handing it to me he says, "Text her fast, you can call her later."

I sneak a quick peek at his bare ass as he walks toward the end of the bed. It is perfect, and I smirk at him. I can't help myself. Sliding the unlock bar on my phone, I send Serena a quick text.

Sorry I haven't called. Been busy. How's Trent? Let me know.
Kiss him for me. <3 :)

Having pulled on his boxers, River walks back over to me and takes the phone. He sets it back on the nightstand. Gesturing toward the bathroom, he says, "Come with me."

I snatch his shirt from the floor and shrug into it, leaving it unbuttoned.

Head cocked, he watches me, his eyes moving over my body. He extends a hand to lead me into the spacious bathroom. It has a black marble floor with HIS and HERS sinks to the right and a large open glass shower to the left with a huge Jacuzzi in the center. I immediately head to use the restroom, which is in its own separate room next to the sinks.

While in there, I hear River softly humming a song. I can't quite make it out over the sound of the water flowing from the sink. When I open the door, I stop and observe him. He's singing and shaving like the two were always meant to be done together. He doesn't notice me standing there as he abandons his singing and starts brushing his teeth. Gazing at him, I can't help but think again how attractive he is, and I laugh out loud at the thought of using that toothbrush this morning.

I cross my arms and bite my bottom lip as I walk over and stand next to him, grinning.

Turning his head, he pulls the toothbrush from his mouth. "What's so funny?" he manages through a mouthful of foamed tooth-paste.

Giggling uncontrollably, I manage to answer, "I sort of used your toothbrush this morning, hope you don't mind."

A devilish grin appears on his face, his eyes narrowing as he sets his toothbrush on the counter while the water continues to run. "Oh, yeah? Then you shouldn't mind this."

Before I can move away, he grabs me by the waist and reaches down to my backside. His lips crash into mine, and he sets me on the counter. His tongue jets back and forth over my top teeth; then he does the same over my bottom teeth before his tongue finds the roof of my mouth. Desire flows through me as easily as the water streams from the faucet trickling into the sink.

Shifting his taut body slightly, he spreads my legs further apart and presses into my core. He moves his mouth to suck my bottom lip before he starts kissing me hard, a little wildly. Yearning pulsates through my body. The toothpaste is now dripping from both our mouths as the water continues to fill the sink, but neither of us cares.

Finally, I nudge him in the shoulder and he steps back. "Hey. That's not playing fair. I didn't say I wanted you to brush my teeth. I . . . ," but I don't get a chance to finish. As his eyes flicker to my lips and down my open shirt, his breathing labors as his lips part and he bows his head. The tip of his tongue finds the small swell of my breast where some toothpaste has dripped and as he starts slowly dragging his tongue up my chest, an unstoppable moan escapes my mouth.

I wipe the toothpaste from my mouth with the back of my hand and try to stop panting as my body heat rises from his touch. When he looks up at me, his eyes are full of passion. Licking the edge of his bottom lip, he propels his hard body back into mine, but this time I wrap my legs around him instead of pushing him back, welcoming the feel of his soft skin against mine.

With a quick intake of breath and toothpaste still dripping down his chin, he says, "What were you saying?"

Moving toward him, I slide my tongue up his chin, licking all the toothpaste off before managing a simple "Nothing."

With his taut body against mine, he reaches and turns the water off. The only sound that can be heard in the room now is our increasingly heavy breathing.

"Actually," I moan as my lips drift down his cleanly shaven chin. "I was wondering." I pause to inhale deeply as my hands slip into the waistband of his silky black boxer shorts. "Why haven't you sung for me yet today?" I barely get the words out between trying to catch my breath and shoving my hands down his boxers.

With a sharp intake of breath, he pulls me forward so my behind barely rests on the counter. My hands fall from his hardness and he exhales deeply as he rocks his hips into mine, his hands traveling down my spine, pushing me even closer. Crying out, I scratch my nails down his back before arching so I can grind my hips further into his.

As his hands travel around my waist and rest on my lower back, he takes a step back. He stares at me with desire.

"You want me to sing something for you?"

Nodding my head, I feel his hands travel right to my sex. He slides them between my legs and trails his fingers up and down my inner thighs, teasing me, torturing me. "Let me turn the music on," he breathes out. But he doesn't leave the room, he doesn't leave me; instead, he glides his hands around my hips and lifts me off the counter, carrying me to the shower, pushing me up against the wall. He turns the water on before setting me down and I get the feeling the water is our music.

He grins and asks, "What do you want me to sing?"

"Anything by Maroon 5, of course."

Even though he frowns at my request, he sings for me anyway.

Showering with River is intimate, very sexy—almost carnal. As he lathers the soap all over my body, he sings "She Will Be Loved." I reward him generously when he sings the part in the song about rainbows and butterflies, my favorite line.

When he finishes, he seductively tells me how much he wants to taste me everywhere, describing what he wants to do to me. Feeling unabashed and very comfortable, completely connected to him, I respond by detailing what I want to do to him, with him.

My brain feels as if it's in overdrive, and my body is driving me into oblivion. God, this man is . . . is . . . I can't even think as he slowly moves his hands, reaching behind me, lifting me and backing me up against the wall.

When we finally emerge from the shower, both sated and satisfied, he wraps a towel around me, and then one around his waist. I run my fingers through his wet, messy hair. I shake my head and grin at how attractive, charming, and just adorable he is before I turn and head into the bedroom. I can feel his stare as I leave the room, so I shake my ass a little, giving him a show, and I hear him laugh.

Heading to the living room, I grab my suitcase and bring it back to the bedroom just as River comes out of the bathroom buttoning his jeans with a towel around his shoulders. He looks overwhelmingly attractive.

He sweetly says, "Why didn't you ask me to get that for you?" His kindness makes me weak in the knees. I'm falling for this guy, a guy I hardly know.

With an enchanted smile, I prepare to speak in a Southern accent while pretending to fan myself and say, "Why, kind sir, do you think I'm a helpless maiden?"

Laughing, smiling and flashing those huge dimples again, he comes over and draws me into his arms, shaking his wet head of gorgeous light brown hair against the crook of my neck.

"No, I don't think that," he says, biting my shoulder, "I just wanted to help."

River's phone rings from the dresser, but he ignores it. He slowly reaches over, grabs a lock of my hair, and tucks it behind my ear in a move that sends shivers down my spine. He circles his index finger around my ear and lightly tugs on my lobe, which sparks a surge of heat in my body.

Grabbing his towel, I pull it off his shoulders and use it to dry his hair while massaging my fingers on his scalp. The rumbling of my stomach stops me from going further. He places his hands on my arms and leans back, his smooth chest glistening brightly in the sunlight. "Hungry?"

"You know how to work up a girl's appetite. I'm starving." And I let his towel fall to the ground.

Pulling the fluffy white towel off my body, River grins and swats my behind with it. "If you'd stop being so sexy and put some clothes on, we could get the hell out of here and get some food." He turns and heads back into the bathroom, leaving me gawking once again at his fine backside. When he enters the bathroom he says, "I know you're watching me," and shakes his ass at me.

I laugh out loud as I begin rummaging through my suitcase. I put my last clean pair of panties on. They are plain white with a little black bow on the back. Then I slip on the matching bra. This lingerie doesn't exactly scream sexy.

He emerges from the bathroom and stands in the door. "I like your bow."

Turning to look at him and meaning to answer sarcastically, I gasp. He's wearing a black AC/DC Back in Black Tour T-shirt. My dad loved AC/DC so of course I do, too.

"Well, I like AC/DC, now get out and let me get dressed."

Strutting, he crosses the room. He passes by me then stops and takes a step back as I continue pulling the messy heap of clothing from my suitcase. He places a kiss on each of my shoulders, and then tugs on the black bow on the front of my bra. "Thank you, Dahlia," he says as he saunters to the bed, sits down, and puts his socks and black boots on before falling back against a pillow and kicking his feet up.

"I'm not giving you a show, you know," I say while slipping on a black lace camisole and pulling my gray long-sleeve Coldplay Viva la Vida concert T-shirt over my head before knotting it to the side. I quickly pull up my faded black jeans and, while looking at him, I start to think about the Coldplay song "Green Eyes." It must have been written for him.

Drawing me from my thoughts, River chuckles as he asks, "Am I making you nervous?"

Swinging my hair over my head, I bend over and brush it. "No, you're not—why would you think that?"

I meet his gaze as he says, "I don't know. It just seems like it. It's good that I don't because I shouldn't—you're much too sexy not to be adored."

He puts his arms behind his head and shoots me a wide grin. "I really like your shirt. Did you go to . . . ?"

As he speaks, I remember my ring. *Where is my ring?* I start to feel dizzy as I grab my neck, running my fingers back and forth, but I know it's not there. River sits up immediately as I frantically say, "Oh, no, I have to go back to my hotel, my necklace is still in the room!" I'm trying not to panic; really I am, but my necklace, my ring from Ben, I have to find them.

River heads over to me with concern etched on his face. He pulls the hair from my eyes and tucks it behind my ear before cupping my cheeks with his hands as his eyes examine mine. "Okay, we can head over there now."

I try to calm myself, but I can't, and tears start streaming down my face. With his thumbs, he wipes the tears away. He doesn't ask why and he doesn't shrug off my concern. He just kisses my forehead and leads me toward the door. Leads me to a journey that can only end with some sort of uneasiness. At the very least, a pained conversation about the man I loved with the man I . . . I don't even dare think about what word to use to describe my feelings for River.

Sensations are swirling through my body like a tornado. But unlike Dorothy, I'm not going to land in Kansas wearing ruby red slippers in a land full of happy people. No, my aftermath will include having to tell the man I'm starting a new relationship with the reason for my panic. I must tell River that the reason he's taking me back to my hotel is so I can retrieve the most significant reminder I have left of Ben.

As we wait outside the hotel for his car, he turns to me and takes both my hands. He looks at me like he knows he can make everything better. "Baby, don't cry. I promise I'll fix this for you. Everything will be all right," he says, drawing an *X* over his heart with his right hand. Baby? Did he just call me baby?

In this moment, standing at the valet stand with rows of cars behind me waiting to be parked, I know. I know I'm not just falling for this attractive, charming, and captivating man. I already fell.

We drive over to the hotel in silence. The strip is so different during the day, even though it's still pretty. It doesn't have the allure it does at night. The lights are on, but aren't shining brightly, not lighting the way. I hope they at least lead me back to the item I need to find.

I'm feeling a little lost sitting in River's car going to get my engagement ring from Ben. Fidgeting in my seat, I keep grabbing for the necklace that isn't there. He isn't holding my hand and he hasn't as much as glanced over at me since we got in the car. I know he must be curious about why I'm so emotional. But I can't talk about it right now. I need to get the necklace back first and for the lump in my throat to go away. Only then can I allow the words to flow.

I wish it were that easy to shut my thoughts off. *Did I betray Ben by taking his ring off? Did I betray him by sleeping with River? How long should I grieve? How long should I wait before getting into a new relationship? Are there even any right answers?*

When we finally arrive, the valet opens my door before River gets out of the car. I wait for him, and he takes my hand, leading us straight to the front desk. I know housekeeping must have already been in the room and apparently so does River since we don't bother going up there. There is a rather long line at the front desk, but River ignores it. Stepping right up to the desk, he nods his head at the gentleman who just handed room keys to a couple and waits for them to leave. Moving to where the couple was standing, he clears his throat to get the attention of the clerk. I'm sure the line of people behind us is not pleased by our blatant disregard for waiting-in-line etiquette.

When the man refuses to look up, River drops my hand and leans forward, placing both elbows on the counter. "Hey, man, I have a situation that needs to be taken care of immediately, and I was hoping you could help me out," he says in his smooth, easy voice. The front desk assistant, obviously impervious to River's charming ways, doesn't even look up as he says, "Sir, I'm going to have to ask you to wait in line like everybody else."

River's jaw tightens as he grips the counter, and in a flat, stern voice he says, "I'm not sure you heard me, but we have a situation that—"

The man narrows his eyes up at River and interrupts him. "I heard you, and once again I'm going to—"

This time River doesn't let him finish before leaning in as close as possible and very politely saying, "I think it's time you call for Mr. Hughes." Then, looking at his nametag and smirking, he adds, "Joe."

Who's Mr. Hughes?

The now completely flustered man stutters before regaining his composure. He stands up straight and manages to nicely say, "Why don't we see if I can fix your situation before I call Mr. Hughes? You were saying?" Swallowing back my nervous laughter, I watch as River cocks his head and winks at me. Then he takes my hand, squeezes it, and sets it on the counter in his so our elbows are almost connected.

Before I know it, the desk clerk is calling housekeeping himself, asking about items that may have been found in the safe in my room. By some grace of God he tells us the necklace had been found and was put in the main hotel safe.

River drops my hand to very politely shake hands with the clerk. Then before thanking him, he removes his wallet from his back pocket and hands the now-jubilant Joe a hundred-dollar bill. He says discreetly, "Joe, please see to it that the necklace gets delivered to us in the bar."

Joe very happily accepts the more than generous tip with a "Yes, sir, not a problem."

We head to the same bar where River waited for me last night. It seems like way more time has passed than just one day. I feel so connected to this man, like I've known him for a very long time. As we're seated, River pulls my chair out for me and I nod my head and grin, but before I sit, I stand on my tippy toes and kiss him on his cheek. "Thank you."

"Dahlia, don't thank me. It's my fault you lost your necklace to begin with," he says, caressing my cheek before motioning me to sit down. Sitting next to me, he grabs my hand and strokes it with his thumb before leaning over and kissing me.

Our waitress arrives, we order two beers and one glass of ice, and of course River snickers. When he asks me what I want to eat, I say, "Anything, right now I could eat the craps table over there," and we both laugh, because, really, couldn't I have just said the blackjack table?

He orders a burger and fries and I order a grilled cheese sandwich, fries, and a chocolate milkshake. I ask the waitress to bring my shake with my food.

River looks at me a little puzzled.

"What? I like to dip my sandwich in the shake."

He shakes his head. "That sounds disgusting."

"Try it. I guarantee you'll love it."

Once our drinks arrive, I gulp my beer down before deciding to say what I should have said in the car. Looking into River's eyes where I see so much kindness, I say, "I'm sorry I sort of freaked, but the necklace isn't replaceable." Pausing, I swallow the lump in my throat.

He continues to look at me and simply says, "I guessed that by your reaction."

Nodding, I clear my throat and tuck my hair behind my ear. "Here's the thing, the necklace isn't just a necklace." I pause again, willing the stinging in my eyes to go away.

River, obviously having noticed my uneasiness, leans forward in his chair, bending slightly into me, and grabs for my hand with both of his. "Go on. What did you want to say?"

Before I can finish, Joe saunters in, smiling like he just hit the jackpot on the casino floor and hands River an envelope labeled: "From Room 716." River nods and says thank you again and Joe walks away to return to his desk duties.

Handing me the envelope, I let go of his hand and open it. I hesitate before pulling the ring out. As I do, I clasp it in my hand and look him in the eyes. "This is my engagement ring—from Ben."

He quickly leans back in his chair and takes a large gulp of beer, obviously not expecting that. Crossing his leg over his knee he asks, "Can I see it?" His eyes now fill with an emotion I can't quite put my finger on. It's not kindness; I think it's more like sadness.

Biting my lip, I hand it to him with shaky fingers. My heart begins beating faster. He stares at it for a few seconds before gently placing it back in my hand and squeezing it shut, as if not seeing it makes it go away. "It's beautiful, just like the woman who wore it," he says, looking intently in my eyes. I notice the use of the word *wore*—past tense.

"Can I ask you something?"

My hands are still shaky as I answer, "Of course."

Pointing to my wrist, he asks, "Is that bracelet from him?"

Swallowing my emotion, I lift my arm and say, "Yes, Ben gave it to me the day he died, and every time I look at it, it reminds me to live life to the fullest, to have no regrets."

"Well, that, too, is beautiful and a great way to live life, Dahlia."

Then he surprises me. "Do you want to talk about it, about him?"

After tucking the ring safely inside my purse, I answer very softly, "Honestly, no. No, I don't. I'm having an amazing time with you. I haven't had this much fun in a long time, and I don't want to drag our weekend down with sad conversations." I say the last part while reaching my hand across the table and caressing his cheek.

He shakes his head and doesn't speak as he takes my hand and kisses it.

On a faint smile I say, "I hope you're okay with that?"

River returns the smile. "Dahlia, for now I'm fine with it, but I'd like to talk about it sometime. I want to know all of you."

Just then, our food arrives. I pull my hand away and silently nod to him. Then his phone rings from his pocket and he continues to ignore it. I remember I left mine at the hotel, but I really don't need it anyway.

We talk and laugh throughout lunch. Before leaving, we decide to hit the casino and then have a casual dinner before heading out to a club.

CHAPTER 14
Alive

I remember Grace telling me on the one-year anniversary of Ben's death as we drove home from the cemetery, "Dahlia honey, there is something beautiful about each and every scar we bear no matter where it comes from." She had to wipe the tears streaming down her face before finishing what to this day had to be the single most important piece of advice ever given to me. "When my son's death, our Ben's death, has healed in your heart, you will know it. A scar will appear and that means the extreme hurt and unbearable pain is over, your wound will be healed—but don't ever let your heart close. Leave it open, let someone else in." She couldn't speak anymore, but I knew she wasn't finished. She put a note on the counter when she left that night that read, "Let your heart heal and someday you will love again. Let someone else love you. You deserve it. Remember, I will always be here for you."

So tonight, as I embark on a first date with this very sexy, charming, and charismatic man, Grace's words come back to me. I know what I'm feeling is *healed*.

Walking into Aqua, I know I'm in trouble. It's dark, and the music is blaring in a loud, seductive beat. I'm already intoxicated by River's charm and breathtaking attractiveness, and this nightclub isn't going to help sober me up. Not to mention the two drinks I had with dinner and the few I had before that.

Earlier in the day, we had taken his car back to the hotel and hit the casino floor. He taught me how to play craps, and we played blackjack and poker. I also tried the slot machines as he watched. Rolling his eyes at me, he teased, "Only sixty-year-old women waste their time on a game of pure chance." And in what I've come to know as true River fashion, he added, "Now, skill games, those are something to spend your time on." Of course, he whispered that in my ear while running his finger down the side of my body. We were having so much fun that we never even made it back to our room. After we left the casino, we walked through the sky tube and then ate a light dinner before coming up to the club.

The nightclub is located on the fifty-fifth floor of the Trees Place Casino. All of its exterior walls are glass, and there is a huge bar toward the back and an even bigger dance floor in the middle. There are also outdoor bars on both sides, just outside the glass walls. Each is a mirror image supported by a brick wall on the backside of each bar, creating a terrace area with trees and benches everywhere. The outdoor bar to the right is serving drinks, but the other one appears to be closed.

Rihanna's song "S&M" is playing loudly as we enter the large double doors of the VIP entrance. We hand our jackets to the coat check, and River turns to me to say, "Stay close, it's a wreck in here tonight."

Does he think I want to be anywhere but close to him? Because I don't. In fact, with all the sexual energy radiating between us, I'm more than willing to forego the clubbing and head straight back to our hotel room. But, since that doesn't seem to be an option right now, I just nod my head and bite my lip. He looks so delicious and I'm hoping I get a taste of him real soon.

Clutching his hand with both of mine, I follow close behind and bump into him as often as I can. Making our way to the bar, he orders two lemon-drop shots. Cocking his head, he hands me the shot. While grinning widely, he declares, "I know up until now you've only done shots to celebrate disasters, but here's to changing that."

As he clinks his glass against mine, I recall my earlier thoughts and know for sure that I have already fallen for him. He remembers everything I tell him, even the most inconsequential things. As I tip my head back to drink the sweet alcohol that smells of lemons, I think about how many times I had to tell Ben something before he remembered. I had chalked it up to typical male behavior, and maybe it was. Maybe River is the exception to the rule.

We order another drink, and he leads me to a high-top table in the reserved section just on the edge of the dance floor. It feels liberating and invigorating to be here with him laughing, drinking, and just having fun. With the humidity reaching record highs, the ceiling above us opens just as the Enrique Iglesias song "Dirty Dancer" starts thumping out a seductive beat. We both look up in awe of the spectacular sight. As our heads tilt back down, our gazes meet. I start bopping my neck and shaking my hips, and River smiles his full-megawatt dimple smile before running his eyes up and down my body. He grins mischievously as he points to the dance floor and whispers, "You sure you want to do this? I'm pretty good."

Out on the dance floor I see a bunch of drunken college boys making obscene gestures with their hands, a group of girls dancing like they have no idea what song is playing, and many couples actually dirty dancing. Having assessed my surroundings, I run my hands down my sides and with a grin from ear to ear I mouth to him, "You're on." He grabs my hand and leads me to the dance floor.

I feel our connection growing stronger minute by minute. What was once an electric pull is now an electric force. We are in the middle of a swarm of people, but I feel like it's just the two of us out here. Having removed my T-shirt long ago, I'm standing on the dance floor in my black lace camisole. With the lights blinking on and off, I know everyone must be able to see my girly white bra. River doesn't seem to mind, though, as his eyes flicker to my lips, my chest, down to my jeans, and back up. He grins at me as I lift my hair off my neck to help cool my extremely overheated body.

Grabbing my hips, he pulls me closer. I snake my arms around his neck as Enrique continues to sing about dirty dancing. As we start moving our bodies to the rhythm, I run my fingers through his beautiful shaggy hair. We move like we have known each other for years; like we're two pieces of a puzzle finally reunited.

At first, our dance moves are innocent. A soft touch here, a light caress there, but the innocence gives way as the song ends. When Havana Brown's "You'll Be Mine" starts to play, it's game on. I no longer just lightly run my fingers through his hair, rather I tug on it. Instead of just running my hands down his back, I wet my finger in my mouth and softly glide it down the back of his neck, and he shivers beneath my touch.

He's playing, too. His hands are no longer resting on my hips. They've drifted down to my backside and he's cupping it. He's no longer just leaning into me; he's now whispering dirty things in my ear.

The song thumps, and we get so completely lost in ourselves that we're oblivious to everyone else on the dance floor. As I turn around so that I'm no longer facing him, my back now to his front, the sexual energy radiating between us grows stronger. My want and my need for him overcome me as he places his right hand on my hip. My body quivers as he slowly slides his hand up my stomach. His nose is in my hair and his hand glides across the front of my camisole. He's breathing against my neck, and I know I'm not the only one losing control. As he continues to softly move his hands up my body, I absorb every caress. When he stops and gently pokes his fingers through the holes of the lace in my shirt, touching my bare skin, it feels like he's searing me with his touch, and I love it.

With one hand traveling up my body, he carefully takes his other hand and swipes my hair off my shoulder to expose the side of my neck. He trails soft kisses down it. As he reaches my shoulder, his kisses fade away. His mouth reappears at my neck, and he seductively drags his tongue back up to my ear. When he reaches my lobe, he jets his tongue in and out, sending shivers down my spine. My body is now a trembling mass of nerves. My awareness of him and my need to have him are heightened.

I smile as Havana Brown's song bleeds into another Enrique song. I no longer hear the lyrics in each verse, but I do hear the words as he sings about fucking someone tonight. The colored lights of the disco ball and strobe lights continue to flicker, and we begin to do more than just dance. He's seducing me, or I'm seducing him; I have no idea which and I don't care. The only thing that matters is that I have an urgent need for him that can't wait to be addressed.

I close my eyes as his hand settles on my breast, and his fingers rub circles around my erect nipple. His hand is now clenching and unclenching my hip as he continues his tongue's assault on my ear and my neck. I'm experiencing sensual overload with his body wrapped around mine, his mouth on me, with his scent so intoxicatingly close, and his smooth jawline rubbing against my tender skin. I can't wait any longer.

When I grind myself into him, I can feel his hardness, and I know that he feels the same way I do. I can hear his erratic breathing and he groans as he grabs both my hips, holding me tight to him. His breathing grows more irregular as his hands drift down the front of my jeans. I slide my hands into his back pockets and push him further into me. He quickly turns me back around. *Hah . . . I got him.*

Facing each other, our eyes flicker and our breathing is ragged.

When he licks his lower lip in a way that screams sexy, I bite mine. I skim my way down his body. I'm amazed my dancing abilities haven't rusted over the past few years, and I'm shocked that I'm dancing far more seductively than I ever have before, ever.

I shimmy my way up his leg and run my hands up the inside of his thighs. As I'm reaching his core, I brush my fingers over his flawless chest and well-defined abs, and they tense up. When I start to untuck his shirt, he grabs my hands and pulls them to his neck, hoarsely whispering in my ear, "Do you want a drink?"

My breathing is beyond controllable as the sweat beads on the back of my neck drip down my shoulder blades. "No, I don't want a drink. I want you," I breathe out in erratic whispers, my desire more than apparent.

River pauses for a moment, as if assessing the situation. He then leans in and touches his nose to mine before whispering in my ear, "You want to head back to the hotel?" I know he knows that's not what I mean.

I shake my head and pout my lips. I've decided it's my turn to drive him crazy; he's not getting out of this that easy. I get up on my toes so that I'm eye level with him, and I kiss him; really kiss him, in a way that communicates what I want. I only stop to suck on his bottom lip before saying, "I can't wait that long. I want you now. I need you now." I know what I just said, and if the words that just purred out of my mouth didn't shock him, they sure as shit shocked me. In fact, I think the only time I've ever had sex in a public place was my first time with Ben, but I push that thought aside. I'm feeling parched, dehydrated, and River is the only drink that can quench my thirst. I need a sip right now, right here, but somewhere just a little more private.

He roughly pulls me to him and growls, "You're just so beautiful. You know I can't say no." Letting go, he trails his fingertips down my arms. Staring intently at me, he scans my body. "You drive me wild.

You know that?" Then he grabs my hand and leads me to the back of the club.

I drop his hand, opting instead to snake my arms around him. The warmth I feel is invigorating, and I need to feel more of him. Right now. When we get to the back of the club, he opens the glass door and leads us to the closed outdoor bar.

The terrace is just as gorgeous as it looked from the front doors, but I don't care about the view. The heat, the humidity, the loud music all fade as we hit the cool fresh air, and I'm finally alone with River. He stops and I walk right into him, giggling. As he turns around, I see the passionate look in his eyes, and I'm no longer laughing.

Cocking his head, his eyes search mine for reassurance. His lips slightly part as he snakes his arms around my waist. I hear a quick intake of breath and the electricity shooting through my body ratchets up to a high voltage. I press myself against him, wrapping my arms around his neck, connecting my lips to his. With a thirst only his soft lips and his hard body can satisfy, I start to kiss him fiercely.

Slowly moving us backward, careful not to separate our lips, we lose touch with reality. Fifty-five floors above the streetlights, cars, and people on the strip, we're in our own erotic world out on this terrace.

After a few steps he pauses, looks around, and then places one of his legs in between mine, sending shock waves through my body. He jets his tongue into my mouth and quickly skims his hands up and down my sides. He breathes heavily in my ear and growls, "I like the way you move."

He's driving me insane! He's always quoting my favorite lyrics, and singing them to me with his rough, romantic voice.

His fresh scent is overwhelming, his hot touch is searing, and his strong body so close to mine, I can't wait for him any longer. Pressed to cure this insanity, I start unzipping his jeans and untucking his shirt at the same time. I move my head down to where his shirt ends. I pull it up and gently kiss his taut stomach. I don't even care that the club's glass wall is not that far away.

I hear myself moan in disappointment as he pulls me up and away from him, just gazing at me with those emerald eyes, now so full of desire. "You're going to end this before we even start," he says before grabbing my hand. "Come with me."

"Gladly," is all I can muster. I want no more talking, no more dancing. I just want to feel his touch, his hard, beautiful body, to feel him inside me.

Turning the corner, we're on the other side of the bar and finally secluded in the dark, cool night. He suddenly pushes me up against the brick wall. I know my face must be flushed, and my body is quivering as I glide my hands down his sculpted chest. Reaching his waist, I finish unzipping his pants. I run one hand down his long shaft while my other hand braces myself on his strong biceps and urges him forward. He groans loudly and pants. "Fuck, I can't control myself around you."

I smirk because this is the first time I've heard him swear without apologizing or not completing the word, and now I know for sure his thirst for me is just as unbearable.

His hands move down my body, and as I continue to stroke him, he moves slowly to unbutton my jeans. His groans and my moans grow louder with each passing second.

Breaking our kiss, he rests his forehead on mine. "You sure you're okay with this? We can take a cab back to the hotel right now if you want."

I shake my head and pull him to me, kissing him hard for a brief second. "No, I want you now," I say as I reach my hand down to grab him.

He quickly pulls my pants down to my upper thighs and just as quickly, his fingers slide inside my panties. As his fingers glide over my sensitive flesh, my thirst becomes a little more manageable. Then he removes them from where I need them to be, placing them on my ass, causing my unquenchable thirst to return.

Grinding my hips into him, I'm pressing myself right where I want to be; he's unwavering, though, not giving up control in the slightest. I even feel him smirk against my lips as he kisses me. A cool breeze passes, but I'm so hot, it doesn't cool me. "I thought you couldn't control yourself?" I murmur, urging him to me, wanting his fingers inside of me. Wanting him inside of me.

"You give me the willpower," he grumbles in a devilish tone.

Okay, sexy, game on! I think as I find my thoughts echoing the words I said before we hit the dance floor.

I sense his wicked grin as I remove my hands from his shaft and run them up his chiseled chest, then under his defined arms, and roughly down his sculpted back. He groans and does the same thing to me, but I restrain myself. I'm starting to enjoy this game way too much to cave.

With alcohol flowing freely through my veins and because of how comfortable I feel around him, I have no inhibitions. I slip my hands inside the back of his pants, run them down his backside, and around his hips to his front. He throws his head back as my hands move up slightly and cup him. I grip the base of his incredible hardness with both hands before sliding them to his slightly moist tip.

I'm pretty sure I'm winning this game of willpower when he says, "Fuck, Dahlia, what are you doing to me?" and quickly pulls my white cotton panties down, ripping them in the process.

With both his hands heading to my core, I brace the wall. He spreads my slick flesh apart using his thumb and finger of one hand. As he plunges a finger inside me, I no longer notice the blinking casino lights in the distance, just the pure pleasure of his touch.

Kissing my neck, he moves one hand to tease my nipple and continues to plunge one finger and then another inside of me. I'm losing my mind. With a panting breath, I mutter, "I surrender, you win." But thankfully, he doesn't stop.

Closing my eyes, I inhale deeply. I drink him in completely as I claw the brick wall for support and scream into the night, "Yes, yes!" My body shudders and pulsates from its core as I come hard and fast. My thirst for River is mildly satisfied, but nowhere near quenched.

Wanting him inside me more than I have ever wanted someone before, I say breathlessly, "River, fuck me now, make me come again." Once again, I'm shocked at my own words, but he's clearly not because he says, "I plan to."

He doesn't wait as he slams inside me quick and hard. Each retreat is followed by another glorious penetration as his thickness fills me. As his pace quickens, he thrusts me against him, into his full hardness, causing it to rub my most sensitive spot with every thrust.

"Stay still," he says, and moves even deeper into me at an increasing rate. When his groans become lower, almost primal, I don't move. I stay still. I want to experience him fully. I realize this has to be the single most fulfilling sensation I have ever felt.

His fingers start digging into my flesh, his own pleasure building at the same pace as mine. Groaning into my shoulder, he's no longer kissing me, no longer able to, I'm sure. Especially if he's feeling anything close to the pure heaven I'm experiencing. As he continues to rock himself into me, I feel my body responding again. I grab his strong biceps for support and start to tremble.

Lifting his head, his green eyes find mine, and they are glazed with passion. He sucks in a quick breath, his eyes closing as he lowers his head to my shoulder.

I lift his head with both hands. "Say it," I command.

His groans grow louder as I continue to clutch his gorgeous face in my hands and experience the mesmerizing transformation that's taking place as he finds his release. He grunts, "I'm coming," as his thrusts slow, and a low cry escapes his mouth.

I know I was wrong before when I feel him fill me and hear him say those words. My muscles clench tightly, and my toes curl. This, right now, is the most fulfilling moment I have ever felt.

As he lowers his head and thrusts into me one final time, I fall apart at the seams, coming for a second time as we both quench our insatiable thirst for each other, further building our connection. As we ride out our orgasms together, he suddenly looks up, his face full of concern, his eyes wide. "Shit, we didn't use a condom."

Lost in the moment, I never realized it, either, but I quickly reassure him, "It's okay, I'm on the Pill."

With both palms pressed against the wall, he leans his forehead to mine. While both of us try to stabilize our breathing, he runs his hand along my shoulder and says, "I've never been with anyone without a condom." He removes one hand from the brick wall and draws a cross over his heart. "I'm clean. I promise."

I nod my head and kiss him, not wanting to talk about other women. So I just say, "River, that was amazing."

"You could say that again." He gives me a sly grin as he pulls up my ripped panties and jeans and I button them as he zips his own.

Once we've put ourselves together as best we can, he curls his arms around my waist and presses himself into me. Bringing his forehead to mine, he starts dancing slowly with me. While we move together in the night, my environment suddenly comes alive, and I see the beauty all around me.

With the blinking lights below, and the stars above guiding our way, River twirls me around the terrace as he sings one of my favorite songs, "Addicted," by Saving Abel.

When he gets to a verse I know really well, I smirk as he makes up his own lyrics. "I'm so addicted to you, everything you do, it doesn't matter if you're walking or dancing, when we're standing here, the sounds you make and the smile on your face, they're unlike anything I've ever seen."

I think of how true those words are and how much they express the way I'm feeling right now. River is unlike anyone I have ever met. And right now I'm so happy to be with him—to be alive.

Finishing our dance by dipping me, he whispers in my ear, "Sorry about your panties."

When he pulls me back up, I joke, "No, you're not, but they were ugly anyway."

He laughs and tenderly cups my chin as we experience our first soft kiss of the evening.

"You ready to go now? We have a hot tub waiting for us back at the hotel."

I smile. "Absolutely!"

He slings his arm around me, and I tuck my hand in his back pocket as he leads me to the coat check, both of us grinning ear to ear.

CHAPTER 15
Kiss You Inside Out

It's Sunday morning, only two days since River and I reconnected. Two days, but it seems so much longer. After all, it only took a minute for me to crush on him that night five years ago, it took less than an hour for me to lust after him two days ago, and, dare I say, it only took me slightly more than a day to know I could feel something more for him.

With our connection so strong, it seems strange that Ben keeps popping into my mind. *Is it because I'm feeling guilty about not being able to recall ever having this kind of budding feeling for Ben like I'm having for River?*

Ben and I never experienced the typical milestones of a new couple. Our relationship simply happened. We just loved each other. I don't recall when I knew for sure I loved him or when I knew for sure he was the one I wanted to spend my life with. One day we were best friends, and then one day we were lovers. There was no single moment where I knew I loved Ben; I just always did.

So yesterday, why did I feel something happening within me that was strange and different? It felt like some alien feelings somehow crashed through the universe and knocked on my door. What were these unknown feelings I had deep within me? Suddenly, after spending two days with River, I'm full of contentment.

I remember waking up next to Ben for the four years we lived together and countless more before that, but I don't recall ever feeling like I do now. We never cuddled with each other when we slept. Ben had his side of the bed, and I had mine. We would usually make love and fall asleep with our legs entwined or arms touching, but by morning we each clearly had our own side of the bed.

Yet, right now River is sleeping soundly, his body wrapped around mine. I'm nestled into his hard, sculpted chest. He's sleeping on the opposite side of the bed than he did Friday night. *Funny, maybe he doesn't have a side, or maybe I don't?*

We had such a magical night, and, yes, my backside is a little scratched from the bricks, but what a pleasant reminder of the amazing time we had. After leaving the club around midnight, we decided to walk back to the hotel and enjoy the sights. We walked arm in arm, slowly; we stopped to kiss, and we stopped to talk. We were in no hurry. Having both been sated by our passionate impromptu romp out on the terrace, we just wanted to enjoy each other's company.

River stopped as we walked past the fountain at the Bellagio. Reaching into his pocket, he pulled out two quarters and handed one to me. He explained that he wanted us both to throw the coins over our shoulders into the fountain while making a wish. He looked adorable as he said, "One, two, three," using his fingers like he was cueing up his band, and then yelled "Go," and we both tossed our coins.

When I looked back at him, all signs of his playfulness had diminished. Adopting a more serious look, he whispered, "Do you want to know what I wished for?"

"If you tell, doesn't that negate your wish?"

Grinning his so-sexy half smile, he shook his head and kissed me. "I wished for you."

Moving closer to see the dancing water perform its show, we stood and watched it, hand in hand. "Come with me to L.A. tomorrow." It wasn't a question; it was a plea. "I just moved so I live alone, and I have some downtime while I wait on contract negations for the new album."

With the brilliant white lights twinkling in the flowing water and the spray misting our faces, I felt like we were living in our own private, enchanted world. As he stared at me, I knew he was completely serious, that he really wanted me to go with him.

It was a moment of pure vulnerability. My throat tightened from his words, and I fought back the tears of joy that stung my eyes. Of course I wanted to go with him, but I didn't know if I should. I didn't really know him. *Did I?* The night had been perfect; our whole time together had been. I had a life back home, with a job, and friends, but it paled in comparison to what I experienced over the last two days. And I knew right then that I couldn't deny this man.

I remembered the first time I saw him that night in the bar so long ago, and I remembered feeling the exact same way I felt right now; like he could see into my soul. So I decided to be happy, to live in the moment. "What time are we leaving tomorrow?"

Even before I could finish my words, he crooked his head in the most adorable way and flashed his dimples. He picked me up as he twirled me around and around. Then before I knew what was happening, he jumped over the fountain wall holding me in his arms. There we stood in the streaming cold water, fully clothed, lights twinkling beneath us, mirroring the stars in the sky above. I looked at him, shook my head, and continued to smile the same smile I'd been wearing for the past two days.

Wiping drops of water off my face, he had gazed into my eyes and winked at me. "See, wishes really do come true—even if you share them."

Lying here now, smiling at the memory of the fountain, I look at our clothes strewn all over the hotel room. As the light outside becomes brighter, I wish we had closed the blinds so I could stay asleep, dreaming of him.

I start thinking about how I really should text Aerie, so I carefully reach over to the nightstand for my phone. *Damn, it's dead.* Aerie is probably so pissed. I forgot my phone yesterday, so I never called her. I'll have to borrow River's phone.

Since I know I won't be able to fall back asleep unless I get up and close the blinds to darken the room, I decide it's time to wake my Dirty Dancer. Sliding my fingers down his chest as it rises and falls with his shallow breathing, I trace every defined crease of his abs.

Waking, he makes a pleasant noise in the back of his throat as he leans down and kisses the tip of my nose. I glance up and when our eyes meet, he mutters, "Good morning," while grinning his crooked grin at me.

With my fingertips heading back up toward his chest, I whisper, "You were sleeping so soundly. Were you dreaming of rainbows and butterflies?"

Chuckling, he quickly untangles our bodies from the sheet and rolls me over onto my back. With him hovering over me, I stare into his eyes, now shining with need as he pins my arms to each side of my head and says, "I'll give you butterflies!" Then he whispers, "Can you wait a bit for your coffee?" before doing just what he said he would do.

❦

I can hear River singing "Beautiful Day" in the shower when I hang up the phone with Aerie. Having already showered, I'm working on the interview as I listen to him and smile ear to ear. Happily I hit the SEND button and finally submit the interview to *Sound Music*—and I think how my dad would have really gotten along well with River.

Actually, I think my dad would have liked him a lot. They share the same taste in music and bands. And of course the same can be said about me and River.

The only disagreement my dad and I ever had about music was concerning Top 40 songs. My dad disliked Top 40 music, as did Ben, but I love it. Ben disliked it because he didn't ever vary his choice of music. He listened to the same things since high school. My dad always pushed for the underdogs and supported indie bands. I'm not sure how River feels about Top 40, but from the songs I've seen on his playlists, I'd say he's not a fan.

Grabbing my briefcase, I pull a Sharpie marker out of it and pick my ripped white cotton panties up off the floor. Under the bow on the front of the panties I write, "You can push me up against a wall and do dirty things to me anytime." Before laying the note at the foot of the bed, I pull out my girly pink lip gloss, apply it heavily to my lips, and kiss the bottom of the note. Grabbing my now-charged phone, I finish the note by adding my cell number and head out the door in my running clothes.

In the nearest boutique, I quickly purchase an outfit on the mannequin, shoes and an extra pair of jeans and a plain white T-shirt. In addition, I've also selected some revealing undergarments, including a pair of slinky black lace boy shorts, a slinky black lace push-up bra, garter belts, and thigh-high hose. I change in the dressing room. My cell begins to ring as I reach for an elastic hairband in my purse. It is flashing *blocked caller*, so I decide against answering and throw my hair into a messy bun. Applying a flick of powder and a touch of blush, I stop to look at myself. Wow, what a difference a few days can make. I no longer wince at the reflection because what I see looking back at me is sexy. Sure, I'm still soft and boney with no breasts to speak of, but none of that seems to matter to the wonderful man waiting for me upstairs.

Happy with my purchase of a short, flared black skirt, a gray off-the-shoulder sweater, and low-heeled, black studded ankle boots,

I set off to get us some coffee and breakfast, feeling better about myself today than I have in a very long time.

When I return I have to set the coffees and scones down next to the door in order to search for the room key I found in River's jeans pocket before I left. As I open the door I can hear guitar chords. My mouth drops open and I almost dump the plastic-lidded cups down the front of my new outfit.

There he sits in faded worn blue jeans, shirtless, his guitar on his lap. The hot Nevada sun streams through the open glass doors, highlighting the magnificently lean muscles of his chest. He's the epitome of sexiness. He glances up at me, and motions with his head for me to come sit next to him, but I stand there mesmerized by the view and the sound of the music. As I watch him play, my eyes dart to his nimble fingers picking the fret board on the neck of the guitar. His fingers move with such ease and the sound they make is mesmerizing. Continuing my visual journey, I eventually land my gaze on his taut biceps, and finally his beautiful face so engrossed in the music.

His whole body seems to be moving to the beat in one single beautiful rhythm. Obviously staring at him, I'm unashamed. I can't help myself, but as soon as the words "I want you to want me" leave his lush mouth, I close my eyes and absorb the music.

Opening my eyes when he stops singing, I glance over at the couch. I see his Cheap Trick T-shirt lying on the back of it and smile. Now I know where he got the inspiration for the song he's singing, or at least I think I know. As he continues to sing the chorus while strumming his guitar, my body comes alive. I can feel my cheeks redden and my pulse quickens.

Raising his head, he looks over my body. When his eyes reach my short skirt, he immediately stops playing. We stare at each other, and he cocks his head to the side as he sets his guitar down. His eyes are simmering. The look on his face tells me everything. He looks like he wants to devour me. His tongue slips slowly out of his mouth to lick his bottom lip and when he pulls it back in, ever so slowly, I nearly faint from his raw sex appeal. I'm a few steps away when he combs his fingers through his disheveled hair, leaving strands sticking up. God, he is so—incredible.

Setting the coffees down, removing my purse, and placing the items on the coffee table, I walk over to him and straddle his lap. "Hey, sexy."

He kisses the very corner of my mouth as he runs his hands from my boots to the bottom of my skirt. "Hi yourself."

Tangling my fingers through his wet hair, I tug on his bottom lip with my mouth. "I really like that song."

My thighs tingle as his hands glide under my skirt. I know the moment he feels my new undergarments because his body stiffens, and he lets out a short gasp. "I really like your . . . skirt."

He explores the soft skin between my garter and my exposed thigh. "Did you buy this just for me?" he murmurs against my lips as he runs his fingers up and down the straps of my garters.

Laughing, I say, "Maybe . . ."

He pauses midkiss to mutter, "Then missing you this morning was worth it."

"Glad you approve."

He gently bites my earlobe before whispering, "I loved your note."

I smirk at him as his lips crash into mine, and he runs his palms up my back.

When his fingers reach the knot in my hair, he pulls out my elastic tie. "I called you."

My hands are wandering down his bare skin, along his torso. "Oh, the blocked caller was you?"

As he's running his fingers down the slight curve of my breasts and along each of my ribs, he says, "Let me see your phone."

The last thing I want to do is break our closeness. "It's behind me."

"Can I see it?"

Twisting around, I reach for my purse and pull out my phone, fully exposing the top of one of my thighs.

"Fuck," I hear him mutter as I turn back and say, "Here you go, sir," with my Southern belle accent, the one I find myself using every time he demands something or does something extremely charming. Odd. Not sure why I'm doing that.

Smirking at me, he takes my phone and taps on the screen before handing it back to me. "There you go, now you'll know who I am when I call you," he says with a wink.

"Do I get a picture?" I ask, standing up to snap one before he answers.

Shaking his head at me with a ridiculously adorable grin on his face, he says, "My turn." He gets up to retrieve his phone from the kitchen counter.

Holy shit! He has my lip-kissed underwear tucked in the back pocket of his jeans. Is he planning on keeping my panties as a souvenir? And that's not all I notice. His jeans are a tad loose, exposing just a hint of the gift that lies beneath them. Of course he turns to see me gawking, but I don't care, and I continue to stand there openmouthed.

He grabs his phone and walks back to the couch. "Yeeesss . . . ," he says while pulling up my skirt and running his phone up my leg.

I look at him quizzically, unable to comprehend anything right now until it clicks. "You are not taking a picture of my garter to store in your contact file," I tell him, pushing his hand away and lowering my skirt.

"What makes you think that's what I was doing? But, thanks for the suggestion," he laughs while feigning innocence.

With a devilish look in his eyes, he raises an eyebrow and moves his phone to playfully finger the inside top of my hose. "And besides, I thought you bought these for me."

Setting his phone down, he picks mine back up. He checks out the picture I took of him before tapping the screen a few more times.

I watch him and remember that it wasn't too long ago that I thought happiness was only for those who believed in fairy tales, that my future held nothing but sadness and a stoic existence. Yet, in this moment, as he juggles our phones, I think that maybe it's our time to be happy together.

As River sets my phone back on the coffee table, he picks his up and turns to face me. "Smile, beautiful girl," and just like that, I melt at his heartfelt words; and for the first time in a long while, I feel hopeful.

CHAPTER 16
Speechless

With the windows open, the sun is shining down on us and the wind is blowing through my hair. The radio is on, but it's not even loud enough for me to identify the song that's playing. River is wearing his black leather jacket and Wayfarer sunglasses, and he looks incredibly hot. I shouldn't even be thinking about this after the conversation we just had, but I can't help myself. My mind is a jumble of thoughts that keep leading back to the man sitting next to me, and how he makes me feel.

His hands are gripping the perforated leather bands wrapped around the steering wheel. His lightly stubbled jaw is tightly clenched. Everything I see, everything about his body language, indicates that he seems uncertain, unaware of how to proceed, maybe even unsure of what to say.

We have been driving for more than two hours. River just exited onto the I-10W merge, and we're closing in on Los Angeles. Even while driving, he oozes confidence. This sexy guy has completely turned my world around in a matter of days. And I'm hoping our recent conversation hasn't put a kink in our connection.

Until about twenty minutes ago we had been talking nonstop since leaving Las Vegas. I found myself telling him things I've never shared with another living soul, not even Ben. He was attentive to my every word and actually wanted to hear more. I told him about my parents, what their hopes were for my future, about the dreams I once had for my own future, the ones that would have had my parents smiling down on me from Heaven. I told him about my life when I was younger, when I had parents I loved and who loved me. I even shared with him how my parents died, which I rarely ever speak of. Something about him just makes me want to open up to him.

He talked about his family. He has a brother named Xander, eighteen months older, and a sister named Bell, fifteen months younger. His father died when he was sixteen, but his mother is very much a part of his life. She has since remarried. His mother's sister lives in Paris and he has a cousin that he's never met. His maternal grandparents died before he was born, and his paternal grandparents died a couple of years ago. He talked openly about his grandparents' deaths, but he never mentioned how his father died and I didn't ask. He was elusive about it, and I felt I shouldn't pry.

He told me about how he started his band back in high school with his two buddies; how their band's name was chosen on a drunken bet and why they kept their band to only three members. He told me about his career goals, which ones he has achieved, and which ones he's still working on. He told me about some of the disappointments life has thrown his way and shared how hard it can be for happiness and fame to exist together. He also expressed his wish to remain an unknown musician and how his brother, the band manager, disagreed and kept pushing the band further into the limelight.

However, now we sit in silence, ever since River asked me, "Can I ask you something?" My immediate response was: "Sure, anything."

I wonder if I should have been a little more cautious before answering. But I wasn't expecting his question or the emotions that surfaced when I answered. Thinking about it, now it makes sense since thoughts of Ben never seem to be far from my mind for long.

Over the last few months, I had become very good at pushing the memories of Ben's murder out of my mind. I had perfected not reliving his death in my nightmares. However, the closer we got to L.A., and the closer I got to the place Ben died, the more persistent those memories became. Not just memories, but feelings overtook me as well. Grief over his death resurfaced, as did guilt over returning with someone to the place where he died.

So, when River asked, "How did he die?" he triggered a flood of every horrid memory and ill feeling bubbling beneath the surface, just waiting to break through. Once I opened the dam, there was no closing it. I couldn't. I had to let it open. I told River about the whole tragic night as I remembered it. With tears streaming down my face, my body shaking with fear, my voice trembling with emotion, I retold the story of my fiancé's brutal attack. This time I was not a witness, I was simply me: the girl who loved a boy who was killed in front of her own eyes.

He listened, nodded his head, held my hand, wiped tears from my cheek, and told me how sorry he was. Ending my emotional and detailed explanation of Ben's attack and his death, I managed to say, "And then I was escorted to a police car as the coroner drove away." With that, I drew in a deep breath and sighed. I wasn't going to tell him about my emotional state after Ben's death now. I mentally pushed everything back far away and simply asked, "Can I tell you the rest another day?"

He nodded, seemingly unable to speak, maybe trying to process what I had just told him. So now as River turns off the I-10W onto the

San Bernardino Freeway, I decide to break the silence and lighten the mood. Plugging my iPhone into the modern radio jack he had installed in his 1960s car, I take a deep breath and run my hands through my windblown hair before asking, "Wanna play a game?"

He gives me a quizzical look before pulling off the freeway. "Can we talk first?" I nod my head, but don't say anything. I don't want to think anymore about Ben today, but he isn't going to let me get away with that.

River parks the car at a gas station and takes off his sunglasses. Setting them on the dash he silently unbuckles his seat belt, twists his body to face me, and reaches over to unbuckle mine. Placing his hands on my shoulders, he turns me to face him.

He removes my sunglasses, and with the pads of his thumbs he caresses my cheeks. He looks at me intently before speaking and I swallow back the emotion I'm feeling from the intensity of his stare; a stare so full of concern I feel like my tears may return at any moment. "What happened to him was wrong, but for it to happen in front of you . . . that is something you should never have had to see, or experience." Placing his fingers under my chin, he tilts my head up. His eyes are gleaming and so full of strength, but his voice is soft, almost broken as he continues. "I mean it, what you went through would break anyone, but here you are . . . so vibrant, so full of life, and still in one piece. Whenever you're ready to talk, I'm here, ready to listen."

He pauses a second to rub his thumbs across my cheeks again, then down my neck. He looks at me with a serene expression and says, "You're so absolutely beautiful." He stops speaking and places a soft kiss on my lips.

As he watches me with such care and concern, I quietly respond, "River, my life the last two years has been . . . nothing, really." I stop to cup his gorgeous face in my hand and then continue. "I'll tell you about it, about me, during that time. Just, not now. You have to understand, it was such a sad time for me, and I don't want to relive it right now. But I want you to know this—being with you these last few days has been the most fun I've experienced in a long time." I stop speaking and kiss him, but my kiss is not gentle like his. It's intense and passionate. He makes me want him every time he touches me and his touch pushes away any sorrowful thoughts lingering in my mind.

He immediately wraps his arms around me, holding me tight. I think again about how we're two people who just connected, or actually reconnected, and it feels like we've known each other for far longer than three days. As we sit here together, we're in no hurry, we have nowhere to be but with each other, and it feels heavenly.

Before breaking our embrace, he whispers, "Did I tell you how beautiful you look today?" Goose bumps ravage my body, and he's grinning as he draws his finger down my bare shoulder. He knows that drives me wild. He's doing it on purpose and I can't help but smile at the thought.

His words are so raw and honest; I know he can only be speaking the truth. My heart is beating faster. I'm smiling so widely, not only on the outside but on the inside as well. It's in this moment that I realize the sweet-nothings he whispers are a part of his gorgeous soul, the soul I already feel so connected to in this very short amount of time we've spent together. I know that coming to L.A. with him was definitely the right choice.

Grinning back at me, he pulls my seat belt across my body. I see him smile when he runs his fingertips across my hip bone before buckling it and then tracing down my leg, slinking his fingers under my skirt before twisting and leaning back in his seat. Fastening his own seat belt, he glances at me. "You mentioned playing a game. What do you have in mind?"

Turning the volume up on the radio, I tap the LIBRARY button on my iPhone and select one of my favorite songs. I allow the song to play for five seconds before hitting the PAUSE button. "Name it."

He looks over at me with a shit-eating grin on his face. "Really?

Come on, now. All you had to give me was the first three beats of that Roland drum machine and I'd know the haunting beat of Phil Collins any day of the week."

Starting to thump out the intro on the steering wheel, he adds rhythm to his beat. Using the dash as his pedal bass and his voice to synthesize the droning, he begins to sing the first few lyrics of "In the Air Tonight."

Thinking, *Wow, he's good,* I shake my head and tease, "Show-off."

"Come on, what else you got, baby?"

Studying my library for songs he may not recognize in three seconds or less, I decide to try Poison's "Talk Dirty to Me." Before I even hit the PAUSE button, he yells out, "Look what the . . ." Then he stops and grins, not bothering to finish the lyrics. Reaching over and running his fingers down my leg, he nonchalantly mentions that "Talk Dirty to Me" was named one of the forty greatest hard rock songs of all time, and as his touch sends shivers down my spine, he says, "But, you must know that, so why are you being easy on me?" Pulling his hand back, he reaches for his sunglasses and puts them back on. "Next."

After nine songs, I say, "Okay, musical genius, last one. All or nothing." Then, flickering my eyes at him, I hike my skirt up just enough for him to catch a glimpse of what lies beneath and ask, "You in?" He's managed to guess every single song within three seconds—so why not distract him a little, knock him off his game?

I hear a sharp intake of breath. "I'm always in," he mutters with a smirk on his face.

Knowing there is not a single song on my playlists he won't know, I decide to just have some fun. Turning up the volume, I let Adelitas Way blare through the car, knowing full well there is no intro or musical chorus. "Dirty Little Thing" starts to play, and I let the first two lines play before looking at his grinning face. On the third line of the lyrics, I don't turn the music off, but instead start singing along. I run my hand up the inside of his thigh as I continue singing about how I like it when he looks at me and before I finish the first chorus, he joins in and we both sing about not being able to say no.

By the third chorus, the song is still thumping but we aren't playing Name That Tune anymore. Reaching over, I take his sunglasses off so I can see his eyes. He immediately places his hand back on my leg. This time his fingers dart quickly to the bare spot between my hose and my garter belt. My body starts to ache with need. His touch does this to me every time.

Placing my hand on top of his, I give it a little squeeze and in a voice somewhere between playful and seductive, I say, "You won, you know."

With a full-blown blinding smile that makes my heart skip a beat and my lips tingle, he cocks his head and glances over at me. "I know." He laughs.

As he picks up my hand and brings it to his mouth, he kisses each of my knuckles and asks, "What do I win?"

Smiling, I remove my hand from his mouth, place it back on his thigh, and lean over the center console to suck on the sweet spot behind his ear before answering. "Anything you want."

I stay close to him, inhaling his fresh scent, rubbing my nose along his unshaven jaw. Funny, I never liked it when Ben didn't shave, but I love the feel of River's slight stubble against my soft skin.

As I lean back, his lips form a slow, sexy smile. "Anything?"

"Anything," I promise.

Laughing huskily, he glances down at my hand on his lap and raises his eyebrows.

I raise one eyebrow in return. "Really?" I ask, but not really questioning it.

"You wouldn't," he says, looking down at my hand again as I begin to slide my palm up his leg to the button on his jeans, slipping my fingertips inside his waistband.

His breathing picks up and he groans when he feels my touch. "Dahlia, I'm only kidding."

I glance at him from under my lashes. Leaning forward, I whisper in his ear, "You might want to pull off the road as soon as you can."

His gaze falls to his lap again as I successfully unbutton his jeans and begin pulling down his zipper. "Dahlia, I wasn't really serious."

"River, you don't know me well enough yet. I never back away from a challenge or from paying up."

"We'll be home in less than thirty minutes," he manages to say.

By this point I am kissing his neck, his jawline, and the outer edge of his ear. "Your choice."

Almost unable to speak, he mutters, "My choice what?"

"You won. You told me what you want. I'm not backing down. So pull over."

Noticing his tight grip on the wheel and the look in his eyes, I know he wants this, but doesn't want to admit it.

"Dahlia?" he asks.

I unzip his pants and tug at the opening of his boxers, freeing his erection before I tease, "Pull over. You can choose—on the road, or off the road. That much you get to decide. But I won't wait." I am physically and verbally making him unmistakably aware that this is going to take place sooner, not later. I am not waiting until we get to his house.

"Fu . . . ," he starts to say, as he quickly moves from the innermost left lane to the outermost right lane, exiting the highway as soon as he can.

Before beginning my descent, I glance up at him. His back is pushed against the seat, and his eyes are slightly hooded and overflowing with desire. Surprising myself again with what I am about to do, what I have never enjoyed doing before, I can only give him a wicked grin. However, I opt to wait for him to safely park the car before finding my way down to his lap, deciding that his state of mind right now might hinder his driving,

I don't waver my seduction in the slightest, though. I reach back and unbuckle my seat belt as River pulls into an underground garage of an office building, obviously closed on Sundays. As he pulls into a parking space in the center of the lot, he unbuckles his seat belt, pushes his seat back.

"Shit, what are you doing to me?" he pants.

Before letting him kiss me, I taunt, "Nothing yet."

I know he's not really referring to what I am doing to him at this moment. I know this because I often want to ask the same thing of him. He has undone me so completely, so quickly, and I think he feels the same way about me.

Capturing my mouth, he kisses me until I am breathless, but I am not wavering. Moving away, I start to trail openmouthed kisses down his neck, over the outside of his T-shirt, down his abs, finally reaching my destination.

His legs tremble slightly as my tongue darts to his very tip, circling it before running it down one side to his base and back up. His hands are lightly gripping my head, and I can hear his erratic breathing. I clench his base with one hand, and he groans as I slide my mouth over his length, moving slowly, up and down. Letting go of my head, he grabs my other hand and starts to suck hard on my thumb.

Passion is bubbling over inside me as I take him in my mouth as far as I can. When his tip hits the very back of my throat, I keep it there, moving just slightly back and forth, but this time with my teeth, not my lips. My tongue continues to lick circles and when it rounds his base, I feel him shudder.

His body's reaction, his groans, his heavy breathing, they're all stoking the fire already blazing in my body. I want to make him feel good, the same way he has made me feel the past few days, so I suck harder and faster. He releases my hand and I wrap both of my hands around his base.

His hands move to grip my hair as he begins to move my head to the rhythm of his body. I follow, taking him all the way in and pulling him out as I bare my teeth gently against his long, hard length. His body stiffens at first before relaxing and I am sure he's going to lose control.

Groaning loudly, he takes his right hand and slides it back and forth across my back, muttering my name. He exposes the skin between my sweater and skirt and runs his fingernails across it while his left hand continues to tangle in my hair, still guiding me.

His breath quickens as I rock my head up and down. His right hand slips under the waistband of my skirt and his fingers splay and grab my ass, causing an ache to build between my legs. I can feel myself getting wetter.

Hearing him suck in a few quick breaths through his teeth, I know he's close to coming. When I flick my tongue across his tip, circling it, sucking it, he hisses, "Fuck." He lets go of my head and grabs the door, his other hand still rubbing back and forth across the soft skin of my backside.

He's nearly panting when I hear him mutter, "Yes." Then as his body stills, his stomach muscles clench. I can taste the salty sweetness flowing down the back of my throat as I swallow.

Raising my head, I can't help but grin at him. His eyes are still closed, but his face is content. As he opens his eyes, his breathing slowly returns to normal. I lick my lips, still able to taste him, and his eyes widen. He starts to say something, but I don't let him speak as I crush my mouth to his.

When he has thoroughly kissed me, he pulls away and then presses his forehead to mine. His warm breath brushes my cheeks. "I have to say, I really enjoy playing that game with you . . . more than any other game I remember playing with anyone. Ever."

Pulling back, he kisses me on the nose and chuckles. "I'm going to have to come up with a really great grand prize for you when you actually win one of these days."

I lean my head back against the headrest as I raise an eyebrow. "Maybe I've just been letting you win. I have mad game-playing skills you haven't even seen yet."

"I can't wait for you to unleash your mad skills." He stretches his legs out to zip his pants back up, shakes his head, and brushes a finger over my lips.

I give him a quick wink before I buckle my seat belt. "In due time. Now let's go check out this new house of yours."

CHAPTER 17
Home

As we pull up to a very affluent neighborhood in the Hollywood Hills, I'm a little surprised by how intimidating it is. There's a large iron gate at the entrance to the community, monitored by multiple guards. I don't see any lane designated for the residents to just pull through using either gate openers or bar codes on their windows.

When we stop in front of the glass booth, a young, skinny blond-haired woman in a uniform approaches the car. River nods his head and greets her. He flashes his sexy dimples and pearly whites. We are immediately waved through. Obviously, this guard already knows who he is.

Scrutinizing the area, I notice a bunch of young women all dressed the same. They are camped outside the gate. I hadn't noticed them when we drove in, but I do now because they're yelling and holding up signs. One sign reads: AUTOGRAPH FOR A KISS? Another one reads: I TRADE FAIR. *Interesting.* I point them out as they shake their signs, along with other body parts, and ask, "Are they your groupies or just groupies in general?"

He glances over and says, "In general, I assume. I'm really not sure. I've never paid attention. But they're basically the reason I moved into a gated place."

"Oh, right. You don't like fans."

"I didn't say that. In the right place at the right time, I do. Sometimes they forget artists have personal lives, too." He stops as if contemplating what to say next. "Don't get me wrong, I love the whole signing-autographs thing and meeting new people after we perform. It's the chaos I don't really like."

The screaming begins to fade as he looks in the rearview mirror. "Xander says it comes with the job, and they're harmless." Shaking his head, he continues. "I'm sure they are, but they can be aggressive."

For some reason, I hadn't pictured River living in one of the most famous Hollywood Hills neighborhoods. But as we drive through the quiet paved streets, I understand. It not only provides privacy and security, but it's also secluded and peaceful, just like the hotel he stayed at in Las Vegas. Like me, he must prefer a more tranquil life. Funny, Ben loved the beach, but not the quiet of it like I did.

As River drives deeper into the community, I think about how Ben would have referred to these houses as *homes of the irresponsibly rich and ass-famous*. Ever since he investigated Mark Hines, the famous football player who lived somewhere up in the Hills, he was irrationally biased toward any famous person from this part of L.A. Ben was the journalist on the team that investigated the money-laundering scheme based on illegal betting. Mark was such a douche, as Ben put it, that he never confessed. He blamed his agent instead. Because of this, he was allowed to continue to play football.

Ben felt Mark used his money and fame to hide his part in the scheme. He also felt it was because of his celebrity status that it worked. His attitude may have stemmed from a mix of his love for football, the injustice itself, and maybe a little jealousy over the power Mark held; I was never certain.

So whenever I mentioned that any well-known person lived in the Hills, his comment was always a derivative of "that fucktard this" or "that fucktard that." He was never jealous of how much money another person had, since both of our families were financially secure. But I do think he was jealous of stars' celebrity status. Even though Ben never actually told me so, I know he had hoped to be a household name one day, like Anderson Cooper.

Ben and I didn't live extravagantly. We grew up on the beach where there was never any pressure to "keep up with the Joneses." We lived our lives easy and carefree for the most part; it was the way of life around there. As I look around, I have to remember—*that* is not my life anymore.

But I should keep an open mind about the city where River grew up, the place where he's most known as a musician. I have no doubt he will be more widely famous soon. I hadn't thought of him like that, until now, but being here drives it all home and Ben's words reverberate through my mind.

Noticing that I seem distracted, River asks, "What? You don't like it?"

His voice snaps me out of my thoughts, and I can't help but laugh. "Of course I do, silly! You just didn't tell me you were one of the rich and famous."

He laughs. "I told you, I got a great deal on this house."

Before he continues, he reaches out to hold my hand. "The previous owners got divorced and just wanted to get rid of it. Xander is friends with the ex-husband, and he hooked me up." He kisses my hand and holds it on his lap. "The view from my backyard is amazing, and that's what sold me on the house the minute I saw it."

Smiling at him, I can't help but think about how much we really do have in common. "Funny, the first thing I do whenever I go anywhere is check out the view. In fact, I think I checked out your view the first time I saw you."

Laughing at me, he says, "Oh? You're finally going to admit you were staring at me?"

"No, I didn't say that. Don't get carried away." I pinch his leg in admonishment.

All the houses are isolated on their own large plots, but I can't see most of the front doors as we drive by because the houses are so well hidden. I'm not really even that interested because the view inside the car is way more appealing.

"You don't even want to start that kind of game," River says, lifting up my hand and gesturing to where I just pinched him. Then he releases my hand and reaches over to tickle me.

I shift in my seat and start squealing. I'm very ticklish but don't want him to know this, so I try to quickly subdue myself. But he's relentless and continues his assault. "You're driving! Put both hands on the wheel. Please!" I yell out as tears of laughter stream down my face.

At a stop sign, he takes his hand back to grab the wheel and hits the turn signal with his other hand. He tilts his head to look at me, and a devilish grin appears on his face. "You didn't seem that worried about my driving ability an hour ago."

"Actually, I was. That's why I waited for you to park the car first," I respond with a sly grin.

"Well, I'll stop for now but only because you asked so nicely," he says sweetly.

He starts to slow down as he approaches a cul-de-sac. He nods toward a house I can just barely see at the end of the street. "Here we are. Home sweet home," he says as he pulls into a long, upward-sloping driveway.

The house has a smooth white stucco finish and looks to be a 1940s-style ranch. It's suspended high above the city with a large, modern circular stucco staircase leading to a beautiful pair of Art

Deco-style double doors. The landscaping is modest but neatly kept; eclectic rocks surround the palm trees. River hits a button in his car, and the large wooden door opens.

The garage is located under the house. As he pulls in, I can see a wide staircase in the back-right corner that must lead into the house. Once he puts the car in park, he switches the ignition off and shifts to face me. "Remember, I already warned you what to expect. I just moved in."

He seems slightly nervous, so I want to reassure him. "It can't be much worse than my house, and I've been in transition for way longer."

As he opens his door, he turns back to look at me. He's wearing a huge smile and his eyes sparkle. "Not sure if I mentioned this, but since I lived with a bunch of dudes, I didn't bring much. The previous owners left a few things, but really it'll be like camping until we hit some stores."

Rolling my eyes at him as I reach for the door handle, I ask, "Are you trying to tell me we'll be sleeping on the floor?"

"Pretty much."

"Well, then, Mr. Rock Star turned Boy Scout, show me the way."

I can't help but laugh, thinking about how similar our carefree domestic attitudes are.

He points at me and says, "Don't laugh. I told you I just moved in."

At the front of the car he takes my hand, leading me up the stairs. Once we reach another small bank of steps that lead to the landing, he ushers me forward. When we get to the top, he reaches above the door and removes a key from the ledge.

Turning around, I notice the key in his hand and make a joke about never letting anyone see where you keep your spare key. As I look at him, my breath catches and my pulse starts to race. Unashamed, I continue to watch him as he reaches around me to unlock the door.

I notice his eyes drift down to my skirt. His fingertips lightly brush the hem before his hands brace the doorframe on both sides of me. The sunlight is peeking through a small round window behind him, highlighting his handsome features.

He dips his head so we are eye level. "Since we've already established you're not a stalker, you knowing where I hide the key just makes it easier." Leaning in, he places his knee in between mine and kisses me hungrily. He kisses up and down my jawline and neck, almost as if trying to find my pulse. It should be easy, since it's racing. This kiss isn't just any kiss; it's a kiss very much full of need. Not just his, but mine. It's a kiss that leaves me breathless and wanting more.

I wonder how it is that one minute we can be having a normal conversation and the next minute I want to strip down in his garage and fuck him right here? It's completely new to me. My inability to control my libido around him is making me a little nervous, so I lower my head and duck under his arm, reaching for the doorknob.

Without glancing back, I open the door and pass him by.

But he moves faster than I do and covers my eyes with his hands, then guides me to where he wants me to stand. "Okay, you're cool to look now."

Opening my eyes, I realize I definitely need a house tour. I'm standing in what must be the most mod-looking kitchen I have ever seen. There is a twelve-light ultramodern fixture hanging from the ceiling—it's at least eight feet long. Stainless steel appliances flank the entire kitchen and where you would normally find cupboards, there are thick glass shelves. The floor is a mix of black and white swirled together, very chic. The counters are jet-black granite with white pearl splashed throughout. There is a high bar with curvy, black stools along it, and on the other side is the living room. It is unlike any kitchen I have ever seen.

"River, this is stunning," I say as I take it all in before moving toward the living room.

He follows and I can feel his eyes on me. "Yeah, stunning."

The living room is painted white, and rich black walnut wood panels the wall in front of me. A large black-and-white picture of River and his band hangs on one of the walls. Underneath the picture is a long gray tufted sofa next to a few vintage guitars resting in their stands. To the left is a huge flat-screen TV sitting on a small stand. Surprisingly, no video game system is attached.

Walking over to the couch, he sits down. "Xander outdid himself," he says, patting the couch. "He picked this out for me and had it delivered." He glances up at the picture and points to the TV and guitars. "He said these are housewarming presents."

"That's really nice of him," I comment while walking over to get a closer look at the picture.

While stretching his arms out on the back of the couch, River says, "He can be, sometimes. You can be the judge when you meet him."

"Well, if he's anything like you, I'm sure I'll like him." I almost said love but quickly caught myself. My emotions are running away from me; I have to rein them in.

"When was this taken?" I ask, still looking at the large photograph on the wall.

"A while ago, maybe four years. It was our first officially released band photo," he says, laughing quietly. "It was a big deal for Xander. The first task he accomplished as band manager."

"Having your brother looking out for you must relieve a lot of stress. I don't have any siblings, but I always wanted a brother and a sister."

"I love my brother and my sister, but they can both be a pain in the ass."

"Well, I would have loved to have had even one pain in the ass growing up with me," I teasingly say.

"Yeah, I guess you're right." He tries to reach for me, but I'm already at the large glass doors that seem to go on for miles. The view is out of this world. In the distance I can see each letter of the Hollywood sign. It's truly amazing—and immediately I long to snap a picture. I wish I brought my camera up from the car.

Opening one of the doors, I step outside to an equally amazing outdoor living area that spans the entire length of the house. The upper deck has a large wooden table-and-chairs set, along with a built-in grill. To the right and left are modern spiral staircases. Each circles down to the lower deck where there is a large rectangular pool and hot tub. Several cloth-covered benches line the half wall made of Plexiglas.

I turn to River, who hasn't spoken while watching me intently. "This is your view?" I sputter out. "You can see the H-o-l-l-y-w-o-o-d sign," I whisper, spelling out the word.

In the time we've spent together, River certainly hasn't given me any indication that he's as wealthy as his surroundings suggest. Sure, he stayed in a nice hotel and spent plenty of money over the weekend, but he's just so laid-back and down-to-earth.

After seeing this house, with this view, I start to wonder what I've gotten myself into.

Snapping me out of my reverie, he comes up from behind and wraps his arms around me. "Hey, you okay?"

"Yeah, I just had no idea."

"No idea of what?"

"That you're one of the rich and famous."

Chuckling, he says, "Hardly. Just in the right place at the right time."

River presses his body into mine and adds, "And I had no idea, either."

"No idea of what?"

His body moves as he laughs, and I feel his strength behind me. "That you're one of those people that has to spell out Hollywood."

I turn around and give him a soft shove. "You're an ass. I'm just surprised. It seems like something you would have mentioned. That's all," I say, motioning to the sign, the view, and his house.

"You mean, like, *Hey, I just moved into a really sweet new place, and, by the way, you can see the Hollywood sign from my backyard?*" he mocks, pulling me back in for a tight embrace.

"Well, I guess not." I don't have a chance to say anything more before he leans into my neck and kisses me so forcefully that I know I'm going to have a mark. My body shivers from his touch, from his warm breath, and I giggle. "What are you doing?"

"I think you know," he laughs against my skin.

I sigh and breathe deeply.

"I've had enough show-and-tell for now, and I have one more room to show you," he says as he leads us back into the house. "Let's finish what we started in the car, in here," he continues as we cross the living room and walk down a hall to an open door at the end.

"Your bedroom," I manage as I look into the very large empty room. There are multiple closed doors inside it. One most likely opens into a bathroom and the others are probably closets. The room also has the same large glass doors as the living room, and I can see the sign and the city from here, too. Everything is just so beautiful.

I laugh when I take a closer look at the room. In the middle is an air mattress with pillows and blankets thrown on it. Turning to face him, I smirk and he smirks right back. He really does light up my insides. So much so, I know my darkest days are behind me.

"What are you smiling about?" I whisper while running my hands up his chest.

"I don't know. What are you smiling about?" he responds while moving some of my hair aside.

"I can't believe you were telling me the truth. We really are camping."

"I never lie," he says, suddenly very serious.

Grabbing his hand, I lead him to the center of the room and turn to face him. "I never meant it that way," I whisper before sucking on his upper lip.

He mumbles something I can't comprehend, but for some reason, I don't ask him to repeat it. He lightly shakes his head and runs his finger over my lips.

The sun is shining so brightly into this room, there is nowhere to hide. I cannot cover up what I once didn't want him to see.

Never taking my eyes off his, I break our embrace and peel my shirt over my head before pulling down my skirt, letting it fall to the floor. Standing in the lingerie that I bought for his eyes only, I smile at him as I run my hands down my body and he gasps.

His fingers trace the skin above my push-up bra and move down to my ribs before tracing circles on my almost-nonexistent stomach muscles. "Do you have any idea what you do to me?" he whispers as he leans to kiss the same trail he'd just etched with his finger.

I stand there, unable to move; having the same thoughts. My heart is racing, and I really don't know what is happening to me. Every time he touches me, my desire for him becomes more of a need and less of a want.

As he stands back up, his powerful green eyes scan my body—slowly. Grinning, he runs his hands down to my garter belts as he says, "I've been wanting to see what these look like since this morning." Then, unsnapping first one, and then the other, he continues. "It was certainly worth the wait."

He leans back a little, catches my hand, and turns it over. Bringing it to his mouth, he gently kisses each fingertip, stopping to suck on them for just a moment before kissing my palm.

"I'm glad you like the outfit," I pant out. My eyelids are fluttering as he breathes on the sensitive spot of my wrist and I continue. "I bought it just for you."

Groaning, he threads his fingers though my hair then runs them down my back, unhooking my bra but not removing it. I pull his shirt over his head and he rips his jeans off before I push him down on the mattress. As I stare into his eyes, so full of desire, I straddle him and he grunts, "I've wanted to do this since your little Name That Tune game."

I hover over him, wearing nothing but my lingerie, and I let his eyes devour me; I can feel our connection growing even stronger. And today, in the early hours of the evening, on the absolute brightest and most beautiful day of the year, we slowly do what we haven't done before. We begin to make love.

CHAPTER 18
Pinball Wizard

Despite having slept on an air mattress, I wake up feeling surprisingly rested and make my way to the bathroom. I look back over my shoulder and grin at the sight of River sleeping so peacefully. I notice again we don't seem to have sides of the bed. I quietly pad over to his closet and find a white button-down shirt on top of a bunch of boxes. While slipping it on, something grabs my attention. The top box has River's boxers in it and Pac-Man catches my eye immediately. *Pac-Man? Really?* I love Pac-Man! When I was younger, my father used to take me to an old-fashioned arcade down the street from the Greek at least once a week. Still grinning, I slip on the Pac-Man boxers and make my way through the empty house to the kitchen in search of coffee.

Walking down the hallway to the living room, I think about how we spent the remainder of yesterday's daylight hours in his room getting to know each other better. I'm constantly surprised by how comfortable I feel with him; the fun we experience together is simply intoxicating. It keeps me wanting more, and I'm pretty sure it keeps River wanting more, too.

When the darkness fell upon us last night, the Hollywood sign glowed in the distance. After stepping outside to take it all in, we made our way back inside to the living room where we ordered pizza. We ate and talked; then we laughed at *Letterman*. Finally, we made our way back to his bedroom and continued what we started earlier.

Looking around the kitchen, I don't see a coffeepot anywhere, so whether or not he has coffee is irrelevant. He actually has nothing in his kitchen. No food, no small appliances, not even silverware.

I stand in the doorway to the bedroom and look around at the blank canvas. It gives away nothing about who River is. But I don't mind because I already feel like I know him so well. Yesterday, I may have been a little taken aback by his home but I know that where River lives is not an indication of who he is. And besides, I love this house, especially the incredible view. In fact, I'm pretty sure that I actually . . . I dare not think it, not yet, anyway.

As I watch him sleep, I can't help but think about how the sound of River's voice melts my insides, how his gaze makes me quiver, and how his touch drives me wild. Everything about him, about us, feels so right. These intense feelings are unfamiliar to me. I've never felt them before, not even with Ben. Suddenly, a wave of guilt washes over me. *Why are my feelings for River so much more explosive than they were for Ben?*

Squinting my eyes while looking out the sheer-covered glass doors, I stare at the scenic view and try to think about River, the man I am enamored with now, and not Ben, the man I loved for so long. But the guilt won't leave me, and I'm racking my brain trying to remember if Ben ever made me feel the way River makes me feel. I can't recall having the same feelings for Ben.

Finally, I hear, "Good morning, sexy girl," and I'm brought back to the present. I glance his way. Stretching and yawning, he looks ever-so-sexy himself. "Whatcha doing over there?" he asks, holding his arms out for me to join him.

"Good morning yourself," I respond, smiling while I walk toward him and almost jump into his arms. "I was looking for coffee."

"Sorry. A coffeepot is the first thing on my list."

Grinning at me, he lightly kisses my nose, almost as if he's kissing each freckle. He rises up on one elbow. "Do you wake up early every morning?"

Laughing, I speak the truth. "I can't sleep when the light shines in from outside." I shift to face him. "My parents installed blackout blinds in my room when I was younger so I would stop waking them up at the crack of dawn."

"Hmmm . . . ," he says before adding, "so you're saying if I want to wake up before you and watch you sleep we'll have to get some heavy-duty blinds?"

"River, no, that would ruin waking up to that stunning view."

"Wouldn't ruin the stunning view I see when I wake up," he says, looking right at me and tucking a loose piece of hair behind my ear.

God, that's what I'm talking about. Everything about him drives me wild. Grabbing his neck, I pull him toward me, kissing him hard. When I release him, he scans my body. A devilish grin appears on his face and I ask, "What's that face?"

He runs his fingers down the buttons of the white shirt, and then he follows with his mouth, tugging on the first button with his teeth. "Do you mean the 'you're wearing my underwear' face?" he asks, moving to the second button.

Laughing as his hair tickles my chest, I say, "Oh, I didn't know people had a face for that."

He lifts his head and narrows his glare at me. "People? Do people have faces for when their girl is wearing their underwear?"

"Well, I love *Pac-Man*," I say before realizing what he just said.

He winks at me adorably and says, "Really? You know how to play?"

"Of course I know how to play!"

"I'll need to check that out," he says as he checks me out, and then says, "You look really hot in Pac-Man."

Our laughter quiets down as his hand starts to trace the outline of the little yellow men located on my hip. "By the way . . . did you just call me your girl?"

"Yeah, I did."

He's staring at me with only truth in his eyes as he laughs again, tugging on the elastic band of his Pac-Man boxer shorts that I am wearing.

Kissing him again, all joking is pushed aside. My kiss is full of want and need, and I make that quite apparent. He instantly groans, then rolls us over so he's now hovering over me.

"Dahlia, I don't know what you're doing to me, but if we don't get off this thing very soon, we may be here all day." He pushes his hand down on the air mattress. "And I'm not sure it will hold up."

"The air mattress or you, River?"

"Watch yourself, girlie, you don't want to mess with me."

"Well, actually, I do, but first I need coffee, so you're in luck. We can't stay in this room all day."

Raising an eyebrow, he jokes, "That's not the kind of luck I want." He presses his warm body against mine and continues. "First, I'll get you coffee. Then we need to hit the stores, and then I'll let you mess with me."

"You want to go shopping?" I ask, surprised by his plan for the day.

He laughs softly and twists to sit on the side of the mattress. "No . . . not shopping, nothing even remotely like shopping, I promise," he says, crossing his finger over his heart.

Leaning back toward me, he chuckles and pinches my ass. "Just quickly stopping in a few retail establishments to pick up some necessities."

"Yeah," I respond, sitting up, but I lean against his back, keeping his body close to mine a little longer. "I'm pretty sure that is the definition of shopping."

As I lean over his shoulder, his head turns toward me and I kiss him. I caress his tongue with mine and taste him thoroughly before pulling away. Sliding over to the other side of the mattress, I stand up and stretch.

Still sitting, twisted with his feet on the floor, his eyes roam my body and my skin begins to tingle. I bite down on my lip at the sight of him and try to focus on what has always been my morning priority: coffee. But even the thought of my beloved coffee can't suppress my insatiable desire for him.

He stands up and lets his unyielding gaze study me for a moment longer. "We should probably take a shower." He has a look on his face like he's trying to convince himself that he should leave the room.

As he stands there, grinning at me, he's completely naked and absolutely sexy as hell. Without saying another word, I grab my bag and saunter off to the bathroom, pushing my shirt off my shoulders and letting it fall off my body, knowing he's watching me. Shortly after I reach the bathroom, I hear his feet padding across the wooden floor, and I know he's headed in my direction. Game on, I win.

Having decided to wear the jeans and T-shirt I bought yesterday since they were my only clean clothes, I slip the clothes on, slide my arms into my black leather jacket, tie my Converse sneakers, the ones I luckily threw in my overnight bag before I left home, and I'm ready to visit a few stores.

I haven't been shopping in so long that I am actually a little excited and my excitement only grows when I walk out of the bathroom and see River texting. He's wearing worn jeans, a black Ramones T-shirt, a black leather jacket, and black work boots. When he smiles at me while slipping on his black beanie, I am transported into the past, to the first time I laid eyes on him, and he's just as sexy now as he was then.

While we're driving, I check my many e-mails and listen to my voice mails. Both Grace and Aerie have left messages. I send Aerie a quick text and call Grace. I hang up just as my phone battery dies and I mention to River that I should be getting back to Laguna Beach by Wednesday. His eyes flicker at mine, and he very quietly says, "How about we take it day by day?"

I want to argue that I really need to get home, but I don't because I couldn't care less about getting home. I just really like being with him. So instead, I smile over at him and say, "I can't stay with you forever, you know." Poking him in the ribs underneath his jacket, I add, "You'll get sick of me and all my games soon enough anyway."

We walk into the Grove shopping center where I've been a handful of times. It really does have the best shopping. I can find all my favorite stores here, including Nike Goddess, Pottery Barn, J.Crew, and H&M.

Coincidentally, the first place we hit is Pottery Barn. I'm quickly learning that shopping with River is rather comical. As we enter the store, he approaches the more-than-willing-to-assist young brunette, who instantly bats her eyelashes at him. She blinks at first, as if trying to place him. I laugh as he jumps on one of the mattresses and tries to take me with him. In thirty minutes, we have selected neutral bedding, soft towels, and fluffy pillows. We also pick out a mattress, box spring, and a black-leather-tufted headboard. The flirty salesgirl didn't have to bat her eyelashes to convince him to add the coordinating nightstands; he would have done it anyway. He quickly pays and arranges delivery for later today.

As we walk through the stores, his arm slung over my shoulder, and my hand in his back pocket, he tells me that he wants to take me to a place called Smitten's tonight. It's a local neighborhood bar that the Wilde Ones have been practicing at every Monday night for more than five years. He says that I'll get to meet his brother, sister, and band-mates, which makes me a little nervous, but I'm excited to finally see him perform with his band.

Our next stop is Williams-Sonoma, where we select the newest Starbucks coffeepot and purchase coffee pods, cookware, modern white plates, and silverware. Once again, he arranges for it all to be delivered later today.

As we continue to walk through the outdoor mall, we pass by an H&M. "Mind if I duck in and grab a few things?"

Nodding, he motions with his head to the side and says, "I'll be over there. I have a few calls to return," then he kisses me, and says, "So take your time." He knows what that does to me.

I smile at him and run my fingers up his stomach. "It won't take that long."

I quickly select a few things to hold me over until I figure out if River has a washer and dryer or until I go home. Approaching the cash register, I hear the urgent pulsing, almost soaring track of a familiar song. The distorted vocals, heavy electronic chords, and pounding bass beat all mixed together are undeniably Justin Timberlake's mas-terpiece "Sexy Back."

Looking around to figure out where the music is coming from, I finally determine that my purse is singing. As the first verse comes to an end, I can't help but smile and step out of line. Reaching into my bag, I grab my phone. The name "River Wilde" is flashing across my screen.

"Heeelllooo." I beam, glancing toward the front of the store. There he is, leaning against the wall between two glass window cases. His foot is propped against the pink flowery wallpaper. He has one of his hands in his pocket and the other is holding his phone to his ear.

He smiles his full, dimpled smile and I smile back. Holding his phone out for me to see, he then puts it back to his ear. "Do you like the ringtone I picked?"

I guess he must have assigned himself that ringtone when he added us to each other's contacts. I watch him push the phone against his shoulder as a couple of fan girls approach him with pens in their hands. He gives them an obligatory grin and signs the back of one of their shirts and the shoulder of another. I roll my eyes about him claiming that no one really notices him. "Yeah, I do, Mr. I'm Not Really That Famous," I say while giving him a thumbs-up. I point at my shoulder, indicating that I want an autograph, too. "But I didn't know sexy ever left."

Shaking his own head, he hangs up the phone. He charmingly waves goodbye to his two groupies and starts walking toward me. "Hey, sexy, didn't you . . . ?" I start to ask when he's close enough, but he ducks his head and kisses me, quickly preventing me from finishing my question.

"Hey, sexy, yourself," he says when he pulls away, and I've forgotten what I was going to ask but figure it didn't really matter anyway. Before taking my hand, he pretends to sign his name on my shoulder, and his touch sends shivers up my spine.

"Thank you, Mr. Rock Star." We step back to the line.

As we leave the store, River carrying the bags, he says, "I have something I want to show you."

"What? The line of groupies outside waiting for you to sign their bare skin?" I joke.

"No, smart-ass, that was random and seriously hardly ever happens."

"If you say so, but you can give me an autograph any day of the week." I smile at him, dropping the subject.

We hop on the Grove Trolley, which travels between the Grove and the Farmers' Market, and get off at the Entertainment Center. The complex has dozens of buildings and is located on a landscaped park with picnic areas in the center. It even has a dancing fountain. There are a lot of people walking around. Some have shopping bags in their hands, and others walk casually while drinking coffee or eating pretzels. The older-looking buildings make the area feel like an old-fashioned downtown.

Exiting the Trolley first, I grin as River steps off and walks behind me. Leaning into my back, he wraps his arms around my waist and guides me into an open redbrick, double-arched building. When my eyes adjust from the sunlight, I see lights and hear sounds everywhere. We've just walked into an arcade. It's very much like the one I frequented with my dad so many years ago. Overcome by emotion, I turn around, throwing my arms around his neck, and kiss him.

With labored breaths, I pull away. I clutch his shoulders while he wraps one arm around my waist, the other still holding my bags. "An arcade? Here at the Grove?"

"Yeah, I thought you'd like it."

"Like it? I love it."

Looking around, I see so many black stalls, all of which house video games from the eighties. There's *Mouse Trap*, *Asteroids*, *Centipede*, *Frogger*, *Pac-Man*, *Space Invaders*, and *Venture*. Along with Skee Ball, driving games, and even a *Chicken Clucker*.

Closing my eyes and listening to the sounds of the machines around me, I'm transported back to the arcade with my dad while I fed quarter after quarter into *Ms. Pac-Man*, *Donkey Kong*, and, of course, the pinball machines. My dad was a pinball wizard, and he taught me well.

His favorite pinball machine was *Flash Gordon*. It was the first multiball table I ever played. It was equivalent to *Black Knight*, but better and faster. The table was amazing, and just the thought of getting that "fifteen seconds" still gives me an adrenaline rush. I remember the first extra ball was easy to land, but getting the second was always a challenge.

My favorite, of course, was *Baby Pac-Man*. It wasn't a game for everyone, and my dad didn't really like it because the flippers aimed at the center of the game instead of at the sides. I liked the challenge; he thought it was a flawed table design. It really did make getting to the mazes difficult, but I thrived on that.

"Look over there," River says, pointing to *Pac-Man*. "How about it?" he asks with a twinkle in his green eyes.

"Game on, hot stuff," I answer as I head toward the machine.

We stay here, playing different games for hours. Challenging each other, I sometimes win, but he mostly beats me. I have no idea how. I decide to try my luck, solo, at the *Drive My Course* game, while River goes to get more quarters. When I finish, I look around the room and spot him walking my way. I melt.

"Close your eyes," he says as he stands in front of me.

"Why?"

"Just close them."

Closing my eyes, I feel him take my hand and attach something around my wrist. It's the same wrist where my Cartier LOVE bangle sits.

"Okay, you can open now."

Staring down, I can't believe what I'm looking at. This adorably sweet and sexy man has just placed a very colorful linked bracelet of the cutest Pac-Man on my wrist. It has a yellow Pac-Man with the blue, red, pink, and orange monsters on it.

"I love it!" I say as I swallow back tears of joy. I throw my arms around him and say, "Thank you."

He lifts me up and twirls me just once before setting me down. "Happy?"

Smiling up at him, I say, "More than happy."

CHAPTER 19
The Secret Is in the Telling

We're walking through the town where River grew up. He has one arm slung around my shoulder and my hand in his back pocket; he's carrying "Stella" on his other shoulder. We are on our way to what River described as his local neighborhood bar. It's dusk, but light enough that I can see the upscale town.

Every town and every city has something that makes it a little unique. For Brentwood, it's the beautiful white dogwood trees that line its streets and the quaint shops. Downtown Brentwood is a small but trendy area. Its old-fashioned streetlights display banners, its stores are covered with different-colored awnings, and its sidewalks are even paved with bricks.

One place in particular catches my eye; a bookstore named Fiction Vixen. My love for literature draws my attention toward the two piles of books in the large windows located on both sides of the front door. The books are displayed in a Christmas tree–like fashion with lights wrapped around them. Pointing the store out to River, he laughs softly and tells me his mother's friend owns it. He goes on to say that she has always been crazy about books and that when he was fourteen she decided to open a bookstore. He spent that whole summer helping her get it ready to open for business. It was his first job. He tells me that he hauled and stacked so many books that he never wanted to look at another book again. Then he jokes that it's why he opted not to go to college. Again, we both laugh and continue toward the bar.

Earlier, he asked me about USC and I asked him how he knew the campus so well. He told me he visited his brother and sister there many times. He also told me his brother was in the Kappa Sigma fraternity, but never lived on campus as an undergraduate or graduate student. I mentioned that Ben was in the same fraternity, but skirted the topic. He told me he went to a few parties at the frat house and then crashed at either his brother's or sister's place. Funny that we only saw each other that one night, but that's good, I guess.

I found out that River's mother moved out of Brentwood a couple of years ago when she got remarried; she and her husband now live in River's neighborhood. His sister lives with them, and his brother lives in what used to be their grandparents' condo in Beverly Hills. His grandparents both died within six months of each other last year and left a sizable inheritance to River and his brother and sister.

As I'm reminiscing about the day we'd spent together, River bumps my shoulder. "Nervous?"

Jostled from my thoughts, I shake my head and say, "No. Should I be?"

"No, of course not," he says, grinning at me. "You just seem . . . somewhere else."

"I'm right here." I squeeze his hand, my Pac-Man bracelet moving as I tilt my wrist.

Turning to walk backward, swinging his guitar to his back, he grabs both my hands and pulls me toward a building that's labeled

SMITTEN'S. "Did I tell you how beautiful you look?" he asks with an adorable grin and a twinkle in his green eyes.

Tonight I'm wearing one of my new outfits. I'm also a little more made up than I usually am because I'm meeting River's friends and family. After our shopping spree, I chose a black lace swing camisole, cream-colored jeans, black high-heeled boots, and my leather jacket. I changed my underwear into something a little sexier, but I had to go without a bra because of the thin spaghetti straps. It really isn't even noticeable. My hair is down, but a little fuller than I usually wear it, and I'm wearing blush, shadow, liner, mascara, and lip gloss. I suddenly feel that electric force between us when he smiles at me.

"Actually, you didn't," I say, moving my head so my hair sways side to side.

He stops and I almost walk right into him. "Even with all that makeup you still look perfect," he says, still clasping both of my hands together, bowing his head, and touching his nose to mine.

"What? You don't like makeup?" I ask, but I'm not in the least bit offended because neither do I.

Standing together on the sidewalk, he slides his mouth to my ear. "I didn't say that. I just think you look amazing with or without it."

He brushes his lips against mine ever-so-lightly and then turns to catch the door for me. The building has a set of double glass doors and one oversize window with the name SMITTEN'S blazoned across it. I walk in first. Redbrick walls border the large square room. There is a stage to the left, the bar is all the way in the back, and the wall on the right is lined with chairs and sofas. High-top tables are scattered around the room, and there is a small dance floor in front of the stage. An archway to the back-left has a sign hanging above it that reads: POOLROOM. The place actually does look like a local neighborhood bar.

With his hand on the small of my back, he starts to guide me toward a cluster of different-shaped chairs and a big black sofa with a wooden coffee table separating them. Pointing in that direction, he starts to say, "Everyone's over . . . ," but before he can finish his sentence, a very cute, young copper-haired woman comes running up to him, throws her arms around him, and gives him a big kiss on the cheek.

River drops my hand to steady her and hugs her back, practically lifting her off the ground. I know immediately this petite, beautiful thing must be his sister, Bell. The resemblance is uncanny. They could pass for twins except her eyes are a much more vibrant green and she has red streaks in her shoulder-length light copper brown hair. She's also quite a bit shorter than her brother. River returns his sister's affections, and I can see how much they adore each other.

Setting her down, he moves back slightly to rest his guitar against one of the four columns in the center of the room. He then laces his fingers with mine, and she thumps him on the chest. "Where have you . . . ?" She doesn't finish as her eyes flicker to our fingers. Her smile turns even bigger, and she eyes us curiously. She actually looks at our hands like she has never seen her brother holding hands with a girl.

Looking at River, she coyly says, "When you texted me that you had someone you wanted me to meet, I assumed it was a guy."

Then she throws her arms around me like we're long-lost friends. "Hi! I'm Bell, River's sister."

"Dahlia. Nice to meet you, Bell," I say as she continues to clutch her arms around my back before finally allowing me room to breathe. She studies me for a few beats. "You look familiar."

"I went to USC. River said you were a sophomore when I was a senior."

Shrugging her shoulders, she says, "Maybe that's it." Gently tugging on some of my hair, she says, "I think I'd remember you. You're so pretty and the shade of your golden blond hair is unforgettable."

She looks at River and gives him a look that he obviously recognizes because he grins at her. Then, twisting sideways, she winks at the bartender and points to me. Why? I have no idea. Then she diverts her attention back to us. I can tell she has all kinds of questions for her brother, but she holds back.

"So where did you two meet?" she asks me as River's name is being chanted from across the room. Looking over, I see a dark-haired, dark-eyed man catcalling him. River smiles at me and gestures with his chin toward his friend as he tugs on my hand. "Come on," then says to his sister, "You coming?"

Bell replies, "I'll meet you over there," then winks at me and says, "We'll talk later," as she walks off toward the bar.

Approaching the seating area, the very attractive dark-haired guy is sipping his beer with an arm draped around the girl standing next to him. As he tilts his bottle back, he eyes me up and down then finishes his drink before setting it on the table. He drops his arm from the girl and grabs two beers out of an ice bucket on the coffee table. Twisting the tops off the Heinekens, he sidesteps the knockout redhead and walks up to us as we approach him.

He's about my height with a very athletic build. I could clearly see the definition of his arm muscles as he twisted the caps, and his tight shirt shows signs of well-defined abdominal muscles. He obviously works out. His hair is short, but long enough that it is wispily styled to the side; his eyes are the color of rich chocolate; and his olive complexion makes him appear slightly tanned.

He hands one bottle to River and the other to me. "River, man, where the fuck you been? You've been MIA!" he says. Then with a big smile, displaying the whitest teeth I have ever seen, he adds, "And who is this beautiful thing you brought with you?"

As I look at this guy, who can no doubt woo any girl, I can tell he must be part Native American. Glancing down at the drinks he's holding out, I notice he has a very detailed tribal tattoo circling his biceps with an intricate feather design running down his arm.

"Phoenix, this is my girl, Dahlia London," River says, dropping my hand to place his arm around my shoulder before he says, "Dahlia, this jackass is Nix Stone."

"Dahlia, like the flower?" he asks, raising his hand to shake mine. "Nice to meet you." Raising one eyebrow, he asks, "What's a sweet thing like you doing hanging out with this douche bag?"

"Language, dude." River says, and he squeezes me a little tighter.

I take a sip of my beer to break away from the other guy's gaze. I hate the taste of beer without ice. I decide to ignore his rude question and shake his hand. "Nice to meet you! You're the guitarist?"

He nods his head and shakes my hand a little longer than necessary but stops as River eyes him.

Shoving River in the shoulder but looking at me, he says, "Sorry, Dahlia. I'm not used to seeing this guy bring a girl to rehearsal. He never stays with one girl long enough to introduce us to her." I glance over at River rather quickly, but he isn't looking at me. My gaze is broken when someone calls Phoenix's name.

"Nix, what crap are you stirring up now?" Bell chimes in, taking the beer out of my hand and handing me some red drink with a lime in it.

"Just ignore him! He's always an ass," she says.

"Bell, you're lucky I love you," Nix responds, winking at her.

Then looking at River, he says, "Meet you onstage, I'm going to warm up." As he walks away he turns, "And, Dahlia, it was really a pleasure meeting you."

Rolling my eyes at his obvious attempt to piss River off, I raise my glass and ask Bell, "What's this?"

"A Cranberry Crown. Try it."

I give it a sip to not be rude, and River bends slightly to whisper in my ear, "Watch out for her drinks."

"I heard that," Bell says as she sticks her tongue out at her brother.

"River, you made it," another voice says. Glancing to my right, I see the cutest blond boy reaching to give River a firm handshake and a manly hug.

"When do I ever miss, man?" River answers, grabbing for my left hand before introducing us. "Garrett Flynn, this is the girl I told you about."

River obviously has a great relationship with this gray-eyed, boyish-looking man. His hair is slightly longer than Nix's or River's, and it almost covers his eyes. His hairstyle and boyish features make him look like he's fifteen. His lip ring only adds to the look, and his tall, skinny stature certainly doesn't help. But honestly, he's so cute and innocent-looking, I know he must make even the hardest of women melt.

"How can I forget the amazing girl you've met twice?" Then he gives me a genuine smile, and I know what he's saying is with the utmost sincerity. "Dahlia, right? I'm Garrett." Extending his hand, he adds, "Nice to finally meet you. I've heard a lot about you."

I shake his hand and smile. "Hi, Garrett. I've heard a lot about you, too." Seeing his easy smile, I know I like him already.

A moment later, I feel someone approach us from behind. Looking over my shoulder, I see another duplicate of River. "This isn't a reunion. Time to rehearse, girls." He's circling around us and I can see some differences immediately between their looks, but there is no doubt that this is Xander.

Raising his hands in an *all's good* gesture, Garrett smiles at me. "Catch ya after rehearsal," he says, and then walks toward the stage to join Nix, who is strumming different chords on his guitar.

Xander is definitely good-looking, but not in the same charming, adorable way as River. His hair color is darker and he wears it shorter. He has the same green eyes, but they don't sparkle like River's. His demeanor, I can immediately sense, is cooler, more controlled. Upon first glance, he seems to be the kind of guy who traded in his college cool-boy uniform of old sports jerseys, worn-out jeans, and broken-in baseball hats for the city cool-boy uniform of button-down shirts, neatly pressed jeans, and a lot of hair gel. He kind of reminds me of Ben.

Extending his hand to me, he keeps his eyes on his brother. "Xander. I assume you are Dahlia," he says with a slight chill in his tone.

I extend my hand and he shakes it once before pointing to the stage. "They're waiting for you," he says to River.

"Yeah, give me a minute."

"One is all you get, bro," he says, walking over toward the bar.

Bell lets out a yelp, claps her hands over her head, and beckons Xander to come her way. "Xander! C'mere!" she yells as she slugs back a second shot of what I think is tequila.

I look quizzically at River as he wraps his arms around my waist and kisses me. "I'll explain my family later." Pulling away, he crosses his heart. "Promise."

Giving him a smile, I lean in to kiss him again.

Drums echo through the room and I hear "Testing, testing. One, two, three" blare through the speakers. Looking over to the stage, I see Nix at the microphone and he says, "Loverboy, your presence is needed up onstage."

River shakes his head. "Come on and sit over here," he says, guiding me toward the high-top table at the end of the dance floor in the center of the stage. "Do you want something different to drink?" he asks as he pulls the barstool out for me to sit on.

"I'm good, Loverboy," I joke as I take my jacket off because it's really hot in here. He takes it from me and drapes it around the back of the chair. I hang my purse on top and sit down as I smile and push him toward the stage. "Thank you. Now go and sing something, will you! I've never gotten to see you with the band, and I'm looking forward to it."

"Forward to it, huh?" He winks as he kisses me one last time and turns to leave. I watch him walk to the stage. He's wearing his trademark worn jeans and a plain white T-shirt. I glance at his ass as he turns to pick up his guitar, and he catches me. He shakes his head and flashes me a wicked grin. I wink back and giggle. I'm used to getting caught gawking, so I might as well embrace it.

Onstage, he takes his jacket off and tosses it to the side before heading over to the microphone stand. He blows into it a few times and our eyes lock as we grin at each other. Damn, I wish I had my camera with me. He's so incredibly photogenic and I'd really love to get some shots of him up on the stage, where he's in his element, so relaxed and comfortable. He starts to sing a few notes, and I can tell this is pretty casual and definitely more like a rehearsal than a show because there are no introductions. Some people stop and watch while others, probably used to the band's rehearsals, continue with their conversations. Once the song starts, I can't peel my eyes away from him. It's an old one, but seeing him sing sends shivers down my spine. He's so serious and when he's more than halfway through it, he seems to lose himself in the song. And I don't want the song or this moment to end. As it does, I slowly recover my composure and shoot him a thumbs-up. He winks at me again and turns to talk to Garrett.

I'm finally able to sip the drink that Bell handed me earlier, when she walks over and sits next to me. She hands me another, this time a blue iced drink, and says, "Bottoms up," then clinks her glass to mine. It's an interesting mix of blueberry and cranberry; I kind of like it. "And this would be?" I ask after drinking a healthy gulp.

"No idea. I just told Tate I love cranberries and blueberries, and this is what he made for us."

"Tate?"

"The bartender, and my very good friend." She smiles over at the Hulk-size man behind the bar who is staring back at us.

Not sure how to respond to her, I point to my drink and give Tate a thumbs-up. He flashes a smile then turns to Bell and mouths, "You like?"

"Excuse me," she says as she gets up from the table. "I just want to thank him properly. I'll be back in a few for some girl talk."

I glance up at the stage and see River watching me. Since I'm in a thumbs-up kind of mood, I shoot him another one as he adjusts the microphone stand and puts his guitar over his shoulder. He turns for what looks like a powwow with the band and Xander.

Glancing toward the bar, I see Bell leaning over it, flirting with Tate. I wonder if he's her boyfriend or just her bar boyfriend, but I can't tell. Then I see her plunk her drink down on the bar and stamp her foot before traipsing into the room marked "Poolroom," Tate following quickly behind. After witnessing their little exchange, I'm guessing he's her boyfriend.

I hear River start to sing a song I know well—it's the one he told me he wrote about me. His eyes find mine as he sings the lyrics to "Once in a Lifetime," and when he hits the chorus he closes them.

Having finished my blueberry concoction, I go back to the Cranberry Crown as I listen intently to River's singing. I love the sound of his rough but smooth tone. Closing my eyes, I take in his voice without any distractions. Then the clanking of a bottle being set on the table makes me open them, and I feel slightly dizzy for a second. I know I need to slow down—I am a lightweight to begin with—and having eaten an early dinner, I don't have much food in my stomach to absorb Tate's drinks.

The song ends, and River lifts his shirt to wipe some sweat off his face. This exposes his firm stomach, and I'm not the only one who notices. Girls throughout the bar are cheering, and I'm torn between doing the same or just running up there and pulling him down off the stage. I choose the former. He looks over at me as he lets his shirt fall and winks. But I stop my cheering when Xander takes a seat next to me. He sets a bottle of Black Label Patrón on the table and adds two shot glasses with chasers.

Xander smiles at me, but his smile doesn't have any softening effect on his cold green eyes. "I've heard a lot about you."

I'm not sure why he doesn't seem to like me but I smile cordially anyway. "I've heard a lot about you, too."

Pouring two shots, he slides one over, but not all the way. He looks at the stage, at his brother, and at the other band members. I get the feeling he's avoiding looking at me, but he manages to say, "You're the reason River didn't answer his phone all weekend."

The music stops and the three bandmates step to the side to discuss something. River is pointing to the fret board of his acoustic guitar, and Nix is pointing to the strings on his electric guitar. Garrett is nodding then shaking his head.

"They'll be a while," Xander says, leaning back in his chair.

He pushes the shot directly in front of me, and I look over at him, about to decline, when a wicked grin appears on his face. "Drink with me, Muse?"

I look up at River, but he's still talking to Nix. Without saying another word, Xander licks his index finger and rubs it in the salt. He motions for me to do the same. So, deciding a drink can only help calm the uneasiness I feel in his presence, I dip my finger in the Patrón, wet my wrist, and coat it in salt. Licking the salt, I quickly down the tequila and grab a lime wedge. He does the same.

When we're done he pours two more shots. "Another?"

"What are we drinking to?"

"Life!"

"Okay, life, I'll drink to that." Then, as I set up another shot, I ask, "What's with the name Muse?"

He doesn't answer as he tips his head back and drinks his Black Label without even a *Here's to . . .*

I do the same, but when I set my glass down I ask another question: "Have I done something to offend you?"

Guitar chords are being played, but the band has their backs to us, seemingly still disputing. After pouring a third round, he leans even further back on his barstool. "Where should I start?" He twirls his glass on the table, some of the liquid spilling out.

"Let's see . . . first, I'm a little pissed at my brother right now. He had a radio interview on Sunday morning here in L.A. that he blew off."

Xander looks directly at me for the first time since sitting down. He actually seems more peeved at me than at his brother as he continues. "I called him all fucking weekend and he never answered his goddamn phone until today."

"I'm sorry. I didn't know." I have no idea why I'm apologizing. River has started to play again, but is still turned to Nix. He's singing a song I've never heard.

"You know what?" he asks, but I don't answer because it seems like a loaded question. He continues anyway. "That's not even what really pisses me off." He drinks another shot, this time straight, and refills the glass again.

Drinking my shot straight as well, I force back the bile rising up my throat and know I have to stop. "So, what is it that pisses you off, Xander?" I ask, equally as cool now. I have had enough of his shit.

"You," he says, not taking his eyes off mine.

"Me! What have I done to you?"

"You don't know, do you? He didn't tell you? No, of course he didn't," he wryly says, pushing a fourth shot my way.

River has turned around and is staring at me with concern. I give him a little smile and return my gaze back to Xander. I have no idea what River's singing now because I am not listening to the words. The alcohol is flowing through my veins and my judgment is more than a little off.

I give Xander a measured glance and push the glass back toward him as if to say enough and I don't just mean the alcohol. "Know what?"

I can see by his glazed eyes that he's more than drunk. Leaning forward he turns to face me, but I lean away. "You should be flattered that I call you Muse. In fact, I've referred to you that way for a long time."

Sighing heavily, he looks up at River for a moment, then continues. "That song he wrote about you is why the band is successful today, so you were his muse."

"He did tell me that," I say, feeling the need to defend River. I honestly have no idea where his brother's anger is coming from.

Shooting me an irritated look, he says, "No. Not about the song." He says it like I'm an idiot.

"Then what?" I ask, even though I need to excuse myself to use the bathroom. I stand up, and the room starts to spin.

He snorts as he answers, "River had brought Bell to the bar the first night you met him. Rather than bring her home himself, he asked me to do it so he could stay and talk to you. She was in a hurry to meet some guy at her apartment, and I wasn't ready to leave so my sister left without me." His sad tone draws me back into the conversation.

Glancing at me, as if he is annoyed that I stood up, I quickly sit back down and he continues. "I was easily distracted back then and had stopped to talk to somebody, and before I knew it, she had left with a friend. When River saw me at the bar with no sign of Bell he tried to call her. She didn't answer and he was concerned so he went to her apartment. She wasn't home so he called me and asked me where to look. I told him to try my frat house, and I think he did. Before I heard back from him, I got a call from my mother."

As this scene plays out, I know what is coming. It's not going to be good. Our eyes lock and neither of us blinks until he finally says, "Turns out the friend she caught a ride with was drunk and ran a red light. Their small car was hit by an SUV. Bell's friend died instantly and Bell spent six months in the hospital recovering. The trauma of the accident affected her so much she didn't care about school anymore. She never went back."

My mouth drops open and I shake my head, telling myself that this is fiction, it's made-up; it's not real. My unfocused eyes narrow in on Xander's sullen expression, and all I see is the truth. Bile rises up my throat and I know I am going to lose it. He blames me. Does River blame me? Does their family blame me? "I'm sorry," I say again for the second time tonight. I'm paralyzed by his words, glued to my seat.

He ignores my apology and continues. "As far back as I can remember, Bell always wanted to be a doctor. Especially when our father died. She wanted nothing more than to save people. But, because of the accident, she didn't take that path. So instead of being a doctor, she works for me as my assistant. She gets drunk most nights and never talks about the life she should have had." Throwing back one more shot, he clears his throat. "So, Dahlia, do you see my problem now?" Then he points to River and says in a louder voice, "You were the only chick he ever even bothered to look for ever, and you didn't stick around that night. Tell me why."

Turning to the stage, I catch sight of River's furrowed brow. His eyes are narrowed in on his brother. Seeing his expression makes my body tremble, and tears fill my eyes as I look away. I don't even know Bell, but my heart aches for her. How can I start a relationship with someone under these circumstances? I stand up again, slightly wobbly, and stumble as I grip the table for balance. I need to remove myself from this situation, but Xander isn't finished. Almost laughing, he adds, "And now, I see my brother tonight, happier than I've seen him in a long time. So, I want to know why you left that night. There's obviously something between the two of you. I could hear it in his voice when he talked to me today." His questions end and then he throws the dagger. "If only you would have stayed . . ."

I grab the tequila shot that he poured for himself from the middle of the table and down it, hoping the quick gulp of this mind-numbing liquid will give me the ability to escape this hell. Then, finally able to stand without fear of stumbling, I give River one last glance before leaving. I feel sick and need to get out of here. He stops singing and quickly removes his guitar strap from his shoulder. I know Xander must be pretty near rip-roaring drunk, but I'm surprised when he suddenly grips my bare arm, preventing me from walking away. With his eyes burning into me, he says, "Have you had enough? Because there's more to tell."

"Excuse me. I need to use the restroom," I manage to say, not able to listen to another word. I take off for the bathroom without even glancing at River again. Barely making it to the bathroom in time, I kneel on the floor, lift the seat, and try not to lean my head against it. The room is spinning as I heave into the toilet. When I think my stomach is finally empty, I sit back on my heels for a minute to steady myself. Once the spinning has stopped, I stand up and make my way to the sink for the cool water I so desperately need.

Leaning against the counter with my head down in the sink, my senses start to return. I wonder why River didn't tell me about this himself—how could he possibly think this information wouldn't impact us? His brother harbors such resentment toward me and I'm sure the rest of his family must as well. Hearing the door open, I already know who it is. As I look in the mirror and see his reflection, all I can do is cry uncontrollably.

Coming over to me, he turns me around and grabs my face with both of his hands. He looks into my eyes, unaware of what I already know. "Are you okay? Are you sick? Did something happen with Xander?" He doesn't even pause for me to answer.

I shake my head no but mean yes. I'm not crying because I'm sick. I'm crying because I might very well be the cause of somebody's life being drastically damaged. "Why didn't you tell me?" I hoarsely whisper while trying to stop myself from crying.

"Tell you what? What are you talking about?" he asks.

"About your sister!" I say, surprised by the hardness in my voice.

"Christ! What the hell . . . ?" he starts to say. With his face so close to mine, I'm sure he can smell the alcohol mixed with vomit on my breath.

Before he says anything else, the bathroom door opens and Xander is standing there. River turns around, but Xander doesn't move toward us. He stays in the doorway, slightly swaying. He looks directly at me. "I'm sorry I was the one that told you, but you had to know." I'm impressed by his ability to speak clearly in his drunken state.

River's eyes narrow at Xander. "What the hell did you tell her?"

I'm startled by River's hostility toward his brother.

"We didn't vow secrecy, and she needed to know," he says in a more humble tone than he's used all night.

My buzz is quickly dissipating as I look at Xander blankly, perhaps a little confused. He was so angry with me before and now he's apologizing?

River's face is pale as he looks back over to me, processing what Xander has said. Running his fingers through his hair, he steps closer to Xander as he says, "What I told you about Bell, those are my demons. I just wanted someone else to blame for once and there you were after all these years."

"Sorry, man, but she had to know."

River slams his fist into the stall door nearest to Xander. "It wasn't your place to tell her!"

He doesn't even flinch from River's punch.

Stepping closer to River, Xander says, "You're right, and River, I know you aren't going to believe this, but I want you to be happy. I know you think you just met this girl but to me you've known her way longer. I know how you are. I don't want you to fuck this up because of your need to always protect women because of . . ."

It seems that Xander has struck a nerve with River because he cuts him off before he can finish his thought. "You don't think I know that you harbor guilt about Bell. I do! But that's your guilt, not mine. I let that go a long time ago. Bell is happy with her life. It's you that's not happy and as for how you see my needs, you're wrong."

It's both heartbreaking and heartwarming to watch these two

brothers tear each other apart over their sister. They must love her so much to care about her so deeply.

Stammering, Xander shakes his head, pointing his finger at River. "You think I don't know that you hide your guilt. You can pretend you are happy with how Bell's life turned out but I know different."

Then he smiles sadly as he says, "You aren't even the one who should feel guilty. A long time ago you asked me to, no, I told you that I would take Bell home so you could find this girl," pointing at me. "You've found her now, so don't let me or Bell or anyone else screw it up for you. But most of all, don't let yourself screw it up."

Pain flashes through me from Xander's words. Am I really to blame for their sister's accident? Should I have told River the truth when I first met him? Couldn't I have just stuck around and told him the truth about Ben? Would it have mattered? My head is spinning and I may be sick again.

Xander smiles sadly, his eyes glassy as he looks from his brother to me. "Dahlia, I'm sorry. It has been a shitty day and I took it out on you."

Then, looking back to River, he puts his hand on his shoulder, but River pulls back. "Bro, I'll call you tomorrow." And with that, he turns and leaves us in the bathroom.

River walks back to me as tears fill my eyes again. Swiping my fingers under my eyes, I scrunch my forehead. "You should've been the one to tell me, not him," I yell, pointing to the door, not in anger, but in sadness.

He stops before me and swallows. Exhaling a shaky breath, he looks into my eyes before whispering, "Dahlia, that's not how I wanted our relationship to start," but I pull away before he can even finish. I don't want his touch or his charm to cloud my judgment about where we stand.

I stare back into his eyes as he flinches from my sudden movement. They are now hazy, no longer gleaming. "River," I say a little softer, feeling the need to make sure he knows that an omission is still a lie. "I didn't want our relationship to start like this, either, but hiding things from me . . . I can't, I won't be in a relationship like that, but what's more . . . what does this mean for us?" I feel bad about my words but a lie is a lie, regardless of why it was told or how it was hidden. This I know well. I experienced it with Ben just that one time and it almost ended our relationship. But this time, with River, I'm more concerned about what this secret will do to our relationship than about the actual secret itself.

He stands there, shaking his head. "I was going to tell you, but I hadn't found the right time yet."

Averting my eyes, with a shaky breath, I manage to say, "I need some air."

I walk past him, through the dimly lit bar, and out the doors into the chilly night. There is a cool breeze in the air, sending a shiver down my spine. As I walk to nowhere I know this time the shiver isn't from his touch. Instead, it's from the secret he kept from me. It's from the cold of the night.

There are still so many people walking through the streets that we happily walked down earlier tonight, but the happiness I felt then is gone. The people seem to be more hurried as well. They are huddling together, almost rushing in and out of the many bars and restaurants that line the street.

November in California isn't usually this cold, but the dampness seems to warn of impending rain. Glancing upward in hopes of seeing some light, finding some answers, all I see are thick clouds covering any stars that I might have seen. They only allow a glimpse of the moon's slight crescent-shaped glow and provide no guidance. Looking ahead instead of up because I know I will find no comfort from the sky tonight, I continue to walk, clutching my body to keep warm, and wondering why life has to be so complicated.

"Here, put this on," he says, taking his jacket off and wrapping it around my bare shoulders. He walks close to me, but doesn't touch me. "If you want to go home, the car is the other way." *Maybe I'm not as sober as I thought.*

Stopping, I turn to look at him. We are toe to toe. With tears in my eyes, I say the words I don't really want to say but know I have to. "River, I think it's time for me to go back home."

Slumping, he closes his eyes and whispers, "Not like this. Not until we talk about everything."

My heart breaks as I look at him but I know I have to go. "I need some time to think, River. I can't do that here."

His eyes snap to mine, and his voice cracks in anger. "What happened to my sister has nothing to do with us. You going home and thinking isn't going to change that or even make you understand."

Looking at him, I hear him but choose to ignore his words. I need time to think and not in my drunken state. "I can call Aerie or Serena to come pick me up if you don't want to take me home." Then, remembering I didn't bring my phone, I ask, "Can I use your phone?"

River's control breaks, ignoring my request; his voice grows louder than he has ever spoken to me before. "Dahlia, are you listening to me? That shit that just happened in there, that's Xander's life." Motioning between us, he continues. "I am not going to let someone's misperception about what happened change this."

Grabbing my shoulders firmly, he says, "You can't just say you are leaving. You can't leave me again."

I shrug out of his grip, and sway slightly as I take a step back. "That's the point, River. I'm not leaving you again. I never left you five years ago because I wasn't with you." Tears are sliding down my face uncontrollably, my teeth are chattering, and I am freezing, but I continue with what must be said. "I met a guy at a bar that I was attracted to and before things got out of hand I left. Now I find out that some unmentionable horror happened to your family because of my actions and you think we're going to be okay?"

He flinches at my tone but tenderly places his arms on my shoulders. Lowering his face so we're at eye level he says, "That's what I'm trying to tell you. It's not like that."

With complete honesty I say, "I just don't know if I can do this. This thing we have is way more complicated than two people who are incredibly attracted to each other. Your brother is going crazy having me here. Does your sister even know any of this? And what about your mother! What will she say?"

"Dahlia! Listen to me!" he says, but I don't. I can't. I don't want my heart to break again so instead I turn around and start walking in the other direction toward his car as he keeps pace. I navigate the sidewalk surprisingly well considering how foggy my brain feels. Neither of us says another word. As we reach the parking garage, with my whole body shaking, I get into the car and wait for him to sit.

I look at him and I see he's shaking as well. With tears in my eyes and sadness in my voice, I say what I know I've felt since Xander told me about his sister. "Here's the thing, River. I've already lost someone I loved, and it almost killed me. What I feel for you is so much more than I ever expected, and I know that if I stay here with you and begin to live again that I won't survive losing you. And losing you is inevitable. We can't be together if your family blames me for your sister's accident. In the end, it will be our undoing."

Shaking his head, he touches my cheek and forces me to look at him. "That's just it. No one blames anyone. Bell is happy. Our family is happy. Xander can't accept what happened. And to answer your question, yes, my family knows about then and about now and they're happy for me, for us." He holds my gaze then leans in and kisses me. With that kiss I feel the air fill my lungs once more and life returns.

I pull away from his soft lips, confused. I don't know what to do, but I feel like this night has been a reality check. "I believe you, but it's still time for me to stop playing house with you. I have to go home tomorrow."

CHAPTER 20
Little Things

"Dahlia," he says, and his tone is as dark and sad as the place I have lived for the past two years. "One day, if you change your mind . . . just know you'll always be my once-in-a-lifetime."

He presses soft kisses to my forehead and nose, then turns, leaving me at the front door to the house I shared with Ben for so many years. The house that is now empty and the house where, once again, I will be alone.

Fear starts to wrench through my body, not from being alone, but of being without him. *Did I make the wrong decision? Can we get past this?* My questions don't really matter because it's too late. I have already said things I shouldn't have. I made the decision to end us.

"Don't leave me," I yell as he walks down the path that leads to another life.

Turning and glancing at me over his shoulder, his eyes are no longer a gleaming shade of green; they're cloudy, hazy. "I'm not," he says as he keeps walking. "You left me, beautiful girl."

Tears stream down my face as I let him go, and he fades into the horizon.

My body thrashes in the sheets, and my fists clutch the pillows as I wake.

"Fuck," I mutter to myself as relief washes through me when I realize it was just a dream. No—it wasn't a dream; it was a nightmare. When I reach over, there is no one there to hold me. It hurts to not have him here with me. Waking up next to him the last few days has been amazing and I feel empty and alone in his room without him.

Licking my dry lips, I lift my aching head. "What time is it?" I ask to nobody but myself.

My heart is still pounding in my chest as I reach over to the nightstand and pick up my phone, plugged into its charger. The screen reads 11:48 a.m. How did I sleep in this late? I never sleep past sunrise. As I set my phone back down, I see a bottle of water and two aspirin on the nightstand.

Hearing the howling of the wind outside, I gladly pick up the water and aspirin. I pop the pill in my mouth and swig the water, hoping it will calm the storm stirring in my head. As I set the bottle and paper down, I notice something written on a Post-it stuck to the nightstand. *Beautiful girl . . . In case you're not feeling so great.*

Stretching and grinning at his note, I glance around the room. Sheets are tacked over the glass doors. He must have done that so I could sleep. How could he be so nice to me after I was such a bitch last night? *Shit, last night.* I remember every minute of the horrible evening, every minute of our painful conversation, but I don't remember getting into bed.

Glancing down, I notice I'm only wearing one of River's T-shirts and my panties. I must have passed out in the car. Did he bring me inside, up all those stairs, and change my clothes? The last thing I remember saying after leaving the parking garage was that I still wanted him to take me home, to my home, not his, but I'd wait until morning.

I need to find River and talk about last night, so I stand on shaky legs and find my clothes lying on the floor beside the bed. Making my way to the bathroom, I look in the mirror. That was not a good decision. Makeup smears my face and my hair is a tangle of knots from all the hairspray. I really need a shower but settle for washing my face, brushing my teeth, and throwing my hair into a ponytail before going to search for him.

I don't have to look far. As I walk down the hallway I hear soft guitar music. I stop at the entranceway to the living room to watch him. He's sitting on the couch in jeans and a plain T-shirt, barefoot, and his hair is a little more disheveled than usual. His fingers are holding a guitar pick and he's strumming a beautiful melody while quietly singing an unfamiliar song that I can't really hear the words to. He has a notebook and pen beside him and he's deep in thought. I stand there awhile just listening, looking, thinking about how unbelievably gorgeous he is, both inside and out, and how sad I am that I'm leaving.

I decide to quietly go get my camera out of my bag in the bedroom. I want to capture his perfect image. As I tiptoe back and stand just inside the living room, watching him through my lens, I snap a few photos while he's playing. He's so involved in his work that he doesn't even hear the click of the camera. When he finishes the song, he adjusts his guitar on his leg and leans over to his notebook.

"That was beautiful."

He glances at me, but the happy grin I usually see on his face is missing.

"What song was that? I didn't recognize it."

Leaning his guitar against the couch, he nonchalantly says, "It's just something I'm working on."

Taken aback by his obvious disinterest in discussing the song, I ask, "You got your guitar back?"

Standing up, he shoves his hands in his front pockets and shrugs his shoulders. "Yeah, Xander brought it by this morning." Then he asks, "How about coffee?"

I enter the room and head for the kitchen while I say, "Yes, I can get it, though."

"I've already made it. I'll grab you a cup."

"Thanks." I put my camera down and sit on the couch, hoping my queasy stomach can hold down the coffee.

"How do you feel?"

"Fine. I took your remedy. I think it's working."

I watch him walk into the kitchen, but he doesn't turn around to catch me like he usually does. Once he's in the kitchen, he pulls out the paper cups we bought at Whole Foods yesterday and pours two cups. He adds cream to mine and I smile. He walks back into the room and hands me the cup. "Do you want me to go get you something to eat?" he asks as I take the coffee, staring at him. For the first time since I met him, I can't read him at all.

"Shit, no," I answer, grasping my stomach. "I hope I can keep the coffee down."

He chuckles and I can tell the River I know is in there somewhere. He walks back over to where he was playing his guitar and sits down. Sipping my coffee, I look over at him. "Was Xander feeling okay?"

He quickly glances my way and answers, "Yeah. He looked wrecked but nothing some sleep won't cure." He takes a sip of his coffee, then continues. "I asked Garrett to take him home last night. I guess he stayed at Garrett's, and on their way back to Beverly Hills this morning they stopped by to check on you and drop off my guitar." Pointing to the bar, he adds, "And your jacket and purse."

"That was really nice." Then I laugh a little. "Shit, I don't even remember leaving my stuff there. I guess since you gave me your jacket, I never thought of mine. At least my purse was still there. That would have sucked to have to cancel everything."

I notice he doesn't laugh at my swearing like he usually does. Instead, he nods at me then says in a flat tone, "Well, your mind was elsewhere. I would have grabbed your stuff when I stopped to talk to Garrett, but I forgot it was even there. At least I grabbed my jacket or you would have been frozen."

For some reason the whole conversation seems strained, awkward, and I sense it's because of my behavior last night. I'm sure he's uncertain about my feelings and upset about what I said.

Needing to make amends for my bitchiness, as in my sober state, I believe that he never meant any foul behavior, I stand up and walk over to the bar. Setting my coffee down, I move toward him.

He scans my body as I approach him. I feel like this one little move on my part, this sign of my forgiveness, has put his mind at ease and by the look in his eyes, I know he's back. Tears sting my eyes as I sit on his lap. His arms instantly embrace me and he lets out a soft sigh.

"I'm sorry," I cry as I throw my arms around him.

He sighs again and pulls me as tightly to him as he can. My head is in the crook of his neck and he inhales before sighing again. Shifting me so that I fit perfectly into his lap, he whispers into my ear, "You have nothing to be sorry for. I'm sorry I didn't tell you. I know I should have."

Pulling back, I sniffle a little and wipe my nose with the back of my hand. He flashes me that grin I adore then shifts to lift his shirt, using it to wipe my tears and my nose.

Resting my forehead on his I ask, "Is your family really okay with me, with everything that happened?"

Cupping my cheeks, he nods. His expression is a mixture of seriousness and sadness. "The accident had absolutely nothing to do with you, Dahlia. Call it coincidence. Call it bad judgment. But Bell getting in that car could've happened even if I was the one who said I would bring her home. She was determined to meet some guy at her place and she wasn't waiting."

His eyes flash to mine. They filled with concern. "I left that night and went straight to her place. When I got there, no one was waiting for her."

"No one," I say, saddened that his sister left to meet someone who obviously never showed up.

He pulls my elastic band out of my hair. "If your head hurts you don't need this pulling on it," he says, tossing the band to the ground before continuing. "Who knows what happened to the frat boy, but he wasn't there waiting for her. He never bothered to visit her and he never knew. After the accident she never mentioned him again."

He spits out, "And I'm glad she never did. I'd have killed him." Hanging his head, he relaxes his jaw. "A guy planning to meet a chick at her place so late after going out with his buddies is just not cool. We didn't even know everything until after."

Pulling away from him I start to say something. "What do you mean by every—?" He puts his finger over my lips to shush me. "Never mind, it's really none of my business anyway."

With a tender hand on my chin, he says, "All of that has nothing to do with us, but I'm still sorry I didn't tell you. I don't want this to impact us, though. Got it?"

I feel exhausted and emotional but I nod and say, "River, I understand and it's okay, but I still have to go home. I can't stay indefinitely."

His gorgeous face looks so sad as he says, "Whatever you want, but you look tired. Can we at least go tomorrow?"

Nodding in agreement because I'm exhausted, I hold him tight, inhaling his scent and loving his warm embrace. "Only if we can take a nap now. I love sleeping while it's raining."

He pulls back and kisses my nose. "Me, too," he says, and then he leads me back to his bedroom.

●

His room is dim when I open my eyes. The rain is still pounding outside, but snuggled into River's chest, I'm calm and at peace. The sheet and a single blanket are tangled around us and he's lightly rubbing his thumbs over the sliver of bare skin between my neck and shoulder. He's awake before me for the second time today.

Lifting my head, I smile at the sight of his adorable face. He's lying on my right side and I cuddle up into his arms. The faint light filtering through an opening in the hanging sheets reflects off his eyes, making them twinkle.

He gives me a sexy grin and asks, "Feel better?"

I nod, lay my head on his chest and say, "Much."

"Good." He kisses the top of my head and wraps his arms around me tightly.

Soon enough I need to use the bathroom, so I slide my body down his and get off the bed.

"Where you going?"

"Bathroom. Want water while I'm up?"

"Nope, I'm good, I just want you back here with me, sleepy girl."

As I leave the room, headed for the bathroom, I turn and ask, "What was that song you were playing earlier?"

"What song?" he asks, watching me like I always watch him.

Turning completely around, stopping at the edge of the bathroom, I bite my lip and answer, "You know, the one you quickly stopped singing when I came in the room. The one I asked you about that you said you were working on."

Sitting up and stretching, his glorious body now in full view, he says, "It's not that I stopped working on it when you came in the room." Then standing up, he adds, "I just want to finish it before you hear it."

"What if I want to hear it now?" I challenge as I quickly turn back around shutting the bathroom door.

"Well, that would depend," he says loudly enough that I can hear him through the door. He adds, "I'll get your water."

When I open the bathroom door he's standing there, water in one hand, guitar in the other. Lifting both, he hands me the water bottle.

I chug it back as he continues to block my path with his guitar. "Yes?"

"Let me stay with you a few days at your house, and I'll play the song for you, even though it's not finished," he propositions, sliding his guitar back under his arm.

Taken aback by his question, I shakily ask, "You want to barter?" Loving the idea of spending more time together but not happy about bringing River to the house that Ben and I shared, I'm not sure how to respond.

"Yeah, barter . . . ," he starts to say, then stops. Pulling me close with his free hand he kisses me. "You know what? Never mind."

Maybe sensing what I'm thinking, or maybe second-guessing his idea, he points to the head of the bed. "How about you sit up there, away from me, so I can concentrate? You're too distracting," he says as he kisses me again.

Summoning all my willpower to not throw him on the floor as his tongue meets mine and his body presses close to me, I pull back from his mouth and sashay toward the bed. "You're so bossy!"

He laughs as I walk away.

I sit down at the head of the bed and I cover my legs with my shirt, wrapping my hands around my knees. "Okay, is this less distracting?" I smirk, resting my chin on my knees.

"Not really." He laughs.

"Well, it's irrelevant anyway since you promised a show."

He looks so fucking attractive as he struts closer and sits at the foot of the bed. "I don't remember promising. That's a whole other type of transaction."

I smile at him and laugh. "I'm willing to pay," I proposition before adding, "as long as the show lives up to my expectations."

He softly smiles at me and says, "I hope it does."

Placing his guitar on his leg, he positions one arm around the neck and his other over the body. "This is something I wrote this morning for you. It's called 'Five.'"

He begins to strum the same beautiful melody I heard earlier. I stare, mesmerized by his soulfulness. As he plays, the chords come to life with his concentration and intensity.

He sings the first two lines of the song and I listen.

5 years, 260 weeks, 1,825 days, 2.3 million minutes.
That was how long ago I met you.

His lyrics immediately resonate with me. I can feel my heart expanding, accepting him as the one who belongs there, the one who is meant to hold it.

As he sings, his focus slips further into his music.

If I did it all again. Would you come along for the ride?
If I did it all again. Could you play this game with me?
I hope so.

Tears are stinging my eyes as I unfold my arms from my legs. He continues to sing, lost in his music, and I continue to watch, lost in him, in awe of him. *Perhaps, in love?*

And 5 years, 260 weeks, 1,825 days, 2.3 million minutes from
*   today, will we still be together?*
Because I love you. Do you believe we will still be together? I
*   hope so.*
Because I really love you. Do you know so?

Shaking with joy and needing to touch him, to wrap myself around him, to show him I feel the same way, I crawl down the bed as he sings his last line.

Now you do—I love my beautiful girl.

Swallowing back the tears, I'm overcome with emotion. He wrote me a love song to tell me how he feels. Sitting beside him at the foot of the bed, I'm rendered speechless for a moment. The tears that have been welling in my eyes begin to slide down my cheeks and he sets his guitar gently on the floor.

As I open my mouth to speak, without knowing exactly what I'm going to say, he reaches over and gently cups my face in his hands. He brushes my tears away with his thumbs. He leans in until his lips almost touch mine. "*Shhh* . . . you don't have to say anything. I'm not expecting you to say anything. I just want you to know how I feel. How much you mean to me."

I kiss him, snaking my arms around his neck as he shifts on the bed to welcome me. When he whispers in my ear, "Dahlia, I love everything about you. I know in my heart you're my girl, so amazing, so fun, so beautiful," I feel my heart pounding and I know it's about to jump out of my chest. Turning my head, I look into his eyes. They are telling me that he's my future.

I can't respond in words. I don't know how. So I close my eyes, knowing I can show him how I feel. I kiss him with all the love I feel. Parting my lips, our tongues meet and explore each other as if they've entered uncharted territory and are looking to claim it as their own.

Pulling back slightly, I teasingly suck on his lower lip before moving my mouth down to his neck. Gliding my tongue across his smooth skin, I plant soft kisses along the way. I can feel his taut muscles through the fabric of his T-shirt as I slowly but firmly slide my hands down his back. When I trace my nails against his skin, I hear a low growl in his throat.

My desire to make love to him is so strong; I can feel my heart beating faster with every passing second. River must feel the same way because he grabs hold of my arms and gently presses me back so I'm lying flat on the bed, looking up into his sparkling green eyes. His hands move to hold mine, threading our fingers together as he raises both my arms above my head while softly running his tongue across my lips. I open my mouth and let his tongue inside as he releases one of my hands but quickly grabs it with his other, keeping my arms restrained above my head.

Still hovering over me, his knees at my hips, he breaks the kiss and slides his mouth to my ear. While running his free hand down the length of my arm from wrist to shoulder, he whispers in his sexiest tone, "I love you, Dahlia. And I want to show you just how much."

My body shivers with anticipation as he runs his fingers down the front of my shirt, over one breast and then the other, and my nipples harden from his touch. At the hem of my shirt, he slowly pulls it up my body, revealing my goose-bump-covered skin. His tongue touches the bare skin just below my breasts and follows my shirt's path up my body as if trying to catch it in a chase. Once my breasts are exposed, his tongue teases my hardened nipples, circling them over and over, and I begin to moan. He's still holding my hands over my head and I cannot touch him, although I want to so badly.

"River," I murmur, my eyes half-closed as I arch my back, offering his mouth better access to my aching breasts. "I need to touch you."

"Soon," he whispers back.

And with that, he pushes my shirt up as high as it will go, sucking on both my breasts, one at a time, as if they are his lifeline. His fingers are lightly tracing patterns on my bare stomach, and the sensation is incredible. I'm so turned on as I writhe under his touch.

Lifting his head, River smiles as he brings his lips back to mine before releasing my hands from his grasp. Our tongues intertwine, and my arms wrap around his body, pulling him into a loving embrace. Breaking away, he pulls both of us up to a sitting position. Without saying a word, he lifts my shirt over my head and tosses it to the floor. Following his lead, I do the same. As his shirt hits the floor, he's already laying me back down on the bed.

I can tell he wants to take the lead, and I'm perfectly happy letting him do just that. His every touch, his every nibble is so overwhelmingly sensual and I love it.

Leaning over me, this time without restraining my arms, he places his hands and knees on either side of my body, supporting his weight. As he glides his tongue down the front of me, my hands travel up and down his naked back. They press into the hardness of every well-defined muscle I encounter along the way and he lets out a deep groan. Continuing his journey, he skims his nose along my skin and dips his tongue in and out of my navel, making me squirm. Reaching the silky edge of my black lace panties, I realize where he's headed, and I'm overcome with desire.

I grasp fistfuls of his hair between my fingers. I gently urge his head downward, encouraging his mouth to reach its final destination. Hooking his index fingers into the waistband of my panties at each hip, he pauses a second before placing his lips between my slightly parted legs. When he softly kisses my most sensitive spot through the fabric of my very damp panties, I can practically see sparks fly from the feel of his touch. I'm getting wetter and I want him badly.

"You're so ready for me, aren't you?" he softly growls against my skin as he yanks my panties down, past my knees to my ankles, and I kick them off onto the floor.

"Oh, God, I am," I manage to whisper, as I raise my hips, offering myself to him, my hands now flat on the bed for support.

Using his hands to further open my legs, he sucks and nibbles on the skin of my inner thigh, trailing his kisses closer and closer to my slick core where I'm so eagerly awaiting his touch. When he finally strokes me with the tip of his tongue, it is pure heaven, and I let out a deep moan. "Oh, God, that feels so good. Please, don't stop."

I feel his mouth turn up in a sexy grin, as he continues to pleasure me with his wicked tongue, never lifting his head. Arching my hips off the bed as a jolt of pleasure runs through me, I grind myself urgently into his mouth, knowing I'm so close to the edge. As my muscles start to tighten, River's tongue massages me with just the right amount of pressure. When he sucks hard one last time, I can't hold back any longer, and waves of intense, fiery pleasure ripple through my body. I cry out his name over and over in ecstasy as his tongue continues to stroke me, prolonging this incredibly wonderful ride.

As my heavenly journey slows, I catch my breath and notice River watching me with a big grin on his adorably attractive face. "Hey, beautiful girl," he says, leaning in to kiss the tip of my nose. His eyes meet mine as I smile up at him, still trying to regain my composure.

"Hey you," I reply, and with that, he raises himself up and moves to stand beside the bed. Reaching into the front pocket of his jeans, he pulls out his phone, and sets it on the nightstand. He turns and quickly yanks one sheet from the glass doors, allowing the small bit of daylight left to filter into the room. I know without even looking that it's still raining outside. I can hear the drops hitting the glass in a constant steady rhythm. It's soothing.

But the calm doesn't last long before River reaches over and grabs me by the ankles, then kneels on the floor at the edge of the bed, sliding my naked body toward him. He lifts my knees, resting them on his shoulders, and I hook my ankles around his neck. I'm very aware of him, I can feel his warm breath between my thighs as he lowers his head and kisses my entrance. His tongue penetrates my already-slick opening and I say, "River, I don't think I can again!"

"*Shhh*, relax," he whispers as he continues to suck and tease every inch of my sex. I feel myself getting wetter, it's like he's kissing me from the inside out, and I don't want him to ever stop. I smile to myself. *Maybe I can do this again?* He slips one finger and then another deep inside me and slides his tongue up and over me. As he brushes over my G-spot, I know I can definitely do this again.

I hear the rain pounding harder outside the window, perfectly mimicking the pleasure building in my body. My eyes close and my head turns to the side as my breathing becomes shallow and quick.

When I feel myself getting close, he suddenly removes his fingers, glides his tongue down deep inside me while he places both hands on my thighs. He's holding me in place and it is incredibly erotic. This is something I've never experienced before. I love it. Tightening my leg muscles as I feel my climax building, I want to raise my hips and thighs off the bed, but I can't. It strengthens the intensity of what I'm feeling.

"You're so close, beautiful girl, just let go."

"Oh, God, River, please . . . I'm . . . I'm . . . ," I cry out and come harder than before. An endless wave of primal bliss overtakes me. It's like I'm being catapulted through a beautiful stormy sea, and I don't want to reach the shore. River's tongue doesn't stop as he wrings every ounce of pleasure from my body, yet again.

I open my eyes as the aftershocks of my release fade away and I focus on his face.

His sexy green eyes are staring back at me. "You. Are. So. Amazing." He follows each word with a kiss as he makes his way up the front of my body, finally landing his lips on mine.

Running my hands through his soft, disheveled hair, I pull him even closer, dragging my lips to his ear. "Make love to me, River," I softly whisper as I suck on his earlobe. I can't quite believe that after two incredible mind-blowing orgasms, I not only have the energy, but also a strong desire to have him deep inside of me. I'm already slightly quivering at the thought of it.

"I plan to," he says, and I know he means it.

While he stands beside the bed, removing his jeans and boxers, I take a moment to sit up and glance out the window behind him. It's getting darker outside, not just from the time of day but the storm clouds that have clearly settled in. The rain is still coming down in buckets and I can vaguely make out the Hollywood sign in the distance, and it makes me smile. The dark, stormy weather outside couldn't be more different than the bright, peaceful, loving atmosphere inside these walls.

Turning to look at River, I admire his naked, gorgeous body, every inch of it from head to toe. He stares at me with a devilish grin and I can't help but shudder with anticipation for what lies ahead.

He climbs back onto the bed, and I reach for him, longing to be entwined with him. With my arms around his neck, he gently guides me up the bed, urging me closer to the headboard until I'm sitting with my knees folded under me, my back against the smooth, cold black leather.

Reaching over my head, I grip the top of the headboard, as he kneels in front of me. Looking at him, I can see he's so ready, his tip already glistening. I can't wait another second. I need him inside me now.

I'm trembling slightly as he parts my legs. With one swift but controlled motion, he smoothly pushes himself inside me, filling me deeply with his length. My hands are still holding tight to the headboard as I hear him let out a deep groan. "Dahlia, you feel so incredible."

Unable to respond with words, I let go of the headboard and put my arms around his body, pulling him closer to me. Pressing my open mouth to his, I feel the velvety softness of his tongue stroking mine, the rhythm matching his thrusts. He quickly takes me and rolls us over so that I'm on top. His head is resting on the fluffy pillows and I watch his face. His eyes close and then so do mine as I push harder and faster. He steadies my hips, holding me right where he wants me to be.

I feel the familiar sensation building in my core. River's motions are pushing me toward yet another release, and I can't hold on much longer.

"Open those beautiful hazel eyes, sexy girl. I want to be looking into them as we come together," he says before he can say no more.

That's all it takes this time. I force my heavy eyelids open, focusing as best I can on his eyes as he pushes me over the edge, shattering me into a thousand glorious pieces, taking me to a whole other universe.

"Oh, River," I moan loudly, panting hard as I slowly drift back down. His movements slow as I catch my breath.

"I love you," he groans, and with only a few more strokes, he shudders as he finds his own release. It's such a beautiful thing, and I know I will never forget this moment.

I want to say the words back because I am in love with him, but the words just won't come. Instead, I kiss him with all the love I have for him pouring from me.

CHAPTER 21

Between the Raindrops

Explaining to River why I didn't want him to come with me to Laguna Beach was one of the most painful conversations I've ever had with someone I love. Funny, I can think *I love you* in my thoughts but I'm unable to verbalize my feelings. I don't understand why. Is it because I've lost almost everyone I've ever loved? Or is it because I've only ever been in love with one other person and those words belonged to him? Saying those words out loud to someone other than Ben scares me. To me, those spoken words convey so much more than just a simple I love you. I feel so much more than that for River. I feel like I have met someone I'm meant to be with.

Neither of us felt hungry all day, and then suddenly we were both famished, so we ordered in. Once we finished eating an obscene amount of Chinese takeout, I decided to approach the conversation cautiously. Sitting cross-legged on his bed, I leaned forward and pressed my palms into his thighs. "River, I want to talk to you about something."

His legs were crossed, his back was against the headboard, and his arms were folded behind his head. Uncrossing his arms, he rolled sideways to face me. He supported his head with his hand and responded with nothing but certainty in his voice as he said, "You know you can."

Gazing into his powerful green eyes, I said, "Promise you won't get mad?"

"You don't even have to ask that, but I promise," he said, taking his free hand and crossing his chest. I found it so adorable whenever he did that.

"I want to explain something to you," I said to him cautiously.

He nodded and ran his free hand down my bare thigh. "Okay."

Clenching his fist with both of my hands, I held his fingers in place as I explained that my house still had Ben's belongings everywhere. That I'd only started to pack up before leaving for Las Vegas. I also explained how I'd just recently decided it was time to move. That I'd actually just put the house on the market.

He listened intently, acknowledging my words, but never interrupting until I said, "I just don't want it to be weird for you, or me, if you come there and see pieces of my life with . . ."

Pulling me down to him, he caressed my cheek. He leaned in close to kiss my nose, then slid his lips to mine and said softly, "I understand, and I want to take you home."

I ended the conversation there and let him kiss me, stroke me, hold me, and love me for the rest of the night. But now, as we're pulling up to my 1940s Craftsman-style bungalow, I'm suddenly not sure this is a good idea. Looking at the purple wildflowers, which have taken over the yard, and the low-pitched gabled roof desperately in need of repair, I start to feel a little uneasy.

Turning the car off, he shifts to look at me and grins. "I never pictured you living in a yellow house with a white picket fence."

"When you want to live close to the beach, you take what's available," I quickly answer, feeling less nervous.

The rain is pouring down so hard, the visibility is close to zero. There are flood warnings and I wonder if the old roof on my house is leaking again. River pulls on his beanie as he opens the door. "Stay there. I'll come around and get you."

I love when he wears that hat; it always reminds me of the first time we met. He grabs my bags out of the trunk and comes around to my door. Of course neither of us has an umbrella, so as I attempt to use my purse for cover, he removes his leather jacket and tents it over my head. We both run quickly up the stone pathway to the covered front porch.

Wiping the drops from my face, I glance at the large arched front door. It is slightly ajar. Terror shoots through me as thoughts of a masked man invade my mind.

Pushing me back with his arm, he asks, "Were you expecting anyone to be here?"

My heart starts pounding out of my chest. "No," is all I can manage.

He moves toward the door and I yell, "No! Don't!" My whole body is trembling, and fear surges through me. My jaw is tightly clenched and I'm feeling sweaty. Ignoring my plea, he continues toward the door, kicking it wide open with his boot.

"You don't have an alarm?"

"Alarm?" I ask with a quavering voice. Then realizing that wasn't an answer, I say, "No. No alarm."

His sharp voice pierces through the open door, "Hello?"

He starts to move inside, and I grab his wrist. "Are you insane? We can't go in there! Let's go back to the car and call the police."

Gently pulling his wrist free, he says, "Dahlia, I don't think anyone's still here. Let me just check it out. See if we even need to call the cops. You stay here."

"No. You're not going in there alone and leaving me out here," I whisper in case someone is in there. I'm scared shitless and not sure why we're even going in, but I follow him.

As we enter the house, my senses are on full alert. River takes small, cautious steps as we enter the foyer and I hesitantly trail behind him. I see Ben's keychain on the tile floor next to the old key-shaped holder we bought when we first moved in.

Peeking over his shoulder I see that the family room is a complete and utter mess. What had been packed in boxes is now strewn all over. The sofa cushions are torn and stuffing covers the hardwood floors, the TV cords hang from the wall, various electronics are smashed on the ground, ashes from the fireplace seem to dust everything, and glass lays shattered in a thousand tiny pieces on top of the hearth.

Running to the fireplace, I fall to the ground, clutching one of the broken pictures. It's a photograph of Ben and me at graduation. The frame is broken, but the photo is still intact. I stare at the face of the man I loved for so long.

I assess the damage done to my most cherished possessions, and I realize they are all broken. My Purple Rain tickets mounted next to my father's smiling face are ripped, but my dad's big brown eyes seem to be looking back at me, trying to offer me comfort. The picture of my parents and me outside the Greek, proudly displaying our newly purchased concert T-shirts, lays shattered on top of another photo. One snapshot is torn in half. It is of my aunt and uncle holding me as the priest baptizes me, branding them as my godparents. My aunt's mother, Grammy, is standing next to them wearing her pearls.

River lightly places a soothing hand on my shoulder as he bends to kneel beside me. "Be careful. There's glass everywhere."

I nod my head as tears trickle steadily down my face. "Who would do this?"

"I don't know," he says in a tone as grim as I feel.

Taking the broken frame from my hand, his eyes narrow as he stares at the picture for a long while. I feel like recognition flashes across his face, maybe even pain as he says, "Is this him?"

Turning to face River, I hoarsely answer, "Yes. That's Ben." I've noticed that just like Aerie, he never actually says Ben's name.

Setting the picture down carefully, he stands up and holds out his hand. "Come on, let's see if anything is missing and call the police. Whoever was here is gone now."

Clutching his fingers tightly, I feel like every muscle in my body is tensing as I force oxygen back into my lungs to avoid hyperventilating.

He points to the small vestibule in the back of the room that leads through the old butler's pantry to the kitchen. "That way?"

I shake my head. "No, follow me."

Heading back to the foyer, we start down the short hallway that leads to my bedroom and Ben's office. He pushes in front of me while I constantly look around for possible intruders, even though I know they're gone. The house is too quiet for anyone to be in here. This is the same quiet I experienced hour after hour, day after day, for far too long.

A crunching beneath my feet makes me jump just before my bedroom. We both stop instantly. He turns around and we look down at my black Converse sneakers as I lift my foot. Underneath it lays a crumpled piece of paper. I recognize the gilded edge of the paper immediately. It is a page from one of Ben's many journals.

Bending, I carefully pick up the wadded piece of parchment paper, caressing the satiny edge and holding it tightly. I try to keep my tears at bay but fail miserably as tears of sadness and sorrow bleed down my cheeks. My heart breaks as I glance into the office. Ben's cherished journals cover the knotted pine floor, along with pieces of his laptop and various books torn from their bindings. Many more journal pages, once pristine, lie ripped, torn, and balled-up everywhere. His beautifully scripted handwriting is still visible through the vile mess.

"No, not his journals," I cry as I completely fall apart. *Who would do this? Why?*

River holds me tightly as we stand between my room and the office. "It'll be okay. I'll fix this for you. Come on, let's go back outside," he whispers.

Wiping the steady flow of tears from my face, I shake my head and pull away. "I want to see everything. This is my life. Broken and destroyed. I need to see it." I sob as I move toward my bedroom where I stand frozen in the doorway, unable to move, but unable to pull my eyes away.

Pillows are torn open, the mattress is upside-down, and a chair is flipped on its side. What I see next, as I glance down at the floor, tears through me like a knife to my heart. Amidst all the mess and chaos are my broken necklaces and scattered dolls, the items I cherish most. Pearls, white and black, cover the floor, stuck in the grooves of the wood planks; some start rolling as I finally find the courage to move toward them, picking up my Ken doll as I walk.

Totally losing any sense of sanity, I put the doll on my dresser and grab the silver-plated coffee mug lying on top of my T-shirt quilt. Collapsing to the floor, I haplessly start pinching the pearls from the ground and depositing them into the cup. Ironically, it is the one unbroken item in the room; the gift given to me by Ben as a gesture to fix what was once broken between us.

River bends down and takes the cup from my shaky fingers. Furrowing his brow, and with concern in his voice, he says, "Let me do this. But first, let's get you a glass of water and take you to the car. I think you've seen enough. It looks to me like random vandalism."

Sadly enough, I think he's right. Nothing seems to be missing, but everything is destroyed. It's like a tornado ravaged my safe, but sad house, taking in its path anything that remained of the people I've loved and lost. As if my world hadn't already been torn apart enough, now I have nothing left but my own fading memories. The house looks the way my soul felt for so long after Ben's death. My internal wounds rip apart and the old feelings of hopelessness return.

River's talking, but I can't hear him. A haunting reminder of my broken days echoes through my mind. Dark clouds begin to settle in before I blink away the eerie feeling. I try to see outside of my own head, but the destruction I'm looking at only exacerbates my grief. Everything is broken. Everything I have left of him, of my parents, has been taken away from me. Even the memories are surfacing less and less, and now my daily reminders are gone. I need them back. I don't want my memories to fade away.

Hysterically, I grab the cup back. "No! I have to collect these." Then, setting the cup on the floor, I crawl on my hands and knees, picking up the glistening pearls. "These were my aunt's. She loved them. They were her mother's, my Grammy's, and they meant the world to both of them."

He crouches next to me and deposits a pearl in the cup. Then he strokes my cheek before gently lifting my chin, and he looks at me with nothing but love. "Okay. I understand. Let me help you."

Pulling myself together, comforted by his simple touch and soft words, I continue to pick up what I can of the pearls before stopping and rising to my knees. He continues to collect all the magical beads and I now feel like I should explain my hysterical reaction.

Wiping my tearstained cheeks once again, I fumble for the words. "River," I mumble before crawling over to him, needing him closer. Glancing at me, he sits up on his knees and pulls me close to him, clutching my arms and not letting go.

As we kneel on the floor that the devil just walked across, he simply presses his forehead to mine. I remain stoic even as the words come out of my mouth, and without looking at him, I begin, "When I was a little girl I would often go with my aunt to her mother's house to visit with her. Even though my aunt's mother wasn't really my grandmother, I loved her so much. I called her Grammy and, really, she was like a grandmother to me, the only one I ever knew."

I pull away and pick up the cup. Fingering the pearls that are no longer connected to their splendid strands, I say, "She wore these pearls all the time. Whenever I visited her house she would put them around my neck and call them magic wishing wells."

Swallowing, I set the cup back down and draw imaginary circles around my neck before continuing. "Grammy would always tell me that wearing these pearls would make all my dreams come true." Sighing, I take a deep breath and add, "When she died, they became my aunt's and then when my aunt died, they became mine."

I hang my head in my hands, unable to bear the pain any longer. His strong arms surround me, and he whispers into my ear, "She sounds like an amazing woman. We'll get her magic back, Dahlia, we will. But right now, you need to take a break."

River's words soothe my pain and as he pulls back, I catch his loving gaze. Exhaling the breath I've been holding, I feel a sense of calmness flow through my veins. New emotions bubble to the surface as I throw myself toward him. Clutching his face and staring into his eyes, the words I've been unable to say suddenly pour out. "River, I love you."

He hugs me tighter than I ever remember being hugged, and after a few moments of embracing each other, he whispers into my ear, "I love you, too. So much. Please let me take care of this for you." Pulling away, he crosses his finger over his heart. "I promise to pick up the rest of the pearls off the floor."

❦

I'm sitting on the front porch, texting Grace that we will be by in a little bit. I assured her I was fine earlier when I called her, but she insisted we come by for dinner once the break-in had been reported. She also invited Serena. I'm a little apprehensive about River meeting her. She looks so much like Ben, same hair color, same blue eyes and after seeing Ben's picture, River might be a little freaked-out.

After nearly three hours, the police finally finished taking their report, collecting fingerprint samples, asking me about missing items, and photographing the damage.

As I place my phone down on the side table, I rock one last time in the antique chair that adorns my front porch. A black Jeep pulls up to the curb. It's still raining, but it's let up a bit. I recognize Ben's best friend instantly as he gets out of the car. Caleb Holt walks the few steps to the porch and hugs me before saying a word. "You okay?"

Surprised, I answer, "Yes. How did you know?"

"Serena called me right after you called Grace. She's concerned about you and asked me to come by and check things out. Sorry it took so long for me to get here, but I was in L.A.," he says, walking toward the front door as River steps outside.

"Dahlia, I think I got everything you wanted. Your car is loaded so I'll just throw this in mine," he tells me while holding a crate of my most cherished but broken items in his arms.

Almost bumping right into River, Caleb's eyes flicker to mine and I can see he had no idea I was here with another man.

They assess each other as they stand there, staring. River sets the bin on the old wooden planks and glances at me, his eyes searching mine for answers. I introduce my once-fiancé's best friend to my new boyfriend. The moment is awkward as neither one of them says a word at first. Finally, River extends his hand and Caleb hesitantly shakes it.

"Sorry. I thought you were alone and needed help getting your stuff together to go stay at Grace's house," Caleb says, moving aside to let River pass.

River strides over to me and stands as close as he can. I grab his hand, reassuring him that I'm okay.

"I think we got it all," River says as he drops my hand and moves back over to get the crate. "Let me just load this in the car while the rain has let up."

As River walks down the pathway to the street where his car is parked, Caleb looks at me. "Sorry. I didn't realize."

"Caleb, it's okay. I wanted you to meet River anyway." Then glancing at my strong but tender boyfriend loading his car, I add, "I'm actually going to stay at his house until I can get this mess cleaned up."

He asks, "Mind if I take a look?"

Scrubbing my eyes with my palms from the mental exhaustion of the day, I say, "Not at all, but it's a wreck. Police think a gang of kids broke in since nothing was taken."

He walks inside.

River comes back and I wrap my arms around him, resting my head on his shoulder. "Thank you."

Snaking his arms around my waist, he kisses my nose. "You don't have to thank me, Dahlia."

Loosening our embrace, I search his eyes. "Caleb is a Navy SEAL and Ben's best friend since we were seven. We all grew up together on the beach."

He shrugs his shoulders as he releases me and grabs my hand. "What's he doing in there?"

"He said he wanted to check it out."

"Why?"

"No idea," I say as I follow beside him, but stop at the doorway. "I don't want to go back in there, River."

"Okay, baby, let me just see if he's finished and we'll go."

Watching River walk down the hall that leads to what used to be Ben's bedroom and mine feels strange. If it bothers River, he does a great job of hiding it, and I suddenly realize that finding my past in pieces has actually brought me closer to my future.

❦

Before leaving the house, River and Caleb walked through each room again, securing all the windows and doors. They didn't really converse, but they did agree they would meet here on Saturday to move the unsalvageable furniture from the house to the curb. The police found no evidence of forced entry, which bothers me. *How did someone get in?* One officer told me the perpetrator knew what they were doing and probably picked one of the old locks. Then he added that maybe they had a key. I found this unsettling and preferred to think that teens broke in for their own sick fun. Either way, whoever did this did it with the intent of turning my home into a battlefield. It doesn't matter who it was, what they did is unforgivable.

Pulling out of my driveway with every salvageable memento in the back of my 2009 white Audi Q7, I can clearly see that my home's exterior is now in need of just as many repairs as its interior. I've known the siding needed reshingling and the roof needed replacement for a long time. Ben and I had planned to make those improvements. They were on the top of our list, but when our list became my list, I just didn't care about the house anymore. For some reason, now I do. Its sad, broken condition reminds me so much of myself before I met River. I just want to reach out and heal it like River helped heal me. But just like me, it's no easy fix. Sure, the outside repairs are simple; I just need to hire contractors to replace and repair the worn items. But the inside will take time.

I wonder how a house left empty for only six days could now look like a war zone—and just like refugees, the battle has left me homeless. But luckily I have a place where I can stay.

As I drive past the For Sale sign in my front yard, I'm sad that I might never spend another night in that house. That I might never get to feel the warmth and comfort that I used to feel there before Ben was killed. Ben and I loved that house, picket fence and all. I remember telling Ben that I never wanted to move. Our house had everything I needed, everything that was important to me: proximity to the beach, the most amazing garden, a tranquil backyard, and a front porch where we could sit and tell stories of our adventures to our grandkids.

The sadness that now burns within me is not without cause. For someone to want to destroy another's personal possessions is beyond

my comprehension. The things they randomly destroyed were my lifeline to my past, all I had left of the people I loved so much. Seeing my
pearls ripped apart like that, taken from a beautiful circle of hope and
turned into small desolate islands, broke me once more but this time I
was not alone. River was there to soothe me.

After silencing my sorrow with his presence and wiping my tears,
we discussed what to do next. Call the police, gather anything I
wanted to take, and head back to his house. I agreed to go back to
River's house, but only for the night. He didn't want me to be alone
and, honestly, neither did I. He agreed to stop at Grace's first for dinner and to unload the things I wanted to keep safe, but didn't agree
with me about staying at Grace's. He wanted me to stay with him. I
explained that I not only need to be closer than sixty minutes from my
house for the repairs, but that I need to work on making myself whole
before I can think of living with him. He didn't question me, but he
also didn't agree. Maybe sensing my confused state of mind, he let it
be. Instead, he kissed me and held me tight.

Once we pull up to Grace's house, I realize the storm is just about
over. The wind seems to be calmer and the huge clouds that loomed
overhead are dissipating.

As I stand in the driveway waiting for River, a cool breeze passes
through as a ray of sunshine gleams down. As I look up to the sky a
small drop of rain falls on my cheek, so small I don't even bother wiping it away. The smell of wet sand surrounds me as the rain clears away
to reveal a beautiful starry night.

I feel slightly nervous about introducing Grace to River. Although Grace is the woman who helped me through my adolescent
years by teaching me how to drive, taking me shopping for my prom
dress, helping me fill out my college applications, and even bringing
me to my first gynecologist visit to put me on birth control, she's also
Ben's mother. I'm sure she will accept a new man in my life, in fact I
know she will, but nonetheless it will be awkward to introduce my

once fiancé's mother to my new boyfriend at her house. But because she's an amazing woman and because I love her as if she were my mother, I want her to meet him and I want him to meet her. She's who I aspire to be.

Grace is shorter than I am, with shoulder-length blond hair. Her creamy porcelain skin never ages and her deep blue eyes are always tranquil. She's not only beautiful, but she sees the world through rose-colored glasses. She very rarely lets anything get her down. She's strong and independent, fun and loving, caring and nurturing. She's everything a girl would want in a mother, and I was lucky to have her willingly take on that role when my own mother no longer could.

Serena is also an amazing woman who I'm sure will accept that I have a new man in my life. She helped me through her brother's death with such love and understanding, I feel like she is my sister, too.

Walking down the stone-paved driveway toward River, I notice he's on the phone in his car. I stop, and glancing over my shoulder, I see the ocean and it instantly makes me smile. I love everything about the beach: its smell, its sounds, the surf. I haven't walked along it in so long. I actually haven't dipped my toes in the sand since . . . I shake that thought out of my head. I have enough sad thoughts I'm trying to push aside. The beach is a constant reminder of Ben. Each time I've come to Grace's over the past two years, I've stayed inside, refusing to recognize or embrace the calm beauty of nature's most magnificent and amazing wonder. Now I welcome it. I've missed it. I want to run toward it.

"Hey, you okay?" he asks, closing his car door.

I turn, and instead of running to the beach, I run to him. Watching him inhale the crisp, clean air, I throw my arms around his neck and breathe in his fresh scent. He feels just like a warm breeze as he wraps his arms around me and hugs me tightly.

"I'm more than okay," I say as I pull back and stand before the ocean, closing my eyes. I open my arms wide, feeling the beauty of the ocean and letting my residual sadness be swept away by the sea air. I hear chuckling, and suddenly, his strong hands hold me. I now know that he's my home. The house we just left is nothing but a house. Tugging on his hand, I pull him toward the front door. "Come on, I have some special ladies I want you to meet."

Grace must have heard the cars in the driveway because she steps outside before we can knock. She's wearing a simple wrap dress and flat sandals with her usual diamond earrings and the wedding band she's never removed, even though her husband died more than twenty years ago.

She smiles at me with relief in her eyes before she throws her arms around me. "Dahlia honey, are you okay?" she asks as she pulls back and clutches my shoulders.

"Grace, the house is a wreck," I say, trying not to cry. "But I'm fine."

She stares at me for a few seconds. I know she's making sure that I really am okay because she's searching my eyes like she does every time she sees me.

Just as I'm about to introduce her to River, she beats me to it.

She smiles and puts her hand out to him. "Hi, you must be River," she says with a warm, comforting look in her blue eyes. "It's so nice to meet you. I've heard so many wonderful things about you."

River immediately responds with an adorable grin. "Mrs. Covington, it's nice to meet you, too. I've heard just as many about you," he says, shaking her hand. He really is charming.

"Call me Grace," she says as she drops his hand and hugs him. I hear her whisper, "Thank you," in his ear, and his grin turns into a full-megawatt smile, which makes me smile and melts my heart.

Looking around, I notice Serena's car isn't here. "Where's Serena?"

"She had to pick Trent up at a basketball game and take him to a friend's, so she couldn't make it."

"Oh, that's too bad," I say, a little sad that she's not here. "I'll call her later."

Staring out toward the beach, I think, *yes*, I'm still upset about my house and everything that was destroyed, but I see hope in my future and that is worth smiling about. Grace looks at me and I flash her my biggest, brightest smile, the one that finally reappeared the day I re-connected with River.

CHAPTER 22
Memories

Leaning into my car, River softly kisses my lips. "You can stay here, you know. You don't have to go back," he says for the second time since we woke up. He pulls back and caresses my cheek. I sigh and look up at his pleading eyes, then shift to take in his beautiful face, strong chin, perfect nose, and full lips.

Looking down to avoid eye contact, I move his hand to my mouth. "River, we've talked about this. We can't move in together after knowing each other for one week." I say this, but I'm aware that he knows it's not my only reason for heading back to Laguna Beach.

"I disagree, you know." He grins as his eyes slide from my face to the words printed on my Smashing Pumpkins Teargarden Tour T-shirt. "You could at least stay one more night."

Rolling my eyes, I look back at him and smile. "Then tomorrow you'd just say the same thing."

"You think you know me that well already?"

"Well, wouldn't you?"

Shrugging his shoulders, he leans in again and kisses me a little longer before saying, "Why don't you stick around and find out for yourself?"

I laugh and shove him. "Enough with the long goodbyes. I'll see you in two days."

Moving away from the car and putting both hands in his pockets, he grins his sexy grin at me. "Catch you later, beautiful girl."

Giggling at his reference to one of my favorite Smashing Pumpkins songs, "Perfect," I blow him a kiss. "I'll call you when I get there. Oh, and, River?" I wait for him to look at me. When he does, I say, for only the second time ever, "I love you."

With a smile, he quickly opens my door and pulls me to him. My heart responds to his touch by beating faster. I close my eyes and lean into him—he smells so good. I press my palms against his chest and swear I not only feel his heart beating but I can hear it, too. He cups my chin and looks at me intensely. "I love you so much."

❧

Traffic is light as I drive the sixty minutes or so back to Laguna Beach. I'm enjoying the tranquility of the enchanting starry night as I reflect back on the past week and how my life has changed so drastically. My emotions range from high to low; I'm happy and I'm sad.

Glancing over at the empty passenger seat while stopped at a red light, I pick up the small black rectangular picture frame I put there yesterday. The glass is gone, but the photograph, still perfect, is of my father, mother, and me at Disneyland. I clutch it tightly against my chest, remembering the fun we always had together. God, I wish they were still here with me. I miss them so much.

Tears stream down my cheeks as I drive, but they are tears of reflection more than sadness. We were able to collect most of my memories from the house. Yes, most are broken and in need of repair, but I still have them to keep and treasure. The only unsalvageable items were Ben's journals. As River packed up the broken photographs and frames, I gathered all of Ben's journal pages, flattened them, and put them in a box. I'd never read his most private thoughts, but I want to keep them nonetheless.

Over the course of the week, I'd finally let Ben go. He will always be with me, but I have made room for someone else in my heart. Grace's words echo in my mind as I recall our goodbye last night while we were standing outside my car. She knew I would be back tonight, but we were both aware that when I returned I would no longer be Ben Covington's fiancé, as I'd often been referred to after his death.

Last night, as I took the engagement ring that I'd tucked away so many days ago out of my purse, I clutched it tightly before handing it to her. River was waiting for me in his car. I was going to follow him home in mine. Glancing over at him, I smiled and took a deep breath. I knew the time was right. "Grace, please keep it safe for me."

She hugged me tightly. "Dahlia honey, I will. You deserve to be happy and you're ready for this, for him," she said, looking over at the man she knew I loved. "Don't cling to the remnants of your life that have been snatched away from you. Instead, look forward to your future. I know I do." We were both crying as we said goodbye. I knew then that when I arrived at her house tonight she would be the same loving woman she had always been, but she would no longer be my future mother-in-law.

Driving down Grace's street I stop at the end of the stone driveway and walk slowly to the beach. I haven't visited our favorite spot since he died, and I've missed it. The moonlit path is visible, and the old weathered planks creak beneath my feet as I cross over them like I've done a thousand times before. Looking up, the dark heavens are shining with twinkling stars, and I truly believe my family and Ben are smiling down on me. The waves splash against the sand, and it's music to my ears. The full moon's beams reflect off the glistening water and make it sparkle like diamonds. The surf moves quickly, crashing against the rocks as the white frothy sea dances across the shore.

I bend down and untie my sneakers. Taking my Converses off, I tuck my phone in one and leave them in the dunes. Inhaling deeply, I hesitantly start my walk through what I have thought of as quicksand for the past two years.

As the moonlight flickers across the beach, it's as if the moon is guiding my way to the shore. I feel like this place is readying me for the peaceful nights that will hopefully come after I leave, after I say my goodbyes.

The soft sand feels like grains of sugar beneath my feet and it comforts me as I approach the shore. Reaching the water, I release the breath I've been holding and think of Ben in the surf, on his board enjoying the waves. Thoughts of all our fun times here make me smile.

A cool wind blows through the air with determination, as if it's trying to get somewhere. The beautiful palm trees, bent back from so many storms, seem close enough to kiss the ground.

I roll up my jeans as the healing water swirls around me, creating a whirlpool around my ankles. Looking out into the darkness, the ocean seems to be laughing as it bounces up and down.

I sit and slowly immerse myself in the water, taking deep, cleansing breaths. I stay here for I don't know how long, and let the water wash away my pain. I know I'll never forget Ben regardless of the tangible things I may have lost; his spirit will always be with me.

Standing up, I look up to the heavens again and smile. I will never stay away from this place again. I love the beach. I realize that although my memories might fade, they will always be the beacons on my path to the future, and I feel surprisingly at ease with that.

As I head back to Grace's house and approach the dunes, I laugh out loud as I hear Justin Timberlake's voice sing through the night.

"Hey, sexy."

I hear laughter on the other end of the phone. "That's my line, sexy girl. Miss me yet?"

"I've only been gone a few hours," I say, walking back to my car. "But, yeah, I do."

CHAPTER 23
Miles Apart

River

December
3 weeks later . . .

Waking up to the sound of water pelting against the windows again doesn't really bother me because I know we won't be getting out of this warm, comfortable bed to go running—not until the rain lets up, anyway. She's lying next to me, and I love how content she makes me feel. I love her, everything about her. She's beautiful, tall, thin, and has these amazingly sweet doe eyes that make her look innocent, and make me want to keep her safe. But her beauty isn't the only thing I love about her. She's fun, playful, curious, and strong. She's always up for an adventure. She loves the outdoors and takes every opportunity to photograph the beauty she sees in it. She might never keep her phone charged and let her e-mails pile up, but she always keeps in touch with the people she cares about. She's simply amazing.

I roll onto my side so I can rest my head on my elbow and start to slide my hand up the inside of her thigh to feel her smooth, soft skin. She shifts to face me. I lean in to kiss her and look at her beautiful face. "Good morning, sleepy girl." I know she must be tired because she never wakes up after me. But at least she doesn't wake up at sunrise anymore, thanks to the blackout shades that we installed in the bedroom.

"Good morning," she says, stretching her arms and smiling at me. She settles back down, snuggling into me, and gives me a good-morning kiss. I love that, in the middle of our kiss, I can feel her smiling.

She pulls away, still grinning, and says, "Ready?"

Looking down the sheet at myself, I smirk, "Yeah, I'm ready." Okay, so I guess she wants to skip the foreplay this morning.

"Great! Let's go, then," she says, pushing me out of bed as she hops off and heads to the bathroom.

"Dahlia! No, really? In the rain? Now?" It's about all I can say because I was so ready, but not for running.

●

After our five-mile run, we stop to walk the last stretch of the street that leads back to the house. We stayed in the neighborhood and didn't veer down the trails. We're walking side by side, and she's telling me about Aerie's new boyfriend and is not bothered at all by the rain. Suddenly she stops, bends down, and starts taking off her sneakers and socks.

I stop, too, breathing heavily from the run, extremely curious about what the hell she's up to. "Dahlia, what are you doing?"

"Taking my shoes off."

"I can see that. Why?"

"Because, silly, I want to jump in the puddles."

She says it like I'm a dumbass and should've known. God, I fucking love her. The raindrops fall, but all I can see is the beautiful girl in front of me. She doesn't have to worry that her broken pearl necklaces won't bring her magic anymore because she's the magic.

As I continue to watch her with amazement and wonder, I no longer simply see rain falling from the sky. In my mind, the drops have become the tiny wishing wells she once described to me and they are gathering all around her. I have this overwhelming urge to grant this girl her every wish, but at the same time, that fucking terrifies me. What if she doesn't want me to be her happily ever after? What if the connection she had with him can't be broken? What if *he* was her happily ever after?

These are the thoughts that scare the shit out of me and keep me from pushing our relationship too far, too fast. What if she loves him more than me? Will she always love him more? As if having to compete for Dahlia's love against a ghost isn't hard enough, knowing the things I know about him just makes me hate him more. But what I know about him, I'd never tell her. I'd never hurt her in that way.

After she jumps from puddle to puddle, she closes her eyes and raises her arms out to the side. She tips her head back and spins in circles like this is something people do every day. Her joy mesmerizes me, and although I never met her Grammy, I know that that woman's spirit is alive inside this girl.

Smiling, I walk over to her and her eyes open. She's blinking away the raindrops when I pull her to me. I kiss her hard, hoping some of her magic will rub off on me. Slowing things down, I never break the kiss as I concentrate on making sure it lets her know how much I truly love her. When she starts to quiver, I know I've accomplished my goal.

❦

"*Surprise!*" she yells, opening her trunk. Once we got back from our run, we took a shower, and she decided to run some errands while I talked to Xander about the contract negotiations.

Cocking my head at her and raising an eyebrow, I peek inside the trunk. "What are we doing with these, running a day-care center?"

She shakes her head, pouting her lips as she points to the boxes. "Do three-year-olds play backgammon?" Every time she pouts her lips, all I want to do is kiss her.

"I don't know what three-year-olds play, but I do know what twenty-six, soon to be twenty-seven-year-olds play, and it's a lot more fun," I answer, pulling her to me and kissing her soft lips.

She steps around the car to open her door, and grabs what looks to be a grocery bag full of food. Walking back to the trunk, she drops it near my feet, waving her finger at me. She giggles as she steps up to me. "You're lucky I love you because sometimes your humor is just wrong."

She's only really said "I love you" to me twice before, but I'll count this one. She's texted the words to me and written them in a note, but verbalizing it seems hard for her. I'm sure it's because of him. But I don't want to think about that now, so I shake that thought out of my head and give my amazing girl my full attention.

Licking my lips, I feign ignorance as I ask, "What? What did I say? And what's in the bag?"

Grinning, she slides her hands up my chest, wrapping them around my neck. "Don't play dumb with me, you know exactly what you said," she mockingly says into my ear. "And as for the bag, you'll just have to wait and see."

In a low whisper, as close to her ear as I can get, I ask, "About the games or having fun?"

She giggles again. *God, I love that sound.*

She unwraps her arms and slides her hands to my face. I hold her as she kisses me on the lips. Her mouth lingers for a few seconds as my palms rub her back. I'm getting caught up in the moment when suddenly she pulls away and swats me on the ass. "You can't put three-year-olds and sexual innuendos in the same conversation! That's just all kinds of wrong."

Crossing my arms, I narrow my eyes and point my finger at her. "I'm not the one with S-E-X on the brain! That word never even came out of my mouth."

I spell the word, pretending to scold her as she shakes her head at me.

"Come on. Help me unload these, and I might not have to punish you," she says, grabbing and twisting my arm toward the trunk as she picks up the bag she set on the ground.

Lifting the boxes out of the car, I turn to her and grin. "If you'd have told me at the beginning of this conversation that punishment was an option, we wouldn't be standing here right now emptying your trunk."

She pushes me forward and grabs some boxes herself as I follow her up the stairs, staring at her beautiful ass.

I set the games onto the counter and I turn around, holding one of the boxes. "I'll only play Monopoly if you play by my rules."

Hands on her hips, she raises an eyebrow. "What rules would those be? Has Milton Bradley called you with a new set? Because as far as I know, the rules haven't changed since the game was invented."

Shooting her a wicked grin, I set the game down and pull out my phone. Holding it out to her I answer, "Dahlia, as a matter of fact, I got a text this morning from Milton himself informing me of one new rule."

Smirking as she walks closer to me, she places her hands on my shoulders and looks right into my eyes. "First of all, I'm pretty sure Milton died over a hundred years ago." She runs her fingers down my arms and holds my hands. "And second of all, only because I'm insanely curious and like to keep up with game changes, what might this new rule be?" she asks seductively.

"You don't know, beautiful girl?"

She flutters her eyelashes and speaks in that cute Southern accent she uses when she's trying to cover that she's being a smart-ass. "Kind sir, if I knew, I wouldn't have to ask. Would I?"

I clutch her hands tightly, pull her up to me, and whisper into her ear, "Every time you pass Go, instead of collecting two hundred dollars, you have to take something off."

"Oh," she says, biting her lip as she takes the game from the counter and heads to the kitchen table, pulling the cellophane off the box. Sitting down, she flashes her irresistibly sexy smile and winks at me as she sets up our first game of Strip Monopoly.

❧

Dahlia decided not to move back into her house. She packed up the rest of her things and has contractors making repairs so she can put it back on the market. We haven't talked about her long-term living arrangements since the day of the break-in, but she knows I want her to stay here with me. She's here most of the time anyway but hasn't said anything about wanting to move in with me permanently.

She's so determined to stay with Grace, she makes a point of going back there at least every other night. Even last night, after we'd finished our little game of Strip Monopoly, she insisted on going back home to Laguna Beach. I'm not sure why she feels the need to do this, but I go with it because it works for her and it's not like I'm unhappy. I'd just be happier if she moved in with me.

We've spent almost every day of the past three weeks together having a blast. Since Dahlia isn't working right now, and I'm waiting for Xander to iron out the band's new contract, we've just been roaming around town and having fun with each other. At first, we spent time picking up a few essentials for the house, including a kitchen table and pots and pans, but lately we spend our days running, hiking, going to the Grove to watch movies, to the arcade to play around, or trying different restaurants for lunch. Sometimes we walk along Hollywood Boulevard and other times we just hang out here at home. Most nights, she comes with me to rehearsals and then we go out with Aerie or meet up with the guys.

Regardless of what we do, Dahlia and I usually end up leaving early because I just can't keep my hands off her sexy little body. I can tell she feels the same way, and it's become a game to see who can hold out the longest before we have to leave. Regardless of who wins, making it all the way home has become a challenge and we've found some fun and interesting things to do along the way.

Tomorrow is Dahlia's birthday. I'm so stoked to celebrate with her, so when Bell asked if she could pull together a small party tonight, I told her yes.

Dahlia's on her way here from Laguna Beach with Aerie, and I just walked in the door. I ran out to pick up her present and was hoping Bell would wrap it for me, but as I look around at the chaos that is my house, I think it might have to stay in the brown paper wrapping.

Bell's entourage is following her through the house with loads of party items as she's barking orders. Shaking my head, all I can do is grin. I should have known better. She points to the table as Garrett trails behind her. "Watch out!" she yells as he sets a bag full of cups and plates on the table. "If you so much as smear a speck of icing on that cake, your ass will be banned from this party!"

"Dude, your sister is so bossy," he says, looking at me.

She's unloading box after box as platters of food fill the kitchen counters, alcohol bottles line the bar, and a giant purple cake in the shape of a flower sits on the kitchen table.

Leaning over the bar, I'm watching the craziness unfold. Bell walks through the kitchen gripping dozens of purple balloons by their white strings.

"Bell, you've got to be kidding me!"

She's smiling, looking very pleased with herself as she ties the balloons to the kitchen cabinet handles. "What? She loves purple!"

258 | KIM KARR

"No, not the color, Bell. This." I wave my hand around the room. "A huge blowout party isn't what I agreed to. It wasn't part of the deal."

She swings her head around to look at me. "What deal? You said I could throw a party, and that's what I'm doing. Now don't be such a party pooper!"

She's got an annoying smirk on her face, and I'm losing patience fast. "You said a small, get-to-know-each-other's-friends kind of a party, and this isn't that!"

I should've known better than to think she could ever plan anything on a small scale. Everything she does is over-the-top.

"River! Don't yell at me! Got it? I'm doing this for you. For your new girlfriend, my new friend, and you should be appreciative about it. Not an asshole!"

Then, pointing her finger at me, she continues. "And yell at me again, I'm so telling Mom."

I decide to just apologize so we can move on. "I'm sorry, Bell, darling," I say in a mocking tone. "Really, we're a little old to threaten to tell Mom, aren't we?" Then I remember I wanted to ask her something.

"And by the way, how do you know Dahlia likes purple?" I didn't even know this.

She gloats for a few seconds before answering, "River, come on, she's named after a flower, and everyone knows dahlias are purple."

"Bell, are you drunk?" I have to ask this because that has to be one of the dumbest things she has ever said.

She frowns. "Nooo, I'm not. Are you?"

I just shake my head and inhale deeply.

She starts uncovering plates of food and is setting them on the bar when she notices me glaring at her.

Pointing my finger at her, I say, "I'm blaming you if she's mad."

"Why will she be mad? Everyone loves a birthday party!" She

gives me her biggest, brightest smile before yelling, "Garrett, where are the other trays of food?"

"I'm getting them. Just wait a second, Bell!"

"Well, hurry up, stop taking your sweet-ass time!"

I'm not finding any of this party prep crap amusing, especially since I'm not sure how Dahlia's going to take it. Just thinking about it again pisses me off.

"Motherfucker!" I hear coming from behind me as static and a loud piercing sound come through the speakers. Turning around, I see Nix has unplugged the sound system and is attempting to connect a mixer board to it.

"What the fuck are you doing?"

He points his chin at Bell. "She wants a DJ setup."

"A DJ? For what? Why? This isn't a fucking dance club!"

Shrugging his shoulders, Nix rolls his eyes and points to Bell as he continues to mess with the sound system like he knows what he's doing.

"Bell!" I yell, my patience with her running very low.

She comes around the bar and pulls me by the arm away from Nix.

Something clings to my head as she opens the sliding glass doors. The balloons are in my face and so is Bell.

"You," she says, handing me the white strings. "Cut the shit and start helping."

I can tell by her tone she's had enough, so I decide to cut her some slack and see what sort of great job she has in store for me. It's cool that she did all of this, but all I really wanted was a small get-together. I figured we'd sing "Happy Birthday," eat some cake, the guests would leave, and then I'd get some alone time with my birthday girl.

Clearly that's not the plan now, so taking a deep breath, I look at my sister and raise my hands in surrender. "What do you need me to do?"

Glancing around, I see Xander busy sucking face with some chick he brought with him.

"See all these balloons tied together? They need to be untied and strung around the chairs."

"Chairs?" I ask because the only chairs I own are the ones around the outdoor table, and there are way more balloons than chairs.

Pinching my chin, she turns my head down toward the pool. "Those chairs, the ones you're going to unfold and put around thooooose tables." She points to a stacked pile of round tables over on the other side of the pool.

"Bell, just how many people did you invite?" I have to ask because there are a lot of fucking tables and chairs down there.

●

Pacing back and forth between the party that is now in full swing and the empty dining room, I continue to look out the window. She should've been here over an hour ago.

Earlier, we exchanged a few texts.

Aerie has issues with my clothing choices and insists we make a stop on the way. Be there shortly :)
Maybe it should've been a clothing-optional party ;)
Hopefully later it will be. ;) <3

I haven't even seen her yet, and I already want to skip the party and go directly to the clothing-optional.

In the meantime, I decide to put in my song requests because the music has been awful. There are so many people here that they're blocking my view and I can't even see the Hollywood sign that Dahlia loves so much.

I stop to talk to a few friends I haven't seen in a while. Then I finally make my way over to Daniel, at least I think that's his name.

He's my sister's new boyfriend and he's deejaying the party. Bell is busy filling the dozens of different types of glasses she brought with wine, mixed drinks, and who knows what else. Garrett and Phoenix are busy staying far away from her to avoid getting roped into being waiters.

I head to the kitchen, grab a bottle of beer from the fully stocked refrigerator, and go sit on the couch next to Xander and some blond. I can't remember her name, but I know he's been out with her before.

"Oh my God, River!" she says, and I instantly regret sitting here. Her voice is like a whiny teenage girl's and her giggle sounds like a five-year-old's.

Taking a swig of my beer, I lower my bottle then raise it in her direction. "Hey, great to see you again."

Xander is grinning at me as he says, "Chloe."

He really can be an asshole sometimes. Calling me out for not remembering her name wasn't necessary. I mean, really, he has a different girl with him almost every time I see him, and this girl isn't one of my favorites. Her voice is so high-pitched it actually makes my skin crawl.

"So, River, I love your new house. When did you move in? Do you have a decorator because my BFF is one and I could so introduce you!"

Her lips are moving, but I'm not even listening. She lost me when she said "BFF," but I smile nicely at her. "Sure, that sounds great."

These are the kind of girls I could never stand. The ones who try to be seductive but sound more like a whining toddler. They think they are sexy but they couldn't be more wrong. I feel like I dated a never-ending slew of them before I reconnected with Dahlia. She is nothing like those girls, and I couldn't be happier about that.

My phone starts buzzing in my front pocket. Setting my beer on the new coffee table, I stand up and pull it out. It's a text from Dahlia.

I'm sorry we're so late. Pulling in the driveway now. :)

Glancing at Xander and his bubbly blond, I say, "Excuse me a minute. Dahlia's here and I want to say hi before she hits the door."

"Dahlia? Who's Dahlia?" Chloe asks Xander.

Xander looks at me and answers, "The girl that has my brother pussy-whipped."

I just shake my head and shoot him a dirty look. I'm not going to argue the semantics of *pussy-whipped* versus *love* with him, especially in front of this Valley girl.

"Aren't I right, Loverboy?" he shouts at me as I walk away.

Opening the door, I brace my hands on the frame and watch her get out of Aerie's car. The driveway reflectors shine upward and highlight her amazing body. The shameless blaze in my eyes must be apparent, but I don't care who sees it. She looks hot as hell in that little black number that Aerie must have talked her into buying.

Her dress is short, the neckline is open, and her legs look a mile long in those shoes. When she turns to close the door, I have to shift a little to control myself. Her dress has no back and her blond hair is up in one of those ponytail things so every inch of her bare skin is visible. Images of her and me alone together instantly flood my mind, and I really regret letting Bell throw this party.

Walking down the steps to meet her, I'm overwhelmed by her beauty. Saying hi to Aerie, I position myself right in front of Dahlia. She's almost as tall as me in those shoes and when our eyes meet, she just looks at me, no smile, nothing—and I can tell, even before her lips turn up, that she's feeling seductive.

Her hazel eyes seem to change color depending on her mood, and tonight they are almost brown. I love when they're that color. I also love when her eyes turn goldish green. There is an almost psychedelic quality to them. It's as if I can see myself staring at the same raw images she sees. Her mind is like a camera, and just looking into her eyes makes any great view even better. I once told her that I noticed how they change color. She laughed and said, "So if you think my eyes are like a mood ring, what color are they when I'm being bitchy?"

Leaning in, I inhale the sweet scent of her hair as I kiss the bare skin of her neck all the way up to her ear and softly lower my voice to an intimate level. "Hey, birthday girl. You look beautiful, perfect, really," I say, pulling her hips to mine.

"Hey there yourself," she says, placing her hands on my arms. "Sorry we're late."

Bending her neck, she allows me full access, and I can't help but grin when I notice her goose bumps. Not one to shy away from an invitation, I slowly work my way down her neck to her exposed collarbone. God, everything about her is just so sensual, and I'm so turned-on right now.

"That's okay. If you're late because of this dress," I say, running my hands down the side of her body. "I definitely forgive you. You look so hot."

"Umm . . . ," she moans softly before saying, "thank you," in an extremely low and raspy voice.

Her seductive grin turns to a smile and she points to the driveway. "I thought you said a few people. This looks like way more than a few people. In fact, I'd say it looks like a party."

Before I can explain, I hear Aerie yell from the top of the stairs, "Caleb, you found the place!"

Caleb approaches us and I let go of Dahlia so she can start walking toward him down the driveway. She kisses him on the cheek and they hug each other. It shouldn't bother me that his hands are on the bare skin of her back, but it does. There's something about him I don't like. Maybe it's just because he was best friends with *him*, and most likely, he knows what I know.

She loops her arm through his, leading him back toward me. I can see the glint of that bracelet he gave her that she still wears. I understand why she always wears it, but it bothers me. We talked about it last week, and she explained that it's her no-regrets bracelet. What am I supposed to say to that? Since it makes her happy to wear it, I'm doing my best to be cool with it.

She walks back down to Aerie's car with Caleb, and I extend my hand. "Hey, man, glad you could make it," I manage, trying to keep it real. I snake my arm around my girl and pull her close. I notice his uneasiness right away. Tonight will be the first time we'll be together socially and I'm interested to see how it plays out.

"How've you been? Sorry I couldn't meet you two last week for dinner. I got hung up in a meeting with a new client who needed an entire security system installed in a matter of days."

"It's cool. We'll plan it for another time," I reply, trying not to grit my teeth. "Come on, let's go in." I guide Dahlia in front of me, putting my hand on the small of her back and tucking my fingers inside the cutout of her dress. I swear I feel her quiver.

We all stand around the kitchen table singing "Happy Birthday," and Dahlia blows out the candles. I slip my arms around her waist, hugging her close to me as I stand directly behind her. Once all the candles are out, I kiss her neck and whisper, "Did you make a wish?"

She turns her head to look at me. "Of course I did, but you know I can't tell you."

I just smirk at her because we have gone through this wish thing so many times, but I plan to grant her more than one wish later, so I drop it.

Bell cuts the cake, and I grab Dahlia and pull her into the empty dining room.

"Happy birthday," I say to her since it's after twelve and officially her birthday.

Glancing at my watch, she smiles at me. "Thank you."

I kiss her and my tongue slips slowly into her mouth. Her fingers comb through my hair and I pull away. "Stay here."

She gives me a questioning look but says, "Okay."

As I walk, continuing to face her, my eyes drift over the length of her body. I mouth, "Stay there," and go back to the kitchen to grab a few things.

Xander is standing near the entrance and corners me. "Did you tell her yet?"

I just look at him and walk away. I told him I don't want to talk about it and that I'm not telling her, so why doesn't he just shut the fuck up?

Caleb is talking to Bell, and I wonder if she knows him. He sees me and turns in my direction.

I've been able to avoid him all night until now, so I make it short and sweet. "Just grabbing a few things before Dahlia and I go to bed," I say directly to Bell, but I see Caleb flinch. "Don't worry about cleaning up, I'll take care of it tomorrow," I tell her as I grab a cup of ice, a bottle of beer, and a piece of cake.

I kiss Bell on the cheek. "Thank you."

"See, I knew she'd like it."

My hands are full, so I say goodbye without shaking his hand. "Hey, man, thanks for coming. Don't be a stranger," I say as I walk away.

"River," he says, and I turn around. "Take care of her."

Not really sure of how to respond, I press my lips together before answering. Bell shoots me a disapproving look; so I know my expression mimics my thoughts: *Fuck off.* But instead I respond the only way I can. "Of course I will."

I feel Dahlia's soft fingers grip my side and turn me around, and as she takes the cake from my hands, she says, "Thank you, is this for me?"

We're standing so close. Her eyes are now dark brown, and her expression tells me what I already know.

"Yeah, it's for you." Leaning in, I whisper, "Come with me. I have something I want to give you."

As we enter the bedroom, I take her cake and set it with the beer and cup of ice on the night table.

She eyes it and says, "Party for one?"

Giving her a devilish grin, I walk over and run my hands down her body like I've wanted to do all night. "No, birthday girl, that's what I call a party for two."

Raising an eyebrow, she grins. "Okay, I'll bite. Spill it. What do you have planned in that dirty mind of yours?"

"Well, first, I want to give you your present, and then I'll be happy to share my plan for your birthday wishes."

I grab the gift from the closet and lead her to the bed, where she sits down. As she unwraps the paper, I know this is the perfect gift for her. I was able to score the original handwritten lyrics to U2's "Beautiful Day." I had them mounted in an old-looking black frame that resembles some of the broken ones I saw at her house.

When she recognizes what it is, she lifts her hand to her mouth. Tears start streaming down her face.

"I love it."

She stares at it for a few minutes, running her fingers across a few lines of lyrics before leaning it carefully against the table. She kicks her shoes off and stands up. I stand next to her and just watch. She unzips the side of her dress and pulls it down. She's wearing a black lace bra and panties. Stepping out of the dress she walks closer to me. Her eyes are a brownish green. A color I haven't seen before.

"God, I love you so much," she whispers in my ear as she wraps her arms around my neck and holds on like she might sink if she lets go.

When she says those words to me this time, I feel like she's trying to tell me something else. She moves her lips against mine and I open my mouth, inviting her in.

I pause for a moment, pulling back to look at her, to tell her how I feel. "Dahlia, I love you more than I've ever loved anyone or anything."

She presses my hand over her heart and hers over mine. "Not only does my heart belong to you and yours to me, but I've known since the first time you kissed me that we were soul mates. I knew it that first night in Vegas."

I try to tell her I feel the same way, but she moves her fingers to my lips. "*Shh* . . . Let me finish." She grabs my hands, holds them tightly, and looks right into my eyes. "River, I don't ever want to talk about this again, but this is something I want you to know. I loved Ben, I really did, but when we were together, I never believed in soul mates. I never even thought about it."

She doesn't have to elaborate because I understand exactly what she's telling me.

I blow out a deep breath and relief rushes through me. She feels the same way about me as I feel about her. I keep my mouth shut, and just nod my head.

She runs her fingers down my shirt, pausing at each button as she undoes it, bending and kissing each bare spot along the way. Her fingers skim my bare chest as her lips make their way back up to mine. She's breathless and I'm panting, but I want to proceed with caution. I no longer want to throw her on the bed and fuck her. I'm not sure what prompted the tears and loving confession, and I want to know, but she doesn't seem to want to tell me right now.

Her hands go to my waist and her mouth returns to my chest, where she starts placing hot, openmouthed kisses on her way down to my stomach.

I pull her back up to my face, so I can look in her brown eyes, but they are focused on my lips.

Teetering between wanting to know and not wanting to know, I just ask, "Dahlia, when you opened the lyrics you seemed sad. Why? Does it have something to do with him?"

Sighing, she inhales deeply and tells me, "No. That concert is the last concert I ever went to with my dad. It was the last time I ever went to the Greek." She cups my cheeks as she continues. "I wasn't sad when I opened it, I was happy. Those were tears of joy because you've given me back a memory."

Now I'm the one trying to keep it together. I feel my body start to tremble, overflowing with the amount of love I feel for this girl. She's had so much sadness in her life. As I gently pick her up and carry her to the bed, I feel so lucky that I'm the one who gets to be her happily ever after.

I lay her down and start kissing her stomach. She sits up on her elbows and points to the nightstand. "You promised to explain," she says, and I laugh.

"Explain what?" I ask, my mind still reeling from her confessions.

"Your birthday wishes, silly."

"Ahh, my birthday wishes for you." I smile down at her beauty and I want to do anything to make her happy. I look at her, kiss her, then move to take a piece of ice out of the cup and let it melt on my tongue.

"What are you doing?"

"Dahlia, I'm granting you three birthday wishes."

"You can't grant me wishes if I haven't told you what I wish for, silly, and there is only one wish allowed per birthday, you know."

"Beautiful girl, you should know by now, I have my own set of rules for almost everything and birthday wishes are no exception."

Running her fingers through my hair, she says, "So tell me, genie, what would those rules be?"

"Since you asked, I'm more than happy to tell. In my world, when I get to be the genie, I get to come up with and deliver the wishes."

She giggles then squeals as I take another piece of ice in my mouth and slide my cold tongue down her body, letting the ice cube dance in and out of my mouth along the way. I pause and look up at her as she watches me. "And this is wish number one."

A low purring sound escapes her mouth. "Oh God, River, I love your rules."

CHAPTER 24
I Was Born to Love Her

River

February
3 months later . . .

Shaking my head, I'm kicking myself for not ordering the necklace earlier. I pace the room with the phone to my ear. Mikimoto's says the package should have been delivered to Xander's house yesterday, and if the dick would answer his phone, I'd know. I'm on hold with Federal Express, waiting for them to check the signature delivery log, when the doorbell rings.

Making my way to the door isn't easy. I smile while stepping over all the boxes Dahlia still hasn't unpacked since officially moving in. Thank God, she only brought what she thought we needed and left the rest at Grace's house or else there would be nowhere to walk. We've managed to furnish the entire house and hire a housekeeper, but the unpacking is another story. For some reason, we never seem to find the time to do it. I don't give a shit about any of the domestic supposed-to-do's anyway, because I got my girl, and we're living life sweet and easy.

When I open the door, my asshole brother is standing there grinning. He pushes me aside as he strides into the living room, planting his ass on the couch. "Why have you called me three times since I got in my car this morning?"

"If you'd answer your fucking phone, you'd know, dickhead."

He flops his head back on the couch and spreads his arms over the back like he owns the place. "Since I was on my way here, I didn't see the point in wasting my breath," he says. Reaching into the inside pocket of his leather jacket, he adds, "Dickhead."

Pulling out the black satin box with MIKIMOTO emblazoned in white across the top, he sneers, "You looking for this, Loverboy?"

Turning my head toward the stairs to make sure Dahlia isn't coming, I quickly head over to him. "You couldn't have let me know it came, assface?"

"Assface? Hmmm . . . Maybe I should have just kept it and given it to the first pretty girl I saw tonight. Since it's Valentine's Day, I'm sure a gem like this would guarantee I score."

As soon as I tuck the box away in one of the many partially opened boxes, I walk over to sit at the counter. Dahlia insisted the movers not block the view, so instead, we're tripping over whatever items she unpacks but doesn't put away every time we come in the room.

Xander heads to the kitchen. "Bro, you live with one messy chick."

Shrugging my shoulders at him, I say, "Some of us have more important shit to do than keep house."

"But really, you have a housekeeper. She can't do it?"

"Dahlia wants to do it herself. She'll get around to finishing the unpacking, don't worry your pretty little head about it."

He pours himself a cup of coffee. "Whatever. Better you than me. This mess would drive me fucking insane." Then raising his coffee mug, he asks, "Coffee?"

Chuckling and nodding my head, I say, "Xander, leaving the mail on the counter drives you nuts."

"Speaking of nuts, you were worried the necklace wouldn't get here. Weren't you?"

I swivel my chair as he walks back into the room and tap my fingers on the counter. "Not worried. Concerned."

"Well maybe next time you'll order your girl's gift sooner," he laughs, taking his jacket off.

I nod my head as he sits next to me, handing me one of the cups of coffee. "So the record contract . . . ," he starts to say.

Dropping my foot to the floor, I spin my seat around to face him. "Xander, I don't want to argue about the label's shitty stipulations right now."

"Look, bro, I know your mind is elsewhere." He taps on his phone's screen and pushes it in front of me. "But we need to get this shit straightened out and sign a contract or we won't have a deal."

Glancing at his phone, he's showing me an e-mail listing the changes to our original unsigned contract. I've seen these at least three times, so I roll my eyes.

"Xander, come on. You know the label doesn't want to negotiate, they just want us to agree before we can move forward and cut the damn album."

Also listed in the e-mail are the promotional requirements. I haven't seen these before.

"This touring stipulation is bullshit," I tell him, standing up and continuing to read. "Everyone knows the only reason a label asks a band to tour for nine months is because they don't believe an album can make it on its own."

"You need to quit being a pussy and get over it, River."

Throwing his phone on the couch, I say, "I don't need to quit being anything, Xander."

"Look, just bring her with you," he says, setting his cup down on the counter.

"That's not it." I slump on the couch and shove my boots on the glass coffee table. "I don't want to be on the road that long. I hate that life. Living on a bus, people in my face all day, eating shitty food and drinking every night, never being alone." I finally admit to him my biggest reasons for not wanting to sign.

"Let me see what I can do," he says, maybe finally resigned to the fact that I'm not going to sign that contract. "So, did you tell her yet?"

I bolt straight up. He knows better than to talk about this when Dahlia is in the house.

"No, and I told you I'm not going to."

"Not a smart idea. What if Bell figures it out and tells Dahlia?"

"Bell's not going to figure it out. You only did because I told you. I asked you not to bring it up again, and I meant it."

"River, I understand your need to always protect women more than you think I do, but I think you're making a mistake here. If she finds out, she's going to be really pissed off at you."

"I don't have a need to protect women, Xander. I just don't see the purpose in unnecessarily hurting someone's feelings."

"Yeah, yeah, I get it. You've always wanted a chick you could talk to, not just fuck around with. That's why you hardly ever went out with someone more than once. I told you I get you, and I do. Really. But now you found an amazing girl, and you have it all, so don't fuck it up. That's all I'm gonna say about it. You know I got your back no matter what."

As I hear footsteps coming up the stairs, I quickly throw Xander a *shut-the-fuck-up* look. I turn my head just in time to get a look at my hot girl coming up the stairs.

"Hey there, beautiful."

"Hey there beautiful yourself," she says in a flirty tone.

Looking over to Xander, she smiles at him. She has the most awesome smile. "Xander," she says flatly.

"Muse," he says just as flatly.

"Did you park your Mercedes out front? Because if you did, I hope it doesn't get stolen while you're slumming," she says to him, barely able to contain her laughter, and then they both start laughing.

They've actually become friends since she moved in three weeks ago. It took a while, but one drunken night and many funny USC stories later, they decided they liked each other. In fact, she gets along great with my whole family. She goes out to lunch with my mom and sister at least once a week. My mom even convinced her to buy a lot of the stuff we have in the house. Since moving in, we've bought everything in here together. It's like I bought this house for us. It fits us perfectly; we both love it and we love living here together.

Dahlia enjoys the view and photographs it all the time. We even planted wildflowers together before she moved in. They bloomed last week, and the look in her eyes when she saw them made me want to fuck her right there in the garden. We run the trails every morning and whoever wins gets to soap the other one down. She thinks she wins every time. God, I love her.

She walks over and plops herself on my lap, and I start kissing her neck. "What are you doing here, anyway?" she asks Xander as he walks over, picks up his phone, and sits right next to us.

He leans over as if he's going to kiss her neck, and I shove him hard. "Get the fuck out of here, man. Don't you have someone else to go harass?"

"Actually, I do have people to see and places to go," he says as he stands up. "I can let myself out."

"Great, man, because I wasn't getting up."

"Bye, Xander," she says, waving as he leaves the room, and I turn to her so I can really kiss her. The sound of her voice sends a jolt of electricity through my body that lights up deep within my soul.

Shaking his head at me, he slams the door as he leaves.

I kiss her soft full lips; I run my hand down the back of her Pretenders T-shirt, then up the front. "Alone at last."

"We've been alone all morning, silly," she says, shoving my hand away as I try to slip my fingers into her bra.

"I know, but you've been downstairs." I suck on her bottom lip before moving in for the kill.

"You can visit me any . . ." She stops talking as I slide my head closer to her ear and dip my tongue in it. I know what this does to her.

She moans a soft purrlike sound, and I grin before scooting her off my lap.

"Hey," she says, trying to crawl back on.

"I want to give you something," I tell her as I stride out of the room and into our bedroom.

"I thought that's what you were doing a minute ago," she laughs. "Should I come in there?"

Now I'm laughing. She really is the funniest person I've ever met. "No. Stay there."

As I come back out into the room, I call out, "Close your eyes. No peeking."

She does and I make my way back over to her. "Okay, this isn't my gift to you for Valentine's Day," I tell her as I string the six or so strands of her aunt's pearls around her neck. "This is just something I wanted to do for you because I know how much this means to you." Before I even finish looping the necklace she's clutching it with both hands. When she opens her eyes she looks down at the pearls—a treasured part of her past she once referred to as her magical wishing wells. I had them strung back together for her.

She's a little teary when she asks, "You did this for me?"

"Of course I did. I know how much they mean to you, and I wanted to make you happy."

She jumps up and kisses me before running down the hallway to the mirror while screaming, "I love you. I love you. I love you."

Yeah, I'm good.

●

That evening my heart is beating so loudly I think it's echoing throughout the extremely noisy restaurant. I hold my breath and bite my lower lip in anticipation. She opens the box and to my great relief, she loves it. Her mouth drops open and tears run down her beautiful face as she fingers the necklace I had custom-made for her. "Pearls and a dahlia? How?"

Putting my finger over my mouth and making a *shh* sound, I say, "It's a secret." I stand up, walk behind her chair, and reach around her as I whisper in her ear, "I love you." Then, removing the one-of-a-kind, three-strand pearl necklace with a quarter-size diamond dahlia connecting the individual strands from the box, I clasp it around her neck.

Swiping her long hair to the side, I lean down and inhale that scent I love so much. It smells like some kind of fruit. Orange or grapefruit, I'm not exactly sure. She bows her head when I do this and I kiss the small freckle on the back of her neck. Then I run my finger up her bare back. She is so fucking sexy. Bending down, I lean into her, dragging my tongue up the nape of her neck to her ear. "You taste as good as you look. I'd much rather be eating you than eating here." Then I wait for the goose bumps to emerge. Sure enough, there they are.

Grinning, I walk back to my chair. "Are you ready to go?"

●

She throws her arms around my neck as we wait for the car, and I hold her close and tight. "I love my necklace, and I love you."

She glides her nose over my jaw like she always does when I hug or kiss her. She likes it when I am clean-shaven, and I love how it turns her on. We break apart and I move toward the car.

I open the door for her as I say, "I love you more."

She's fumbling through her purse as I start up the car and pull away, and she pulls out a small black bag. Pointing to the valet's temporary holding spaces, she asks, "Can you pull over there a second?"

Glancing at her, in a dress that leaves little to the imagination, I reach for her hand and grin. "Sure, baby. But can't you wait until we get home?"

I can't help but laugh to myself over my own wit.

She playfully slaps my hand away and doesn't let me grab hold of hers. "River, just pull over."

"Okay, beautiful girl, your call," I say, winking at her, thinking she wants me now.

I put the car in park and turn to face her. She looks like a knockout in that short, strapless black number. The dress exposes so much of her soft skin, it's just calling for me to lick her and the bottom is so short, it's just screaming for me to run my fingers along her thighs. What's really killing me are those high boots; they made me hard the minute I saw her. Honestly, I'm having a hard time keeping my shit together around her tonight. I really should've just taken her into the bathroom, but it's Valentine's Day, and I wanted to make it romantic.

I've never spent one of these heart-filled days with someone I really cared about, so this is all new to me. My sister suggested taking Dahlia to a nice hotel for the night, so that's what I'm doing. I actually made a reservation at the Beverly Wilshire last month. The suites were all taken, but I was able to book a room.

She touches her pearls for a minute while the black bag rests on her lap. She seems pretty happy. Then, with that seductive smile that could thaw the Artic, she says, "Close your eyes, and hold your hands out."

I swallow and nod, squeezing my eyes shut and holding my palms up over the console. As I do, I can feel cool metal objects being carefully placed into them.

"Happy Valentine's Day, River."

Opening my eyes, I see six metal guitar picks, all uniquely engraved. I scan each one before looking up at her. My smile must be wider than any dam ever built to stop a flood.

I transfer all of them into one hand and hold up the one that reads: I LOVE YOU. I stare at her with amazement. "I love you," I whisper while trying to rein in my emotions. I lean over and kiss her, slipping my tongue in her mouth because I want to taste her so badly. I squeeze my palm shut so I won't drop any of the picks and grab her with my free hand. I run my hand through her soft hair and over the smooth bare skin of her neck and shoulders.

She giggles and pulls away, breathing just as hard as I am. "I love you more."

Shaking my head in disagreement, I decide not to engage in our little who-loves-who-more game because I know I'll win. I love this girl more than anybody has ever loved anyone. Instead, I just look at her as she moves her hand to my tightly closed palm.

She begins to pull my fingers open, one at a time, exposing the engraved picks. She takes all of them out of my hand, leaving the I LOVE YOU one in my palm. Selecting one at a time, she reads each engraving to me as if she's whispering sweet nothings.

"Hold Me," she whispers, running her fingertips over the words before gently placing it in my hand with the I LOVE YOU pick. Then she does the same thing with the others as she whispers, "Touch me, kiss me, and love me." Finally, she giggles as she says, "And this is my favorite, 'Loverboy.'"

Once all six gifts are safely in my hand she opens the bag for me to pour them back in. Before I do, I take the Touch Me one and stick it in my front pocket as she looks at me quizzically.

"What? I'm saving it for later. You know, in case I want to cash it in."

"They're guitar picks, silly. They're not sexual-favor chips!"

"I know what they are!" I say, sitting back in my seat and putting the car in the drive. Then, with a glance over at her, I ask, "Did you give these to me as a present?"

Her lips purse in that adorable way she has when she's trying to explain something. "Yessss . . . "

"Well, then, they can be whatever I want them to be."

She just shakes her head at me. "Okay, Loverboy."

We're driving down the highway listening to music when the Mighty Storm's "Through it All" comes on the radio. Dahlia is quiet as she listens to the lyrics. It's almost as if she's trying to memorize it. Once the song finishes, I turn down the volume and look over at her. "Did I ever tell you we opened for Jake Wethers a couple of years ago?"

"Before Johnny died? No fucking way! You knew both of them?" she asks, practically jumping out of her seat.

"Yes fucking way," I respond, but without any of her enthusiasm. I don't apologize for using the F-word since I consciously decided to use it to make my point.

"Wow, you really met Jake Wethers? That's amazing! I would love to meet him. I think he's a musical genius."

"Yeah, the whole situation sucks. He had it together when we met him and his band and I'm sure he'll get through it." I stop to think how hard it would be if I lost someone.

"We even hung out after the show. All of the guys were pretty cool. We actually learned a lot just from playing with them that one time."

"I'm impressed. Jake Wethers. Hmm . . . Who else have you met? Any of the guys from One Direction?"

"No," I laugh. "Their music isn't exactly my type of music, but do you like the D-bags?" I ask her, knowing what I'm about to tell her will definitely freak her out.

"Of course I do! I love Kellan Kyle! You know him, too?"

I nod. "I met him once before we went on our first tour. He was in L.A. with his friend Evan, you know, the drummer in his band?"

"Of course I know who Evan is! Kellan met him on his way to L.A. while passing through Oregon."

"Anyway, they came to Smitten's to jam with us, but that was the last I saw of them. They met a few guys here in L.A. and I think that's when they formed the D-Bags. I never heard of them again until they went on tour last year." I look over at her again as I say, "Bell met Kellan, too. She spent most of the night he jammed with us talking to him in between sets and then met up with him after we were done."

"Your sister went on a date with Kellan Kyle?"

"I wouldn't call it a date, and please don't ask me for the details because I never asked."

"See, you are famous," she says, smiling over at me and finally sitting back down.

"No, I'm really not. I've told you this." I think it's cute that she loves music so much, and that certain artists get her so excited.

As I pass the exit that leads to our house, she points to the sign as I zoom by. "Wait a minute, where are we going?"

"It's a surprise. You'll see, but we're not sleeping at home tonight."

"So, where are we sleeping? Please don't tell me we're sleeping on an air mattress."

Laughing as I turn the music up, I say, "In a bed."

She pouts her lips and reaches out her long, slender arm to turn the volume back down. "In a bed—where?"

I love when she pouts her lips like that. She looks so hot.

"Where are we going?" she huffs again.

I have to laugh because I think she might be having a fit. "You're not going to stomp your feet and cross your arms, are you? Because if you are, I'm going to have to pull over to watch this."

She sticks her tongue out at me, and I try to grab it, but she moves away too quickly.

I turn the music back up and sing along, waiting for her next question, but she's good at playing any game I throw her way. She doesn't say anything as she shifts in her seat and hikes her dress up just a little higher. I give her a quick glance and look back at the road. I can play, too. She stretches and her top slips down slightly. Damn, she's good. I keep singing and humming, thumping my fingers to the beat on the steering wheel, trying to ignore her.

Then, she breaks and starts to speak. I grin over at her.

"So, are you going to tell me where we're going?" she asks again.

"Nope."

"Well, that's too bad because I have a secret I want to share. And I was thinking a trade was in order. You know, one for one," she says, twisting a little, leaning her elbow on the console, and placing her chin in the palm of her hand.

"Not interested."

"Oh, I think you might be, especially since it has something to do with what I'm wearing . . . oh, I mean, not wearing."

I whip my head around at her. "You're lying."

Sitting up straight, she runs her fingers from the top of her boots to beneath her skirt where I can't see them anymore. "Tell me where we're going and find out for yourself."

Instantly reaching my hand over to her lap, I blurt out, "The Beverly Wilshire." I drive faster so I can just get there already.

Okay, so she's good.

"Oh, my God. I've heard it's amazing there! How'd you manage to get a reservation for Valentine's Day? I thought they book out almost a year in advance."

I have to laugh because she thinks she knows me so well already, and actually she does.

Tapping my fingers on her leg, I say, "I'll never tell."

"Fine, be that way."

"Providing details wasn't part of the trade. But a deal's a deal."

My fingers start to creep up her thigh. I get hard instantly at the feel of her soft skin. Actually, I feel like I've had a raging hard-on since she put those thigh-high boots on. I don't give a shit about hearts and flowers anymore. I want her. I need to taste her. I want to be inside her. So I drive even faster.

I run my fingers all the way up the inside of her legs. Fuck, she wasn't lying. She's not wearing panties. I start to move my fingers and I can feel how wet she is. She's just so fucking hot. Then suddenly she presses her hand on top of mine and pushes it away.

Grinning mischievously, she says, "That's enough for now." Shocked, I look over at her, and she seems to be the perfect picture of calmness.

On the other hand, my pulse is racing, and I feel like I'm now the one who's going to have the tantrum. "What? Why?" I mutter.

She takes my hand and holds it in hers as she crosses her legs. "Because, providing details wasn't part of the trade."

I'm horny as hell as I pull up to the hotel, and I hope the evidence in my jeans isn't too noticeable as I hand the valet my keys. I've already checked us in, and I have the room key in my pocket, so we head straight to the elevators.

We're finally alone in the elevator. My heart is beating about seven times too fast as I reach out and grab her. Pressing her body against the wall, I pull her mouth to mine and enjoy the taste. This is not a loving, romantic kiss. That moment has passed.

"I want you—now," I manage between my wet, tongue-filled kisses.

"I want you, too."

Staggering out of the elevator, not wanting to unlock my lips from hers, I try to pull the key out of my back pocket, but she's distracting me. Her fingers are in the waistband of my boxers, and she's sliding them around to the front, trying to unbutton my fly as I blindly reach behind me and pull the key card out.

We make our way to the room, and I somehow manage to open the door. As we enter, I shove her dress down, and it immediately falls to the ground. Fuck, she isn't wearing a bra, either. I step back to look at her. She's standing in front of me in only her fuck-me boots and pearls. I really want to take a picture of her. I know I'll never forget her image like this, right now, but I want to be able to see her whenever she's not with me.

She stands there watching me watch her. I see her breath picking up speed as she runs her fingers through her hair.

I take another step back and glance around the room. "Champagne?" I ask, pointing to the bottle chilling on the table near the window and the bowl of strawberries next to it.

"Absolutely," she says, standing there biting her lip.

I pop the cork and pour us each a glass, adding two strawberries to hers. "Can I ask you something?"

"Sure, anything," she answers, and I love that she feels completely comfortable with her body around me.

"Can I take your picture?" I'm a little nervous asking because I really have no idea what she will say, other than call me a pervert probably.

She slowly walks over to me and takes her glass of champagne from my hands. She takes the berry I pushed onto the rim, dips it in the liquid, and bites. "Maybe we can barter?"

Swallowing at the sight of her, all of my nervousness is gone.

I take another berry from the bowl, dip it into her glass, and press it to her lips. "Oh, yeah. What did you have in mind?"

"I want a picture, too."

"You want a naked picture of me in pearls and boots?"

Giggling, she says, "No, I want a picture of you . . ." She sets her glass down and quickly unbuttons my shirt, tossing it aside. "Wearing only your jeans and . . ."

Moving my mouth to hers, I lick the champagne off her lips. "And?"

"Take my picture first," she says, sucking on my bottom lip for a second before moving back.

Shrugging my shoulders, I reach into my front pocket and pull out my phone. The TOUCH ME pick is in there as well. I smile as I pull it out. "I'll save this for later," I say, holding it up before placing it on the table.

She starts to make all sorts of absurd poses, and I pretend to be a fashion photographer telling her what to do. We do this for at least five minutes as her poses go from nice to naughty, and my horny meter shoots off the charts.

"Okay, playtime is over. Time for the real picture."

"Okay, bossy pants," she says with her hands on her hips. "Where do you want me?"

"Right there." I point to where she's standing as I lean over and gently kiss her. "Thank you."

She gives me a soft smile, and I hit the camera button three times to ensure one of the pictures is good. I scroll to the camera roll and look. "You really are so beautiful, Dahlia." I hand her my phone to look.

"I don't want to see myself naked, you pervert," she quips, and I start laughing. I grab our glasses and, handing her hers, I toast, "Happy Valentine's Day, beautiful girl."

"Happy Valentine's Day, River. I love you."

We both take a sip and I grab another berry from the bowl and dip it in her glass, but this time I don't run it over her lips. I trail it down her chest. Then, with the tip of my tongue, I follow the path I made with the champagne. Her nipples harden instantly as I circle one then the other before sliding my tongue back up her chest, her neck, and to her ear where I whisper, "I want you now."

"Ah ah ah," she says, waving her finger at me.

Walking over to the bed where she threw her purse, she pulls out a tube of lipstick and smears it on her lips.

"You don't need that, you know. It's not like we're going anywhere," I tell her.

"I know. It's for my picture."

"I already took your picture, Dahlia."

"No, silly, the one I'm taking of you."

"Oh, no, I'm not wearing lipstick," I warn. "That wasn't part of the deal."

Walking back over to me with that tube in her hand, she says, "Oh, you're wearing it, just not on your lips."

She starts firmly pressing her lips all over my shoulders, chest, and stomach. When she finishes, she pushes me over to the bed. "Lie down."

"Who's the bossy one?" I laugh.

She ignores me and grabs for her phone. If I'm lucky, it will be dead. *Shit. I guess not.* She starts snapping pictures of me.

"I'm not posing," I tell her as I just lie on the bed with my hands behind my head.

"Suit yourself."

I love how easygoing she is.

"Done," she says.

Now, finally we can do what I've wanted to do since I saw her in those boots—well, actually, what I want to do every time I look at her. And since it's Valentine's Day, I'm going to take it slow and make love to this beautiful, fun, sexy, and simply amazing girl.

I stand up, shove my jeans and boxers off, step out of them as quickly as I can, and tell her, "Good, because I'm not."

CHAPTER 25
Diamonds

River

6 months later . . .

I jerk him toward me and get right in his face, gripping a fistful of his preppy shirt. "She's *mine*. You don't deserve her, you never did."

He stares at me, unfazed, before angrily shaking me off. "Is that how you see it? I see things a little differently. You filled a void I left behind, but that's all you'll ever be; a substitute for the real thing."

Lunging at him, I punch him square in the jaw. He doesn't move to hit me back; in fact he doesn't physically engage me at all, but the pain he causes is deeper than any physical impact could have ever been.

Wiping his mouth with the back of his hand, his eyes narrow on mine. "Believe whatever the fuck you want, pretty boy. She was mine first, and she'll always be mine. Nothing you ever say or do can change that." Then he turns and walks into the night.

Yelling, "She's not your anything!" I feel a tug at my arm. I open my eyes and pop up on my elbows. The room is pitch-black. I can't see anything. She shifts in the bed and a flick of the light switch has me instantly squinting. The light from the lamp shines on her golden hair as she strokes my cheek. "Are you okay?"

I try to shake it off. It was just a dream. It wasn't real. I will never lose her. I swallow a few times before answering, "Yeah, I'm fine."

When I lie back down, she rests her head against me. Settling onto the pillow, she kisses me just under my jaw. "Want to talk about it?"

"No. I can't even remember what it was about," I lie. I've been having these dreams almost every night for the past week, ever since I bought her engagement ring.

"You sure?"

With a deep breath, I push back the dread that's making its way up my throat. I don't need to answer her. I'd rather show her I'm okay. I look over at her, and I think about how much I love that we don't care what side we fall asleep on as long as we're together. Running my slightly trembling hand down her back, I roll her on top of me.

A small smile forms on her lips. "Are you sure you even had a bad dream? Or did you just want to have sex in the middle of the night?" She leans her head down to my mouth and runs her nose over my stubbled jawline. I inhale her citrus scent, feeling thankful she is here with me.

I laugh and wish that were true as I brush strands of her hair out of her face. "I didn't think I had to fake a bad dream to have sex with you. But now that you mention it, I certainly like the idea. And I figure since we're both up, why not?"

I roll my tongue along the exposed skin of her neck as my hand glides up the inside of her thigh. The moment I slip my fingers inside her, a small moan escapes her lips and her body arches, preparing for what I hope to give her forever.

●

$\mathcal{I}$ had to approach the subject cautiously. I knew she had to go back there to be okay with it again. Before I can ask her to move forward with me, she has to accept her past. And the fact that she refuses to return tells me she hasn't. My father used to say that scars are the road maps to one's soul, but her soul is beautiful and I don't need a road map to find it; I reach it every day that we're together. What bothers me is what he said about scars that can't be seen—the emotional ones. We all have them but hers are deep. I want to be the one to help her heal those wounds.

This is why I want to take her back there. Not only so she can see my band perform, although of course I want her to be there. But I know I can't help her with the scars *his* death left on her. I can't even talk about *him* with her. I know it's wrong and I try, I really do. I just can't. I hate him and can't get past that. I can only hope that loving her enough and being there for her has already started the healing process.

I was reluctant at first when Xander told me he arranged for the Wilde Ones to perform at the Greek. Yes, it was definitely a great opportunity for the band to preview some of the songs from our new album, but I wasn't sure if I could get Dahlia to go. Then I realized this was my opportunity to bring her back there and make it a happy place for her once again. Also, truth be told, I want her there with me to kick off this tour, especially since I'm not really into it. Trying but failing miserably to come up with the right way to persuade her, I decided to call Grace and ask her to meet me for lunch. I thought about calling Serena since she and Dahlia talk almost every day, but I decided Grace was the better choice because she knows Dahlia so well.

Meeting *his* mother to ask for advice seems odd but I know it's the right thing to do. Grace has been like a mother to her, ever since she lost her own. I just had to forget about *him* and push away my feelings like I've done since I saw *his* picture at her house.

On my way to the restaurant, I stopped by Dahlia's house to check on it. She still owns it. She's gotten a few offers but none close to her asking price, so she's refused them all. I don't want to push her, but I know her refusals aren't based on money. I think she's just having a hard time letting go.

I arrived at Caffe Riace before Grace and asked for an outdoor table. I knew, just like Dahlia, that Grace loved being outside. So now I'm sitting in the late-afternoon sun, wishing I hadn't left my sunglasses in the car. I blink the bright sun out of my eyes as I type out a text to Dahlia.

> *Just thought you should know how hot you looked this am in those boots I love so much. BTW not sure I'm crazy about you wearing them to meet with your first client. I love you.*

Her response is immediate.

> *LOL since my first client is a 50 yr old woman I don't think u have anything to worry about. BTW even if I were meeting Adam Levine you'd have nothing to worry about. I love you more. <3 :-**

I laugh to myself. I love her more than she could possibly ever know, but we have fun debating who loves whom more. Suddenly a shadow blocks the sun as I sit here grinning. Before I can respond to Dahlia's text, I look up and see Grace approaching me. She reaches the table and unbuttons her jacket as I stand and give her a kiss. I pull out her chair. She sets her purse on the table and immediately puts her napkin on her lap.

We order lunch, and the waiter brings our drinks. I decide to first tell her about my upcoming proposal. Her reaction is pure happiness, as if Dahlia is truly her own daughter. She even sheds a few joyful tears

as she congratulates me and gives me her blessing. Once our food arrives, we talk about my upcoming tour and the impact it will have on
Dahlia's new photography business. I explain to her that Dahlia didn't
take on a heavy load of clients who needed album covers completed
during the tour. For the ones she did offer to style and photograph, she
plans to fly back to L.A. to complete the jobs.

I push my plate aside and rest my hands on the table. "Grace," I
say as she looks up at me. "I'm hoping you can give me some advice."

"Of course, you know you can ask me anything."

"Well, it's about Dahlia's parents, her dad, really. My band is going to be performing at the Greek in a few weeks and I really want her
there. Not just to see us perform but because I want it to be a happy
place for her again. And maybe if she does, she'll let some of her demons go."

She finishes her salad and sets her fork down, wiping the corner of
her mouth. "River, that is so special. I think you simply need to tell her
how you feel, how much you want her there with you. She'll go, knowing how important it is to you. I know she will. She loves you so much."

The waiter clears the table, and Grace orders a cup of tea. "I think
it's just the anticipation of going back there that frightens her. She's
been afraid to be surrounded by memories of all those special times
with her father. But knowing how much she loves you and how you
make her feel so safe, I believe she's ready to confront her past. And,
yes, I do think it will help her put some of her ghosts to rest."

❦

The drive to the Greek was quiet. I held her hand as she fidgeted
the whole way there. I knew she was nervous, and so was I. Not
because I was performing, but for her. After meeting with Grace, I'd
waited a few days and then, just as she had suggested, I asked Dahlia
straight-out to go with me. She was hesitant at first but didn't say no. I
explained to her that Xander had arranged the gig to help straighten

out some contract issues involving the band's upcoming tour and that I really needed and wanted her to be there with me. That was true, but not the entire reason. After thinking about it for only a moment, she reluctantly agreed. I even arranged for Aerie, Grace, Serena, and Trent to sit with her.

Once we arrived, her doubts passed immediately. This was evident on her face and in the color of her eyes. It was like watching a child at an amusement park. As we walked through the gates, I knew her happy memories were pushing the sad ones aside.

Now, lying together on our bed, I smile about beginning to take that step together. I look at her and run my fingers over her bare stomach while we kiss. She smiles and pulls me closer. As we lie in each other's arms, she thanks me again for taking her back to the Greek. She laughs as she reminisces about all the concerts she saw there with her dad.

When she's finished, I lean in to kiss her as my hand gently rubs circles down her back. "Thank you for agreeing to go back there. I know it wasn't easy for you, but I thought you needed to go, and it was important to me that you be there for our kickoff show."

As I gently press kisses along her mouth, she moans against my lips. "I know, and I'm so glad I went. You were amazing, and the Greek was just as amazing as I remember it. The whole night has been truly amazing."

I pull back to look at her lovingly. "Dahlia, you're the amazing one, and I'd do anything for you. I want you to be happy, always."

She doesn't say anything else; she just crashes her lips to mine as her fingers knot into my hair. I respond instantly. My hands wander up her naked body, touching each rib, sliding along the curve of each breast until they meet her hands in my hair where I clutch them and pull them down to our sides, holding her tightly, just for a moment.

Letting go of her hands, I softly trail my fingers back up her body, playfully teasing her along the way, but stop at her heart to trace it. I can feel the goose bumps form on her skin as I lower my head down to kiss the line I just etched. "I love you."

I kiss my way back up to her lips and gently cup her chin. I look into her eyes and tell her exactly how I feel. "Dahlia, I will love you forever." Then I kiss her and say, "In this lifetime and in the next."

She clutches my face, and I see love and desire in her slightly hooded eyes. "River, I love you. So much."

I smile at her. "You are everything I have ever dreamed about; you are my dreams." I see tears welling in her eyes, and I don't want them to spill, so I kiss her softly, deeply, pouring all of my love into it. Her head falls back further into the pillow and her breathing picks up speed. I can't hold back any longer. I want nothing more than to be buried deep inside her, to feel our bodies as one, our souls forever connected.

The feel of her lips as she drags them down my jaw, along my neck to my chest makes me shiver with need. Tracing circles along the inside of her thighs, I slip one finger inside of her, test her wetness, and I know she's so ready for me. I tease her a bit as I gently circle around, in and out, until she can't take it any longer.

"River," she cries out as she arches her back, her breathing quick and shallow, her eyes shut. "Please, I want to feel you inside me, make love to me." As I easily slip inside her, her arms lace around my neck and her legs wrap around my body to pull me closer, and I know this is the woman I always want to be with.

●

A few weeks after the concert at the Greek, I decided it was time to ask her to be my wife. I wanted her to be mine, more than anything I had ever desired. My plan to pop the question was simple—take her to one of her favorite places and ask her. Getting her there was just as simple. All I had to do was suggest we go for a sunset run; she always wants to go running. But arranging it all to go as planned was not so simple. There were so many variables, so I decided to stick to the basics.

We pull into the parking lot in the late afternoon, and it's one of the hottest days of the summer. Walking up to the hiker's entrance, she steps forward, leaving just a few inches between us. "You sure you want to do this? Because I know just as well as you do that this little climb isn't going to be easy in the scorching sun, and I'm not afraid to admit it." She steps back, and I can see her eyes are deep brown as she smiles at me.

She lunges forward to stretch, touching her fingers to her toes as her sweatpants ride down her hips a little. Damn, she's good. She knows I'm powerless against her when she struts her body around like that. It drives me crazy—but what she doesn't know is the reason why I'm making this four-mile uphill hike in the blistering sun. So I play her game and act indecisive so she thinks I really don't want to do this. Damn, I'm good. I even paid off the guard to stop anyone from following behind us. This way, when we reach the top of the hill, we will be all alone. Just the way I need it to be.

I fold my arms over my chest and watch her.

She walks down the path and turns her head over her shoulder. "You coming?"

I run up behind her and pick her up. She squirms to try to free herself and she could if she really wanted to because her backpack prevents me from holding on tight. I set her down and laugh, "You know I never turn down a challenge."

She is still laughing when she turns to look at me, and her beauty takes my breath away. She is just so natural and carefree. I have no doubts this is the girl for me—forever. With her I've had the best days of my life and I know there are only better ones to come.

As we approach the top, we're walking single file up the dirt trail. My eyes follow her every move as she leans forward, stepping up onto the plateau.

She takes her camera out of her backpack. "I just want to snap a few photos before the sun loses its glow."

Before handing it to me, she slips her Pac-Man bracelet off and zips it safely away. "Do you mind holding this while I climb up the *H*?"

"You sure that's safe?" I ask because I've never heard of anyone actually climbing up the letters.

She sees the worry on my face. "Hey, sure it is." She points to the letter and says, "It's not that high."

"Beautiful, first of all, it is that high but I'm not thinking of up," I say as I gesture below us into the valley. "I'm thinking of down."

Taking a sip of water, she nods and kisses me. "I'll be right back." She hands me her water bottle.

"Hey," I yell as she climbs the fence to get closer to the letters, leaving me holding all of her shit. "What do I look like? A pack mule?"

She looks over and winks at me. "Never thought of you that way. A jackass maybe on occasion, but not a mule."

I take a gulp from her water bottle, set everything on the ground, and follow her. Does she really think I'm going to let her climb up there alone?

Standing below the *H*, the letters are enormous. "Umm . . . Dahlia, I'm not sure you can do this. There is nothing for you to grip onto. You'd have to pull all of your body weight up the pole."

"Are you saying I can't?"

"I'm saying you more than likely won't be able to."

"Care to make a bet?"

All I can do is laugh. "Baby girl, I'm not even going to bet you on that because it would just be plain wrong."

With her camera hanging from her neck, she pouts her lips and folds her arms in front of her, surveying the letter.

"Dahlia, just give me your camera, I'll take the picture."

She stands there, still pouting. Removing the camera from her neck, she hands it to me.

I take it and whisper in her ear, "Watch out. You know what your bitchy mood does to me. That look was so hot."

True to form, she rolls her eyes and then takes a seat on the ground.

Somehow I manage to pull myself up to the first rafter and balance against the crossbeams to take the picture my girl really wants.

As I descend, I give her the camera and she hands me the water. I finish the bottle and toss it next to our stuff.

She comes to stand between my legs and presses up against me, chest on chest, cupping my cheek with one hand and slipping her other hand into the waistband of my track pants. "Thank you."

My pulse jumps and my whole body responds, but I have a question to ask her—a plan that I have to stick to right now.

My voice becomes husky. "Unless you want to be naked very soon, I think it's best if you don't touch me like that up here."

Pulling up my T-shirt, I wipe the sweat from my face as her hands instantly find my bare abs. I do my best to ignore the overwhelming need I have for her by chanting, "Stick to the task at hand, stick to the task at hand," to myself. I walk over to the backpack and unzip one of the compartments and discreetly tuck the box in the waistband of my pants, careful for her not to see.

"What are you looking for?" she asks.

"My phone, I wanted to see what time it was," I tell her as I quickly pull out my phone.

I know she's watching me from behind, so I twist my head. Her smile, her eyes, her amazing beauty stops me in my tracks. I don't even wink or make a comment. I just know by the way she's looking at me right now, that this is the right time.

Walking back over to her, I lean in, clutch her face with both hands, and start to kiss her. I trace the seam of her lips with my tongue and she opens her mouth. Pressing my lips harder against hers, our tongues meet and I feel our souls connect, in the exact same way she described it to me on her birthday. The moment couldn't be any more perfect. The sun is starting to set over the horizon; the city we live in together is below us; and the sign she loves so much surrounds us.

Dropping down on one knee, I look up at her beautiful face. I can already see tears starting to form in her eyes as I begin to speak. "I never imagined I could feel so connected to someone as much as I feel connected to you. I knew I loved you from the moment I saw you. How could I not? Loving you is as easy as breathing."

I open the box where the custom-made, diamond-encrusted pearl ring sits. Like her necklace, the pearl sits inside a flower, a dahlia, attached to an eternity band of diamonds, representing my everlasting love. My hands are shaking so badly as I take the ring out of the box and stand. I want to look directly into her beautiful eyes when I ask her the most important question I will ever ask anyone in my life.

"Dahlia London, you know I love you more than any man has ever loved a woman. My love for you runs deeper than any words can convey. My heart is yours forever. Will you marry me?"

I'm still shaking, I'm so fucking nervous; this girl owns me and the fact that I want it that way scares the living shit out of me but makes me the happiest man alive.

Her words are the words I've been waiting to hear since the minute I laid eyes on her. "Yes, yes, yes, yes . . ." Her yeses continue until I pull her to me and kiss her like I've never kissed her before. All the love I have for her is pouring out of my heart and into hers. She wraps her arms around my neck as tightly as she can and I swing her around in circles. Once I set her back down, I take her hand and slide the ring on her finger. It's the perfect ring for the perfect girl.

Tears are streaming down her face, and they are not letting up. I hug her as tightly as I can. Whispering into her ear, I say, "Hey, baby, it's okay. This is a happy time. Not a time for all these tears."

Kissing her neck, I graze my teeth over her skin, and she giggles. I pull back and wipe her tears with my fingers, and I can't help but smile when I see goose bumps on her arms. I want to cry with her, I'm so happy, but I don't. Instead, I just look at her. At the same girl who, when I first saw her across the room our eyes met and our souls were forever connected.

CHAPTER 26
Victim

River

September
10 months later . . .

Picking the location for our weekend getaway was simple. I know Dahlia loves beautiful views and the outdoors, so I picked a place where we can enjoy both. The band finished the album and the label is getting ready for it to drop, the promotional bonanza has begun, and the tour starts in six weeks. With all the chaos about to unfold, I wanted to spend some time alone, just the two of us, so I didn't tell anyone where we were going and wanted to surprise her.

Once the album promotion begins, I know our life together will change for a while. I've been through it before. It will be months of craziness. We'll be living on a bus, in a different city every night, crammed together without any privacy. I'm doing this for Garrett, Nix, and Xander, because if it were only for myself, I'd gladly stay in L.A. playing small venues.

Even though I'm not looking forward to the album launch, Dahlia's extremely excited for me. She's agreed to start the tour off with me but has to return to L.A. to complete some jobs that have to be shot before the end of the year. I hate that she'll be by herself. I feel like she's already spent so much time alone in her life. Now that she has me, I don't ever want that for her.

Bell suggested Monterey Bay for our escape, but I nixed that idea immediately. Dahlia grew up on the beach; she loves it, and actually, so do I. But the reason that it's not one of my favorite places to take her is *him*. We've gone to the beach a few times, mostly when we go to Grace's house. But when we're there, I feel like she's not truly with me. She stares out into the water almost like she's looking for him. I've thought about discussing it with her, but as soon as we leave the beach, she's always back to herself, and it seems unnecessary to bring it up.

Right now, as we ride the ski lift and I look over at her goldish green eyes, I can see what she sees. There are hundreds of miles of beauty below us. The wet snowflakes fall down onto the mountaintops as the crisp, cool wind carries them across the summit. The tall evergreen trees are reflected in the lake below us, as their branches bend back and forth. We can see the trails we ran earlier that lead to a breathtaking view of the stream. Now, as we sit under the blue California sky, waiting to ski down Pinball Mountain, I can see all of that. Before I met her, I would have only seen the snow-topped mountain that I'm about to ski down.

I ask, "You sure about this?" She insisted we ski this mountain because of its name. I tried to discourage her when she told me she wanted to try it because it's a black diamond.

Thinking back, it was pretty dumb of me to have agreed, but who am I to say no? Now that we're about halfway to the top of the mountain, she's fumbling with the goggles on her head, and I think she's second-guessing herself.

I pull her hat down to keep it from falling off. "You nervous?"

She looks at me, her cheeks rosy from windburn, but still doesn't answer.

"Did you hear me?" I ask, tapping my pole against her ski before leaning over and kissing her. She still doesn't answer me so I suck on the corner of her bottom lip before gliding my head closer to her covered ear. "Can you hear me now?"

Even though the skin on her neck is not visible, I know she's covered in goose bumps. She blinks her eyes a few times. "Sorry. Just thinking. We're pretty high up, aren't we?" she says, and I know she's nervous.

"Hey." I grab both poles in one hand so I can tilt her chin to look at me. "I'll stay with you, and we'll zigzag down the mountain or walk if we have to. It'll be fun and you'll be able to say you skied Pinball Mountain."

She nods her head, and I decide it's time to take her mind off her poor decision to graduate from the much easier blue trails and go directly to the black.

"So are we having sex in the hot tub again tonight?" I ask, not that I really care where we have sex but more because I love thinking about her cute naked body all the time.

"River!" she says as if she's shocked, but she's not. "If we decide now, that takes all the spontaneity out of it." But she grins, bumping her shoulder into mine.

Pointing to the mountain I know will take us forever to get down, I say, "Sorry, beautiful girl. I forgot how spontaneous you are. I just want to know what to expect when we finally make it to the bottom."

She laughs and pulls her goggles down, preparing herself to exit the lift. Pulling mine down as well, I adjust my hat and get ready to ski down Pinball Mountain.

After cautiously making our way down most of the mountain, we finally get to the last slope, and I ski ahead of her. Swooshing my way to the bottom, I chuckle as I watch her snow plow down the last stretch.

She catches me watching her and comes to a stop next to me. "Show-off."

"Had enough?"

She nods her head emphatically.

Moving around her, I put my pole into each of her rear bindings and she steps out of her skis. I do the same. I lean our skis against the rack, and the valet comes over to take them. With my arms wrapped around her waist from behind, I lean my chin on her shoulder and whisper, "Let's go inside and get a drink." I walk with her in front of me, my arms still holding her tightly as we head into the lodge.

As we approach a table near the stone fireplace, she takes off her gloves, goggles, and hat. Her beautiful but messy hair hangs around her head. She runs her hands through it trying to tame it, then reaches in her pocket and pulls out a hair tie.

As she pulls her hair back, I say, "Don't put it up. I love your hair like that."

"Messy and windblown?"

"I just love it down. You know that."

She smiles and shrugs her shoulders. "Whatever. You're the one who has to look at it."

As she takes off her coat, I can't help but think how fucking hot she looks and she doesn't even know it. She has these tight little black pants on with a snug white turtleneck. I laugh to myself when I see she's wearing black-and-white-striped socks. In the past ten months, I've never seen her wear anything that wasn't a shade of white, gray, or black. She looks hot in everything, so she obviously knows what to wear.

"How about we try a hot toddy?" she says as we sit down in the chairs near the fireplace.

"I'm not drinking anything with the name *toddy* in it. It scares me. I'll stick with hot chocolate," I say just as the valet brings us our boots.

I bend to put my boots on and notice she's watching me. "What is it?"

"Thank you."

"For what? Not wanting a hot toddy?"

"No, silly. For helping me down Pinball Mountain."

"Well, you know that did take an exceptionally long time."

"Yesss," she says in her standard-response tone when she knows I'm fishing for something.

Sitting up, I roll my shoulders, one then the other. "I'm feeling pretty *sore* from catching you so many times."

She drags her eyes slowly across my shoulders as she bites her lip. "Well, then, I think you might be in need of a massage."

Wiggling her fingers, she adds, "And as luck would have it, you're in the company of one of the best masseuses around."

Shooting her a devilish grin, I say, "A massage? Or anything of my choice?"

She laughs and shrugs her shoulders. "Anything of your choice, like what?"

"You'll see."

She shakes her head at me, and I can't help but smile. Watching her now, so natural, so beautiful, I know why it only took that one meeting so long ago to know she owned me. It's like I was hers from the very first time I looked into her beautiful eyes.

We decide to head to our room after we finish our hot chocolate. Once we're in the elevator, I grab her and kiss her. Her response is immediate, and we have a full-blown makeout session. We can hardly keep our hands off each other long enough to open the door, and we stumble into our hotel room practically wrapped around each other. Crushing my mouth into hers, I kick the door shut behind me.

As I trace my tongue over the seam of her soft lips, I can taste the hot chocolate she just drank downstairs.

"Mmmm . . . you taste like chocolate," I whisper in her ear, my hands now resting on her cute ass.

"You like that?" she answers back in a sexy whisper.

"Mmmm hmm . . . ," I moan again.

"We could order some more from room service. Or better yet, chocolate cake."

"Whatever you want. As long as I get to taste it on you, I'm in."

She turns her head and playfully bites my earlobe while her fingers trace patterns up and down the back of my sweater. I'm so turned-on right now, but I need to take a shower. This sweater is itching the shit out of me and has me sweating my balls off.

Reluctantly pulling away, I give Dahlia a quick kiss. "Order whatever you want. I'm going to jump in the shower. I stink and I don't want you spending the night having to smell me," I tell her, walking backward toward the shower.

Giggling, she throws herself onto the huge bed and hangs one leg off the side. "Go ahead. You've kind of killed the mood anyway."

"Just keeping it real." I wink at my beautiful fiancée, lying on the bed where I can't wait to join her after I clean up. Then I add, "I won't be long! And, Dahlia, I can bring the mood back in two seconds flat."

She shakes her head and rolls her eyes. "Whatever you say, Loverboy."

"Care to make a bet?"

"Actually, I'm going to pass on this one because I think I just might lose," she laughs. "Go shower, I need to call Aerie and Serena and check in with them anyway."

She sits up and grabs her phone as I turn around.

Twisting my head back, I see my girl, once again checking me out from behind. I catch her doing this all the time, and I love it. She's used to getting caught, so she just shrugs her shoulders and blows me a kiss. I wink at her as she's dialing, and then I hear, "Hey, Aerie, it's me."

I hear her laughing and giggling with Aerie, and it makes me smile. I love that sound. I could listen to it all day; it's like one of my favorite songs.

The glass walls are starting to fog up as I step inside the steamy shower. The hot water feels great on my muscles after skiing and bending down to pick Dahlia up off the ground all day. The itching from my sweater slowly lets up as I soap up my back. Thinking of Dahlia's face as we stood at the top of that black diamond trail on Pinball Mountain, I can't help but laugh out loud. She looked slightly petrified, but she was determined to make her way down that mountain on her own—and she did, well, most of it, anyway.

Closing my eyes as I rinse the shampoo from my hair, I sense her near me. When I open my eyes I smirk because she's standing against the sink, arms crossed, just watching me.

"Hey, beautiful girl, whatcha doing?" I want her to be standing next to me, not way over there.

Attempting to lift her tight sweater off she asks, "Mind if I join you?"

"Hmmm . . . Let me think about that," I say, and then I quickly dunk my head under the water to rinse the last of the soap off before exiting the shower and heading toward her. She has her sweater halfway off when I grab her and pick her up, clothes and all, and haul her ass back inside the shower with me.

"Do you really think you have to ask me a question like that?"

Her breathing is hitched and I know she knows she doesn't.

Setting her down under the showerhead, I lean back against the glass wall and watch as the warm water pours down her body, drenching her clothes. She's giggling, not whining like a lot of girls would. God, she's so amazing.

But right now, I'm thinking I'd love to see her sexy body naked.

Enough of the giggling. Pointing to her soaking wet sweater, which looks like it weighs a ton, and her wet pants clinging to her long legs, I say, "You've got too many clothes on for what I have in mind. Why don't you take them off?"

"You want me to take this off?" she asks, pointing to her clothes.

"Yeah, I do."

"I'll try," she says, looking at me coyly, intentionally taking her time pulling off her sweater. I know she's attempting to tease me.

"Let me help." I walk over to her, undo her jeans, and shove them down.

She wobbles a bit, but I hold her hips steady. She smiles down at me as droplets of water spill down her angelic face.

Standing up, I push her back against the wall and start to kiss her.

She pushes me back a little and runs her hands up her breasts. Then, with the most innocent smile I have ever seen, she asks, "Do you want to take this off, or do you want to fuck me wearing it?"

Normally, I would laugh at her saying "fuck," but I'm having a hard time controlling myself. I practically growl as I turn her around and undo her bra. Running my hands down her hot body to her panties, I slowly slide them off, feeling every inch of her soft, slick skin.

"Does that answer your question?"

She reaches around to grab me but I shift to redirect the showerhead. Moving back over toward her, I kiss one of her shoulders and then the other as I reach my hands around her and touch her everywhere.

Turning her around, I press her against the wall. "You were supposed to give me a show," I tell her, bowing my head down to her hard nipple and sucking on it.

"I never agreed to any such thing." She's panting now, but I know I can get her to give me one anyway.

"Remember you said massage or anything I choose? My anything is a show."

I continue to lick and suck her breasts as her hands slide down my shoulders to my arms.

"Okay, anything," she says, and I can't help but grin.

When she starts to moan, I move to the other breast as she braces her hands on my shoulders. When I pull her nipple forcefully with my mouth, she screams out, "River, please!"

I know what she wants, but I ask anyway. "Please what, Dahlia?"

"I want you inside me. Now."

She's watching me. I grin at her and suck harder, tugging a little with my teeth as I rub circles around her other nipple.

"I will be soon, I promise."

She has the tiniest, most beautiful breasts, and as I slide my tongue down her stomach her hands come up to cup them. I'm torn between watching her and pleasuring her. The thought of either, or both, has me throbbing. Slipping my tongue in and out, I move it faster and then I slip two fingers deep inside her. As soon as I do, I watch pleasure wash over her face and I know she's coming hard. "Oh God, River!" she screams out as I continue to move my fingers until the trembling subsides.

Standing up, I take a minute to admire her. Her once too-thin body has taken on the most sensual shape. I can't get enough of her, regardless of her body type, but I know she looks the way she looks right now because she's happy.

Grabbing the soap, I start washing her arm. I slide the soap up toward her shoulder and then drop the bar to the ground to run both my hands up and down her soapy skin. As the soap lathers, I move my hands upward and with my legs, I gently move her back and press her against the glass wall.

She gasps when I rest one of my legs between her thighs, and as my hands find her chest I gently rub circles around her nipples. The soap makes my fingers slide easily. The water sprays down, and I move the showerhead so just a slight trickle is hitting us.

I decide to lather her leg. I do the same thing that I did with her arm, but this time, once I meet the top of her thigh, I press a little harder and rub smaller circles around her.

She moans softly and as I look up, her eyes flutter shut. I brush my thumb over her and she squirms in a way that tells me she's enjoying it.

"Please, River," she whispers, her eyes still closed.

I plunge my fingers deeper then pull them back. I grin as she tries to follow my hand with her hips.

"Please, River, please!"

I know she wants me and her asking for it really turns me on, but I'm not giving in that easily. Even if I want to.

"What, Dahlia? Please what?" I tease her.

She moans a little louder as I continue to plunge my fingers inside her, sometimes slowly, sometimes quickly, and she begs, "Please fuck me now."

Kissing her jaw, I can't help but chuckle at her use of the word *fuck*. I remember when we first met how cute I thought it was when she would swear, something I always tried not to do in front of her.

But hearing her say "fuck" is so hot, and really, all I want to do is fuck her now.

Sliding my tongue up to her ear, I whisper, "I swear I will. I swear I won't stop until your legs are shaking and every hotel guest on this floor knows my name."

I feel a smile form on her mouth. She's breathing very heavily as she bites my earlobe.

I press her back further into the wall and replace my fingers with my cock. She instantly responds, trying to wrap her legs around me, to push me further inside her, but I resist and just barely slide in and out of her.

I'm torturing myself, but I'm enjoying watching her more. She's trying to grip the wall, but there is nothing to hold on to. I stand still for a few moments, drawing out her anticipation, trying to get myself under control as she continues to try to push her body closer to mine.

I enter her with my tip only, over and over. As she moans, she continues to call out my name. When I see her body start to tremble, and she's screaming my name, "River, please!" I have no willpower left.

In one swift motion, I grab her and lift her up, pushing her body up against the wall. She responds instantly, wrapping her legs around me as I plunge inside her hard and fast. I have to remember to breathe, she feels so good. I continue to watch her, as her eyes start to roll, and I know she's so close.

I want to take it slow and make her come over and over, but I need her too much. I start moving faster, thrusting into her over and over again, each time harder and faster. When I see the look of pleasure spread across her face, I know she's there, again. She screams my name one final time as I hold her hips in place and yell out her name. Leaning in, I kiss her hard as our bodies quiver together.

Citizens' "Amazing Grace" startles me awake. It's playing from Dahlia's cell phone and I know it's her ringtone for Grace. Reaching for her, I realize she's not in bed.

"Dahlia, your phone!" I yell, yawning and covering my head with the pillow.

She doesn't answer. I call out to her again, but the room is too quiet. I realize she's not here.

As I try to find and silence the fucking phone, I see a note on her pillow.

*I know how tired you are from "skiing" so I thought
I'd let you sleep in. Just running the shorter trail then
I'll bring coffee back. I love you more.*

Blinking the sleep out of my eyes, I remember she woke me up earlier and wanted to run the lake trails to see the sunrise. I told her to give me a minute, but, shit, I must have fallen back asleep.

Lifting my head off the pillow, I see her phone. I grab it from the bedside table where it is plugged in. The battery must have died again, so she left it to charge. The song keeps playing, and the message light is blinking ten missed calls. The time reads six fourteen a.m.

I decide to answer it. "Hello," I mumble into the phone as I balance it on my shoulder and sit up.

I'm surprised to hear Serena's voice instead of Grace's. "River?" she asks, and then she's oddly silent.

I flop my head back on the pillow and stretch out. "Serena? What's—?" I start to say when she interrupts.

"I need to talk to Dahlia." Her voice is a little off, and she sounds sad or nervous, I'm not sure which.

Taking the phone in my hand, I sit back up immediately. "Serena, she's not here. She went running. Is everything okay? Is it Grace?" I have to ask, but pray it's not.

"River, you need to find her. We need to talk to her now." Her tone is urgent, and I have to know what's happening.

"Serena, what's going on? What's the matter?"

Her voice is muffled for a few seconds, and I can't really hear what she's saying when Grace gets on the phone.

"River, we've called the police," she tells me, her voice quavering as she speaks.

"Grace, I'm lost. What do you need the police for?"

"Didn't she tell you?"

My heart is racing, and I really just want her to tell me what the fuck she's talking about. "What are you talking about? What's going on?"

"I left Dahlia three messages last night. They let him out on a technicality."

"Grace, who did they let out?"

"The man who shot Ben. He's out," she's saying, and I'm trying to process what's going on.

I look at Dahlia's phone and hit the HOME button. I see three messages from Grace that haven't been listened to, and fifteen missed calls from Grace and Serena.

"Grace, she hasn't listened to your messages yet."

She's crying and I think she is unable to speak but she manages to say, "Hold on."

Caleb gets on the phone. "Hey, man. Where is she? I'm not sure what's up but we need to keep an eye on her."

I'm trying not to get annoyed at this prick and his use of "we." "She went running. What the fuck is going on?"

I can hear him inhale a deep breath. "Look, man, I think the guy that shot Ben is looking for something. I drove by Dahlia's house last night just to check on it, and someone broke in again. I drove over to your house looking for her, but they wouldn't let me in the gate and neither of you answered their calls. I called your sister and she gave me your number. I called you all fucking night."

I bolt out of bed and look frantically around for my pants. Running to the bathroom, I find them on the floor. I pull them on and find my phone still in the pocket. My hands are trembling. "I'll call you back when I find her," I tell him, and hang up.

Calling hotel security, I quickly explain the situation. Whether it's necessary or not to send someone to find her, I have no fucking idea, but I want her found now.

Just as I throw on my shirt and sneakers and head for the door, the hotel phone rings. I'm torn between answering it and running out to find her but since I did call security, I turn around and go back. I silently pick up the phone.

"Mr. Wilde?"

"Yes."

"Sir, we'd like you to come down to the lobby and we'll take you to the hospital."

I swallow a few times, trying to catch my breath as all the air leaves my lungs, and my knees buckle beneath me. As I'm searching for the courage to ask the question I already know the answer to, I hear the ambulance sirens in the distance and I don't need to ask anything.

Wiping a tear from the corner of my eye, I bolt out of the room and take the ten flights of stairs down to the lobby where security is waiting for me. I can hardly think, but I know I can't lose her. I can't lose my best friend, my soul mate, my smile, my laugh—my everything.

❧

They say she's already on her way to the hospital in the ambulance. I want them to take me to see her now. No one knows what happened, just that someone heard screaming and called security. This car ride feels like the longest fifteen-mile drive of my life. My phone keeps ringing, but I can't answer it. I just have to see her, my beautiful, perfect girl. I need to know she's okay.

I slide open the photos I have of her. Some are serious, some are funny, some are quirky, and some are downright hot. All of them show her beautiful face, and the tears I've been holding back start to flow as I unleash the sorrow I feel about my inability to keep her safe.

Absorbed in my thoughts and the quiet of the car, I can barely even hear my own breathing. The heat is blasting and even though I'm not wearing a coat, I'm sweating. The security chief is talking to me, but I'm not listening until I realize he's telling me we're at the hospital. Rushing through the emergency room doors, I make my way through a very packed waiting room toward the small glass window at the reception desk. As I get closer I think I see Dahlia behind it, but once I'm there, I realize it's only wishful thinking.

Holding myself up against the counter, I feel slightly queasy. My nerves are getting the best of me. My heart is pounding a thousand beats a minute, my stomach is in knots, and the chill running through my body is making the shivering painful.

"Can I help you, sir?"

"My fiancée was just brought in and I need to see her now!" My voice is raised and I'm attracting dirty looks from the people standing in line, but I don't give a shit. I'm desperate to find my girl.

"Sir, are you family? Only family members are allowed back," she says, handing me a form to fill out that reads: "Nonfamily Member Patient Inquiry."

I'm trying to keep my patience but am losing the battle as I take the clipboard from her and repeat, "I told you, we're engaged."

She looks up at me with an expression that says she's heard this before. "Sir, like I said, access is for the patient's family only. Please fill that out, and have a seat. We'll inform you of her condition once we get her permission."

"She has no fucking family! I am her family!" I frantically yell through the window.

Taking a deep breath, I pull myself together. I complete the form and hand it back to her. I stand there, trying to figure out what to do, when I see the doors to the emergency room corridor open as a patient is wheeled out with her leg in a cast.

I see that the nurse behind the desk is engaged in conversation, and I know I have to do something. So without thinking of the consequences, I quickly walk through the open doors and enter the never-ending hallway. Once inside, I pause for a minute, deciding the best way to go about finding her. I'm praying she's actually back here and not in some operating room. Starting with the first curtain, I poke my head in, trying not to disturb the person behind it.

After I've done this a few too many times, I see a doctor walking down the wall. "Excuse me, Doctor," I say to the short brunette woman in a white lab coat. "Do you think you could help me? My wife is back here and I can't remember what room she's in. I had to go out to the waiting room to use my phone to call and check on our daughter." I'm making this up as I go, and I'm actually wishing it were true, hoping it will be true someday. "And now I can't remember what room she's in."

Smiling, she says, "Sure. What's her name?"

"Dahlia London," I tell her, and I really wish I were saying Dahlia Wilde.

She walks over to the desk and looks on a clipboard. She then directs me to curtained room number ten. It's no more than ten feet away, but the walk feels like miles.

Memories flood my mind with visions of her dancing in the rain. Her carefree take on life and the beauty she finds in everything is awe-inspiring. What's ironic is she thinks everyone around her is amazing, but she's the amazing one. The one I was supposed to take care of and failed miserably.

My phone is ringing again and the nurse walking down the corridor shoots me a look. "Sir, your phone is supposed to be turned off when you're back here."

I hit the vibrate button. "Sorry, miss," I say as I see seven missed calls in the last thirty minutes, all from Caleb.

I hold my breath as I open the blue curtain. Fear and dread flow through my veins until I not only see but hear the voice of the girl I've fallen so deeply in love with.

"River, is that you?"

I yank open the curtain to see her sitting in the bed with her head propped back. There's a bruise on her cheek, and her lip is swollen. She has a bandage wrapped around her wrist where she wears the bracelet from *him*. But thank God she's sitting up and talking to me.

Swallowing hard, I can't suppress my tears and they instantly start flowing down my face. I jet over to her side and gently wrap my arms around her, careful of the wires connected to her body through the hospital gown.

She pulls me to her even tighter.

I whisper because I'm barely able to speak, "Are you okay?"

Crying, she nods her head. "Yes."

I gently cup her face in my hands, and stare at her. I press my lips to hers, careful not to actually apply any pressure. As relief washes over me that she's all right, I put my head in the crook of her neck and stay there, unable to move. She's become so much a part of me in such a short period of time; I can't imagine my life without her. She holds onto me, and her crying continues as I attempt to soothe her. Each of her tears tugs at my heart.

At this moment, I not only feel the strong physical connection she needs from me right now but also the deep emotional connection that binds us together.

I want to ask her what happened. Who did this? Did he touch you? How did he touch you? I want to fucking kill this man, but right now what she needs from me most is just me. So I save my questions for later and just hold her tight, thanking God she's alive and okay.

Her cries turn into my cries as I kiss her on the forehead. "Everything's okay now, baby. And I promise I'll never let anyone hurt you ever again."

CHAPTER 27
Connected

River

3 days after the attack . . .

With her concert T-shirt blanket wrapped around her, she's wedged in between my legs on a lounge chair as we gaze out on the sunrise and the Hollywood sign before us. Her head rests on my chest, our fingers laced together, and my arms are wrapped around her, holding her tight, as they've been since the attack.

She was released from the hospital yesterday. Caleb and Xander drove up to Tahoe the day of the incident and stayed until it was time to leave. Caleb asked her more questions than the police, but the story was always the same. She offered very few details and only had a vague recollection of what the guy said.

She didn't see him. He grabbed her from behind and threw her down, shoving her face-first into the ground. The only thing he said to her was to give it up and she wouldn't get hurt. Those words still send shivers down my spine. He pounded her head into the stony trail a few times as she tried to scream around his hand. When someone started yelling from a distance, the guy fled.

Xander insisted on driving us back home from the resort, and Caleb took my car. Dahlia is physically all right, but she's shaken. Caleb has really stepped up, and I've decided to set aside my dislike for him and let him help. He's installing a state-of-the-art security system and has a rotating crew of bodyguards on call.

We decided to wait a few days to tell her about *his* shooter's release. We hope that because of this attack, he will be picked up again, and she won't have to worry. I felt bad deleting her messages, but I had to, for her.

Not being able to see her when she was in the emergency room weighs heavy on my mind, and I wonder why we decided to wait until after the tour to pick a date to get married. So, as we lie together, I ask her, "Why are we waiting to get married?"

I kiss her hair and continue. "It seems like all I was really doing was waiting for you my whole life anyway, and I don't want to wait anymore."

She shifts her body so she's lying on her side and looks up at me. Laughing a little, she responds, "I'm not really sure. But, when you put it that way, I don't want to wait, either."

"How would you feel if we charter a plane to Las Vegas and get married today? I can have it arranged in a matter of hours. We can fly up there, get married, and be back here by sunset."

"You don't mind if your family's not there?"

Sitting up straighter, I pull her to me and straddle her legs. Gently tucking her hair behind her ear, I gaze into her beautiful eyes. "I won't be satisfied until I wake up next to my wife every morning. Dahlia, all I want is you and me forever. We can celebrate later once you're feeling better. We can even have another ceremony here. But what happened in the hospital I never want to happen again.

"So will you marry me today?"

Tears drip down her face, but this time they're not tears of sadness. She leans in and kisses me. When she pulls away, she says, "River Wilde, I would love to marry you today."

❦

Six hours later, she's wearing the most beautiful white dress. We had decided not to tell anyone what we were doing, but when Aerie stopped by unexpectedly this morning, Dahlia caved and shared the news. Aerie ran out and bought her a dress. It's short with pearls embroidered all over it, and she looks amazing. The bruises on her face are still evident, but neither of us cares. Pictures can be taken another day. Today is about us, for us. Once she marries me, we will be connected forever.

Caleb has security all set. He wasn't exactly happy about our impromptu trip. I'm not sure if it was for personal or professional reasons, but he insisted he be the one to accompany us. I agreed because I know she means a lot to him, and he would do anything to protect her.

We're ready to go and I glance over at Dahlia, where she's plugging her uncharged phone into the wall. "Come on, beautiful. You don't need that today." I'm laughing because I'm usually telling her she needs to charge her phone earlier than five minutes before we're walking out the door.

I walk over and pull her to me as I gaze into her now brownish green eyes. "Are you ready to become my wife?"

Pulling back, she looks at me. "Only if you promise to love me forever."

I cup her cheeks and say, with absolute certainty, "Beautiful, I made that promise to myself the first time I kissed you." I cross my finger over my heart and add, "I promise to love you always. How could I not?"

Hugging her as tightly as I can, I know I will never let her go. After I kiss her, I slide my mouth to her ear and whisper, "And the instant you become Mrs. Wilde, I'm going to show you just how much."

She nods her head and I see the goose bumps emerge, and I can't help but smile. Grabbing her hand, we head toward the door. "Amazing Grace" starts playing from her phone in the kitchen just as we're about to take our last steps as River Wilde and Dahlia London.

EPILOGUE
Breakeven

Ben's Journal

February 19, 2010
Caleb called me today and told me he had a story for me, if I dared listen. Of course I wanted to hear it. I've always been game for a dare. He told me it was not a laughing matter, but that it might make me go down in history as one of the best investigative journalists. I agreed without hesitation.

February 21, 2010
Caleb and I met today and what he told me blew me away. I didn't believe him at first. I found it odd that someone would contact him just as his tour in Afghanistan ended with an offer like this. He told me their initial contact with him had been immediate. He gave me a USB drive with information I needed to research it. When I came home, I loaded it and, shit, when he said he had a story that would

rock my world, he wasn't shitting me. I was actually a little sickened by what I saw and knew the story had to come out. This was going to be a walk in the park and I'm going to be famous.

February 23, 2010
I've been up for twenty-four fucking hours straight. This is so much bigger than Caleb ever thought. I called him and left him a message over six hours ago, and the asshole hasn't called me back.

February 25, 2010
Fucking Caleb Holt. He's been missing for two days, and then he calls and tells me I have to kill the story. He wants me to forget he ever told me. Well, he knows me better than that. I'm not fucking doing that. I started writing the article today and plan to release it the night of my awards show. I have to because it's not only about me, it's about helping other people.

February 26, 2010
When Caleb told me today what he told me, at first I didn't believe him. I thought he'd gone fucking nuts. He told me if I didn't disappear, die, actually, Dahlia and I really would end up dead. I walked out of the bar planning to ignore every fucking word he said and publish that article. When I got to my car there was an envelope on the window. Sitting in my car, I opened it up. Someone had been photographing Dahl everywhere she went. There was even a picture of her with a man behind her at a coffee shop pointing a knife to her back. I threw up instantly. I know these people aren't messing around. Fuck, what am I going to do?

February 27, 2010

I spent the last eight hours with Caleb planning it. He had it all figured out. He paid someone off to take the fall for killing me. They would eventually be released on a technicality. He even managed to acquire a bag of blood that matched my type so that when I'm shot it looks like I'm bleeding. He wanted all the evidence for the story back. Fuck that, why would I give it all back? I gave him enough and hid the rest in the house, a place where no one would think to look.

February 28, 2010

I have less than a week left with the girl I've spent my whole life with. Fuck, this is killing me, but I can't bring her with me. She wouldn't be happy living on the run. Today I sent her flowers even though I never do that. I know she's going to think something is up, but I want her to remember how much I love her—forever.

March 1, 2010

I took my Dahl to lunch today. I don't know why I never did that more often. I even brought her a bag of her favorite Peppermint Patties. I would've gotten her some fancy chocolate, but I know she loves chocolate-covered mint the most.

March 2, 2010

Fuck. Fuck. Fuck. I met with him less than two weeks ago, and tomorrow I have to die. I've tried to back out but I'm in too deep and *they* want me dead. So today I'll spend every minute with her making sure she knows how much I love her.

March 3, 2010

Today was the happiest and the saddest day of my life. I love her like I've never loved before. I knew it was our last time together, and I needed her in a way I can't even explain. We shared a bond I've never felt with her before. Maybe it was because I knew I'd never see her beautiful smile again, touch her body again, kiss her soft lips again, or even walk this sandy beach with her. She had no idea what was going to happen or why I was so emotional and that just tore me apart.

I gave her a bracelet to symbolize my love for her, and I hope she never takes it off. Saying goodbye was tough, but I had to do it to protect her, to save her. Leaving her alone in the fucking car wrecked me. She pleaded for me not to be the hero. I was no fucking hero. I was doing what I had to do to save her. When I looked at her one final time, I wished I were really going to die. I left her lying on the floor of the car. She believed I was getting out to save her from a crazed lunatic. I guess in a way I was, but her calling me a hero made me want to throw up. I certainly wasn't her hero. She was in danger because of me. Still, you'd think that I'd sleep better knowing she will always have those thoughts of me, but I know that I won't.

I made Caleb bring me here one last time. I just can't leave without seeing it. This was our favorite place. I may never be able to come back so I want to say goodbye. Goodbye to the beach, goodbye to my mother, sister, and nephew, and goodbye to her.

I have visited this place many times, but today it's different. I'm alone. There are no comforting arms around me. My body trembles. Not from the cold, but from the realization that fate hasn't worked in my favor. A single tear slowly drips down my face as I look into the night and scream, "Why couldn't we just stay together?!"

As the wind moans in the distance, thunder crashes and lightning strikes. I stand here hoping the impending storm will carry me away and erase the shadow that looms over me. A slow, soothing rain falls from the blackened sky, but it provides no relief for my ravaged soul. A mist slowly rises into the night, and the cold air sends shivers down my spine.

I huddle to the ground, feeling lost and alone. As my tears merge with the rain, they fall into the darkness. No one is here to see me. No one knows where to find me. Only the vultures notice me as they fly swiftly overhead, seeking shelter against the cold rain. I'm not looking for refuge in this place I now despise, but I have nowhere else to go. I have no hope. I have no future.

March 4, 2010
I was killed in a random carjacking gone badly. I'm in New York City now. Caleb dropped me off at some apartment he rented under my new name and got me a job as a college professor. Shit, I fucking hate him. If it wasn't for him, I'd be alive today. I left everything behind except this one journal. I have nothing, and I'll never see my Dahl again.

November 17, 2011
Caleb showed up at my apartment after one of my classes. He told me something was going down, he didn't know what and he was worried. He informed me that the house Dahlia and I shared together was ransacked, like they were looking for something. He asked me if I had given him everything.

I lost my shit and just started pounding him uncontrollably and he let me. He never even tried to hit me back. I only stopped when I saw that the blood running down his nose had soaked into his shirt and down onto the carpet. He grabbed a towel and held it to his nose but continued talking as if nothing happened.

I didn't let him finish. I couldn't bear the images of my Dahl hurt, lying on our floor, that flashed through my head. I think he sensed what I was thinking about and he told me Dahlia wasn't around that weekend.

All I could think was *thank fuck*, but then I asked Caleb where she was. At first he shrugged his shoulders and turned away from me to sit on the couch, but I pressed him until he finally told me. He said Dahlia had come back to the house with some guy. I pressed further; I wanted to know what guy. Who was he? Was he using her to find the information I'd hidden so well?

My fifty questions continued, and I never paused to let Caleb answer. I didn't know if I wanted to know the answers. All I knew was I had to get back there to see her, to be with her, but Caleb insisted I stay dead for her safety and for mine. He said they wouldn't hurt her since she didn't have anything to do with it, and I was dead.

I went to sit on the couch next to him. I told him he owed it to me to tell me what he knew. So he did. He said he was pretty sure Dahlia was fucking the guy he had seen her with. He told me he was really sorry. Caleb went on to explain that he had followed them to some swanky L.A. neighborhood in the Hills. And as far as he could tell, she was staying there. Dahlia in the Hills. What the fuck?

I was fucking furious at him, at me, at her. She's already

shacked up with someone? I really wanted to kill the guy, and I wanted to beat the shit out of Caleb. The thought of my Dahl fucking someone else drove me to the verge of insanity.

I knew she'd move on eventually, but to know that it's happened is something else entirely.

I walked over to the CD player on a table in the corner of the room and just stared at it. The song playing was "Go to Hell" by Go Radio. Fucking appropriate, huh? I couldn't help myself. I pounded my fist on the player so hard it smashed into a thousand pieces on the floor, and I broke my fucking hand.

Caleb took me to the ER where they put a cast on it. God, could they just put a cast on my broken heart? I sat there in the ER, thinking back to Dahlia, and wondering why I hadn't just insisted she marry me when I first asked her. Not that it would have mattered that much. Shit, either way I would never see her again.

Caleb left the next day. He assured me he'd watch out for her and said he wouldn't contact me again.

September 21, 2012
Sitting here now at the large wooden conference table with a room full of suits from some government agency I still don't even know the name of, I can hear every tick of the clock hanging on the fucking wall. All I can think about is that, after almost three years, I'm finally going to see her again, touch her again, love her again. I gave up everything to keep my Dahl alive, and now I'm going to be able to finally get it all back.

Caleb told me she's with some douche bag, supposedly it's pretty serious, but I know the minute she sees me here in the flesh it'll be over. We just have too much history for it not to be.

Damn, why did I have to be so fucking good at my job? Losing it all in the blink of an eye wasn't worth it. Back then I was hungry, and nothing else mattered. Well, that's not true. I cared about what was happening and wanted to stop it. I really did care.

I hadn't heard from Caleb in almost nine months until he called me a few days ago. I knew something was up, but had no idea what. He asked me again if I had kept information, and once again, I lied and assured him I hadn't. I tried to ask how my Dahl was, but he just hung up.

So when they called me yesterday and told me they were bringing me back in, I knew something must have happened. All they told me was that it wasn't over, but they wanted me back here. I was accompanied by one of the suits on the next flight from New York to L.A. The only thing the suit told me was that my house had been broken into again. I wondered if this time they found the information, but how could they? I asked if she was okay, but he didn't answer.

And now I sit here. Where the fuck is Caleb? I asked them but got no answer. The only answer I have received in the last twenty-four hours is, "Yes, we have notified your family." But I'm hanging patiently here because I can't believe it's actually going to happen when I never thought it would. My story will eventually come out. I will be free of *them*. Free to be with my Dahl. It seems surreal but so fucking real at the same time. My mother is on her way, and once I see her and tell her my story, I'll finally get to call my Dahl.

Don't miss what comes next for River and Dahlia
in Kim Karr's next novel,

TORN

Available in e-book now from InterMix and in
paperback from New American Library in April!

$\mathcal{A}$ glimmer of light catches my eye through the partially open curtains across the room as I wake. It must be dawn because the sky is turning various shades of pink, red, and orange. Before I know it, the sky blazes with color; it's as if it's on fire—just like my body, but I push my pain aside. It's a glorious new day. And I'm here to share it with him. I look at the gorgeous lines of his body slumped over in the chair next to my hospital bed. He's asleep, but not very soundly. I study him, taking in his strong jaw, sculpted nose, and toned body. But it's his soul, his playfulness, and his amazing personality that made me fall in love with him. He's so much more than I could ever have asked for—he's my soul mate in every sense of the word.

Carefully removing my hand from his, I try hard not to wake him. Then I slowly ease myself up from the bed and make my way to the bathroom. When I return, the sun has fully risen and so has he. He's staring out the window with the curtains now completely open. I sweep him with my eyes so that I can appreciate every little thing—at just over six feet he's glorious. Strong shoulders, a lean waist, abs that seem to flex with his every movement. Arms crossed, tilt of his head cocked just so, his T-shirt tucked into his jeans haphazardly, and his stance so straight and sure. The soft bluish gray sky of the early morning is almost as breathtaking as the sight of him.

Trying to see what he's looking at, I only notice the fluffy clouds drifting by. They appear so white against the morning sky; they make me start to smile. But I know that's not what he's seeing right now. When a blue jay flies by and he turns around I want to erase the pain I see in his sorrowful expression and sad green eyes.

I don't want to dwell on the events of yesterday's incident, but he seems to be preoccupied with it. His mood has been somber ever since it happened. He calls it an attack—I prefer incident. After all, I'm here, alive and merely bruised. I'm not going to waste my time thinking about one bad day—I'd rather celebrate the good things in each new day. But he blames himself. I haven't been able to convince him that if anyone was to blame it's me. Then again a random act of violence couldn't have been prevented and thankfully, I'm all right. I just want to leave the hospital and go home.

Grabbing my clothes from the chair, I throw them on the bed. I'm standing in front of him on the cold linoleum floor in nothing but a hospital gown. I make a twirling motion with my finger impatiently. "Do you mind turning around?"

Sighing, he runs his hands through his already messy hair. "I'm not turning around. I want to help you. Seeing what he did to you can't make me feel any worse. Believe me."

I swallow the lump in my throat and try to gather the right words to respond—to help put his mind at ease. "River, it was *not* your fault. Some perverted animal, looking to get his kicks by attacking women, that isn't your fault."

He can't hide his shudder from my eyes. "Dahlia, it wasn't a fucking incident. You were attacked. If I had been with you it wouldn't have happened. I shouldn't have been sleeping. It's really just that simple."

I stand there shocked by his tone, even though I know he doesn't mean to be so harsh. "No, it's not just that simple . . . ," I start to argue, but he cuts me off.

His shoulders sag. He promptly diverts his eyes to the ground and shoves his hands in his jeans pockets. "I'm sorry, Dahlia. I don't mean to yell. I just can't stand that you got hurt. It kills me to see you like this, to know what could have happened to you. It just kills me."

We've had this conversation twice already. I already know my re-assurances will go nowhere. So I repeat myself and contemplate making my way to the duffel bag lying next to the chair to get my socks and shoes and then go into the bathroom to change. But I plead one more time, "River, please turn around."

He's standing in front of me with only the bed between us but for some reason it feels like we're miles apart. He doesn't move toward me, but I can see the overwhelming emotion in his face and in his eyes. He's hurting. I can also hear it in his voice and his sorrow not only makes me sad, it tears at my heart.

I've never been shy around him. I just know that I'm covered in bruises and I want so badly to spare him the heartache of seeing me this way.

"No, let me help you," he whispers. His tone is barely audible.

With a deep sigh I resign myself to his plea and pointing near the chair I ask, "Can you please hand me that?"

Grabbing my bag, he sets it on the bed.

As I untie the ugly green gown and slide it down my arms, he watches me. But not in an, "Oh I want to see you naked" kind of way, more like an, "Oh God, I might be sick" way.

The gown puddles on the floor and I stand there completely na-ked in front of him. I watch as he looks at me. He scans my body from head to toe before his eyes drift back up to meet mine and he swallows.

In an attempt to lighten the mood, I pick up the hospital gown and playfully toss it at him. "Your turn to play dress up."

His lips finally turn up in a semblance of a smile, but his eyes are still filled with sadness. "I think I'll pass this time, if you don't mind," he says, holding the gown up to him. "Green isn't my color."

Both of us smile, and I know he's looking beyond my bruises. At last. And all his love for me is now reflected in his eyes—it means everything to me.

He strides around the bed and insists on helping me put on my panties and jeans. I want to comment on how easy it would be for him to get in my pants right now, but I refrain. However, when he ever so carefully starts to tug my sweater over my head, I can't hold back. Grabbing his hand, I press it over my heart and look at him. "See, you can touch me. I won't break. I'll even let you get to second base," I say, sliding his hand down to cup my breast.

He resists at first, but eventually he sighs and brushes his thumb over my nipple. A slow grin crosses his lips. "Second base, that's it? I think I had a better chance with the pants."

We both laugh a little and I continue to hold his hand in place. His eyes burn into mine as he moves his hand to cup my cheek. Leaning into my ear he whispers, "You'd better stop it. You're going to get me all worked up and when Nurse Smiley Face comes in here she's going to kick me out."

He pulls back and I roll my eyes as he pushes my sweater down the rest of the way. I silently wince a little in pain. My shoulder is sore, my wrist is sprained, and my body is bruised. The doctor wanted to cut off my bracelet, the only jewelry I was wearing, because of the swelling, but I begged him not to. It's the one thing of Ben's I have left and I need it to always remind me to live my life with no regrets.

Once I'm dressed, River gently places his arms around my waist and tenderly embraces me. "I'm sorry. Did I hurt you?" he whispers.

"You could never hurt me," I respond in a low, comforting voice.

Leaning back, he crosses his finger over his heart. "I promise I will never let anything happen to you again." The ache in his voice cuts through me and I have to take a deep breath to prevent tears. I just want to throw my arms around his neck but my aching body won't let me so I settle for circling my hands around his waist instead. He in turn slips his strong arms around me and we just hold each other.

Then he kisses each of my eyelids and rests his forehead against mine. With each passing second I can feel our love growing stronger, if that's even be possible. We stay like this in silence until the nurse enters the room.

She clears her throat and he whispers, "Nurse Smiley Face caught us again, I'm in trouble now."

I giggle and we step apart. She's nice, but she didn't like it that River stayed the night. And once last night when I asked him to lie next to me, she came in to check my vitals and made him get off the bed.

She takes my blood pressure one last time and goes over the discharge instructions left by the doctor—basically rest, no strenuous activities, and if I experience headaches of any kind I am to see my doctor immediately.

Once I've signed all the paperwork, the nurse calls for an orderly, and when he arrives, he wheels me to the door. River gets his car and we are finally allowed to leave the hospital. He decided earlier that we should spend the night in Tahoe and head home in the morning. On the way to the hotel, he looks over at me. "Did I tell you Xander and Caleb are here?"

I look at him questioningly. "No, you didn't. Why are they here?"

He laughs a little and says, "What do you mean why? They're here to make sure you're okay."

"But we're going home tomorrow, they could have just checked on me then."

Shrugging his shoulders, he answers. "I know but I wanted Xander to drive us back so I can sit with you."

"Oh that's really sweet of you, but not necessary. I'm fine."

"Well, even if you're fine, it's not a short ride, and I want you to be able to stretch out on the backseat. I want to be able to be close to you. To take care of you if you need anything."

I look at him lovingly; he really does always say the sweetest things. "Thank you. But why did Caleb come? Do Xander and Caleb even really know each other?" I have to ask because it wasn't so long ago that I thought River didn't care for Caleb and now his brother is riding up to Lake Tahoe with him.

"Yeah, of course they know each other. They've met a few times actually. And since I decided yesterday to hire Caleb to install additional security in our house, I thought it would be a good idea to discuss the upgrade with him before we get home. That way he can start on it as soon as possible."

"We don't need additional security at home because of what happened. River, I think that's a bit much."

"Dahlia, I never had the security system upgraded when I moved in, so I'm just taking a precautionary measure, that's all. You'll be coming back to L.A. alone during the tour so I want to make sure you're safe."

Shaking my head, I throw in, "I didn't even think you liked Caleb and now he's working for you."

"I never said I didn't like him."

"No, you didn't say it, but I felt it every time you talked to him."

"Hmm . . . well, regardless of how I feel about him, I know he's good at what he does and when I called him he said he had time. Oh and one more thing: Caleb or someone who works for him will be escorting us places."

I narrow my eyes at him. "You mean like bodyguards?"

"Well, I wouldn't call them bodyguards, just additional security."

"That sounds really awkward."

"Dahlia, I promise you won't even know they're around."

"I doubt that." I rest my head against the window and close my eyes. I find the whole amp-up-the-security thing a little absurd, but since it makes him feel better, I won't protest.

When we get to the hotel, we learn that Caleb had our room changed and he and Xander now occupy the adjoining room next door. I want to tease River—"Yeah, we won't even know they're around"—but I don't.

The doctor gave me some pain pills at the hospital and they've made me so tired that I spend the rest of the day in bed, snuggled in River's arms. I must have fallen into a deep sleep because when I wake, I look at the clock and it's almost eight. The first thing I do is reach for him only to find that he isn't next to me. Looking around the room, I'm a little disoriented at first. But I see River huddled in the corner with Caleb and Xander, discussing something in hushed whispers that I can't hear. When he sees me try to sit up and move to get off the bed, he hastily rushes over.

"What do you need, baby?" he asks in almost a whisper. His face looks worn, tired, and worried.

"I need to go to the bathroom and get some water." I try to smile at him, but my mouth tastes like it has a wad of cotton balls in it and my body feels completely detached from my mind. I'm not sure I can actually walk to the bathroom without falling. I also feel light-headed.

"Let me help you," he says as he moves my legs to the floor and carefully helps me stand up. But when I start to wobble a little, I grab his shoulder for support. I think the pain medication has not only made me light-headed, but also unstable.

He's already wrapping my arm around him as he picks me up. "Dahlia, let me help you."

Xander and Caleb look over at me, appearing worried. They stand and both say good night, disappearing through the adjoining door.

Once we reach the bathroom, River gently sets me down and removes my pants. I grip the counter and begin to regain my stability.

"Can you grab me a T-shirt?" I ask him quietly.

"Sure, beautiful girl, whatever you need," he replies with a smile.

When he leaves the bathroom I push the door slightly closed and frown as I take the first real glimpse of myself in the mirror since the incident. I look much worse than I did earlier this morning. The bruises have turned purple, my wrist is still swollen, the scrapes on my cheek from where my attacker held my face to the ground are crusted over, and my shoulder aches from where he shoved his knee to hold me down.

I carefully take my sweater off and hastily wrap a towel around me. I consider a shower, but decide against it. It seems like it would require too much energy right now. I do manage to brush my teeth. Once I finish I look back into the mirror and see that he's standing behind me in the doorway with such sadness in his eyes. He walks over to me as I wipe my mouth with a towel.

"Let's put this on you," he says while pulling his long-sleeved 30 Seconds to Mars T-shirt over my head. "It will be easier to get on and off than one of yours and it will keep you warm."

Setting the towel down, I let him dress me like I'm a small child. Happy memories of my father getting me ready for school pop into my head. My dad would help me get dressed and drop me off at school when my mother had to leave early for work. I loved those days. I loved every day my parents were alive.

"You all right, Dahlia?" he asks with concern.

"Yeah, yeah, I'm fine."

His gaze is doubtful.

Smiling, I tell him, "You dressing me now just reminded me of happy times when my dad would let me pick out whatever I wanted to wear to school whether it matched or not. Since my mom wasn't home to make me change I usually wore his concert T-shirts."

He smirks. "You mean your mom, the fashion designer, didn't like it when you wore your dad's grungy T-shirts to school?"

"How did you guess?"

"Intuition." He shrugs. "Personally I think you make everything you wear look incredible, but I could see where your mom might have a different opinion."

I lean into him just to feel his warmth and nuzzle his neck. "I wish you could have met my parents."

"I may never be able to meet them, but I know them through you."

Pulling away, I smile at him and press my palms against his chest. "That means everything to me," is all I can say because it does.

He nods and we stay silent for a few moments.

"I think you should lie back down." Carrying me back to the bed, he sets me down on the opposite side I woke up on. But I don't care which side I sleep on as long as he's next to me. I take his hand and squeeze it. "Thank you."

"You don't have to thank me," he says, kissing the top of my head.

Love fills the air between us and I have to suck in deep breath to calm by breathing.

Running his fingers down my cheek, he too seems to be settling his breathing before speaking. "I ordered you something to eat while you were in the bathroom."

"I'm not really hungry. I'm just really thirsty."

Pulling the covers up over my legs, he sits beside me. "You have to eat something when you take these pills." He opens the medicine bottle on the night table and pours two oblong white horse-size pills into his palm then sets them down next to the open bottle.

"There's no way I can swallow those."

He laughs quickly and then stands up and walks toward the TV. "I ordered you grilled cheese and French fries to eat and a milkshake to swallow the pills with." He opens the adjoining room door calling out, "Hey, Xander, just bring the food over here when it comes."

I'm staring at his backside when he turns his head over his shoulder and catches me. He throws me a wink and I smile back. We don't exchange words but we both start laughing and I have to say, that is my all-time favorite sound. God, I love it when he laughs. It's soft but husky and oh so sexy.

I hold my bruised ribs in pain, and he apologizes for making me laugh.

"River, it's okay. I want to laugh. And really I just couldn't resist the view."

He stifles back more laughter and I ask, "Why did you order food and have it delivered to Xander's room?" I pause a moment before adding, "And why are we sharing a room with Xander and Caleb anyway?"

His laughter stops and he becomes more serious. "We're not sharing a room with them. The door closes between us, silly girl." As if to prove his point, he opens and closes the door in a swinging motion. Leaving it open, he walks back over to the bed and sits next to me again. He cups my unbruised cheek before leaning in to kiss my forehead. "And I ordered food to be delivered to their room in case you fell back asleep. I didn't want the knocking to disturb you."

"Oh, that makes sense. Well, now that you mentioned my favorite—grilled cheese dipped in a chocolate milkshake—I might be feeling a little hungry."

"Have I told you how gross I think that is, by the way?" he asks, raising his eyebrows.

"Only a thousand times, and yet every time I order it you manage to steal a bite. And don't think I haven't noticed you dip it in your shake first."

Chuckling, he pinches his thumb and index finger together and says, "Well, I might like it just a tiny little bit."

I smile at him and lay my head down on the pillow just as Xander brings in the tray of food. River points to the empty spot next to me on the bed. "Thanks, man, just put it down right there."

"Dahlia, do you want anything else?" Xander asks.

"Just a gallon of water," I say jokingly. "My mouth feels like a desert in the middle of July."

He grins at me and starts to pour the liter of bottled water into a glass as River takes my giant pills along with a knife from the tray and comes over to the table.

"I'll take the whole bottle please. No need for a glass."

Xander hands me the water as River cuts the pills in half.

"Stop looking like you're going to someone's funeral, Xander. I'm fine. You and Caleb really didn't have to drop everything to come up here when we're just going home tomorrow anyway."

"Will it make you feel better if I tell you I came for my brother?"

I take a huge sip of water and eye him before giving him a full smile. "Since I know you'd never admit you came for me then, yes, it will."

He kisses me on the forehead. "Good night, Muse. If you weren't such a pain in my ass I might find you funny. I might even like you." I don't mind him calling me Muse since he repeatedly tells me the Wilde Ones' claim to fame is the song "Once in a Lifetime," which River wrote after meeting me that first time.

"I'll keep hoping and wishing for the day you say you love me."

He looks at me with all trace of humor gone. "I'm really glad you're okay Dahlia. Good night. See you in a few hours."

Glancing over at River, he gives him a nod before closing the door. Our plan is to leave in the middle of the night to get home early enough for Xander to get to work. River flops on the bed and once I swallow the disgusting horse pills we share the tray of food and then fall asleep in each other's arms.

❦

Moonlight cascades through the windows and the stars shine bright above us as Xander drives us home. Lying on River's lap, I'm listening intently to him. He's strumming his fingers through my hair and singing along to "Losing My Religion" but his voice sounds sad, reminiscent of something almost. When the song finishes I reach my hand up to caress his cheek. "I love that song. I saw R.E.M. perform it at the Greek the year it came out."

He takes my hand and kisses my knuckles. "I have a love-hate relationship with it myself."

Xander snickers from the front seat. "Yeah, more like it had a love-hate relationship with you."

Combing my fingers through his hair, I tug on a strand and he grins. "Why?"

He slouches a little more so I can rest my head on the tautness of his abs. His fingers tap my arm and he laughs. "When it hit the top five my dad decided I should learn to play the mandolin. He studied hit songs all the time trying to dissect them for what drove them to the top. He took note of anything different used in its production and 'Losing My Religion' was only the second hit song to ever feature a mandolin prominently."

Xander starts laughing so loud it surprises me. I don't think I've ever heard him laugh like that. River shakes his head. "Shut up, Xander."

River's eyes seem to dance in the moonlight at the memory and it thrills me to see him laugh when he mentions his father. He doesn't mention him often but on the rare occasion he does it's never with any sign of emotion. I'm glad he has happy memories of his dad, like I do. I have a sudden urge to kiss him and pull his head down closer to mine so I can press my lips against his. "Tell me," I whisper, tracing the outline of one of his perfectly defined pectorals.

"Don't laugh but you know the saying it's all in the wrist?"

I nod.

"It's absolutely true. Subtle, nimble wrist movements are the key to playing the correct note on the mandolin and no matter how many times I tried, I just couldn't get it down."

"Tell her the rest," Xander interjects.

River rolls his eyes. "Okay, so my dad knew I was getting frustrated and tried teaching me by using the only other hit song featuring a mandolin."

Xander laughs loudly again. "Man, I can still picture it," he manages between snorts.

I move to sit up but River reaches out to stop me and continues, ignoring Xander. "My dad was teaching me how to play 'Maggie May,' so I watched some of Rod Stewart's music videos and Xander walked in when I was practicing Rod's walk from the 'Hot Legs' video. I had decided to give up my attempts at the mandolin and decided I'd rather learn to move like Rod."

All three of us burst out in a chorus of laughter and the vision in my head is priceless. God, sometimes it feels like my heart will burst with love for him. Everything about him drives me wild but especially his sense of humor.

His gaze captures mine and although we're having a conversation with his brother we've somehow moved from playful touches to sensual caresses. His hand rests on my stomach and his fingers are under the hem of my shirt resting on my bare skin. I'm drawing lines back and forth across each muscle of his washboard abs. The lower I get, the heavier he breathes. Leaning down, his soft lips meet mine and I wrap my arms around his neck and press harder. We get lost in each other for a moment and a small moan escapes my throat.

Xander clears his throat. "The windows are steaming up. Could you stop acting like a couple of teenagers?" Then he turns the radio up.

It's shortly before dawn when Xander drops us off at home. With coffees in hand we sit outside and watch the sunrise. I'm content to sit quietly near him with my head resting on his chest and appreciate the company, but in the calm of the bright crisp morning River asks me, "Why are we waiting to get married?"

I twist my head to catch his gaze.

He kisses my hair and continues. "It seems like all I was really doing was waiting for you my whole life anyway, and I don't want to wait anymore."

I shift so I'm lying on my side and can look at him. "I'm not really sure. But, when you put it that way, I don't want to wait either."

"How would you feel if we charter a plane to Las Vegas and get married today? I can have it arranged in a matter of hours. We can fly up there, get married, and be back here by sunset."

"You don't mind if your family's not there?"

He hesitates only a moment before pulling me closer. His arms tighten around me as the green depths of his eyes stare into mine. "I won't be satisfied until I wake up next to my wife every morning. Dahlia, all I want is you and me forever. We can celebrate later once you're feeling better. We can even have another ceremony here, but what happened in the hospital I never want to happen again. So will you marry me today?"

He's romantic, fearless, and full of life and I love every inch of him. I loop my arms around his neck and my lips find his. Smiling at him as the sun rises and with the Hollywood sign as our backdrop I say, "River Wilde, I would love to marry you today."

He groans against my mouth and the sound echoes through my skin making me smile even more. He kisses me. Then he kisses me again. Then some more. Once we're both breathless he moves me enough to stand up. His smile, the real one, breaks across his face. "Stay here. I'll be right back."

I have no intention of going anywhere, so he's safe. When he comes back he has Stella firmly in his clutch. Joy radiates from him and there's a familiar gleam in his eyes as he sits down at the end of the lounge chair with the guitar. The slight breeze in the air blows his hair. I move toward him and rest my chin on his shoulder, my front to his back. His hot skin awakens all my senses.

I peer down and watch as his hand dances over the strings and he starts singing "You and Me." As he plays I can feel every motion of his body as if I'm the one playing. Curling my hand around his hip, I feel him shudder as heat travels through my arm. My eyes shift to his face and it's a picture of what is real, what is right in my life, and what we have . . . true love everlasting.

He sings the final verse, "The clock never seemed so alive," into my ear and I shiver as his warm breath grazes the skin of my neck. I could watch him play and listen to him sing a thousand times over and never grow tired of it. Not ever. When he cocks his head to mine, picking the last notes on his strings as the sound of his music fills the air, I can't help but think how lucky I am to get to spend the rest of my life with him.

ACKNOWLEDGMENTS

My family. And those words aren't nearly enough. You have truly supported me through this crazy, fun, invigorating, and inspiring process of writing a book. You not only dealt with a messy house, dirty laundry, and many lists of groceries that were never purchased; you also gave me the time I needed to write this book. So thank you to my wonderful husband and my four beautiful kids. XOXO

To the woman who very quickly became my best friend, Jennie Wurtz. We have spent countless hours on the phone, have sent so many texts I've lost count, and with the amount of PMs I'm surprised Facebook didn't reprimand us. You're not only a great friend but you assisted me all the way and provided invaluable input. I will love you forever!

My dear friend, Kerri Coakley. You are the first person I met in the Facebook Indie world. How lucky am I? You always read whatever I wrote over and over again and smiled about it. You encouraged me, supported me, and pushed me every day. I will forever be grateful to you!

To the best beta readers—ever. As a new author, I couldn't have asked for better. Jessica Hayes and America Matthews, you were with me from the start. You have my utmost gratitude. And a special thanks to Jessica for your help in music selection and for letting me use your quote: "Everyone has a destiny, it just matters which road you take to get there." Also, Kristina Amit, Rebecca Berto, Kathryn Crane, Melanie Dawn, Jessica Dow, Ellie Lovenbooks, Nichele Reese, Nacole Stayton, Erika Taylor, Deb Tierney, and Summer Van Vynckt, who all beta-read *Connected*. Your input was invaluable and you helped shape this book into its final product.

To Sarah Hansen for going out of your way to make sure I got the picture I asked for and then taking that picture and turning it into a work of art. To me it will always mean the world that you went above and beyond!

To my editor Mary Kelley of Adept Edits—T.H.A.N.K.Y.O.U! Your kind words, support, friendship, and just plain funny comments were more than any first-time author could ask for. And thank you for taking my words and making them so much better. You helped make the publication of this book a reality.

Thank you to Samantha Towle for granting permission for the use of fictional character Jake Wethers. And thank you to S. C. Stephens for granting permission for the use of fictional character Kellan Kyle.

To Aerie for the countless hours spent helping me, teaching me, and just talking to me. Your assistance was invaluable, and you will always be a friend. I am so thankful for the first day I PM'd you and you agreed to work with me. P.S.—My medicine cabinet is always open to you!

To Kimberly Brower of Book Reader Chronicles—All I can say is I will be forever grateful.

To B&X for agreeing to appear on the cover of *Connected*. You are an amazing couple.

To everyone who helped me along the way who I did not, or could not, thank—you know who you are! And know that I do appreciate everything you have done very very very much!

To all the amazing readers and bloggers. I hope you enjoyed reading *Connected* as much as I enjoyed writing it.

To Amy Tannenbaum of the Jane Rotrosen Agency, who believed in *Connected* enough to sign me up. It's been a dream come true to have such an amazing person as my literary agent. Honestly, words cannot express my gratitude.

And finally—to Penguin. When I began this journey I never imagined I would land a publishing deal. So, thank you, Kerry Donovan and the team at New American Library, for so eagerly and enthusiastically taking me on. Truly a dream come true!

Courtesy of Photo One to One Photography

Kim Karr lives in Florida with her husband and four kids. She's always had a love for books and recently decided to embrace one of her biggest passions—writing. *Connected* is her first novel.

**And don't miss the third book
in the Connections series,**

MENDED

***Music has the power to heal,
but not all broken hearts can be mended.***

Always in control, Xander Wilde considered life on the road to
be a perfect fit for him. But when disaster strikes on the Wilde Ones'
latest tour, fate intervenes . . . and a newly single Ivy Taylor, the only girl
he has ever loved, steps back into his life.

After moving past her painful breakup with Xander years ago, Ivy
was poised to become the next big name in pop music . . . when suddenly she withdrew from the limelight—the same day she announced
her engagement to her controlling agent, Damon Wolf.

Xander knows he should keep his distance. But once they're on
the road, he can't resist pursuing her for a second chance. Yet a jealous
Damon can't let her go—and he's keeping dangerous secrets that could
destroy them all.

When the three of them come together, everything falls apart. But
if Xander and Ivy can hold tight to the bond that connects them, they
just might have a chance at reclaiming the powerful love they thought
they had lost forever. . . .

**Coming out in June 2014 wherever
books and e-books are sold!**